THE BISHOP

A Novel

BROOKS BROWNLEE

NEWMAN SPRINGS PUBLISHING
320 Broad Street
Red Bank, NJ 07701

First originally published by Newman Springs Publishing 2021

ISBN 978-1-63692-685-8 (Paperback)
ISBN 978-1-63881-609-6 (Hardcover)
ISBN 978-1-63692-686-5 (Digital)

Printed in the United States of America

To Jim Garvey, Bob and Grace, Jane, Mike, Rob and Kate and Tom and Little Brooks and Omer Rains. Thanks for your inspiration and love and help.

ACKNOWLEDGMENTS

On January 30 of 2014, I had a severe stroke, which left the use of my left arm and leg impaired. I am blessed to have recovered 100 percent of my cognitive abilities.

For most of my life, I have wanted to try my hand at writing fiction. The stroke removed me from employment and thus was beneficial by providing me with the time to write. I began *The Bishop* in my daughter Kate and son-in-law Tom's living room one evening during Thanksgiving in 2017.

Along my journey since the stroke, I have had the great benefit of guidance and inspiration from several people, some of whom are published authors. These include:

Omer Rains. Omer is a retired California State Senator and celebrated author of *Return to the Summit,* a chronicle of his wonderfully inspirational recovery from an aneurism that impaired all four of his limbs. After recovering the use of his limbs he climed Mount Everest and thus demonstrated his unfailing devotion to exercise and achievement.

Omer's example showed me how dedication to physical therapy and writing a book could be key elements of success in recovery. Omer has been a good friend and mentor and cheerleader throughout my physical recovery efforts. He introduced me to an impressive occupational therapist, a fellow named Waleed Al O'boudi. At Omer's request, Waleed initially treated me without charge. A generous philanthropic couple in my hometown paid for an additional two weeks in Waleed's care. Waleed's treatment left me inspired to believe I could recover the use of my left side limbs.

Wayne Glass. Wayne is a retired USC professor of Governmental Affairs who lives in my hometown. We met through the local Rotary Clubs in our hometown. In 2019 he taught on Semester At Sea. The ship stopped at several cities in Brazil. Wayne developed an interest in the Portuguese language as spoken by Brazilians. He speaks fluent Russian. In early 2020 he asked me to teach him the language. We began early in the year and he now has progressed as I would expect a fifteen year-old would. His skill is uncanny and his accent very good. I cannot wait to travel with him in Brazil.

I owe him thanks for his excellent effort. Teaching him has refreshed my capability with speaking the language; in doing so I have learned new vocabulary and honed my proficiency. In our time working together on his studies we have become good friends; Wayne has contributed to my positive attitude and sense of enjoyment in my recovery efforts.

Laurent Ebzant and Fred Findlen. Laurent is the general manager of the Grand Hyatt Rio de Janeiro. My friend Fred introduced me to Laurent via email. Laurent generously spent over one hour out of a hectic day to provide background on his property that was critical to the authenticity of my description of Fernando and Marta's time there. Fred Findlen is the general manager of the Hyatt Maui Resort and Spa; he ran the Hyatt in my hometown and is a close friend.

Terry Jones. Terry is the founder of Travelocity and Kayak. He is a published expert and speaker on the topic of innovation. His books have been impressively successful. They are *On Innovation* and *Disruption Off.* He is highly sought as an inspirational speaker on innovation.

We met through the morning Rotary Club in our hometown. Terry has provided me with encouragement and guidance while I have been writing *The Bishop* and throughout my stroke recovery. He further was a member of the advisory board for a start-up company I began in the spring of 2012 with my friend named Tom Bryan.

Tom is president of a highly successful community bank in Rantoul, Illinois. He is a valued friend and has provided me with good humor and encouragement in the years since the stroke.

Peter Mountford. Peter is an acclaimed fiction author from Seattle, Washington. Peter was an adjunct faculty member teaching in the masters of fine arts in writing at a local private university near my home. His award winning novel *A Young Man's guide To Late Capitalism* is fantastic.

In 2018, I enrolled in Peter's section and began learning how best to write my book. Initially we worked via Zoom and Skype. We met in person for the first time over lunch in August 2019. Peter offered encouragement and guidance and a critique that had me start a complete rewrite of my manuscript. In October of 2020, I provided Peter with my then draft of my revised manuscript. Despite his busy schedule, he graciously reviewed my draft and provided helpful suggestions and encouragement.

Throughout my interactions with Peter, I gained critical insights on point of view and descriptive language and a homicide detective's perspective. Peter is always very busy teaching and writing and speaking. I am blessed to have had his guidance.

Omer and Terry and Peter have treated me with great respect and consideration despite my disabilities. Their attention has been highly beneficial while I have struggled physically and emotionally in my recovery.

My psychologist, Dr. Monique Stanfield, has been a great help in keeping me grounded and humored and focused optimistically on my potential recovery.

Brazilian actor, Wagner Moura, is one of my favorite Brazilian actors. He portrayed Pablo Escobar in the Netflix series *Narcos*. While watching *Narcos* I asked myself why Wagner is frequently cast as a bad guy. I created Fernando Carvalho as a good guy character modeled physically on Wagner.

Carl Caen is my quad-based cane; he has served me loyally for the six years since a friend gave him to me. He is my Wilson like the volleyball in the movie *Cast Away*.

My wife, Jane, has been a self-sacrificing supportive inspiration throughout the burdensome effort to deal with my incapacities.

I believe the stroke has been harder on her than me. She was thrust into the role of caregiver and breadwinner, both of which she has carried out marvelously.

I owe her huge thanks, and she has taught me what true love is.

Our children, Mike, Kate, and Rob, and son-in-law, Tom, have been sources of wonderful optimism and confidence and encouragement throughout my recovery.

I owe a great deal to my parents Bob and Grace for sending me to Brazil for thirteen months as an exchange student, in addition to their love and support throughout my life up to the age of fifty-eight when Grace passed.

It was in Brazil I fell in love with the country and its geography and people.

My high school language teacher Jim Garvey was also instrumental in my becoming an exchange student. Jim convinced my parents to send me on a tour of Europe he led in the summer of 1971.

There Jim exposed my classmates and me to the evils of totalitarian rule in Eastern Europe and the USSR. What I witnessed were prisons masquerading as countries at the expense of human dignity and liberty and opportunity for self-realization. That exposure provided my passion for having totalitarians as bad guys in my story; my intent is to depict totalitarian regimes and the evil they are regardless of their political philosophies. I strongly support democracy and peoples' right to self-determination. During my time in Brazil the then military dictatorship decided to transition the country to democracy. My high school best friend's father was a colonel in the army. I asked the colonel his opinion on the transition away from dictatorship, and he replied, "Several of us in the army command were required to go to Leavenworth Kansas to study at the Command and General Staff College (CGSC) of the US Army there. A key lesson they imparted to us was that the military is intended to defend one's country from foreign threats, and should, therefore, not play a role in domestic politics. We in the Brazilian Military have embraced that thinking and are backing away from involvement in domestic politics." In the tumultuous years since democracy was restored in 1985 the military has remained hands off of politics.

In recent years the nation experienced political strife leading up to and following the fall of presidents Dilma Rouseff and Lula Ignacio da Silva. The military admirably stood by and did not intercede in domestic politics. The restored democracy is referred to as the New or Sixth Republic. The first constitution was enacted in 1824 following successfully achieving independence from Portugal in 1822. The 1985 constitution is similar to that of the USA but is uniquely Brazilian in its number of articles and amendments.

I was fortunate to be there to witness the events in advance of the restoration of democracy. I lived in Brasilia and was, therefore, near the center of the 'action'. I learned a great deal about human character and wisdom from my friend's father. My first host parents taught me a great deal, as they were Holocaust survivors. The father had been a resistance fighter in the Czech Underground in WWII.

The mother was the sole survivor of her family's internment in Auschwitz and she still had her serial number tattooed on her wrist. They had met in a refugee camp for Jews in Italy. He made money racing motorcycles and later, automobiles, in Italy. They used the money he won to migrate away from Europe.

Their choice of Brazil as their final destination had proved fortuitous. There they had built a highly successful furniture business in São Paulo that they had brilliantly expanded to Brasilia prior to its completion in 1960, on the strength of the opportunity with the new capital being built there. I have found humor to be the best medicine in combatting the dark shadow cast on my spirit by the disabilities. To that end I make jokes about my condition. Naming the cane is an important piece of this.

I asked Dr. Stanfield if it was okay I talk to my cane. She didn't miss a beat and turned toward Carl and asked, "Carl is it okay with you that Brooks talks to you?" Carl did not respond of course. Great therapeutic laugh! Laughter dampens the tough parts of my condition.

Without Jim Garvey and my parents, there would be no *The Bishop*.

Jim was a treasured mentor and friend until his death in 1999. He was a groomsman in Jane's and my wedding in 1980.

Newman Springs Publishing is high on my list of those to thank. I submitted my initial manuscript to five publishers and four said they wanted to publish *The Bishop*.

Newman Springs' committee that read and evaluated my submission was complimentary and enthusiastic as no other. They understood what I was trying to accomplish.

CHAPTER 1

Edifício Boas Vistas (Beautiful Views Building), Jardim Botânico, Rio de Janeiro, Brazil
Friday, December 27, 2019

Roberto Cavalcanti, founder and CEO of Brazil's leading private equity firm, O Grupo Roberto Cavalcanti, was hosting an event in his exclusive apartment home located in a luxurious apartment building in Rio de Janeiro's prestigious Jardim Botânico or Botanical Garden neighborhood. Cavalcanti had thought up the gathering as a means to introduce the nation's top university graduates to potential employers represented by the country's leaders in business and government.

Cavalcanti's large five-bedroom residence boasted luxury furnishings and beautiful décor with a dark red theme augmented by beautifully carved wood accents. The living room area provided the primary space for guests to assemble. The overflow was being accommodated outside on a massive deck with sweeping views of Guanabara Bay, the harbor, and Flamengo and Copacabana beaches.

The sun sat in the sky, casting shimmering light on the rolling waves in the ocean. The Yacht Club of Rio de Janeiro was holding a regatta in celebration of the start of summer. Their sails rippled in the breeze while the boats bobbed in formation.

Attendants circulated through the assembled guests, offering appetizers and taking drink orders. Three portable bars were set at the corners of the deck to accommodate guests wishing to be served without waiting for the attendants. Cavalcanti was serving generous quantities of each of Sonoma-Cutrer chardonnay and Veuve Clicquot champagne. An assortment of premium wines and liqueurs from Argentina and Uruguay was also offered. A fountain stood in the center of the deck, serving caipirinhas.

The party began exactly at 5:00 p.m. Several gorgeous young women from Rio's top samba clubs danced seductively among the attendees. The dancers were accompanied by a quartet playing samba music. The dancers wore tasseled skirts colored indigo blue, white, yellow, and green as the Brazilian flag. They also wore translucent blouses open at the midriff.

Guests lounged on sofas and chairs as the attendants circulated.

Among the male graduates was the handsome twenty-eight-year-old Fernando Carvalho. Fernando was a passionate athlete. He stood just less than six feet tall, and he had thick brown hair and large brown eyes. Well-dressed and confident, he caught the curious eyes of many of the females present as he strode about, mimicking the gait of John Travolta he'd seen Travolta use in the movie *Get Shorty*. He had adopted the gait as part of his personal image and branding.

One of the dancers, an enchanting beauty named Marta, approached Fernando.

He smiled and spoke, using his best radio announcer-like voice, "Well, my, what a beauty you are."

"How am I so lucky as to be the object of your attention?"

He paused for a moment and continued, "I am Fernando Carvalho. My university friends call me 'The Bishop.'"

"The Bishop?" asked the blushing Marta coyly.

"Because of the way I dress." He routinely wore a black mock turtleneck sweater with a lightweight black suit with black loafers or cowboy boots and black leather belt. The outfit gave him the appearance of being a member of the Catholic clergy.

Marta replied, "Well, my friends call me Cutie because I am a living doll, but my name is Marta Esteves." Her eyes were large and brown and her hair brunette with a hint of blond in highlights.

The weather was a lovely early summer combination of clear blue skies and temperatures in the mid-to-upper-seventy-degree-Fahrenheit range. Uniformed guards with automatic weapons patrolled the perimeter of the deck as a precaution against potential attack by either criminals or political insurgents. The Cavalcanti home was on the seventh or top floor of the building and was, therefore, securely above the street level below.

Fernando was further entranced while Marta bit her lower lip and appeared unnerved by his attention. The sun glistened in her beautiful eyes and in the blond highlights in her hair. Fernando found himself unable to pay attention to anything other than the beautiful woman before him. He was unaccustomed to being so captivated by a female and tried to refocus on his discussion with Marta. He felt the warmth of the air and sun enveloping him and providing the strength to act sophisticated and not stutter.

They exchanged phone numbers, and he again spoke, "I am from São Paulo. I am only in Rio this evening for this gathering. I will call you as soon as I can to arrange our first date. Please be patient as I have no idea as to when that might be."

Marta blushed even more and replied enthusiastically, "I promise, handsome. I cannot wait!"

Fernando was a top honors graduate in economics from Universidade Católica de São Paulo in São Paulo, Brazil. Fernando had passed on an opportunity to receive a full-ride scholarship for a master's degree from a prestigious US institution in Massachusetts.

Cavalcanti sought out Fernando, and they spoke at length at the commencement of the gathering. Marta smiled seductively at Fernando and walked away while waving goodbye over her left shoulder. Her perfect violin-shaped figure and how it swayed while she walked mesmerized Fernando.

Cavalcanti invited Fernando to join him in one of the seating areas on the deck so they might speak in a confidential setting. Once there, he said, "Well, young man, I am intrigued by and hopeful to learn your story and how you rose up from poverty. I'd love to know how you obtained the support and motivation to attend Universidade Católica. What do you want to do in life now?" All the while, he was greeting other guests and making sure his party was unfolding perfectly.

Greatly flattered by Cavalcanti's attention, Fernando replied, "Senhor Cavalcanti, I want to help my country by taking a role that provides benefit toward our national progress in our quest for full recovery from the economic and emotional damage wrought by the Lula da Silva and Dilma Rousseff presidencies. I am highly encouraged by the direction being set by our newly elected president, Ricardo Voss. I very much want to serve and help him in his quest to restore our economy and place in the international business community. I am definitely interested in achieving financial independence and security for my mother and aunt and me. I also am convinced Presidente Voss will succeed and restore our national pride."

Cavalcanti listened to Fernando and was captivated by Fernando's sense of national duty and devotion to himself and his mother. "Fernando, I am intrigued by your focus and story and will speak with my management team at my firm regarding how we might find a role for you on our analysts team." Then he gave Fernando his card and said to call him any time. "I will get back to you soon regarding what opportunity my firm may offer to a fellow of your caliber."

Fernando had garnered the nickname of O Bispo or The Bishop. This arose from his unique choice of a routine outfit. Starting early in his collegiate life, he had begun wearing his distinctive black outfit. On the evening of the Cavalcanti party, he had elected to top his costume off with a black Stetson cowboy hat. He felt the hat gave him an air of authority. In that, he was definitely correct. He had laid the hat carefully in his lap and toyed with it self-consciously while speaking to Cavalcanti. A prankster classmate at Universidade Católica had begun calling Fernando The Bishop as a kindly jest. The nickname was bestowed with respect because Fernando was a straight arrow and respected for his dedication to academic purposes and success. The outfit gave Fernando a strikingly good look and accentuated his powerful physique.

Cavalcanti caught the attention of Ronaldo Amaraes and asked him to sit down and join them and introduced him to Fernando. Their seats were in an area filled with potted fragrant flowers, and the aroma combined with the warm air and light of the setting sun produced a pleasant feeling for the men while they drank caipirinhas and chatted.

Amaraes was the chief economist for O Banco do Brasil. The Bank of Brazil is Brazil's largest by total assets and is the largest bank by total assets in all of Latin America. It was founded in 1908 and is the oldest and longest-active bank in Brazil, even older than the country's central bank. Amaraes and Fernando spoke at length and exchanged contact information.

Amaraes became increasingly animated in his sales pitch to Fernando about why O Banco do Brasil would be his best career choice. Amaraes was a strong supporter of Presidente Voss and a senior member of Voss' inner circle of advisors.

"Senhor Amaraes, I am excited about the potential of my assisting Presidente Voss and you and O Banco in the correction of the economic problems that have developed and plagued Brazil in recent years," said the enthusiastic Fernando.

At the end of their conversation, Amaraes offered to host Fernando in his Rio offices and introduce him to his economics team and see if there might be a fit for a role for Fernando. Amaraes told Fernando his personal assistant had recently resigned to take care of an aging parent, and he, Amaraes, was filling that role along with performing his normal duties. Amaraes apologized for being distracted and said he was watching his cell phone with care and would look to reconnect with Fernando at his earliest convenience.

The two had to strain to hear and be heard above the din of the party. While they spoke, the musicians turned their playlist to a collection of bossa nova hits; they played while dark descended.

Once dark, outdoor lighting turned on, the lights were strung on lines from poles at the sides and corners of the deck. Other lights were placed in the plant pots and were aimed up into the plants. The lighting's effect was magical, and quickly the pace of the party accelerated. Several of the students were soon in discussions with Petrobras, the state oil company, and General Motors and Chrysler and Volkswagen.

In the course of the conversation, Amaraes learned Fernando had grown up in poverty in Heliópolis in São Paulo. Heliópolis is a vast slum, or favela, as they are called in Portuguese. Amaraes was impressed with Fernando and his story of how he had overcome poverty and the associated lack of opportunities.

Fernando explained his father, Carlos, had died of cancer when Fernando turned eleven years old. His mother, Maria, was left without financial resources and was compelled to find work as a domestic servant. Following several brief employment stints, a wealthy businessman named João Carlos Diamante hired Maria. Maria was a beautiful woman of five-feet-seven-inches height with large green eyes and brunette hair. Diamante lived in the penthouse of a luxury highrise apartment building in central São Paulo. Maria received Diamante's permission to bring the then-twelve-year-old Fernando to work with her so she could keep an eye on him. Diamante was very impressed with Fernando and his quiet, polite demeanor and amply evident intelligence. Diamante was inspired by Maria's and her boy's struggle against poverty and allowed Maria to bring Fernando into his home with her with her so and be sure Fernando studied and didn't get distracted and get into trouble. Diamante further offered to pay Fernando's tuition so he might attend the excellent local Catholic elementary school. The school was named Colégio Maria Imaculada.

Fernando was allowed to study in Diamante's personal study in the apartment while Maria wrapped up her daily obligations. Fernando blossomed into an exceptional student with the benefit of studying in Diamante's home office. The quiet environment was vastly different than the Carvalho home in Heliópolis. Their house was a modest structure made of cinder blocks with a corrugated aluminum roof. It was set between several other similar houses that were crowded together. When Fernando was born, Carlos Carvalho had painted the exterior in colors from the Brazilian flag. The paint had faded noticeably, and that was offset by the neighboring homes' pink and orange and magenta colors. The Heliópolis home was in a busy, noisy neighborhood, and Fernando's friends would frequently interrupt Fernando while he struggled to find the time and quiet to study.

Over time while he enjoyed Diamante's generous support and provision of refuge, Fernando became a top honors student at the elementary school. Diamante was so pleased with Maria's work he wanted to anchor her in his employ for a long period of time. He told Maria he was very pleased with her work and Fernando's academic progress. He said he would pay for Fernando's enrollment in the premier private middle and high school in São Paulo, an institution named Colégio Pre Universitário de São Paulo or Pre for short.

There was a string attached. Diamante told Maria his payment for Fernando's tuition at Pre would last for as long as Maria remained satisfactorily in his employ and Fernando was showing continued promise as a student. Mindful of the generosity of Diamante's support and his need to show progress, Fernando became a star student at Pre. In his final year at Pre, Fernando applied for acceptance at Universidade Católica de São Paulo.

With Diamante's help and encouragement, the university accepted Fernando. Fernando achieved one of the highest scores in that year's national university entrance exam. The exam was demanding and highly competitive and covered several disciplines.

Diamante had, by that time, taken a deep near-fatherly interest in Fernando's academic direction. Diamante was a graduate of Universidade Católica. Combining his enthusiastic support of Fernando and his love of his alma mater, Diamante offered to pay Fernando's university tuition. With Diamante's guidance, Fernando decided to study economics. Fernando was intrigued by Diamante's wealth and obvious financial security and wanted to be able to support both himself and Maria in a comfortable lifestyle in the coming years. Diamante introduced Fernando to friends of his who'd all been economics majors as undergraduates. The friends each had financial well-being akin to Diamante's, and Fernando was intrigued.

Fernando was a competitive materialist by nature. At the age of fourteen, Fernando and two of his closest friends were invited and successfully persuaded to join a gang in Heliópolis called the Sombra Preta or Black Shadow. Through their activity in the gang, the boys were able to steal small but costly electronic items they had longed to own, like portable CD players and pagers. They were able to obtain cash through robbery and burglary. They additionally learned to be effective as hand-to-hand combatants.

One of the adult male leaders in the Sombra Preta raped Fernando's friend and fellow gang member, Luis Antonio. The rape was quite violent in response to Luis Antonio's resistance and attempted defense. Luis Antonio was left with a badly bruised face and scarring from the blows delivered by his assailant.

Fernando and another Heliópolis friend and gang member named José Vargas swore an oath to avenge the attack and one evening tailed the adult gang member and cornered him in a cul-de-sac at the end of an alley. The cul-de-sac was in shadows while the sun was setting; this and the drop in temperature in the sun's absence gave the scene a macabre feeling. Soon, their target was illuminated by filtered light coming from windows of neighboring homes. Using automatic weapons they purchased on the black market, they shot Luis Antonio's assailant to death.

It was Fernando and José Vargas' first exposure to violent death and the first and only ever intentional killing committed by either of them. They never again engaged in or considered participating in a killing. For Fernando, the exception would be accidental or in future engagements that demanded violence for good causes. Fernando could vividly remember the look of shock on their victim's face. The boys were long haunted by the memory of the man's passing. Over several minutes, life clearly drained from him while he bled out. At the end, their victim's face and eyes lost all evidence of life and finally became fixed. The filtered light and evening air made the scene memorable. For years, the memory and images of the fellow's death haunted Fernando and José Vargas. Fernando vividly recalled how the fellow sobbed and swore at both Fernando and José Vargas while he vainly struggled to survive the bullets' impacts.

The boys grew old during the episode and were emotionally hardened to an extent that they could survive any physical or emotional threat thereafter. They were emboldened by the knowledge they could defend themselves and their families and close friends from significant threats. Fernando saved and revisited the memory as a keen reminder of that which he should never do again. He felt reassured by the confidence that should he need to protect himself and others close to him from danger, he could.

From that day forward, Fernando and José Vargas and their friends continued their criminal activities, without killing or physically harming anyone else. They grew concerned their parents or some authority might question them about their new belongings and cash wealth. They conjured a cover story. The story was they had obtained jobs at a car parts factory near Heliópolis. They said they were hired for the graveyard shift. The shift hours provided a good cover to explain the boys' late-night absences during their active hours in the Sombra Preta.

Relieved to have an explanation, Fernando was able to share and explain his new wealth and belongings with and to Maria and her identical twin sister, Celia, and Diamante.

Fernando was careful to manage his time in order that his studies didn't suffer. This gave rise to a marvelous skill for time management that would serve him well throughout his academic and work careers and personal life.

In his discussion with Amaraes, Fernando carefully withheld the details of his time in the Sombra Preta.

Cavalcanti stepped back toward Amaraes and Fernando and had two gentlemen in tow that took seats with Fernando and Amaraes. Cavalcanti sat with a flourish and joined them. "Fernando Carvalho and Ronaldo Amaraes, I'd like to introduce you to two of our esteemed guests from the government. They are Colonel João da Silva and Director Marton Vargas of the Polícia Federal. Colonel da Silva is the most senior and successful investigator in the PF."

Fernando's defense mechanism was aroused because he feared the police and any potential discovery of his activity in the Sombra Preta as well as his and José Vargas' hands in the killing of the rapist.

Vargas and da Silva expressed interest in Fernando and, in the conversation with Fernando, learned of his impressive and successful effort to exit poverty.

Fernando struggled in the dark and lighting to study the policemen's faces for a sign of suspicion about him. Fernando and his story intrigued da Silva and Vargas. They showed no sign of suspicion but only inspiration.

Colonel da Silva showed keen interest and spoke first, "Fernando, I work with underprivileged youth in our inner cities throughout our great nation to help them learn how to best succeed. Might you be willing to join the director and me in our efforts and act as a role model? Director Vargas and I are here looking for talented and intelligent graduates with desire and technical expertise that might be helpful in our fight against crime and the evils wrought by deprivation. Unfortunately, corruption and embezzlement are still a fact of life in our country. I am seeking a young talent, such as yours, to help in the battle against those old and persistent problems. You and your story of accomplishment against tough odds would inspire and encourage young people struggling to overcome the shortcomings of life in the favelas throughout our land. Here is my card with my cell phone number. I hope to be in contact with you soon to discuss a possible career for you with the PF."

Encouraged by the attention, Fernando replied, "Thank you, Colonel da Silva and Director Vargas. Here is my card with my cellphone number and home phone number and email address. I look forward to hearing from you and speaking again soon. Colonel da Silva, I would be pleased and honored to join you and Director Vargas in your efforts to help underprivileged, inner-city youth."

Fernando was elatedly fulfilled by the interactions and introductions at Cavalcanti's party.

CHAPTER 2

Edifício Boas Vistas, Jardim Botânico, Rio de Janeiro, Brazil
Friday, December 27, 2019

The Cavalcanti party came to an end around eleven o'clock in the evening.

Fernando made his rounds to bid his new contacts good night. He reassured Marta Esteves he was still interested and planning to call her as soon as he could; he felt like a young schoolboy filled with romantic excitement. He breathed in deeply as he watched her walk away and turned his head toward the sky and spoke to Carlos, "Well, my dear father, I don't want to seem to be too overanxious, but she could well be the gal I fall in love with!"

He thanked Cavalcanti and Amaraes and Colonel da Silva and Director Vargas along with his several other new contacts. Fernando left Edifício Boas Vistas feeling confident in and excited about his future career and romantic prospects.

Fernando drove a distinctive vintage sports car, a 1973 Volkswagen SP2 that he stored at the home of a friend in Rio in order to have transportation during his frequent visits there. While he approached his car on the street outside of the building, he saw a dark Chevrolet sedan approaching. The street was empty. Fernando's defenses were aroused, and he realized his wonderful silver car with distinctive red interior had betrayed his presence.

The sedan slowed, and the driver was easily visible through his open window. It was Carlos, a criminal who went by just one name. Carlos was a stocky fellow who stood 5'7" tall and weighed just over 180 pounds with brown eyes and dark hair dyed an unconvincing blond.

Carlos spoke first, "Well, well, Fernando Carvalho or Senhor O Bispo, what brings the Sombra Preta to Rio?!Are you so foolish as to think Regimento A would tolerate your presence here in Rio?!"

Fernando looked around sheepishly to see if anyone could overhear the conversation. He was relieved to note there were no witnesses in sight. "Well, Carlos, I wasn't aware you and Regimento A owned Rio de Janeiro," Fernando intoned in a sarcastic voice.

Carlos replied, "Well, my friend, I apologize because we do own the city. And we do not appreciate your presence here!" Carlos was the leader of Regimento A, a crime gang that was a lead competitor of the Sombra Preta in several cities throughout Brazil. Fernando and Carlos had unfinished business arising from a conflict between Regimento A and the Sombra Preta that had taken place two months before in Porto Alegre in the state of Rio Grande do Sul.

"Okay, let's finish our business. I will not be dictated to regarding where I may be," said Fernando, standing his ground.

Carlos revved the engine of his Chevrolet and departed with tires squealing.

Fernando jumped into his Volkswagen and started the engine and took off in pursuit. The chase took them through the heavy pedestrian traffic in the streets near Copacabana Beach.

While Fernando slid his car expertly sideways through a turn at a corner, he struck and instantly killed a slow-moving elderly homeless man suffering from elephantiasis. He realized he had acted stupidly and could imagine his new momentum gained at the gathering that evening quickly evaporating. Carlos had quickly disappeared from sight, and Fernando was soon flush with regret at having jeopardized his great fortune gained from his contacts at the Cavalcanti party. He noticed several witnesses observing his car and license plate.

He was to take an early morning flight home to São Paulo and immediately drove to Galeão International Airport to be in place to catch his flight. He was excited to report to his mother Maria and aunt Celia and Diamante about his successes at the Cavalcanti gathering.

Upon arrival at Galeão, he found an off-site parking lot and carefully hid his car from view from the adjacent street. The car bore a wicked dent in the front of the hood from the impact with its handicapped homeless victim. Fernando left a spare key atop the front driver's side tire and left the parking ticket in the glove box. He quickly called a university buddy and asked him to retrieve the car and deliver it to a high-end body shop for repair. He slept in the car until he needed to go to the terminal for his flight. He ate in the terminal and boarded his flight to São Paulo at seven o'clock in the morning.

Once back in São Paulo, Fernando got into Maria's car he had borrowed to get to the airport and drove home to Heliópolis.

While he approached his house, he saw several police vehicles from both the São Paulo Civilian Police Force and PF parked on the street outside the home. His heart sank in recognition he was the target of the activity he saw.

He entered the house and found his mother and his aunt Celia in tears. The civilian officers had evidently been searching the home and had located several of the items he had stolen along with his stash of cash. All this was piled high in the middle of the living room like a vivid monument to his sordid criminal behavior.

One of the PF officers read him the charges he was to be charged with and handcuffed him. He was informed he was under arrest for the death of the pedestrian he had struck in Rio, and the officer continued he'd likely be charged pending his explanation of how he had come to possess everything in the pile in the living room. He was removed to a waiting PF car and transported to the regional PF headquarters where he was placed in a holding cell pending an arraignment planned for the following morning.

The next morning, Monday, December 31, dawned early. And Fernando was served breakfast and informed he had a visitor. He was escorted into an interrogation room in which Colonel João da Silva was seated and greeted him. The circumstance felt to him like a surreal nightmare, and he second-guessed his actions in a sharp, repeated personal reprimand that was so persistent he could not put it aside.

da Silva informed him his case was being referred to a grand jury and he was to be held pending an arraignment. The arraignment was handed down within three days, during which he languished in his cell.

His mother and Diamante arranged an attorney to handle his defense. On Thursday, January 30, 2020, the attorney expressed concern she had been unable to obtain a change of venue and explained the trial was to begin on February 5 in Rio.

On Friday, January 31, Fernando was taken to a private jet operated by the PF for the flight from São Paulo to Rio in the company of two PF agents.

Upon boarding the plane, Fernando was greeted by Colonel da Silva and a PF agent of significant size. "Well, Fernando, it is good to see you again. But I regret the circumstances, as I am sure you do as well. Director Vargas and I were quite surprised to learn of your past criminal activities. It was a work of art hiding your criminal life while obtaining your degree in economics."

Fernando was not prepared to play along with the colonel's banter and replied, "I have no reason to explain my past to you, Senhor Colonel da Silva. I am prepared to cooperate in any fashion that may secure a good future for my mother and aunt Celia."

Upon landing in Rio de Janeiro, Fernando was transported by da Silva and the large agent and two additional PF agents in a PF sedan to a holding cell at the Rio PF offices.

In the car from the airport, da Silva sat close to Fernando in the back seat and spoke while looking him straight in the eye, "Fernando, you are confronted by the potential of a likely sentence of many years. I know how much you care and are concerned for your mother and aunt Celia. If you would cooperate with me after you are sentenced, I believe I may be able to help you gain an early release in exchange for your commitment to assist Director Vargas and me in our efforts to fight crime. You and your network of Sombra Preta contacts represent an untapped wealth of information I am convinced would be invaluable in solving cases. Let's wait to see what happens after your trial and see what can be done."

"Senhor Colonel, I would be more than pleased to assist you if the terms of the offer were attractive." The conditionality of this phrase was emphasized by the subjunctive case in Portuguese, leaving the opportunity clearly open to da Silva.

Upon arrival at the PF facility in Rio, da Silva patted Fernando on the knee and spoke while Fernando exited the car and was whisked by the two PF agents assisting da Silva into the building and into his holding cell. da Silva followed along, observing his young charge while continuing the discussion, "Please be patient, my friend. I am not going to let you off the hook on your offer to help me with inner-city youth development. I fully intend to find a means to engage you and your Sombra Preta network in Director Vargas' and my crime-fighting efforts."

Fernando sat in the holding cell, contemplating the burdensome outcome of his poor choices in life. Within days of his arrival in Rio, his trial began.

While in the holding cell, he was consumed with regret over his poor choices in life. He resolved to not be consumed with negativity and swore an oath to find a way to make good out of his dire circumstance.

CHAPTER 3

The defense was sorely at a loss to counter the wealth of evidence against Fernando on the charges arising from his Sombra Preta activities. In a negotiated sentence following a guilty plea, Fernando was sentenced to serve five years for the manslaughter of the elderly man in Rio during his pursuit of Carlos.

At trial, the prosecution was aggressive in pointing out Fernando had been sentenced for the death of the elderly homeless gentleman. The prosecution refused to give Fernando any leniency in consideration of his academic success and success in overcoming his impoverished youth.

He was sentenced to six years in federal prison for his Sombra Preta activities. Both the five years for manslaughter and six years for his gang activities were to be served concurrently.

Maria and Celia and Diamante all attended the trial, hoping to see Fernando receive some leniency. da Silva sat in the audience as well.

On Friday, February 14, at the trial's end, Fernando was remanded to Porto Velho Federal Prison in the state of Rondônia. He was swiftly transported to the prison and placed in the general population. Rondônia is far distant from São Paulo and Rio in a highly rural setting and thus separated Fernando from potential frequent visits by his São-Paulo-based friends and family and Rio acquaintances. The prosecution asked the judge to sentence Fernando to Porto Velho to augment Fernando's suffering from his punishment. By unfortunate coincidence, Carlos of Regimento A was also serving time at Porto Velho. Carlos had been returned to Porto Velho for a parole violation. Carlos had assumed the leadership of the prisoners through several acts of violence and generosity intended to convince the prisoner population they should follow his orders. This was accomplished with the aid of members of Regimento A who were also imprisoned. To effectively maintain control, Carlos elected to suppress prisoners who were affiliated with the Sombra Preta.

Upon his arrival at Porto Velho, Fernando developed a circle of friends comprised mainly of past residents of Heliópolis and members of the Sombra Preta. These men became his students in classes he held to teach them basics in mathematics and personal finance and reading and writing. Fernando's intent was to help the men improve so they might qualify for parole later on and be prepared to succeed once out of prison. Fernando proudly considered the effort to be his chance for redemption by doing good.

Carlos felt threatened by Fernando's effort. Fernando's intellect and good intent were oddly out of place in the violent world of Porto Velho. One day, Carlos approached Fernando and threatened him with a makeshift weapon. One of Fernando's Sombra Preta buddies, a large fellow nicknamed Leopardo or Leopard for his unique choice of spotted tattoos, stepped in to aid Fernando. A fight broke out among the prisoners. The fight cascaded rapidly into an all-out war between Regimento A and Sombra Preta.

Over three violence-filled days, twenty-five prisoners died at the hands of other prisoners and at the hands of guards.

The guards in the prison were all remarkably huge fellows who were dedicated to punishing the inmates and keeping them in line, as opposed to rehabilitation. The guards misinterpreted the initiation of the fighting to have been caused by Fernando.

This struck the warden as odd because he knew of and supported Fernando's efforts to assist other prisoners. At the warden's direction, Fernando was placed in a solitary confinement cell for protection.

CHAPTER 4

Porto Velho Federal Prison, Rondônia, Brazil
April 1–5, 2020

The warden and da Silva remained in contact pursuant to da Silva's desire to keep Fernando safe for future crime-fighting collaboration. The warden called da Silva and informed him of Fernando's circumstance and risk with the prison violence.

da Silva quickly arrived at Porto Velho and was ushered into a meeting room. As da Silva entered, he found Fernando seated, awaiting his arrival. "Well, young man, you're in quite a pickle here. I hear you are doing wonderful things to aid the other inmates. The warden and I believe things would be better if we kept you safely in solitary confinement under protection of the guards so you may continue the teaching effort. If we secure you in a solitary cell, Carlos won't be able to threaten or harm you. We believe you should be allowed to spend several months proving yourself to be an exemplary prisoner so you may qualify for and receive our support for parole. Here are the terms under which your successful fulfillment of this assignment could and will be rewarded." da Silva handed Fernando a piece of typed paper that outlined Fernando's path to parole. "Here you are, Senhor Carvalho. I will wait in the area until tomorrow morning and hope to have breakfast with you here in this room then and receive this copy back with your signature so you may qualify for and receive our support."

The document outlined a customized program prepared for Fernando at da Silva's and the warden's direction. Under its terms, Fernando was to serve another nine months in Porto Velho in protective custody in solitary confinement with a personal attachment of guards to protect him. His meals were to be prepared at his direction and served to him in the company of his inmate students in their classroom. The students were to receive the same meals. da Silva's and the warden's intent was to erode Carlos' position of authority among the inmates and elevate Fernando to a higher stature than that of Carlos in the inmates' eyes. The meal menu was a complement of numerous traditional Brazilian favorites and delicacies.

Should he perform as requested, Fernando would be paroled on October 10 of 2020. His parole would require him to perform 250 hours of public service; 120 of those hours were to be spent assisting the PF in solving crimes and 130 hours of work in conjunction with da Silva to help inner-city deprived youth. After completion of his obligations as outlined, Fernando would be allowed to obtain employment in the business world with an assurance he would be left alone so as to perform his employment duties, without conflict against his service to the PF.

Fernando read the document and broke into a smile. "Thank you, Senhor Colonel. I look forward to our breakfast in the morning. I need to reassess my future objectives this evening and decide if I will sign on with you. My thanks to you and the warden for protecting me and my teaching initiative."

Fernando was returned to his protective cell, and he found himself thinking of Marta Esteves. He anxiously dug through his personal items to make sure he still had and could find her phone number. He was delighted when he found it. His guard detail arrived to take him to dinner, and he went with a big smile. After dinner and lights out, he lay in pleasant agitation, contemplating a future with the charming gorgeous woman he had met at Cavalcanti's party. He further relished the mental image of reuniting with Maria and his aunt Celia and driving the SP2. He had learned the car's repair was progressing very well along with a modernization effort to replace the suspension geometry to be on a par with better-handling modern cars. The electronics were being brought up to the level of those found in new cars of the current era. The idea of a "brand-new" classic automobile was exciting to Fernando in a way that surpassed his thrill on the day he bought it from a private party in Brasília.

He was unable to fall asleep until four o'clock in the morning when he called to one of the guards in his protective detail and obtained a flashlight. He read the proposed plan from da Silva and the warden again and sat in excited contemplation until five o'clock in the morning. He resisted the temptation to be angry over the time he had lost in his life and gracefully concluded it was his own damned fault and he should accept that and focus on redeeming himself. In the balance, things looked to be getting better, and his life ahead held renewed promise. Imagining his father Carlos watching over him proudly from heaven, he executed the document and folded it carefully into a square and placed it into his pocket to store it safely for his morning meeting with da Silva. He felt a profound sense of gratification and optimism over his own future and fell asleep imagining being with Marta and his family and friends in a new promising life.

At six thirty, one of his guards knocked on the door to his cell, and Fernando stood and faced the door and found the guard holding clothes on hangars. The guard was smiling broadly and additionally held shoes and socks and boxer shorts. The guard spoke first, "Good morning, Fernando. Colonel da Silva asks that you wear these clothes to your breakfast meeting."

On the hangar were a black mock turtleneck sweater and lightweight black suit. The shoes were black loafers and the socks black. A black leather belt completed the garb. Fernando smiled in recognition of a pleasant future working with a wonderful man like Colonel João da Silva.

The guard ushered Fernando into a secure private showering room where he found toiletries unlike any found in any prison. These consisted of a brand-new high-end shaving razor with flawless German blades and exotic shaving cream and aftershave. A note was placed in the middle attached to a shampoo and a hair dryer and hairbrush and toothbrush and toothpaste and mouthwash. The aftershave was wonderfully aromatic and made Fernando feel refreshed and reinvigorated and confident. The note read:

> Good morning, young man. Welcome
> to the first day of your new life. Your future
> is filled with renewed promise. I look for-
> ward to seeing The Bishop at breakfast.
>
> Your fan and friend and future partner,
> João da Silva

Fernando felt a huge weight lifted from his shoulders. Never had he enjoyed a shower so much in his life. By seven o'clock, he was dressed and shaved and ready to go. At eight o'clock, he was seated across a table from da Silva in a meeting room.

Fernando spoke first, "Well, Senhor Colonel, I am invigorated by your generosity with the clothing and toiletries." da Silva smiled a broad, warm smile, like the smile one would bestow on a favored child or younger sibling. "Well, it is such a pleasure to see you relaxed, Senhor Carvalho. I felt it was damned well time O Bispo reappeared! Have you considered my offer?" He noticed Fernando was holding the offer document tightly in his right hand.

"Well, yes, I am prepared to deliver the signed agreement if you will allow me to place a couple of phone calls." Fernando was smiling in a way that accentuated his appearance of being a cleric.

da Silva imagined the priest from his boyhood church and felt reassured that he was choosing the correct fellow to trust going forward. da Silva agreed to allow the phone calls.

Fernando made two calls. The first was to Marta Esteves' cell number.

Marta answered, sounding seductively happy and upbeat; in the background could be heard the sounds of a samba club practice. "This is Marta. To whom am I speaking?" She giggled when she spoke.

Fernando had practiced his introduction in his head in his cell. "Senhorita Esteves, this is Fernando Carvalho. We met at the party at Roberto Cavalcanti's in Rio last December. I am very sorry I have taken so long to reach out. I have had several weeks of challenges that, once explained, will allow you to understand, if not excuse my delay. I am wondering if you would meet me in Rio in mid-to-late October. I have a commitment that will keep me away until then and am hoping you'd pick me up at Galeão Airport and spend time with me."

"Well, man of mystery, I am intrigued and very interested in seeing you again. I feared I had offended or scared you in some fashion, or you had lost interest or misplaced my phone number. I am very pleased and excited to be hearing from you."

Fernando's voice deepened, and he replied, "Well, I was so intrigued and captivated by you in our first encounter I had been savoring the idea of our next meeting. Your charm and beauty and vivaciousness captured my interest."

"Well, I'll be." She chuckled. "I'll make sure to still be around come October! And I will await your next call with great anticipation and an excited heart," cooed Marta in reply.

Completely satisfied with the outcome of the call, Fernando hung up and dialed again. This call was to Maria.

"*Olá*," she answered.

"*Mamãe*, it's Fernando. I am calling from Porto Velho with wonderful news." He laid out the deal with da Silva in great detail. In so doing, he described his tutoring effort with the other prisoners. He mentioned some of the tutored prisoners his mother knew.

"Oh, Nando, I am so pleased your future path has had its promise restored. I have prayed and believed all along you would find redemption. I am impressed that your work with the other inmates elevated you in the eyes of the government. I love you with all my heart. Celia and I will come to see you at Porto Velho in late September so we may discuss your return home!"

"Maria, I would love to see you both, and I have other news. I met a wonderful girl in December. I just spoke to her, and we plan to reconnect in October and she and I will spend the end of the month exploring what potential we may have together."

"Oh, Fernando, that is wonderful news that a mother longs to hear. I look forward to meeting her and will keep you both in my prayers. I am so excited! I have prayed for your release from prison and return to a normal life."

Pleased with the calls, Fernando returned to da Silva and ceremoniously handed him the signed agreement. "Thank you, Senhor Colonel, for returning my life and identity to me. As October 10 approaches, I will arrange for a place to live. If it is acceptable, I will reside in Rio. There is a woman there I am interested in, and I am hopeful it may prove to be a lasting relationship."

The two shook hands and hugged.

"Fernando, my boy, Rio would be an excellent choice. I have spoken to Roberto Cavalcanti and Ronaldo Amaraes, and they have agreed to understand your misfortunes and consider you as a potential employee. Your passionate expression of desire to assist Presidente Voss and many of us in the restoration of our national economic strength was the proof we all needed to believe you are a good risk and are likely to be rehabilitated and thus still desirable. Your tutoring initiative is further proof of your character and capabilities! Amaraes comments he has an opening for an analyst on his team and reports he replaced his personal assistant with someone he isn't happy with. He believes your introduction to work with his team would be enhanced if you were to be his assistant. In so doing, you would be exposed to a great deal of valuable knowledge critical to assuming a more senior role on his team. You could as well be assigned meaningful and challenging analytical tasks."

Fernando and da Silva each devoured their meal of fresh fruits and pastries and scrambled eggs and coffee.

"I have been planning to work from the PF offices in Rio, and it will be convenient for us to be close to each other."

Fernando marveled at the irony of having developed the respect of da Silva and having become his friend.

Following the breakfast, da Silva bid Fernando good-bye and promised to fulfill his promises, provided Fernando would continue his exemplary behavior in prison.

"Senhor Colonel, you have my promise and endless gratitude. I cannot thank you enough for your support and trust."

His guards then escorted Fernando to the exercise yard. In the exercise yard, he saw Carlos at a slight distance.

Carlos was glowering at him from fifteen yards away. "I see you, Fernando Carvalho. You'd better stop making the inmates happy at my expense. They are worthless to me with knowledge and a sense of self-worth. I know where your family lives, and you'd better take care."

The guards formed a physical barrier between the two, extending their separation to thirty yards.

"That's just fine, Carlos. I know where your family lives too, so we are even," replied a sniggering Fernando. He recited Carlos' family's home address in the Rio favela of Rocinha. He had anticipated threats from Carlos and researched Carlos' family as a potential target for revenge.

The guards could sense the potential direction of the tension between the two and quickly escorted Carlos away to his bunk where he was left to spend the remainder of the day.

Fernando conducted an aggressive workout consisting of forty-five bar dips and thirty each of pull-ups. He continued with crunches on a padded mat on the ground. He concluded with two sets of twelve repetitions of bench-pressing two fifty-five-pound dumbbells. Following the bench presses, he took two forty-five-pound dumbbells and did two sets of twelve repetitions of seated curls. He then ceased the weight work and ran for one hour on a treadmill at a demandingly brisk pace.

He returned to his cell feeling an exultant contentment with his life and future prospects.

CHAPTER 5

Heliopólis favela, São Paulo, Brazil
Friday, April 10, 2020

Fernando's aunt Celia Donegal was seated in a streetside café, drinking coffee with a male friend. The day was dark because of a heavy cloud layer. Thunder rolled ominously through the clouds, suggesting an oncoming heavy rainstorm and producing a sense of foreboding.

A dark-colored sedan approached their position at speed, and two passengers and the driver sprayed Celia and her companion with automatic weapon fire, killing them both and three other patrons instantly.

The São Paulo Civilian Police responded to the scene quickly and recognized the indication of a clear threat to Maria Carvalho whom, they suspected, was the actual target of the attackers. The police called Maria and alerted her they were dispatching several officers to guard her in her home. The police described the circumstance to Maria, and she understandably broke down in hysterics over the loss of her beloved identical twin.

João da Silva was in São Paulo and soon arrived to express his regrets and condolences and assurances for Maria's safety. A motor home was placed on an adjacent vacant lot, flanked by an armored military police or Polícia Militar (PM) vehicle. A team of eight consisting of three regular army troops and two PF agents and three military policemen, all heavily armed and dressed in tactical uniforms took up position in the motor home on the vacant lot and stood watch. da Silva assured Maria her safety was a top priority for the Brazilian government and that he was working to secure Fernando's near-term parole from prison so he might be at his mother's side.

Maria was deeply shaken by the loss of her twin sister. da Silva and his driver took Maria and escorted her, flanked by the armored PM vehicle and dropped her at Diamante's apartment for safety.

With Diamante's and other residents' and the building management's concurrence, armed policemen and troops were left to secure the garage and lobby of the building. As part of the effort, they camped in sleeping bags on Diamante's living and dining room floors and in the elevator lobbies on each floor of the building.

da Silva arranged to travel to Porto Velho Federal Prison and meet with Fernando and break the news of his aunt's loss.

The police found the gunmen's car cruising quietly on a street and pursued it in a high-speed chase through Heliópolis. The driver stopped in a cul-de-sac where fellow gang members were waiting. The criminals opened fire on the officers who were pinned down by a hail of automatic weapon fire. A call to the military police for pre-planned backup resulted in a dispatch to the officers' aid.

Truckloads of armed troops with a helicopter were sent for cover. Upon arrival on scene, the truck stopped, and the troops fanned out throughout the neighborhood and engaged the criminals in a ferocious gun battle that threatened innocent bystanders; the battle was similar to and as violent as any officers had seen in a war. The troops had far superior weapons of a much heavier caliber than the assailants. The helicopter's door gunner expertly took out several of the assailants with his 60-millimeter gun. The troops and helicopter acted with extreme caution and avoided injuring innocent bystanders.

After several minutes of fierce fighting, the troops made a brilliant flanking move, and shortly, the three men from the car who had killed Aunt Celia were killed, as were four or five of their fellow criminals. The PF and PM officers in charge of law enforcement on scene described the effort as the most daunting challenge they had yet witnessed. This was surprising because gun violence was common throughout Brazil.

On the morning of Saturday, April 11, 2020, da Silva arrived at Porto Velho and was ushered into a meeting room with Fernando.

The room had green paint that had faded with age to an odd gray. Moisture from a leaking ceiling above had accelerated the paint's decline. There was a single aging bare bulb of low wattage hanging at the end of a cord from the ceiling. There was an odor of damp decay and mold in the room. The paint and odor and low-light level combined to give the windowless room a macabre feeling.

A surprised Fernando struggled to see his guest, and he spoke first, "To what do I owe this honor, Senhor Colonel?!"

"Well, my lad, I am afraid this isn't a social visit. I have disturbingly tragic news to share. Please promise me to not overreact. I am very sorry to report your aunt Celia was murdered by heavily armed men driving past while she was seated with a male friend at a street-side café in Heliópolis. The gunfire was not aimed with any care, and her friend and other people nearby died as well."

The emotional blow to Fernando was elevated by the dark dank room's environment.

da Silva continued, "The civilian police and PF and PM are with your mother for protection, and you needn't be overly concerned. Fortunately, the three men whom we believe killed Celia and her companion were killed in a gun battle with our authorities and are not loose to harm anyone else. Two of the dead assailants were brothers of your 'friend' Carlos, so he too will be suffering and grieving. The warden is telling him now. Your mother is currently at Senhor Diamante's apartment, and the building is under heavy guard by the PF and PM We suspect your aunt was killed while being mistaken for your mother. I believe it would be in your and your mother's best interests if you were soon released to return home to be with her. The warden and I have agreed to try to secure your parole on or about May 1 under terms identical to those we agreed upon for your contemplated October parole."

In the dark room, da Silva noted Fernando's face betrayed an understandable rage and heartbreak and painful sadness.

Fernando spoke after fighting back the urge to lash out, "This is the work of that *filho-da-puta* Carlos, isn't it?!"

"Well, now, Fernando, please remember how things play out when Carlos gets under your skin! He is why your night ended so unfortunately after the Cavalcanti party. For your own sake, do not do anything to reverse your current positive trend and optimistic outlook," said da Silva in an attempt to counsel and console Fernando.

Fernando sighed heavily and fought back a tear and replied, "Yes, Senhor Colonel. I want to see my mother and friends again and be available to explore the potential Marta Esteves and I may have. You have my word I will stay calm."

"Well done, lad!" replied a relieved and enthusiastic da Silva. da Silva continued, "On Monday morning, the warden and I plan to phone and speak with a friend who is a federal judge whom we believe may be helpful in securing your parole. We additionally intend to obtain Ronaldo Amaraes' assistance in asking Presidente Voss to grant you clemency. Our argument will be clemency is needed to make you available to work at O Banco do Brasil and to assist the PF in fighting crime. I will return next Tuesday to tell you what is planned. I recommend you locate a place to live in in Rio. Ronaldo Amaraes says he will welcome you to start work with him at O Banco do Brasil on Monday, May 11, 2020. Do not mistake my friendly tone to indicate I will tolerate any wrongdoing by you or your friends in retaliation for your aunt's death. Be assured your mother and Senhor Diamante will definitely be safe under the guard we have positioned at Diamante's apartment building. I look forward to rewarding your good behavior. Be sure to continue teaching your classes to the inmates. I will return within one week to report back regarding the possibility of the clemency."

"Thank you so much, Senhor Colonel. If I do receive clemency, you have my word I will become an exemplary and productive citizen. I so want to return to my mother's side. I won't make a mistake."

The two shook hands and hugged vigorously.

da Silva spoke again, "Fernando, the warden and I will work hard and passionately for your early release. We feel it is critical for you to be home in time for Celia's funeral. João Carlos Diamante has offered to pay for and help coordinate the funeral. I believe you can again be that impressive fellow I met at the Roberto Cavalcanti party."

CHAPTER 6

Porto Velho Federal Prison, Rondônia, Brazil
Morning of Saturday, May 2, 2020

Fernando's entourage of guards escorted him to a meeting room where he found João da Silva waiting for him, looking somber.

"Good morning, Senhor Colonel. To what do I owe the honor of your company?"

"Good morning, Fernando."

The two shook hands and hugged each other.

"Fernando, I promised I would return to report on progress in obtaining clemency from Presidente Voss for your early release. He asked us to proceed in our effort to obtain your parole. He promises he will pardon you if and when you complete a time of positive behavior and success in your work while meeting the terms of your potential parole. The warden and I have obtained your parole commencing on Monday, May 4, and Ronaldo Amaraes says he is prepared to have you start work for O Banco do Brasil on Monday, May 11. We have arranged for you to live in the home of one of our PF agents in Rio. His name is Paulo Coberto. Paulo lives in the Rio suburb of Niterói. He's single as are you. The home is a wonderful bachelor pad. It has a rooftop garden complete with barbecue and bar and sound system and hot tub, all with wonderful views of the mountains and beaches and ocean. Our research revealed an added benefit. Marta Esteves also lives ten minutes away by car in Niterói. You are scheduled to move in with Paulo on Saturday, May 9. You are also welcome to stay at João Carlos Diamante's home with him and your mother on the night of May 4. Things will be moving very quickly for you now, Fernando. I hope you will be able to manage the exhilaration of civilian life and reintroduction to your mother and friends. Presidente Voss and senhores Diamante and Amaraes and Director Vargas and I are all convinced you will do well." da Silva took Fernando's right hand and gripped it firmly in his powerful hand and shook it vigorously.

Fernando marveled at da Silva's seductively persuasive personality and engaging smile and felt he was truly blessed. "Thank you so much, Senhor Colonel. Several months ago, I was convinced my life was heading in a tragic direction. Now I realize God intends for you and me to work together to help our beloved Brazil. With Presidente Voss, we are destined for a return to greatness. I owe you my life, João da Silva."

da Silva was impressed with Fernando's graciousness and sincere expression of gratitude. He continued, "Fernando, your gratitude and dedication inspire us all. I will be here on Monday morning to pick you up for the trip home to São Paulo. A fresh set of clothes and toiletries will be ready for you to prepare for your trip home. I am happy to tell you your mother and Senhor Diamante have invited your friends José Vargas and Luis Antonio to dinner for your welcome-home celebration on Monday evening. God bless you, young man. Your slate has been wiped clean. Be sure to earn your continuing freedom, my friend! I have a backlog of cases, the solving of which would benefit from your and your network's guidance. The warden and I ask you to please arrange to have someone carry on with your tutoring initiative for the prisoners. It would be fantastic if you leave Porto Velho as a better place than when you arrived. An impressive fellow like you needs to leave a strong legacy in his wake. I will see you on Monday for breakfast. Enjoy your weekend. You may now call Marta Esteves."

da Silva noted with joy that Fernando had an incredulous smile on his face.

The then-giddy-with-excitement Fernando accepted and borrowed da Silva's cell phone and dialed Marta Esteves.

She answered on the fourth ring. "Is this the dreamy fellow nicknamed O Bispo?!" she asked while giggling.

Using his radio announcer's voice, Fernando replied, "Well, Senhorita Esteves, yes, it is I. I am happy to report my return to Rio has been accelerated. I will arrive in Rio on Friday, May 8. And on Saturday, May 9, I will move into a new home in Niterói to live with an agent from the PF. Would you like to pick me up at Galeão Airport slightly before seven o'clock that evening? I will text you the details to my flight in a moment. I will arrive dressed as O Bispo. Would you please wear a sundress and sexy shoes? I will begin work for O Banco do Brasil on Monday, May 11."

"Well, handsome, that is marvelous news. I look forward to learning what kept you away from a tantalizing morsel like me for so long now!"

"Well, it is a very long story, and as long as we have been apart. I look forward to telling you about it over dinner at the Grand Hyatt Rio on the night of Friday, May 8!"

"Oh, Fernando, I cannot wait!" cooed Marta in her wonderful Carioca accent. The Carioca accent is the accent customary to Rio de Janeiro. It may be jokingly referred to as sounding like Spanish spoken by a drunken French person.

Fernando could feel her warm smile through the phone and felt a building excitement around getting fully acquainted with Marta. He had been without a romantic female companion for so long he felt he would explode with anticipation.

Fernando next called the auto body repair shop working on the SP2 to let them know he intended to drop by on the afternoon of Tuesday, May 12, for a look at the progress on his car. The shop was ready to accept Fernando's visit, and they scheduled an appointment at three forty-five that afternoon.

CHAPTER 7

Porto Velho Federal Prison, Rondônia, Brazil
Monday, May 4, 2020

At precisely 6:30 a.m., Fernando's guard attachment arrived with a fresh set of clothing for the O Bispo outfit. Fernando arose excitedly and was shown to the private shower room where he found the same toiletry assortment that da Silva had provided before.

While preparing himself for breakfast with da Silva, Fernando studied his image in the bathroom mirror. He marveled at the exhilarating flood of the returning sensation of freedom. He fought a nervous excitement that bordered on disabling ill ease while contemplating his reunification with his mother and Diamante and friends.

He was ushered into a private dining room and was greeted by da Silva and the warden who stood and applauded Fernando.

da Silva spoke first, "Fernando, you and I have much to discuss, and I believe it would be best to speak to each other confidentially on our flight to São Paulo."

"That sounds fine to me," replied Fernando.

The warden then turned and spoke to Fernando, "Fernando Carvalho, it has been an honor to have you housed in Porto Velho. Colonel da Silva and I feel it would be best for us to all eat with your prisoner students for one last hurrah in your honor. They deserve the inspiration of seeing you gain your freedom after you helped them prepare for theirs," said the warden enthusiastically.

Fernando's guard detail then escorted the three men to the central dining hall where there was a head table elevated on a platform next to a podium with a microphone. The warden ascended the podium and addressed the assembled men, "Gentlemen, it is my distinct pleasure to host you all for this send-off breakfast celebration to honor Fernando Carvalho."

The room burst into applause and warmly enthusiastic supporting cheers.

The warden continued, "Gentlemen, Fernando Carvalho is known by his nickname earned for the manner in which he dresses. His focus on you all for your learning and improvement and personal enrichment elevated him to the level of a member of the clergy. We all owe him a huge vote of thanks! Hip, hip, hooray! Hip, hip, hooray!"

The warden invited Fernando to step to the microphone. And Fernando spoke, "Many of you are aware of how much pride and joy I derived by teaching here at Porto Velho. I am very fortunate to be departing today because I will be reunited with my dear mother this evening."

Fernando could see Carlos glowering at him with ferocity while flanked by two huge guards who kept hold of each of Carlos' wrists. Fernando smiled a victorious smile at his rival and chuckled to himself.

"I bid you all a bittersweet goodbye. I fully expect to maintain contact with the warden to know about your collective progress. Ricardo Dolor has agreed to continue the tutoring program, and I have offered to remain available as an advisor should he need advice. I am convinced he will bring the same passion and wisdom to the program as have I.

Please remember knowledge is power, and knowledge without wisdom and intelligence is a sinfully dangerous thing. I will miss you all. Warden and Colonel da Silva, I cannot thank you enough for lessening the pain of my time here. Porto Velho allowed me to find a solid footing for my life. God bless you all."

The food was served, and the warden invited everyone to eat. At the back of the room, a chant arose, a rhythmic repeating of Fernando over and over, accompanied by clapping in the same timing.

Fernando rejoined the warden, and da Silva at the head table, and Fernando's guard attachment joined them.

da Silva smiled his signature seductively engaging grin and placed his right arm around Fernando's shoulders and spoke, "Well, Senhor O Bispo, you are as good and blessed as any man of God. I look forward to being your partner against crime and evil in this great land. The Cavalcanti party was one of your and my luckiest nights. I look forward to being your friend and coworker for life."

Fernando laughed with emotional warmth over this fortunate outcome and fought a growing tear at the corner of each eye. He thought back on each terrible mistake he had made and swore to himself to be dedicated to doing good with well-reasoned thought as he had learned to. "Well, Senhor Colonel da Silva, perhaps you are Batman and I am Robin?!"

da Silva looked very pleased and broke into his signature smile. "Well, Robin, it is time to get in the Batmobile and head to our airplane to return you home to your destiny."

They drove to the airstrip and were greeted by a small Embraer jet dedicated to serving the PF. The pilots were PF agents whom Fernando recognized from the Cavalcanti party. da Silva cheered the pilots upon boarding.

A male flight attendant served cocktails and beer and coffee. Fernando chose to drink Brahma Chopp, his favorite domestic beer (chopp is Portuguese for draft beer), because he wanted to be awake and active throughout the coming evening's celebration of his return home to São Paulo and Heliópolis.

da Silva and Fernando sat side by side in luxurious lounge chairs.

"Well, Fernando Carvalho, I hope you will have time before work early each morning to speak with me to discuss the challenges I could use your help with. I know you will be in a new world, and I do not wish to disturb your opportunity for success at O Banco. I invite you to determine the timing and pace for our ongoing contact."

Upon landing in São Paulo, the plane's engines were powered down by the crew.

da Silva turned toward Fernando while they removed their seat belts and secured the items they had carried onto the flight.

Fernando had a small carry-on-style suitcase in which he had stored most of his casual clothing and some gifts for his family and friends he had purchased in the airport gift shop in Rondônia prior to takeoff.

CHAPTER 8

João Carlos Diamante's apartment building, São Paulo, Brazil
Evening of Monday, May 4, 2020

Fernando and da Silva arrived at Diamante's apartment building, and da Silva spoke to the PF and PM commanders overseeing the security precautions. These consisted of a truckload of six PF agents and five PM officers all dressed in tactical fighting gear and armed with Colt Automatic Rifles. The Colt Automatic Rifle is a lightweight 5.56-millimeter light-combat weapon utilized with great success by NATO (North Atlantic Treaty Organization) and other forces around the world.

The security detachment was in place to prevent any attempted revenge effort by Carlos and Regimento A to hurt Fernando and da Silva for having undermined Carlos' influence over the prisoners at Porto Velho.

Satisfied with the security, da Silva and Fernando took the elevator to the penthouse level and were greeted by Diamante and Maria and Luis Antonio and José Vargas.

"Oh, welcome home, Nando," said Luis Antonio and José Vargas in unison.

A tearful Maria put her arms around Fernando and spoke, "Oh my god, Fernandinho, I thought I might never see you again, my beloved son!" Fernandinho is the endearing diminutive form of Fernando. "I am so excited to have you back as a free man. Thank you, Colonel da Silva, for taking an interest in my boy!"

da Silva broke into his most charming smile and shook Maria's hand. "Senhora Carvalho, it has been my great fortune to meet and know such a smart and capable young man as Fernando Carvalho! Securing his freedom was a selfish act I performed for my and our country's benefit! Fernando is the younger brother I have always longed for and never had. I am blessed to know him and so pleased to meet you."

da Silva turned to Diamante. "Senhor Diamante, I understand you are to be thanked for taking Fernando and Maria under your wing and watching over them. Fernando is now destined, as he always was, to be a national treasure! I am convinced you've known this all along."

Diamante smiled broadly and replied, "Well, Colonel, you and I both have the distinct pleasure and honor to know O Bispo and to be his friends and supporters! His mother is a superior human being and did a superb job of raising him in poverty. They each had determination and passion commensurate with the other's. Additionally, Maria served as an inspiring role model to Fernando! We should not let Fernando and his friends escape our continued focused criticism of their youthful choice of a life of crime!"

Fernando and José Vargas and Luis Antonio all nodded their emphatic agreement and smiled proudly in concurrence.

"I completely agree and expect these young men will assist Director Vargas and me and the PF and Presidente Voss in our efforts to stop crime and corruption throughout Brazil!" replied da Silva in an elevated tone with his arm around Fernando's shoulders.

Diamante replied, "Amen, Senhor Colonel da Silva! Well, now it is time for dinner. Please all follow me."

Diamante led them all through the home's luxurious living room and into an elegant dining room with a grand dining table set with expensive silver and glassware. The room was painted in a dark red and had a formidable carved hutch sitting on the side of the room. The exterior wall was floor-to-ceiling windows. The sun was low in the sky and cast a calming progressively lower light through the windows. A light rain began to fall, accompanied by a subtle thunder. The hutch was made of brazilwood, matching the material and design of the dining table.

A sommelier stood to the side in a corner, holding two bottles of red wine she had just withdrawn from a wine-chilling case in the kitchen. She was a striking beauty, and Fernando was captivated by her similarity of appearance to Marta Esteves. He realized he was longing for his coming reunion with Marta. The wine was a favorite of Diamante's he had discovered on a trip to a venture capital conference in San Francisco, California. It was a 2012 Stags' Leap Petite Sirah. The sommelier placed large red wine glasses made of crystal in front of all at the table. She ceremoniously opened and decanted the two bottles and poured an approval taste from each for Diamante.

The chef and three waiters appeared, and Diamante asked to have the meal served. A selection of jazz was playing softly through speakers in the ceiling and walls.

With the music as a mood-setting background, Diamante explained the wine and its unique characteristics and qualities. Diamante swirled the wine in his tasting glass and held it up to observe the color and viscosity. He drew a deep breath to appreciate its aroma, and he looked very pleased and asked the sommelier to leave each bottle to decant for a few minutes and then pour a glass for each guest. "Everyone, it is with great pleasure I welcome Fernando back to the real world. I am sure he hasn't had a meal like ours this evening in a long time and pray he accepts and enjoys it as a token of Maria's and my love for him. Job well done, Fernando Carvalho!" Everyone touched their glasses with the others at the table and echoed Diamante's welcome to Fernando. The servers returned with plates covered by silver domes concealing the meal.

With the rumble of the thunder as backdrop, the chef made an introductory announcement, "This evening, my team and I have prepared butterflied leg of lamb which we cooked over an open fire to medium rare. We seasoned the lamb with rosemary and salt and pepper and garlic and basted it with olive oil and its own juices. There is mint jelly to accompany your meat. Please use it as you please. As an aside, the meat will be delightful without the added flavor of the jelly. On your plates, you will find mashed potatoes covered with the juice from the meat along with grilled asparagus and sautéed mushrooms. You will find the lamb and entire meal and the wine complement each other in magnificent fashion. Following the main course, we will serve a salad. Please enjoy your food. Welcome home, Senhor Fernando. We have missed you terribly and are so pleased your ordeal at Porto Velho is over."

Fernando blushed at the attention and spoke, "I offer a toast to Colonel João da Silva, without whose support and attention, I may not have survived in prison, where I might yet be trapped. I owe him much more than the simple obligations I must fulfill under the terms of my parole! I further toast João Carlos Diamante for his love and attention to Maria's and my needs. Without his support, we would not have been able to survive my dear father's death. God bless you, João. I further salute our new president, Presidente

Ricardo Voss. The future of Brazil is looking very promis-ing! I additionally salute my dear mother who so successfully cared for me in my father's absence. I look forward to work-ing with O Banco do Brasil and the Polícia Federal in over-coming the damage wrought by the da Silva and Rousseff administrations! Long live, Brazil! To my great surprise, my life has become bright and inspiring!"

Everyone toasted Fernando's comments and relished the lamb and Petite Sirah.

CHAPTER 9

João Carlos Diamante's apartment building, São Paulo, Brazil
Evening of Monday, May 4, 2020

The chef returned and spoke, "Well, everyone, I trust from the way your plates have been swept clean that the meal was to your satisfaction. We will serve the salad shortly."

Diamante spoke again, "Well, Diego, that was too good, and I am convinced Fernando enjoyed it immensely!"

In advance of the arrival of the salad, the sommelier returned and presented Diamante with another bottle to approve. She showed him an unopened bottle of 2018 Catena Zapata Adrianna Vineyard White Stones chardonnay from Mendoza, Argentina. Diamante nodded his approval, and the bottle was opened. Diamante directed the sommelier to pour the approval tasting for Fernando.

Fernando felt somewhat out of practice and swirled the wine in his glass and lifted it and studied it in the light of the candles on the table. He relished being able to remember the ritual he had learned at Diamante's side some ten years before. He drew a deep breath through his nose and savored the fruity aroma of the wine. He took a sip and swished it around in his mouth; he smiled and nodded his approval, and the sommelier poured each of the others a glass of their own.

Throughout the meal, Fernando kept thinking excitedly about his upcoming reunion with Marta.

The chef spoke again, "Well, my friends, this salad is made with lettuce that was grown in the state of Rio Grande do Norte as were the tomatoes. The olive oil in the dressing is from Uruguay as is the red wine vinegar. Bon appétit. I will leave you to savor the wine and salad and will return in a few minutes."

Diamante was looking at Fernando and beaming. "Well, young man, are you glad to be home?!"

"João, this is a dream come true! Ever since Colonel da Silva suggested my parole, I've been dreaming of how things would be when I returned home. I am blessed and overjoyed to be sharing this evening with all of you. I intend to be a model citizen and make you all proud. I know I must bear the burden of my sins. I propose a toast in honor of the poor fellow I hit and killed in Rio."

da Silva and Diamante were seated next to each other and shared appreciative expressions while congratulating each other for their and Maria's roles in creating and freeing O Bispo.

The chef returned to the table and announced, "I hope our modest offering brought you all pleasure." Everyone smiled and congratulated the chef and service personnel with a collective positive murmur. "Very well, please wait while we prepare to serve a white cake with lemon frosting for dessert. Thank you. You are all too kind."

The sommelier returned with a bottle of Uruguayan ruby port that she presented to Diamante for approval. He waived the tasting and asked the sommelier to pour for everyone. A contented feeling descended over the table and its occupants, and everyone chatted happily.

Fernando looked around the table and winked at Maria who broke into a glorious smile and started to shed a tear of joy. Fernando rose up and stood behind his mother and wrapped his right arm around her shoulders below the neck and whispered in her ear, "Well, Maria Carvalho, it appears the road ahead for us in life is clear. I am very fortunate to be your son and love you with all my heart. I so wish Celia and Carlos were here tonight. I believe they are here, in spirit, as well! I love you deeply." He kissed her cheek passionately and stood to join Diamante and da Silva in a conversation over the port.

The evening's tranquility was suddenly shattered by the sound of squealing tires and shouting and automatic gunfire from the street below. In a vain attempt to gain entry to the building, three pickup trucks loaded with armed insurgents attempted to attack and kill the security force in the street. The attackers were untrained amateurs who proved no match for the law enforcement officers and military men standing guard in the street. Following a few minutes of brutal fighting, all the attackers were dead.

da Silva rushed down the building's fire-exit staircase to speak to the security commanders to obtain a report and to possibly join in the defensive efforts in the event his help might be required. Upon his arrival at the ground floor, he found the on-site commanders speaking to the São Paulo regional commandant for the PM. da Silva knew the commandant well from their days together in the army where they had become good friends.

The commandant updated da Silva, "All of the attackers have been killed. All in, we suffered four casualties, Colonel. Two military policemen were killed, and two PF agents suffered non life-threatening wounds to their legs. They are being tended to by our medical corpsmen and should be fine soon. Ambulances are on their way, being escorted under the protection of armored vehicles belonging to the military police. Albert Einstein Hospital has been notified to expect the wounded and reports they are ready to receive them. The civilian police have identified the deceased attackers as members of Regimento A who reside in São Paulo. We suspect our old nemesis, Carlos, is behind this atrocity."

Enraged by the casualties inflicted and destruction of the serenity of the evening's gathering in Diamante's home, da Silva called the warden at Porto Velho and described the circumstance and suspicion of Carlos' responsibility. He sought out and thanked the wounded PF agents and made sure they were properly cared for.

The warden and da Silva agreed da Silva would fly to Rondônia that evening and participate in an interrogation of Carlos late the next morning.

da Silva asked for and received a handwritten list of the dead attackers to be used in the interrogation. While confirming reinforcements to replace the casualties were on the way, da Silva learned seven members of the GRUMEC were on the way from their São Paulo position. GRUMEC is a Portuguese language acronym for Underwater Combat Group. It is a branch of the Brazilian Navy as skilled and hardened as the US Navy SEALs. They were instructed to fan out in coordination with the law enforcement agents present to ensure the area was secure.

da Silva smiled briefly to himself and returned to Diamante's apartment and explained the dire circumstance that had unfolded in the street. He enthusiastically thanked Diamante for his hospitality and reiterated his thanks for Diamante's role in Fernando's upbringing and bid everyone a good night.

He took Fernando aside, and they spoke, "Well, Senhor Carvalho, your new life will begin in Rio this coming weekend. I look forward to speaking with you on the morning of Tuesday, October 12, regarding what we may accomplish together. As I promised, I will call you early that morning in order that I do not interrupt your focus on starting work with Ronaldo Amaraes. Good luck in your introductory time with Marta Esteves. I hope she is everything you have hoped for as you may be for her. Good luck as well with your initial time at O Banco do Brasil. Remember to keep yourself focused on the straight and narrow path, my boy. Your country needs you to be of service, and those of us who've invested our faith and energy and effort and time on your behalf deserve the reward of you proving you can be and are rehabilitated. Please give my best to Senhor Amaraes. Please also give my best to Paulo Coberto when you move in on Saturday. Paulo is one of our best agents. I'm convinced you will enjoy living with and getting to know him. His home is, by far, superior to your cell at Porto Velho!"

Fernando smiled a warm smile back at da Silva and spoke, "Senhor Colonel, you have my word I will live up to everyone's expectations. I understand I am blessed to be out in society and free of the dark tedium of Porto Velho. Thank you so much for all you have done for me. I hope you can corral Carlos and his Regimento A team and protect the country from more of their evil mischief."

da Silva smiled a sly smile and responded, "Well, Senhor Carvalho, I do have a plan for your friend Carlos that I believe will coerce him into cooperating and standing down. It is designed to force him into a corner from which he cannot escape."

The two hugged firmly, and Fernando returned to the apartment to wind up the evening with his friends and mother and Diamante.

*　*　*　*　*

Fernando was filled with excitement about the days ahead and realized he was feeling much as he had as a youngster at the beginning of a holiday break from school. He sat back down with Diamante and Maria and José Vargas and Luis Antonio. Fernando reveled in the experience while the evening passed slowly in a languid slow motion that felt like a fantastic dream to a man who'd been facing years of confinement.

He spent several days resting up prior to departing for Rio on Friday, May 8.

On Tuesday, May 5, Celia's funeral was held. Diamante delivered a joint eulogy with the president of an education nonprofit Celia had been a passionate volunteer for. The eulogy was wonderful and filled with humorous recollections of Celia's life and behavior. Maria and Fernando were freed of their deepest grief by their laughter. The service and burial concluded with a gathering at the Diamante home in which the chef and sommelier delivered a delightful celebration.

The day passed quietly until a team of Carlos' insurgents attempted to interrupt the calm with an attack on the celebration at the Diamante home. The GRUMEC troops fought the attackers ferociously and expertly killed five. The commanders called da Silva to let him know of the continuing Regimento A threat. The day's weather was clear and warm until a massive rainstorm arrived as grim reminder of the somber nature of the day's events.

Fernando was prepared to move in with Paulo Coberto and spend the following days immersing himself in his work at O Banco do Brasil while absorbing everything he could learn from Amaraes and members of his O Banco do Brasil economics team.

Fernando remained in touch with da Silva and obtained a few leads that helped the colonel in his crime-solving efforts.

* * * * *

Upon his arrival at Porto Velho for the interrogation of Carlos, da Silva was greeted by the warden and the guard detail that had watched over Fernando. He was ushered into the dark interrogation room in which he had told Fernando of Celia's death.

Seated at the table in shackles was Carlos. The day was very hot, and the humidity from the exterior found its way into the room. Carlos was drenched in sweat.

"Well, good afternoon, Carlos. I hope you are in a mood to listen to me because I have a clear message and warning you'd better listen to and heed."

Carlos glared at da Silva, and his anger and hatred were visible in the light of the single low-wattage bulb suspended from the ceiling. "What the hell do you want, Colonel da Silva!? I hold the high ground! You are in no position to dictate to me!"

Two large guards stood in the room's corners. They edged toward Carlos in response to his agitated voice and stood behind him, ready to pounce when necessary.

da Silva spoke in reply, "Carlos, we know you and your Regimento A buddies are responsible for the recent violence in São Paulo that caused the death of Fernando Carvalho's aunt Celia, and we will not tolerate any more of your senseless violence. The warden and I have agreed to terminate your visits to the exercise yard. Additionally, the PF and PM and GRUMEC are, as we speak, positioning a blockade around your home in Rocinha. The blockade will be like an international border crossing. Everyone entering or exiting the home will be compelled to show identification and be fingerprinted and to provide DNA samples as well."

Carlos stared at da Silva with hatred while listening and replied, "Do what you want with me. I am immune to your punishments of me. You have no right to harass and burden my mother and father and siblings!" The sweat grew noticeably on Carlos' forehead and in his armpits, leaving him looking much as though he had fallen in a pool of water. "I demand to see my attorney!"

da Silva smiled a smile of victory. "Well, Carlos, we do have the right to take this action. A judge in Rio has authorized these measures. We have served your attorney with the court order permitting the blockade." da Silva ceremoniously placed a photocopy of the judge's order onto the table in front of Carlos. "You do not appear to hold the high ground nor do you have any leverage here. If you promise to cease the violence and it doesn't reoccur, you have my word I will work to prevent the blockade and to restore your exercise yard privileges."

da Silva noticed Carlos was crying, not aloud but in frustration in silence. Tears streamed down the cheeks below each eye, and he was gritting his teeth and clenching his fists.

"Okay, Senhor Colonel, I promise no further violence, provided you do not place the blockade. If you do place the blockade, there will be hell to pay. If you do not, there will be peace."

da Silva smiled enthusiastically and signaled the guards that he intended to approach Carlos. The guards moved in close enough to strike in the event Carlos acted up. da Silva moved next to Carlos and took Carlos' shackled right hand and shook it vigorously. "Well, Carlos, we have a deal. You will be allowed to exercise today and tomorrow. You have my word there will be no blockade of your home. I instead will hold that option open in the event you disappoint the warden and me. Have a good rest of your day and a good night. Do not disappoint me or the warden. The court ruling gives us flexibility in deciding how difficult we should make things for your family and friends, in the event you are not cooperative. Have a good completion to your week."

da Silva was shown to the prison gate and reentered the PF car he had used to get to the prison from the local airport. He had flown in on the Embraer private jet assigned to the PF. He then flew home in the plane.

That evening, he was back with his family in his home in Brasília and feeling content over his achievement with Carlos.

da Silva poured himself a drink and called Director Vargas with the positive news. They agreed Carlos couldn't be trusted and discussed what other measures could be employed to exert influence over him in the event he wasn't true to his word.

Vargas called the warden and directed him to carefully control and monitor Carlos' contact with the world outside of Porto Velho.

After careful observation, the prison guards determined that Carlos was using a kitchen staffer as the conduit for his contact with the Regimento A leadership in Rio. The kitchen staffer was fired quickly.

Carlos demanded a conversation with the warden after that. The conversation was held in the interrogation room in which da Silva had spoken with Carlos.

"Good afternoon, Carlos. How may I be of help, and what are your concerns?" began the warden.

Carlos smiled impishly and replied, "Warden, I am very unhappy with how you have cut me off from the outside world! I have given the Regimento A leadership clear instructions as to what they should do in the event they are not able to communicate with me."

The warden sat down across from Carlos. Three guards moved behind Carlos and secured his arms and legs. The warden responded, "Well, Carlos, that is a threat and a direct violation of the agreement we have under which we abstained from the blockade at your home in Rocinha. For the sake of your family's and friends' comfort and convenience, I urge you to retract the threat and renew and amend your previous pledge to include no violence nor threat of violence."

Carlos laughed at the warden and responded, "Well, Warden, we seem to be at an impasse. I demand you allow me to communicate with the Regimento A leadership. In the event you do not and you impose the blockade on my family, I warn you there will be a cascade of further violence!"

The guards then picked Carlos up from his seat and abruptly removed him to his bunk.

The warden calmly replied, "All right, young man, I too have no choice. You will be removed from your current bunk and placed in solitary confinement without contact with anyone but the guards. The blockade of your home will take effect immediately. Your return to the prison population and removal of the blockade will require your making a new pledge just as I have requested. You will spend tonight and the next three nights in solitary, and the blockade will begin this evening."

Carlos spat on the floor and replied, "Warden, I have given the Regimento A leadership a list of targets to be killed in the event I am unable to contact the leadership."

"Very well, Carlos, my law enforcement colleagues and I have arranged to send you to a solitary cell in the brig at Porto Velho Air Force Base. You will be held without visitation rights and without external communication. Your mail, both in and outbound, will be severely limited to include communication with only your family and will be read by law enforcement censors. The censors will be instructed to take note of your communications' content and to alter your outbound communications to prevent any undesirable outcomes," concluded the warden with a firm nod and brief smile. "Should any violence occur, your sentence would be extended to life. Game, set, match, my friend!" The warden quickly departed the room.

Carlos erupted in anger, "You cannot do this to me! I demand to see my attorney!"

One of the guards injected Carlos with a strong sedative, and the three guards took him to a waiting van that was prepared to transport him to Porto Velho Air Force Base and his new home.

* * * * *

The warden called da Silva and Director Vargas to let them know of his action with Carlos.

Director Vargas was relaxed and enthusiastic. Marton Vargas and his wife, Lara, were moving into their dream home on Lake Paranoá in Brasília. The home was located in the tony neighborhood in which the federal cabinet members resided. Marton and Lara had scrimped and saved in order that they could move from their modest middle-class home in central Brasília.

The new home had a striking contemporary look. In order to save cost, they had elected to utilize concrete set in a form with a pattern to simulate wood. The concrete was stained to have an appearance of real wood. A massive glue lam beam that ran the length of the home supported the roof. It was set on vertical concrete pillars at each end of the home. The roof was constructed of wood and curved to a height of three feet above the glue lam beam. The external walls of the home were primarily made of glass, with the exception of walls at either end constructed of the formed concrete. The curved openings between each end wall and the roof were glass as well. The home was 75 feet or 22.8 meters long from side to side and 50 feet or 15.2 meters deep; the interior was slightly less than 4,000 square feet or 372 square meters. The garage was oversized and could accommodate three of the smaller cars customary among the Brazilian population. The home was set on a lot of under 1 acre or 4,050 square meters. The backyard was naturally landscaped, and the Vargases planned to have it formally landscaped.

During the call, Vargas was walking on the property, admiring his new home while enjoying a caipirinha.

As evening turned to night, Lara Vargas turned on exterior floodlights, illuminating the home's exterior for Marton's enjoyment. She additionally lighted interior lights, making the modestly elegant interior visible from Marton's vantage point in the yard.

He sat down in a yard chair and reveled in the warm feeling of success at having achieved the ability to build and own and occupy his dream home. He studied the yard, imagining a planned landscaping project having been completed. The work on the landscaping was to begin within one or two weeks. Marton Vargas was feeling at the top of his career and life.

As he assumed office, the newly elected Presidente Ricardo Voss had made a serious effort to place individuals of the highest caliber in each and every leadership position in the nation. After careful study and contemplation, he decided to name Colonel Marton Vargas as director of the Polícia Federal. Vargas was a career PF agent who'd risen up by leading the investigations of and solving numerous high-profile crimes involving murder and theft and extortion and corruption. Through the news broadcasts and print media publishing that covered his successes, he had become a folk hero throughout Brazil.

He found a tree stump and placed his drink on it and told the warden and da Silva he was adding Fernando to the call.

Fernando answered quickly, "Good evening, Senhor Director. How are you, and to what good fortune do I owe this call?"

"Fernando, I am well. I am walking blissfully in the backyard of my new home. I have Colonel da Silva and the warden of Porto Velho on the line. It appears the warden has constrained Carlos against any further violence. Following the death of your dear aunt Celia, I thought you might like to hear about it."

Fernando replied with a short chuckle, "Well, of course, I'd like to hear, Senhor Director!"

The warden and da Silva then said hello to Fernando, and the warden described his exchange with Carlos and action in moving him to Porto Velho Air Force Base. They chatted for a while, trying to guess what Carlos' threat of continued violence might be about. They agreed to offer bonuses to the brig guards at Porto Velho Air Force Base in the event Carlos was unable to communicate with the outside world and if they succeeded in preventing his committing violence while he was at Porto Velho Air Force Base.

While they chatted, Carlos was raising a huge fuss in his cell in the brig at Porto Velho Air Force Base.

Two weeks earlier in Rio, the leaders of Regimento A in place in Carlos' absence while in prison had opened a note Carlos had left in a safe deposit box. The note outlined a set of heinous acts to be carried out against Fernando and the warden and the PF in retribution for any potential act to expand on Carlos' punishment. The readers jumped into action rapidly and made phone calls to coordinate the fulfillment of their boss' vile hate-filled plans.

Having no knowledge of this development, Vargas and da Silva and Fernando agreed they had taken the steps necessary to contain Carlos.

Lulled by this false sense of security, Marton Vargas felt safe. Perhaps he could and should have implemented heightened security measures in his neighborhood and around his home. But his reverie, looking at his new home, had a narcotic-like effect, and he avoided any further action and continued about his daily routine thereafter.

As the morning of Thursday, May 7, 2020, came to Carlos' Porto Velho Air Force Base cell, his guards again gave Carlos a heavy dose of sedatives in order that he might remain silent. They were concerned he might do himself serious harm while flailing wildly.

Colonel da Silva was in Rio, awaiting Fernando's planned move in with Paulo Coberto. PF Director Vargas was at home, feeling comfortable with his wife and daughters. Fernando was equally comfortable and still in São Paulo, pending his departure for Rio the following day.

* * * * *

On the evening of May 7, Fernando called Marta to confirm plans for his arrival in Rio at six o'clock in the evening on May 8; Marta agreed to pick Fernando up at Galeão International Airport. They chatted excitedly and planned to then go to the Grand Hyatt Rio for dinner.

Fernando explained he intended to spend the night there in advance of going to Paulo Coberto's to move in.

"Do you really think you will want to stay in a hotel? You are very welcome at my place," Marta cooed at Fernando.

"Well, Senhorita Esteves, I hadn't been so bold and presumptuous as to consider that option! It sounds like a wonderful idea. I should warn you I am coming with three large suitcases filled with my belongings to move into the house in Niterói. I am due there at ten o'clock on Saturday morning."

"Oh, that will not be a burden!" enthused Marta. "I cannot wait to see you, Fernando Carvalho. My heart is pounding in anticipation. I believe I will struggle to stay focused throughout the upcoming days!"

"As will I," he replied. "I'll see you on Friday evening, beautiful," intoned Fernando in his best sexy voice.

CHAPTER 10

João Carlos Diamante's apartment building, São Paulo, Brazil
Morning of Friday, May 8, 2020

Fernando arose at five thirty in the morning to allow time to arrange his things for departure. He had been to the Heliópolis house to collect his things for his move to Rio and had three large suitcases loaded to the hilt with many of his life's possessions sitting in the entry area. In this collection were included some wonderful paintings made by his father Carlos.

Three PF agents dispatched by da Silva arrived to take Fernando and his belongings to the airport for the flight to Rio scheduled to depart that afternoon at 3:00 p.m.

Maria and Diamante each arose at six o'clock in the morning, and the chef arrived at seven o'clock and prepared a wonderful breakfast of eggs and bacon and pastries and fruit. Everyone washed their food down with ample quantities of strong coffee mixed with foamed, heated milk.

Fernando promised his mother and Diamante he would stay in touch and return soon for a visit. Maria and Diamante excitedly wished him well in his meeting with Marta.

Around noon, the PF agents took Fernando's belongings down to the building lobby and loaded them along with Fernando into a large Chevrolet sedan for the drive to the airport.

da Silva had made the Embraer jet he and Fernando had flown on available for Fernando's relocation.

Galeão International Airport, Rio de Janeiro, Brazil
Evening of Friday, May 8, 2020

At 5:45 p.m., Fernando's plane touched down at Galeão International Airport.

Fernando was excited in a way he was unaccustomed to being. He dialed Marta's cellphone to report the landing and coordinate their meeting. He was surprised as the phone rang several times and no one answered.

On the third attempt, he went to voice mail and nervously recorded a message, "Hi, Marta. This is Fernando. I hope you haven't been delayed in coming to Galeão. I just landed and will be at the curb near baggage claim anxiously awaiting your arrival."

Frustrated by the failure to connect, he dialed back a few times, and in each case, the call went to voice mail.

On the first voice mail opportunity, he left a message, "Olá, Marta. It's Fernando. I have landed at Galeão and will be at the curb by six twenty-five. I cannot wait to see you, girl. Call me back!"

He then called the hotel to confirm his arrival and reserved a table for two in the restaurant at seven fifteen that evening.

Fernando tried Marta's number several more times with an equal lack of success. As he began another attempt, his phone rang, and he was relieved to see it was Marta. Fernando answered and said, "Well, there you are. What a pleasure it is to be hearing from you."

Marta was laughing and replied, "You are obviously unclear about the effect you have on me, Senhor O Bispo! I am excitedly arriving at Galeão and will be at the curb at six thirty. I cannot wait to get my hands on you! I hope you're rested up from your time in São Paulo, and I am looking forward to learning what delayed our getting together since our first meeting last December."

"Wow, that is enticing, and I can assure you I am at full charge on my battery!" Fernando chuckled, trying successfully to sound convincingly self-assured.

The PF agents were following him with his luggage and joked about his evening of amorous opportunity ahead.

At the curb, they found Marta waiting in a small Chevy pickup truck. She was dressed in a fashion that demonstrated what was on her mind. She was dressed in a tight-fitting black dress cut very short with no sign of a bra. She had a pair of provocative black high-heeled shoes open at the toes, exposing her toenails polished with a white finish matching her fingernails. She had obviously had her hair permed and colored with blond highlights and had striking white imitation fingernails and false eyelashes and marvelous deep red lipstick.

The PF agents continued goading Fernando and were dumfounded by Marta's sexy beauty.

Once his gear was stored in the load bed, Fernando got into the passenger's seat, and Marta kissed him with a long deeply erotic kiss that lasted for two minutes. Music was playing, the song "Glorious" by British singer Foxes. Fernando thought he would always remember the moment when hearing the song.

"Welcome back to Rio, silly man. I have been counting the minutes and seconds since we first planned this meeting. Am I correct you are nervous and thought I had forgotten our date and were worried I might be a no-show?! You will shortly see how invested I am in our nascent relationship!"

She started the truck's engine and chuckled while putting it in gear. "Well, Fernando, you are a very fortunate fellow. I surely know my way around a stick!"

Fernando thought to himself how fortunate he was to be in her company and thought through how he intended the night should unfold. "Well, Senhorita Esteves, I am happy to say I have a marvelous stick."

Marta laughed seductively and said, "Well, Fernando, I don't want you to think I am an easy, slutty woman. I do intend to find a path to being your romantic partner but not at the drop of a hat."

CHAPTER 11

Grand Hyatt Hotel, Rio de Janeiro, Brazil
Evening of Friday, May 8, 2020

They arrived at the Grand Hyatt and handed the truck over to the valet attendant on duty. Fernando exited the truck and held the driver's door open for Marta.

Marta stepped toward Fernando and said, "I retract my suggestion we stay at my place. I love the feeling of this hotel and would love to stay here with you tonight after our dinner."

Fernando smiled and nodded yes and took her arm and motioned to the bellmen to collect his things from the pickup. They entered the lobby arm in arm and approached the front desk where Fernando checked in. Fernando was offered a chance for an upgrade to a suite on the floor with concierge service. He jumped at the opportunity. Fernando's collection of bags was sent to the room while he and Marta went to the restaurant for dinner.

At dinner, they began with a bottle of a wonderful Argentine Cabernet Sauvignon.

Marta sat very close to Fernando's left side and held his left hand tightly in her right hand. She made certain Fernando could feel the press of her right unharnessed breast. Fernando was excited and intrigued and carefully looked her over and noticed she had nicely sized but not-too-large pouty breasts. She dropped her right hand from his left hand down to rest at the top of his left leg. He noted she was wearing an intriguing perfume that created an impression of magical seduction.

He realized she had succeeded in arousing him physically, and he looked at her. And she said with a huge grin, "See, I do know my way around a stick!"

"And I noted I have a marvelous stick!" he replied.

"Well, I intend to be the judge of that" came Marta's giggled reply.

Fernando had passed his life carefully avoiding being emotionally attached to a girl or woman and marveled at how intrigued and enchanted he was becoming with Marta.

They each wanted to get through dinner and head to their room. They chatted idly while finishing their first glasses of wine and ordered a barbecued steak and a pan-grilled halibut that they shared.

Fernando signaled the waiter for the check and had the bottle of wine recorked, and they headed to their room.

In the elevator, Marta held Fernando's left arm and looked him in the eye and said, "I don't want to seem too easy without our getting truly familiar. I'd like to spend time talking and getting to know each other before we engage physically."

Fernando, the consummate gentleman, nodded his concurrence. Just as he opened the door to their suite, the concierge butler arrived to welcome them and showed them the room's layout and features.

Marta asked the concierge butler to position an ottoman two feet from the room's lounge chair. That arrangement made, she motioned for Fernando to sit on the chair. She sat down on the ottoman across from Fernando and asked his permission to step away.

He nodded yes with a bemused chuckle.

"Thank you, Senhor O Bispo," said Marta while standing back up and kissing Fernando's forehead. "May I use one of your T-shirts as a nightgown?" she asked with a giggle.

"You'll find one in the green suitcase," he replied while being even further intrigued by his companion.

Marta dug through and found two shirts with the logo of the Rio football or soccer team Fluminense. She sniffed each critically and selected the larger of the two. "This is the one!" she announced ceremoniously. "May I use it?"

Completely confused and intrigued, Fernando said, "Of course, you silly thing!"

"Oh, thank you so much, Fernando. It has your smell and feels wonderful. May I put it on?"

"I insist," he said.

Marta stood in his full view and unzipped the back of her dress and took it off, exposing her incredibly gorgeous body. She stood in her shoes and dramatically pulled the shirt over her head, then sat, and seductively removed her shoes.

Fernando sat grinning from ear to ear in the lounge chair.

Marta returned to the ottoman and sat facing Fernando and started talking to him about her and kissing him.

He responded with a passionate hug and kiss and touched her hair and stared into her large wonderfully beautiful brown eyes. "I am fighting my natural instinctive response and simply want to talk with you to become acquainted as you wished earlier. Would you like to have some more wine?"

"Of course, handsome man," she almost sang in response.

The smiling Fernando then moved to his suitcase and removed a bottle of the Stags' Leap Petite Sirah he'd received from Diamante before departing São Paulo. Diamante told

Fernando it was a gift for his introductory time with Marta. He sat back down and called the concierge butler and asked him to bring wine glasses and a bottle opener.

The concierge butler knocked quickly and opened the bottle and filled two crystal glasses.

Fernando and Marta returned to the lounge chair and ottoman and resumed their kissing.

Fernando explained his past to Marta, including the death of the homeless man on the night they met and his Sombra Preta past and how he and Luis Antonio had killed José Vargas' attacker. He described his arrest and imprisonment and parole and loss of his aunt Celia.

Marta said she was terribly sorry and somewhat relieved to learn all of it as she had suspected he was out chasing women and partying and ignoring her the whole time since Cavalcanti's party. She offered she was relieved to learn he hadn't been intentionally avoiding her while involved with someone else. She apologized for doubting him and the intensity of their kissing grew dramatically, fueled by the marvelous wine.

Marta placed Fernando's right hand on her left breast, and she made a groan of pleasure while he responded to the invitation.

She took the wine glasses and placed them within easy reach of the bed on the nightstands. She connected her cell phone to a speaker in the room and started to play a playlist she had created in Spotify for their introduction. She stood in front of Fernando and took his hand and guided him to the bed. He marveled at how he found her choice of his T-shirt as a nightgown to be extremely erotic and exciting.

Two hours later, they were quite exhausted by their athletic lovemaking.

Fernando observed he had to get up in a few hours and be ready for Paulo Coberto to pick him up to move into the house in Niterói.

Marta agreed that they should indeed finish the Petite Sirah and make further love.

CHAPTER 12

Grand Hyatt Hotel, Rio de Janeiro, Brazil
Morning of Saturday, May 9, 2020

At 6:30 a.m. the following morning, Fernando's alarm sounded, and he got up and started to pack. He dressed for and took a long run of ten kilometers and returned to the room looking very tired and damp from sweating. Marta was aroused by his appearance and scent, and they again made love with abandon.

Fernando was soon in the shower and was pleasantly surprised when a cascade of cold water poured over his head. Marta had filled a pitcher from the room with cold water and jokingly had reached above the shower door and poured it over his neck and back.

"Come here, you vixen!" he said jokingly while grabbing Marta and pulling her into the shower with him.

"Stop. I still have your shirt on!" she protested while giggling and grimacing.

"Well, I can solve that problem quickly!" he responded while pulling the shirt over her head and off.

They embraced in a passionate kiss and were interrupted by the ringing of Fernando's cell phone. It was Paulo calling to announce he and some PF agents were in the lobby waiting for Fernando to come down for the move to Niterói.

Marta looked very disappointed by the interruption and spoke, "Well, lover, I am sorry our little getaway is coming to an end. I want you to know I do not feel you have an obligation to me, but I have really enjoyed myself being in your company."

Fernando smiled contentedly and replied, "I hope to see you again soon. Marta, this was a fantastic time and more than I'd hoped for. I do want to see you again. I will call you once I am settled in Niterói. You can count on it."

Fernando took a piece of paper from the desk in the room and wrote down Paulo Coberto's address in Niterói and handed the paper to Marta. "Marta, you are a charming and wonderful woman. I enjoyed our time together here. Please wait patiently for me to call you again once I am settled in my new home and job. I promise I will not get arrested and produce an interruption such as occurred before last night."

Marta's obvious vulnerability was exciting to Fernando, and he walked with her to the lobby and tipped the valet for her pickup.

CHAPTER 13

Grand Hyatt Hotel, Rio de Janeiro, Brazil
Morning of Saturday, May 9, 2020

Marta turned to Fernando and looked him in the eyes with a disarmingly seductive smile accented by her gorgeous eyes and mouth. She seemed to radiate light and energy. Fernando felt regret over the ending of their night together.

"Okay, I am really glad you want to see me again." Marta continued, "I'm betting you were really surprised by how much you enjoyed being with me. I am very attracted to you, Senhor Carvalho."

Coberto and the PF agents accompanying him to retrieve Fernando's belongings could not resist staring at Marta dressed again in her seductive black dress without bra and with her sexy shoes. They took Fernando's room key and went to fetch his luggage while Fernando checked out and settled his account. Fernando was pleasantly surprised to learn João da Silva had arranged to have the bill paid by the PF.

Unnoticed by Fernando and the others, a spy for the Regimento A and Carlos was employed as a houseman janitor; he recognized Fernando as an enemy of his boss Carlos. He had seen Fernando with Marta entering the restaurant for dinner the previous evening and had been trying to locate them again. He followed behind Fernando and Marta, observing them and intending to follow to see where they went. He entered a cab and instructed the driver to follow Marta's pickup truck.

Fernando walked Marta to her pickup and kissed her passionately and said goodbye.

"Well, Senhor Carvalho, I must be careful to not fall madly in love with you!"

"As must I be careful in your case, Senhorita Esteves," replied Fernando in his best announcer voice with a huge smile on his face. "You truly do know your way around a stick, Marta. All of my expectations were fulfilled."

"As were mine. Your stick is truly marvelous, as you had declared," she cooed at Fernando. Marta put the pickup in gear and smiled at Fernando as he watched her depart. She blew him an impassioned kiss and pulled away to head for her home, which was in Niterói.

Fernando did not see the cab with the Regimento A spy in it pull out to follow Marta's pickup truck. Fernando tipped his Stetson deferentially toward her as she pulled away.

Coberto and the agents then pulled up in a van they had loaded with Fernando's belongings, and Fernando jumped in.

CHAPTER 14

Home of Paulo Coberto, Niterói suburb, Rio de Janeiro, Brazil
Afternoon of Saturday, May 9, 2020

Thirty-five minutes later, Fernando was in Coberto's house, seeing his new bedroom and getting acquainted with the house's features.

Moments after Fernando's arrival at Coberto's house, Marta parked in the surface lot for her apartment building in Niterói. A cab then dropped a suspicious-looking passenger in the nearby street, and the individual stood watching Marta and taking note of her destination.

Coberto showed Fernando to the rooftop area at his home. Two gorgeous women in their mid-to-late twenties dressed in string bikinis were tending the bar on the rooftop deck and offered Fernando his choice of a beer or wine or caipirinha or shot of cachaça.

Coberto told him to unpack and get in a bathing suit and return for before-dinner drinks and a dip in the hot tub.

The young women were seductively attractive, each a curvaceous blond. They joined the men in the hot tub, and Fernando learned the one named Heliana was Coberto's live-in girlfriend. The other was named Denise and was Heliana's sister.

Fernando got acquainted with Heliana and Denise and told the women and Coberto his life story, including his birth and early years in Heliópolis and history with the Sombra Preta and arrest and imprisonment at Porto Velho. He described his introduction to da Silva at the Cavalcanti party and da Silva's role in Fernando's parole.

The women were somewhat sheltered by having been the roommates of a top PF agent for a few years. They were excited about meeting a reformed criminal and told Fernando about their lives. Heliana and Denise had been born and raised in Brasília because their father was an ex-minister of defense named Fred Santos. They each were executive assistants to high-powered attorneys in Rio's financial district.

Fernando's cell phone rang, and he saw the call was coming from Luis Antonio.

"Good evening, Fernandinho, my friend. How are you?"

CHAPTER 15

Home of Paulo Coberto, Niterói suburb, Rio de Janeiro, Brazil
Afternoon of Saturday, May 9, 2020

"**H**i, buddy. I am very well. I am at Paulo Coberto's home, getting settled in and finding it is a fantastic place with wonderful amenities. How are you?" asked Fernando.

"I am fine. I am in São Paulo, visiting my family and missing you. Am I interrupting something?" explained and asked Luis Antonio.

"My old friend, you aren't a bother at all! What may I do to help you, my brother?" asked Fernando in enthusiastic reply.

Luis Antonio continued, "Nando, I have learned some disturbing news that may be of great interest to Colonel da Silva and I feel compelled to share it. I have been visiting with and talking to many of our old Sombra Preta friends to get caught up. One of my sources reports there is a retired army major making trouble in Porto Alegre. He is behind a large gunrunning and theft ring and selling weapons to young people in the favelas. Does that sound interesting? Fernandinho, I have learned his name is Major Strock, and he is in Porto Alegre arranging a large shipment of guns and ammunition to Rio and São Paulo. Here is the address where Strock and his group and the weapons may be located. Strock is a despicable human being, Fernando. We need to handle him carefully," said Luis Antonio, rereading an address in an industrial park in Porto Alegre to Fernando to confirm he had it correctly written down. Luis Antonio concluded, "He is like a disease or insect, Fernando, and we must contain or destroy him and his current initiative."

Fernando took notes on his phone and determined to quickly contact da Silva. He spoke to Luis Antonio at length and collected the full extent of the story. "Thanks, Luis Antonio. I will report this to Colonel da Silva as soon as I can."

Fernando excitedly dialed da Silva's cell phone.

The colonel answered, "Good evening, Fernando. How are things going?"

Fernando relished the warm tone from his mentor and replied, "Hello, Senhor Colonel. I apologize for the late hour of this call. I am happily settled in at Paulo Coberto's home and just had a call with my friend Luis Antonio. He tells me there is a retired major of the Brazilian Army who is leading a conspiracy focused on trafficking in stolen weapons and ammunition and selling them to a hungry audience in the favelas throughout the country. The initiative is the product of a partnership between the Sombra Preta and Regimento A and is a brainchild of Carlos forged in his old cell in Porto Velho. I have suggested to Luis Antonio there might be a monetary reward for our assistance in capturing the perpetrators in an incriminating circumstance. We suspect the other participants are involved in some related killings and bribery of army and navy supply personnel and other government officials. The retired officer's name is Major José Strock," said Fernando. "I again apologize for the hour, Senhor Colonel. My impression from my conversation with Luis Antonio is there is a need for immediate action. There is a warehouse in

Porto Alegre filled with weapons and ammunition destined for sales and delivery in Rio and São Paulo pretty soon." Fernando read the address to da Silva. "The magnitude of the activity is very large. Luis Antonio's source estimates the monetary volume of the sales to be in excess of one hundred fifty thousand US dollars per week."

da Silva replied, "The hour is never too late for this kind of knowledge, Fernando, and there is no need for apology. This is precisely the sort of thing I'd hoped you'd be able to discover and share with me. I'll fly to Rio tonight. Let's meet for breakfast at the Grand Hyatt at nine o'clock in the morning to discuss the next steps."

Brazil has strict laws regarding gun ownership and possession, which mandate no one under the age of twenty-five may own or possess a gun and/or ammunition. Sadly, contrary to the intent of the law, many young people and gang members in the large cities manage to obtain guns and ammo, which they utilize in street violence and crime, which is rampant. One must assume there is a flow of illegally obtained guns from the military and other sources that exacerbates attempts to control the violence, which frequently requires the PF and PM to intercede along with civilian police authorities. The resistance by the criminals turns neighborhoods and entire sections of cities into war zones. Brazil is a wondrously beautiful country blessed with an abundance of natural resources and populated by a peaceful and graceful people who deserve a better life without all the stressful and threatening violence.

Colonel da Silva concluded, "I know Strock from my days in the army and remember him as a violently angry man who is a disturbed, manipulative zealot whom no one trusted nor could argue with."

Fernando agreed to the breakfast meeting and got another beer and returned to the hot tub to relax before dinner. He sat reflecting on his great fortune to be free from Porto Velho and to have met Marta. The attractive women on the rooftop caused Fernando's thoughts to wander back to Marta Esteves, and he called her cell phone.

The phone rang five times and went to voice mail. After three more failed attempts, Fernando was surprised by the lack of connection and left a voice message and retired to bed.

CHAPTER 16

Niterói suburb, Rio de Janeiro, Brazil
Morning of Sunday, May 10, 2020

The following morning, having received no call in return, Fernando resolved to go by Marta's home to find her on his way to the Hyatt to have breakfast with Colonel da Silva.

Upon his arrival at the apartment house, he was relieved to see Marta's pickup was parked undisturbed on an adjacent surface lot. He entered the building and took the elevator in the lobby to the floor upon which Marta resided. He found his way to the apartment with the number she had given him at the Hyatt.

Her front door was suspiciously ajar and unlocked. Fernando knocked and announced himself and entered. He went through her apartment and found the bloodied corpse of his attractive brunette lover with a gunshot to the head on the bedroom floor, dressed in her tight-fitting black dress and stunning black high-heeled shoes.

Stunned by his discovery, Fernando steeled himself against an emotional reaction. He resisted the inclination to touch Marta or anything in the apartment for fear of disturbing evidence. He touched the back of his right index finger to her throat and wrists and found no pulse. Her beautiful eyes had lost their sparkle and were unfocused and fixed on the ceiling above. He choked back tears and said a quick prayer for Marta's safe and quick passage to heaven and bent and kissed her forehead.

A note addressed to him was lying on the floor next to the body. He was wearing a long-sleeved T-shirt. He stretched the right arm's fabric with his left hand so his fingers on the right hand were covered and bent down and cautiously picked it up. It read, "Fernando Carvalho, Regimento A is coming for you and swears an oath you will not be happy on any future day."

Fernando called da Silva to report the death and postpone their breakfast meeting.

da Silva was just arriving in Rio and arrived at the apartment quickly with Paulo Coberto and his best investigator, a fellow named Sergio Viana. A team of forensics experts arrived and began a thorough search of the apartment for evidence.

Coberto and Viana went door to door at neighboring apartments and found a woman who had seen a suspicious man walking around just after she had heard a loud bang. Nosy by nature, she had followed the suspicious fellow and had taken note of his car's make and model and license plate. She offered she was no fan of Marta because Marta was a noisy neighbor, what with her samba club lifestyle and appreciation of loud music. The woman stated firmly that she liked Marta very much because she had a sweet and accommodating personality. She confessed to having a great fear that such a thing could happen in the neighborhood.

Coberto assigned one of the agents to run the information they'd received in search of the name and location of the car's owner. Within forty-five minutes, they had a name and profile of the targeted individual. His name was Alberto Fiel; he lived in the Rocinha favela in Rio and was a ten-year employee of the Grand Hyatt.

CHAPTER 17

Niterói suburb, Rio de Janeiro, Brazil
Morning and afternoon of Sunday, May 10, 2020

Fiel had a criminal record and had recently been released from prison where he'd served ten years for assault and battery. He was known to be a member of Regimento A and very dangerous. He was suspected to be Carlos' choice to be his successor to the leadership of Regimento A.

The forensics team found a shell casing on the apartment floor near Marta's corpse and was able to fortunately extract a fingerprint from it, offering the possibility of providing conclusive evidence of Fiel's presence, if not guilt. No additional prints were located, and a forensics team member departed for the local PF lab to have some of the collected evidence tested and checked. The note to Fernando was removed as evidence and later tested for fingerprints. Fingerprints were indeed found on the note; it appeared that the author had sloppily written the note with greasy fingers from eating something.

An enraged da Silva turned to Fernando and spoke with gritted teeth, "This will require your and the Sombra Preta's assistance to solve it!"

Fiel's identity and tie to the fingerprint and other evidence made him a clear candidate for arrest.

da Silva continued his angry comments, "We will find the cretin responsible for Marta's killing, and he will have his day in court," swore da Silva.

In a conversation with Coberto and Viana, they all agreed with da Silva's direction that they should only go to Fiel's home after careful preparation. Coberto convinced da Silva they'd best go after Fiel quickly for fear he might harm someone else or flee.

Arrangements were quickly made with the PM to provide officers and an armored vehicle for their entry into Rocinha and approach to the Fiel home. Regimento A was known to have numerous heavily armed members on the lookout throughout Rocinha, and it was fully expected they would present an armed resistance to any law enforcement presence near or on approach to the Fiel home. The PM additionally provided a helicopter gunship.

CHAPTER 18

Rocinha favela, Rio de Janeiro, Brazil
Evening of Sunday, May 10, 2020

At 7:25 p.m. that evening, Coberto and Viana and two other PF agents met the PM at a helicopter landing pad on the roof of one of the buildings in Rio's financial district.

A plan was set in which the helicopter would transport ten men in tactical uniforms to the Fiel home where they would meet another seven men in an armored vehicle. Coberto and Viana were to ride in the helicopter and oversee the assault. The armored vehicle was to arrive at the Fiel home at 7:50 p.m. just as the helicopter was arriving in place.

At 7:35 p.m., they lifted off and confirmed the armored vehicle would be on time. A spotter reported there were seventeen heavily armed Regimento A members in the area around the Fiel home standing guard over Alberto.

CHAPTER 19

Rocinha favela, Rio de Janeiro, Brazil
Evening of Sunday, May 10, 2020

The distinctive rhythmic sound of the helicopter's engine and rotors echoed in the warm and damp air made thick by humidity.

As the helicopter hovered above the Fiel home, Coberto spoke through the ship's loudspeaker, "Alberto Fiel, this is the Polícia Federal. You are wanted for murder. Come out with your hands over your head and lie down in the street."

The only response was automatic weapon fire aimed at the helicopter by the Regimento A guards. The helicopter's door gunman expertly returned fire and killed six of the Regimento A gunmen. The armored vehicle arrived, and the officers in it spread out around the house and engaged the guards in a fierce gun battle that lasted for several minutes. With the helicopter providing continuous cover, the resistance was quelled. The atmosphere around the battle felt very much like a war, such as the Vietnam War or the French occupation of Somalia or Chad.

The PM officers involved were exhausted by the effort and soon retreated from Rocinha. The remaining officers approached the house and kicked in the front door.

Fiel resisted by hiding in the house and later capitulated and called out, "I surrender! My family is in the house, and I do not want to place them at risk."

The ground commander had a megaphone and ordered Fiel to comply with the direction to exit the house with his hands over his head and lie face down in the yard. This Fiel did quickly.

Within minutes of their arrival, the authorities had handcuffed Fiel, and he was transported to the regional PF headquarters to be held, pending arraignment.

Coberto and Viana called da Silva and Fernando with the news, and they were each ecstatic.

da Silva turned to Fernando and closed their celebratory discussion. "Fernando, you have had a hard day and need a friend to comfort you. Let's have lunch at the Grand Hyatt. You need to talk to a friend and disburden your mind. I want to share my plan for Major Strock so we may quickly go after him. I called the Hyatt's manager, and the room service cooking team will remain in place to serve us lunch by the pool when we arrive. We will need to eat so we may manage the quantity of alcohol I anticipate we will want to consume. I am terribly sorry for your loss today, my friend."

Fernando and da Silva soon arrived at the Hyatt, and they proceeded to the pool area. Fernando tried as best as he could to hide a tear forming in the corner of his left eye. Being in the hotel was a grim reminder of his joyous time there with Marta.

Upon their arrival at the hotel, they found the hotel manager waiting for them with a table set with a tablecloth and elegant place settings and a waitress awaiting their orders. The manager and da Silva were old friends since da Silva had begun utilizing the property as the venue for retreats with his Rio PF investigative team.

da Silva and Fernando placed drink orders with the waitress and began studying the menu.

da Silva looked across the table at Fernando and spoke, "Well, my friend, I have no way of knowing the pain you are experiencing, but I want to try to cheer you up. You have been on a wild emotional roller coaster for days now, all at the fault of Carlos and Regimento A. I want to salute you with my wishes for good fortune on Monday as you begin your work with O Banco do Brasil and Rogerio Amaraes. I want to go to Porto Alegre to stop Strock and believe you would be an excellent addition to the team for that effort. I called and spoke to Rogerio Amaraes on my way over here, and he has agreed to hold your position open to start on Monday, May 18. I hope that will provide the time we need to get Strock. We will depart Sunday morning at nine o'clock for Porto Alegre to get the major."

The drinks arrived, and da Silva continued speaking, "Our first challenge together will be to bring Carlos and his squad down legally. I want your promise to resist the temptation to take violent action against them. As my partner in the PF, you will be in a position to defeat your enemy and see him stuck in Porto Velho for many years beyond his current sentence. Your sources inform us Carlos and Regimento A have struck a deal with the Sombra Preta to participate in an effort to steal and sell military firearms and ammunition from the weapons depot in Porto Alegre. We intend to catch them in the act and tie the effort back to directions from Carlos. Should we succeed, we believe we may extend his sentence in Porto Velho indefinitely. To that end, we will require your and Luis Antonio's and José Vargas' ability to gather intelligence from your Sombra Preta contacts. Let's put this murdering filho da puta away forever!"

Fernando thought back to Marta and said a word of prayer to her, promising to get those guilty for her death. Fernando smiled an agreeable smile while nodding his concurrence with da Silva's emotional pitch. "Senhor Colonel, nobody wants Carlos punished more than I after how he murdered my dear aunt Celia and sweet Marta Esteves. I will call Luis Antonio and José Vargas and arrange their cooperation and see what we may learn."

They sat in quiet conversation, and each departed to prepare for their departure for Porto Alegre in the morning.

CHAPTER 20

They reconnected in the restaurant at eight o'clock in the morning to have breakfast.

Paulo Coberto arrived soon with a driver and collected Fernando and da Silva's belongings for the drive to Galeão Air Force Base to catch their flight to Porto Alegre. Fernando had returned to Coberto's home to sleep and prepare to depart with the PF team for Porto Alegre.

Fernando called Luis Antonio to find out how he was doing. Luis Antonio had flown to Porto Alegre to infiltrate Strock's operation. He planned to obtain advance intelligence for the coming police action.

da Silva held a conference call to prepare for the action against Strock. Fernando and Luis Antonio were each equally excitedly interested in addressing the gun problem. They had grown up as participants in and victims of gun activity in their neighborhood in São Paulo. Fernando and Luis Antonio each agreed they could imagine themselves feeling justifiably like heroes in the event they could help da Silva stop Strock and his gun flow.

Fernando hung up and went out for dinner with Coberto and Heliana and Denise. They had drinks and pizza at a local Niterói eatery. Both Fernando and Coberto were anxious to get a good relaxing night's sleep. They and the women returned to the house, and all sat in the hot tub, having nightcap drinks.

The men went to bed at ten o'clock to sleep until they departed the house at eight o'clock in the morning to go to the Grand Hyatt for breakfast with da Silva.

By ten thirty in the morning, they were with da Silva and a PM commander on board the Embraer jet dedicated to da Silva's purposes. They were bound for Porto Alegre.

A small detail of GRUMEC troops was left in place at the Niterói house, standing guard over Heliana and Denise Santos.

Maria Carvalho had a blossoming love affair with João Carlos Diamante. With Fernando's and da Silva's guidance, Maria moved into Diamante's home. A security force of GRUMEC troops and marines and PF agents and PM officers stood continuing guard over the apartment building and its occupants.

At exactly 11:00 a.m., the pilots ran the jet's engines up and released the brakes, and they were soon aloft from Galeão Air Force Base.

CHAPTER 21

Porto Alegre, state of Rio Grande do Sul, Brazil
Afternoon of Sunday, May 10, 2020

Three hours later in Porto Alegre, Strock and his men were working at a loading dock at a warehouse in an industrial park. The park was filled with planting beds full of colorful flowers and small shrubs set around the bases of palm trees. A strong wind of over twenty-five miles per hour was bending the trees while a light rain began. Strock and his men had stored numerous cases of stolen weapons and ammunition intended for street sale through the Regimento A and Sombra Preta gunrunning collaboration.

Major Strock was standing in a laughable commanding pose somewhat akin to Benito Mussolini's favorite side profile stance and was finishing a coffee and cigarette. He saw a group of PF vehicles followed by several PM vehicles with marines and PM troops driving into the facility and shouted a command to his subordinates to prepare to defend the building.

At da Silva's signal, the marines and PM troops spread out throughout the industrial park and took positions with a clean line of sight to the building occupied by Strock and his men. da Silva was in the lead car with Paulo Coberto and Fernando.

He addressed Strock through the microphone and loudspeaker in the car, "Major, this is Colonel João da Silva of the PF. My associates in the marines and PM and I intend to capture you and your men and all of the contents of the warehouse. If you do not immediately surrender everyone and everything to me and my men, we will sadly be compelled to take you by force."

Strock smirked at da Silva and intentionally flicked his cigarette in the direction of the car da Silva and the others occupied. "Colonel da Silva, you and I have a marvelous history of having worked together successfully. If I must kill you and your companions, I will be heavily saddened," mocked Strock.

da Silva and Fernando and Paulo had made their way quickly out of Porto Alegre's airport, thanks to a ride in a Brazilian Marine Corps helicopter. They were leading a combined effort of the PF and PM and regular army troops and officers. The Brazilian Marines are called Fuzileiros Navais. It literally means navy marines. The force was established in 1908. Upon departing the airport, they met up with their PF comrades and a combined marines and PM group intent on supporting the effort against Strock.

As they approached, they were waiting for Strock to make the first move.

Fernando turned to da Silva and asked, "Please, Senhor Colonel, let me handle this man. Please tell him you are sending in an emissary to speak with him."

da Silva protested the thought of Fernando taking such a risk and sighed heavily in acceptance. da Silva picked up the microphone and slowly depressed the on button and spoke, "Major, stand by for one of my men who will come in and speak with you."

Strock laughed and warned, "Please tell him he comes here at the risk of his life, and he will become my hostage. I respect you too much to engage you in battle, Colonel!"

da Silva reluctantly motioned for Fernando to get out of the car and proceed.

Fernando opened the car door and placed his Stetson hat firmly on his head and walked in purposeful style in his routine rhythmic fashion straight toward Strock.

Strock appeared somewhat surprised and amused by Fernando's appearance. "Are you Carlos' 'friend' The Bishop?!" asked the bemused Strock. "I want you to know we have your friend Diego Alamaraes held at gunpoint inside!" Diego was one of Luis Antonio and José Vargas and Fernando's old Sombra Preta friends who were active in the gunrunning initiative.

"Diego, we are here to rescue you!" shouted Fernando.

"Please do not be silly." Strock chuckled. He was standing in full view inside the roll-up door entry to the warehouse.

Strock moved clumsily without success to grab Fernando and place a gun to his head. Fernando walked straight to Strock and pushed him so hard that he lost his balance and fell out into the daylight. The crack of a PM sniper's rifle echoed through the air, and Strock collapsed with a mortal wound to his temporal lobe.

One of Stock's men reacted quickly by grabbing Fernando and dragging him out into the light with a gun pointed at his head. "Colonel, I have your boy, The Bishop, and I intend to kill him if you and your men do not fall back!"

Another, in turn, pulled Diego out in similar fashion.

One of Strock's other men assumed command and addressed da Silva, "Senhor Colonel, there are fifty of us in here right now, and we stand prepared to defend our position to the last man!"

da Silva ordered his reply, and the sound of the sniper's rifle echoed twice through the facility, and the men holding their guns to Fernando and Diego collapsed, each with a massive head wound. Ten of the remaining men in the warehouse quickly surrendered.

One of the other men inside assumed command and exposed himself and addressed da Silva, "Senhor Colonel, there are fifteen of us in here right now, and we are equally prepared to defend our position!"

da Silva ordered his reply, and the sound of the sniper's rifle echoed once through the facility, and the man shouting out the defiance fell dead with a mortal wound to his chest near the heart.

One of the remaining men assumed command and addressed da Silva, "Senhor Colonel, there are only fourteen of us left in here. We surrender."

The captured men were removed for interrogation and provided a wealth of information regarding other criminal activities.

Diego and Fernando turned to each other and embraced.

In a trembling voice, Diego whispered, "Thanks," to Fernando, and they walked to da Silva and Viana and Coberto.

"Wow, do I ever have the best roommate!" enthused Coberto.

"Well, Senhor Carvalho, my instincts about you have been proven correct!" said the highly pleased da Silva. "In a few minutes, you and I will speak to Director Vargas and Presidente Voss. The president was hoping we'd succeed and thereby would send a message to criminals throughout Brazil that they cannot escape the law."

Fernando felt a twinge of anxiety about speaking to the president.

da Silva's cell phone rang, and he motioned to Fernando to keep quiet and get ready. He answered the call on the phone's speaker, "Good evening, Senhor Presidente. How are you? May I speak with you on the speaker?"

"But, of course, Colonel da Silva, my friend. I have Director Vargas sitting with me. We are so happy to hear you have brought Major Strock's little escapade to a close! Congratulations! Is Fernando Carvalho there with you? Was he involved in the effort?"

da Silva smiled warmly at Fernando and replied, "Why, yes, Senhor Presidente and Director Vargas. Fernando is here and was actively involved. Fernando's friend, Luis Antonio, discovered the existence of the gunrunning operation. Were it not for Fernando Carvalho, Major Strock could well still be alive and active. Fernando has confirmed my suspicion he can be of great value in our security and crime-fighting efforts. Fernando brought the matter to my attention and was heroic in his actions in taking Strock down. He was bravely instrumental in Strock's defeat. He is now the model citizen we had hoped he would be after his release from prison." da Silva explained the effort against Strock in detail.

Voss interrupted, "Well, now that is marvelous news. If you're there, Fernando, may I say I now realize why Colonel da Silva and Director Vargas wanted you to be pardoned. To that end, I am, while we speak, executing an executive order pardoning you. Your country and president and director of the PF are very proud of you and pleased to have you out in society and helping us."

da Silva continued, "Gentlemen, Fernando was exemplary today, even in the aftermath of losing a woman he was very close to in a senseless murder intended to scare and punish him in revenge."

Voss added, "Well, Fernando, Director Vargas has told me about your loss. I extend my and our country's condolences. I hear you are preparing to join Rogerio Amaraes' team at O Banco do Brasil on the eighteenth. I look forward to following your career and being inspired by you even further."

Fernando smiled, and da Silva patted his back and shook his hand vigorously. Fernando tried to reply to the president while being hugged tightly by da Silva, "Senhor Presidente, I don't know what to say. I am ecstatic! This is so wonderful coming from you, sir! I hold you in the highest regard and cannot imagine how the pardon could be more gratifying! Thank you so much. I am dedicated to protecting and improving our country and serving you in those causes. I will reward your trust through my continued efforts and focused good behavior."

Voss listened and wrapped up, "Well, thank you, Senhor Carvalho. I am blushing. I've no doubt we could be greatly improved as a country if all our people were as dedicated and capable as are you. Good evening, gentlemen, and thank you again for stopping Major Strock and his nefarious efforts."

Vargas followed up on Voss' comments, "Fernando and Colonel da Silva, this is Director Vargas. After our first meeting, I was as sure as Colonel da Silva that Fernando would be of great benefit in our crime-fighting efforts. I must confess I had no thought Fernando would be as courageous and capable in a dangerous situation as he was in the effort against Major Strock. I am thinking of some challenging assignments that might pair Fernando and Colonel da Silva again. Congratulations on your highly deserved pardon, Fernando! I am waiving the training in our academy that would be routinely required for an initiate in a case like Fernando's. He is demonstrating a great propensity to learn and execute wisely on the fly. He may work at Colonel da Silva's side but has absolutely no authority to act as an agent of the law. Fernando, you may engage in any action in a defensive role but may not initiate any offensive combat action."

Presidente Voss concluded the conversation, "This has my full support, gentlemen! I look forward to seeing what you can accomplish together in the future. Good luck in your work with Ronaldo Amaraes, Fernando."

CHAPTER 22

---✦---

Leblon neighborhood, Rio de Janeiro, Brazil
Afternoon of Thursday, June 11, 2020

João da Silva arrived at an apartment building in the upscale and exclusive Leblon neighborhood in Rio de Janeiro, Brazil. da Silva had been called to the apartment to oversee an investigation of a brutal murder that appeared to have potentially troubling political implications.

A dark, threatening, and powerfully ominous storm sat over the city. The storm's intense rain gave the psychological impression of lowering the outside temperature by over ten degrees Fahrenheit. This was false as the temperature remained well above ninety-five degrees Fahrenheit and was unchanging. It was weather typical for early June and a bit difficult to manage while dressed in a policeman's uniform as da Silva was. This was because the relative humidity remained moderately high at around 75 percent or more. The storm's thick, dark clouds made the sky dark. This made the day appear as if to be night. It was although as early as three thirty in the afternoon.

da Silva arrived in an official black sedan. After the car came to a stop, the driver got out and dutifully moved to open the rear passenger's door for da Silva.

The driver was dressed in a raincoat and waterproof wide-brimmed hat. The heavy rain fell from the hat and raincoat like a waterfall. The driver, a junior PF agent, stood at attention awaiting da Silva's instructions.

da Silva sat for as few moments, listening to the rhythmic pound of the rain on the car's roof and finished smoking the first of his three daily cigarettes. Smoking was at odds with his disciplined interest in athletics. He found smoking to be of great benefit to the focus required for his investigations. He sat reflecting on the task ahead and motioned with his right index finger to the driver to open the door. The driver opened the door, and da Silva stepped from the car to the curb in the drenching rainstorm. The driver opened an umbrella for da Silva and helped him to put on the left sleeve and entirety of his raincoat.

da Silva sidestepped the umbrella in order to see better and stood in the rain, holding a pad of paper over his head, studying the exterior of the building, and envying those who could live in the neighborhood. He crushed his cigarette absentmindedly with the toe of his right shoe. The act was out of habit and entirely without purpose. The deluge had already extinguished the ember.

The driver reentered the car and took refuge from the driving rain.

da Silva walked to the entry to the building and entered the modest lobby and took the elevator to the top floor. On the top or fourth floor, he checked the apartment numbers for the address he was seeking and knocked forcefully on the entry door to the apartment he sought.

A PF agent named Arturo Mel answered the door, and the two shook hands immediately after Mel had saluted da Silva.

da Silva entered the apartment and somberly surveyed the scene inside. He noted the apartment must have been gorgeous prior to the events that had occurred on the previous night. da Silva noted there was no sign of forced entry and concluded the victims must have unwittingly allowed the perpetrator or perpetrators to enter.

João da Silva was an athletic man of 6-feet-2-inches height and weighed 195 pounds. He had a physical stature and demeanor that commanded equally the respect of his subordinates and suspects and witnesses.

He shivered and wiped his brow with his handkerchief and realized it was a psychological reaction to the weather outside and the horrific scene in the apartment in front of him. The owners' housekeeper had discovered the murder scene. The apartment was in disarray, and it appeared there had been a fight. There was blood everywhere, and the furniture was strewn randomly about, clearly the result of a desperate and violent struggle. The apartment's air-conditioning had failed to offset the exterior heat and humidity, and one of the investigators had opened a sliding glass door to the home's balcony a small bit in the vain hope the exterior air would provide some relief against the interior heat and dead air and stench from the corpses inside. The deceased had defecated and urinated at death, and the interior odor was unconscionably bad. The remains of the victims littered the floor and sat in the blood they had lost.

da Silva noted the remains were near the sliding door that led to the home's balcony and at the entry to the hallway leading to the bedrooms. He also noted the positions of the remains and surmised the victims had been fleeing the perpetrator or perpetrators in an attempt to escape to the balcony or to hide in their own or another bedroom.

da Silva had a powerful imagination, and while he looked about, he believed he could envision the murders in his head just as they had unfolded. The imagery in his mind was like a horror film. The images saddened him greatly. He sighed heavily and tried to refocus himself for the task at hand.

CHAPTER 23

Leblon neighborhood, Rio de Janeiro, Brazil
Afternoon of Thursday, June 11, 2020

The victims were Jorge and Veronica Azevedo, the owners of Gastronomia, a highly successful disruptive technology company aimed at Brazilian and United States consumers. da Silva knew the Azevedos resided permanently in São Paulo, and this apartment was their weekend and holiday home.

It was Thursday, June 11, 2020, Corpus Christi Day. The Azevedos had planned to be in Rio for several days to participate in the scheduled events for this key Catholic holiday and celebration. Brazil has the largest population of Catholics of any country on earth, with an estimated 130 million Catholics out of a total population of roughly 210 million.

On his way into the home, da Silva noted the walls and furniture had gouges that appeared to have been caused by a sharp object of indeterminate type. There were gouges in the sheet rock of the walls and leather and wood of the furniture.

The remains bore defensive wounds. The defensive wounds appeared to have been caused by the same item as that that had caused the gouges in the sheet rock and furnishings. da Silva looked at the gouges carefully and took a tape measure from his coat pocket and carefully measured each gouge. He found each was 3 inches or 7.6 centimeters in length and 0.13 inches or 0.33 centimeters wide. He focused on the defensive wounds and found them to apparently be of equal length and similar width. He noted the wounds had blood on the skin around them, indicating they had been inflicted while the victims were alive.

He noted the measurements on a notepad he meticulously withdrew from his raincoat's pocket. He used a beautiful fountain pen that he treasured. He replaced the pen in his coat's pocket with equal care to that he employed in the measuring. The pen was made of mock ivory with a nautical scene etched into it, depicting two sailing ships engaged in a naval battle with cannons firing. A gold clip and accents completed the pen's elegance.

The murdered victims were indistinguishable one from the other, except for their severed heads that were still recognizable and genitalia that were still intact.

da Silva knelt in contemplation and put his left hand to his chin and thought at length while surveying the scene in front of him. The tip of a machete was his assumption as to be the likely cause of the gouges in the walls and furniture and the defensive wounds on the remains' arms and legs. A machete could also explain the means of the dismemberment of the victims.

He instructed the forensic team leader to have the medical examiner inspect the suspected defensive wounds to see if they matched the gouge measurements.

The victims had been dismembered by what appeared to be an unknown sharp object, and their extremities and internal organs littered the stylish living room in a manner that appeared to have been staged by the killer or killers as an intentionally ominous and frightening warning. The blood lost by the deceased was disturbingly puddled on the beautiful wooden flooring as if in ponds.

The couple was politically well-connected, and for that reason, the PF had jurisdiction over the effort to solve the case. There was to be a presidential election in late 2022, and da Silva knew the Azevedos had been involved in a series of large and extravagant fundraiser events. They were close friends and supporters of Presidente Ricardo Voss. This caused da Silva to wonder if the murders had a political motive.

Prior to Ricardo Voss' election in 2018, Brazil had been embroiled in a series of astounding corruption cases involving presidents past and present of the republic. da Silva was concerned the murders might have been the work of an extremist political group bent on capitalizing on and dramatically increasing the past corruption's destabilizing impact on the confidence and choices of the electorate.

CHAPTER 24

Leblon neighborhood, Rio de Janeiro, Brazil
Afternoon of Thursday, June 11, 2020

Da Silva stepped gingerly around the blood puddles and remains in order to avoid disturbing any critical evidence. He directed the forensics team toward footprints in the blood puddles.

He studied the home and the remains and blood with his expert eye he'd developed over twenty-five years of service. The entirety of the expensive brazilwood and leather furnishings in the home were askew, and several were overturned, and all were covered in blood and the weapon gouge marks.

da Silva removed his pack of Minister brand cigarettes from the right breast pocket of his uniform shirt and sighed while he searched his pants' pockets for matches. He was relieved to find the matches and sheepishly extracted a cigarette from its distinctive blue-and-white pack.

The still-evident splendor of the home caused him to feel as though he should obtain permission to smoke. He then put that concern aside and lit the cigarette and placed the pack back in his shirt pocket and returned the matches to his pants' pocket. A subordinate looked for and located an ashtray for da Silva's use. da Silva relished the smoke and nicotine and composed himself.

João da Silva was, without question, *the top* investigator for the PF. He had successfully solved in excess of twenty complex cases involving murder, theft, kidnapping, and financial corruption. PF Director Vargas had assigned him to the Azevedo case with the expectation he would solve it expeditiously and conclusively.

The apparent, obvious staging of the crime scene in the home appeared intended for the purpose of taking threateningly impactful photographs. da Silva suspected the photos could be useful in forcing potential victims to comply with future monetary demands to be made by the perpetrator or perpetrators. Additionally, da Silva suspected the photographs could be utilized to provide evidence of the successful completion of an assigned killing by a hit man or men.

da Silva stared at the magnificent view visible through the apartment's windows. Outside was a sweeping view that included the Atlantic Ocean and Guanabara Bay and Pão de Açúcar (Sugarloaf) Mountain and, off slightly to the left, Corcovado mountain with the Christ the Redeemer statue. A sudden burst of thunder and a concurrent lightning bolt gave the room a strange macabre Gothic feel. The lightning gave the eerie impression the statue was animated. The magnificent Art Deco statue was awe-inspiring in its beauty and obvious fixed inanimate strength. Animation seemed obviously impossible and creepy.

da Silva shivered and wiped his brow again and paused to refocus his mind and energy on the job at hand.

The ocean was churning from the storm's wind and was slate gray in the shadow of the clouds. The bobbing of the water gave the impression the room was moving up and down as though it were a boat in the water. The movement of several powerboats in the water carrying holiday celebrants amplified this impression. The boats struggled to make forward progress and fought to avoid the churning of the waves driven by the gale-force winds of the storm.

da Silva scratched his jaw and noted the television was still on. It was tuned to a politically biased news program, and da Silva took note and wondered how that might play into his suspicion of a political motive in the killings. The station was definitely not broadcasting views in keeping with his understanding of the Azevedos' political beliefs. da Silva soon cautioned himself to avoid focusing on the broadcast, as it might be completely irrelevant to the investigation.

He looked around for a place to sit and rest his legs. He noticed the sofa was still somehow close to what he assumed was its original position on a rug facing the television. This he gauged by observing marks in a rug under the sofa. He noted there were permanent indentations in the rug from the prolonged presence of the weight of the sofa's feet. From this, he observed the sofa and rug had moved together 2 meters or 79.4 inches out of place during the fray in the home. The sofa too had gouges and had blood on it. da Silva decided the sofa was too rich a source of potential forensic evidence. He, therefore, would not sit on it. He asked one of the forensics team members to right an overturned chair on which he could sit and smoke and think.

He instructed the forensics team to dust for fingerprints on all the furnishings in the hope the assailant or assailants had been so sloppy as to place items for their suspected photographs by bare hands without gloves.

In disarray on the sofa sat the Rio newspaper *Jornal do Brasil*. He surmised the victims must have been reading the paper and watching the TV when the killer or killers attacked.

He sat for three minutes and looked around the room and collected his thoughts. He rubbed his temples because he was exhausted from days and hours on end of challenging work. He then stood and stretched and proceeded to walk through the apartment, admiring the contents and the collective "feel." He tried as hard as he could to spot something that gave him a clear path to the truth. The effort made his attempt to not disrupt the evidence more difficult. He walked with his left hand behind his back at the waist.

Suddenly, he caught site of the fantastic décor in the home's office. It was decorated as a tribute to Formula One automobile racing. The décor focused in particular on the Brazilian Formula One hero driver Emerson Fittipaldi. da Silva deduced that the Azevedos were friends of Fittipaldi based on several framed photographs, including one taken a few years earlier in the pit at the Grand Prix of Monaco where the retired Fittipaldi had been acting as an advisor to the Ferrari team.

da Silva was so soothed by the impact of the smoke and nicotine that he resolved to put out the cigarette and smoke another, thereby raising his total smoked for the day to his limit of three. He returned to the chair and ashtray and ceremoniously deposited a length of ash in the ashtray.

da Silva motioned to Sergio Viana.

Viana had now filled the role of chief assistant investigator and had been on the scene for two or more hours, and da Silva questioned him at length about the success of the forensic evidence collection efforts conducted until that point.

"What a tragedy, Sergio, the contrast between the ugliness of this crime and the beauty of this home is incredible," said da Silva in a melancholy tone.

CHAPTER 25

Leblon neighborhood, Rio de Janeiro, Brazil
Early evening of Thursday, June 11, 2020

"I have never in my career been so horrified and revolted by a crime in a wealthy home!" he continued. "What is wrong with our country, my friend?! The violence and anger and death are draining me of any optimism for their eradication."

Viana nodded his concurrence and rubbed his now-excessively-tired eyes and looked around the room and fell into a concurrent reverie.

da Silva looked into Viana's eyes and recognized his subordinate was equally interested in solving the case. "On the phone, Sergio, you told me the housekeeper reported this disaster. Where is she now?"

"Senhor Colonel, she was so distraught she was near to a breakdown. Her name is Felicia Ontiveiros. I had a female officer and a grief counselor take her home to Rocinha. We have placed a car with two PM officers and a PF driver outside of her home. They are to keep watch and ensure her safety and make sure she stays put. I have placed her address and telephone number in your contacts file. We informed her we will want to speak to her again soon and told her to not leave Rio without our permission. She was so distraught

I was concerned about her ability to keep focus and provide any information we might need."

da Silva continued to walk through the apartment, admiring the contents and their feel.

Viana walked with da Silva, and the two chatted about what they saw. Another picture depicted a joyful Azevedo couple with their eyes agleam, standing with Fittipaldi on the sidelines at Interlagos racecourse in São Paulo. Interlagos raceway is the pride of Brazilian car racing and one of the greatest tracks in the world. Fittipaldi held the trophy from the race that day as he had just won the Grand Prix of Brazil.

da Silva sighed an envious sigh in recognition of how long ago that day was, as it was in 1973. He marveled at it having been forty-seven years before. He caught himself drifting into an emotional reaction while recalling he had been ten years old that day and was now fifty-seven. He was born on January 25 of 1963.

His father, Pedro, and he had watched the broadcast of the race. It was the last time they had been together as father and son. A drunk driver soon killed Pedro in a head-on collision. da Silva sadly recalled that had been the beginning of some hard years in which his family struggled in the wake of his father's death.

Pedro had been a homicide detective for the Rio Civilian Police Force. The force is known as the Polícia Civil do Estado de Rio de Janeiro (Civilian Police of the State of Rio de Janeiro). As a young man, da Silva had worshipped his father and was entranced observing his father preparing to head to work each morning no matter how late Pedro had returned home the night before.

"Remember, João, a policeman's duty is to the people of our city and country. One cannot let tiredness or feeling ill be an impediment to fulfilling one's duties." da Silva's youthful memories were filled with such lessons, and he had pursued his career in a passionate drive to follow his father's inspirational guidance.

da Silva remembered the day and Fittipaldi's win clearly and was touched by the memory. da Silva remained transfixed on the photograph and drifted to memories of his father who had been a rabid Formula One fan.

Viana had to coax him back to the effort at hand.

da Silva could not imagine the joy that an experience like that depicted in the photograph could provide and felt a surge of envy. On his modest salary, there would very likely be no such adventure in his life. For years, he had wanted to attend a Formula One race and could not afford to do so.

da Silva was excited upon discovering another photograph of the Azevedos, this one with deceased Brazilian racing legend Ayrton Senna, a favorite and personal hero of da Silva's. Senna had perished in a wreck on May 1, 1994, in Imola, Italy, at the San Marino Grand Prix, a memory that saddened da Silva deeply. Senna had been a promising star and perished at thirty-four years of age. Senna was leading the race when he crashed and perished. Senna was a Brazilian national hero, having won three Formula One Drivers' Championships in 1988 and 1990 and 1991. He was killed when his car struck a concrete barrier head-on. His death was a great tragedy both personally for his family and for the Brazilian racing fans who had placed so much of their hopes on the likelihood of his continued successes.

da Silva's and Viana's excitement grew as they encountered a collection of racing memorabilia, and the two became engrossed in their study and appreciation of it. There were car models and photographs and replicas of trophies from races around the world.

da Silva and Viana saw a signed photo of the Azevedos with seven-time Formula One world champion Michael Schumacher, this also at Interlagos in 1994 after Schumacher's win that year in the Grand Prix of Brazil. In deplorable Portuguese, Schumacher had written an awkwardly worded tribute to his "well friends," the Azevedos.

da Silva felt a twinge of pity for these poor people who had been robbed of an enviable life by some scumbag creep or creeps. His investigatory prowess was awakened and reinforced by his anger and outrage.

Viana interrupted da Silva. "Senhor Colonel, we are making good progress and have collected more evidence than we could have hoped for. We should be finished with our work within two hours," reported Viana.

"We must solve this gruesome and despicable crime, Sergio," concluded da Silva. "The fate of our country counts on us to stand watch over its people and catch those who would act in this manner. The ages cry out for us to be successful in our effort to solve this crime!" intoned the somber da Silva with his jaw clenched in resolve.

Upon receiving the satisfactory report regarding the progress of the investigation from Viana, da Silva ceased his tour of the home and pondered how beautiful the exterior view must be at night when the statue was lighted. He thanked and encouraged Viana and the entire investigating team and stepped to the home's balcony off the living room.

He wondered how someone with that wealth and lifestyle had come to be in jeopardy of a fate such as that lying before him and his team.

CHAPTER 26

Leblon neighborhood, Rio de Janeiro, Brazil
Early evening of Thursday, June 11, 2020

The expert forensic team from the regional PF offices was busily taking samples of everything they could locate in the apartment, including fragments that could have come from the clothes of the killer or killers and any possible fingerprints or genetic evidence.

da Silva was an avid runner and weight lifter and was imposing when dressed as he was in close-fitting clothing. His hair was thick and brown, and constant exposure to the sun from his athletic endeavors gave it the impression of being blond. He had large green eyes that, set against his bronze-colored skin, gave him a movie-star-like appearance. He was an imposing figure standing on the balcony with the wind blowing his hair. The relentless rain quickly drenched him despite his having wrapped his raincoat tightly around his torso.

He turned and looked into the apartment and watched his team with pride. da Silva's personality and physical appearance were seductively engaging such that men and women alike took to him immediately. This was highly valuable in his line of work because witnesses and suspects found it exciting and rewarding to provide him with information, which would garner his effusive and disarming praise.

The entire living and dining area of the Azevedos' apartment was drenched in blood, which provided ample opportunity for the investigators to remain busy in their evidence-gathering effort for a very long time. The forensics team and homicide investigators each wore nylon booties and latex gloves so as not to disturb any evidence.

da Silva stepped back into the living room and toward the severed heads of the victims and noted there was no evidence of head trauma, except small cuts by a sharp blade around which the blood had completely dried, which indicated the cause of death had been the blood lost from the dismembering of what he assumed were live victims. The facial wounds' dried blood could not have been spilled following death and the blood loss seen in the room. The victims' eyes remained wide-open, giving the eerie impression they were pleading for his help in solving the crime.

"If only we could see what those eyes saw," mused Viana.

da Silva continued his study of the victims' remains and nodded somberly toward Viana in agreement. da Silva recognized the victims as he had met them two years before at a reception at the home of the governor of the state of Rio de Janeiro. He and Jorge and Veronica and da Silva's wife, Katia, had all had an animated conversation about the terrible influence the previous dishonest leaders of the country had by engaging in despicable corrupt embezzlement and bribery activities.

da Silva stared at their severed heads and wondered who had killed them and why. He said a prayer asking for guidance. The cuts to the heads, he surmised, must have occurred in random fashion while the Azevedos fought to fend off and/or escape their attacker or attackers. They could as well have been inflicted in a threatening action prior to the death-producing cuts.

da Silva continued into the kitchen and noted the faucet in the sink was dripping. He motioned to Viana to have the forensics team collect blood that was sitting in the sink and on a bar of soap. The suspicion was the perpetrator or perpetrators might have used the sink to clean up and had in their haste understandably failed to turn the faucet completely off. da Silva additionally hoped the perpetrator or perpetrators had been caught in the act of the killings and in their haste had left evidence that would identify them. The forensics team rapidly collected everything they could from the sink and its surrounds.

da Silva shook his head and contemplated from whom he might receive help in obtaining information about the crime. He felt urgency due to the late hour, now past four thirty in the afternoon, and worried they might be running out of time to locate the criminals responsible for the awful scene he surveyed.

He stepped into the home's front hall off the living room and pulled out his cell phone and dialed Fernando Carvalho. The noise from the rain and wind heard through the still-open exterior door was perturbing, and da Silva pressed his phone to his right ear in order to be able to hear and be heard over the sound of the wind and rain and thunder. The call was a long shot, as da Silva had no idea as to the whereabouts of The Bishop. To da Silva's great relief, there was an answer.

"Well, hello there, Senhor Colonel. This is Fernando Carvalho. What a pleasure it is to hear from you! I was about to call you to see if we might get together soon! I have been studying a wealth of information I have received from O Banco to prepare me for my start there next week. I arrived in Rio last night. I was in São Paulo visiting João Diamante and Maria. How may I be of assistance to you, my friend?"

CHAPTER 27

Following da Silva's fascinating description of the crime, Fernando immediately agreed to go meet his friend the colonel at the crime scene and to determine how he might help with the case.

A rigorous search was undertaken in the home's office to locate anything indicating who the murderer or murderers might be, and papers and electronics and all the collected forensic evidence were meticulously catalogued and removed to waiting vans on the street outside.

da Silva stepped back out on the balcony to watch his team packing themselves and the evidence into their vans.

To heighten the dismal scene's depressive impact, the rain began to fall harder as if from a waterfall. It gave the impression the falling water was like a reminder of the blood lost by the victims.

da Silva stepped back into the living room and sat down on the chair one of his men had righted for him to sit in while smoking. He was soaked from standing in the rain and took his raincoat to a bathroom in one of the bedrooms to hang it up to dry in the shower. He patiently resolved to wait in the living room chair for Fernando's arrival. He left the sliding door to the home's balcony open in the hope it would freshen and cool the stale odorous air in the apartment.

The aromatic exterior air had found entry through a failed exterior vent and created an overly warm and seductive atmosphere inside that conflicted with the brutal reality of the images hidden within the apartment and lingering stench of death. The smell of the sea air was like a tonic and caused da Silva and the investigating team to wish they were outside to participate in the holiday celebrations. This contrast between the exterior air and that in the apartment was exaggerated by da Silva's choice to leave the sliding door open, which allowed more exterior air in. da Silva closed the sliding door in the hope the air-conditioning might be able to return to normal function in the absence of the influx of exterior air.

da Silva continued to ponder his options to conduct the investigation. He concluded Fernando Carvalho was the person from whom he had hope for guidance or help in unraveling the puzzle before him. He believed this firmly because he suspected there could be word about the crime in the criminal network Fernando and his contacts had access to.

da Silva stepped again to the balcony and took in the sweeping view while contemplating how best to proceed. He decided to return to the chair and rest. He stepped back in, looking like a wet animal. With the sliding door again closed, the heat and humidity outside were ineffectively fought by the apartment's overworked and aging air-conditioning.

da Silva returned to the chair and sat in thought while looking around him at the incongruity of the horrid violent scene inside in contrast to the beauty of the home and its view.

CHAPTER 28

Leblon neighborhood, Rio de Janeiro, Brazil
Early evening of Thursday, June 11, 2020

There came a knock at the entry door to the apartment, and one of da Silva's team members opened the door, and in stepped Fernando Carvalho dressed as The Bishop. His customary outfit was extraordinary in the city's tropical environment.

Members of the investigative team who had not met Fernando before were transfixed and realized they were seeing the legendary man known as O Bispo. Fernando's successful role in the effort to stop Major Strock had intentionally not been announced publicly. Presidente Voss and Director Vargas and da Silva wanted him protected for potential future covert assignments. The rumor mill in the PF ranks had been afire with word of Fernando's approach to Strock. Thus, The Bishop entered onto the scene.

da Silva stood to greet his friend, and he and Fernando shook hands and exchanged greetings typical of two close friends and hugged each other. "How are you, Nando, my boy?!" inquired da Silva, holding Fernando at arm's length with each hand. "How is the life of The Bishop?! Are you well past the grief over the loss of Celia and Marta? I want to hear all about your preparations for your work with Ronaldo at O Banco."

da Silva ceremoniously introduced Fernando around the room.

Fernando walked through the home with da Silva, learning about the awful crime. "I am doing very well, João. It was such a pleasure to receive a call from you, my mentor and surrogate older brother! I am sorry it took this terrible circumstance to bring us back together!"

da Silva looked at Fernando and thanked him for coming to the crime scene. da Silva then asked where Fernando's vintage sports car was and how its repair had come out.

Fernando replied, "Thanks, Senhor Colonel. I picked the car up just two days ago, and it is just like new. It performs marvelously, thanks to the improvements I ordered. Let me show it to you. It is just there on the street outside. Come with me if you can, and I will show it to you."

da Silva stepped again onto the apartment's balcony, accompanied by Fernando. The balcony was overlooking a traffic circle below where the car sat in the circle of light from a streetlamp. And da Silva took the moment to finish his cigarette. He extinguished the one he had started in the living room and immediately thought to light another. This he stopped because he was nearly over his daily limit of three. He also stopped because the rain was so hard as to make lighting another impossible.

Fernando pointed toward the car and described its improvements. "I had a new engine and transmission installed and the horsepower increased to two hundred seventy-five and had new suspension geometry achieved by installing new struts and sway bars. The electronic system was converted to twelve volts, and the gauges and sound system were upgraded."

da Silva put his arm around Fernando's shoulders while they looked down and said, "Well, my lad, I'd love to go down and say hello to and see your 'new' car."

The street was filled with holiday celebrants moving to and from Leblon beach. Brazilians treat beach activity like a reverential experience, and the rain and heat had in no way impeded the crowd's appetite for beach activity.

Several male celebrants had surrounded the SP2 and were admiring it carefully without touching it. da Silva made a hand motion toward his men in the street, and several of the PF agents soon surrounded the car like a protective shield.

A break in the rain lengthened, and Fernando and da Silva descended to street level and approached the car.

da Silva spoke while looking at the car with evident envy, "Please excuse me while I spend a couple of moments sitting in the driver's seat of this marvelous machine. I regret there was an unfortunate time that a man in my position could have contrived a reason to seize the car and keep it."

Fernando chuckled in his response. "Well, Senhor Colonel, that could put a hold on my crime-fighting cooperation and enthusiasm. Well, Colonel, I am disappointed I am not the object of your attention!"

da Silva inspected the car wistfully while staring at its marvelous analog gauges and running his hands over the steering wheel and stick shift knob and turned to Fernando who stood next to the opened driver's window. "Well, laddie, they don't make automobiles this beautiful anymore. There was a time the SP2 was very popular, perhaps even on the level of the Chevrolet Camaro today. Modern cars do not have the magnificent appeal of this VW and are not proprietary designs of our people's own invention and creation such as this. I envy you for owning it and would be honored if you would trust me to be its caretaker in your absence one of these days."

da Silva returned to the apartment with Fernando and confirmed the forensic work was wrapping up well. Satisfied with what he learned, he took another walk through the apartment with Fernando and Viana at his side confirming the progress in the investigation and discussing next steps.

He started to withdraw another cigarette from the pack and sniffed it and thought better of smoking another. He placed it unlit between his lips and chuckled and returned it to the pack.

da Silva and Viana discussed what had been accomplished, and da Silva gained satisfaction that the effort was well toward complete.

CHAPTER 29

Leblon neighborhood, Rio de Janeiro, Brazil
Evening of Thursday, June 11, 2020

"Who could have committed this atrocity?" da Silva inquired of Fernando.

"I have no idea, but I have several contacts I can ask about this," replied Fernando.

Fernando proceeded to make several calls of inquiry from his cell phone, looking for a lead, and continued the effort well into the evening while dark established its permanence for the coming night.

There came another knock at the apartment's door, and the coroner's team entered. A long discussion ensued in which the coroner's team and forensics experts discussed the acceptable timing and method for the removal of the remains of the victims. Upon reaching agreement, the coroner's medical examiners commenced the grim effort of loading the remains into body bags. This seemed tragically absurd as, in addition to the torsos, there were only relatively small bits here and there.

da Silva hoped for further evidence from the coroner's and forensic dentist's study of the body parts, which would be examined carefully for evidence of any kind. Final establishment of identity would require painstaking work to genetically identify each of the deceased and examine the wounds evidenced on each of the collected body fragments. A forensic dentist had arrived with the coroner's team and was standing by to accompany them to their lab and use the severed heads to obtain a sound identification of each victim. The victims' hands were intact on the severed arms and offered the potential for fingerprint identification.

Fernando quickly and luckily connected with his close friend and ex-fellow member of the Sombra Preta, José Vargas, who worked at the US Consulate in São Paulo. He was a waiter for social gatherings.

José Vargas said, "I believe I may have a thought about your investigation although I've no direct knowledge of such an endeavor. There was a gathering here at the consulate, and I overheard the venture capitalist CEO of a sizeable US technology firm expressing concern over the developments at your victims' company as a significant competitive threat. He was speaking in an agitated and angry voice to a fellow who appeared to be a security guard or bodyguard. Perhaps this could be worth looking into? The name of his company was, I believe, GastroApp. And the CEO's name is David Melkor." José Vargas then went on, "GastroApp offers a robust online gastronomical resource for people to determine their preferred meals and menus. It earns revenue in the form of royalties from suppliers whose products GastroApp recommends. The victims' company was threatening to Melkor as it posed a challenge to GastroApp and its market position. Gastronomia had developed an innovation that could allow a visitor to its website to determine with absolute certainty if a food item would be tasty to them and precisely how it would taste. They too earned royalties and appeared poised to dominate the online food referral space. This threatened the valuation of GastroApp, which has a market capitalization of in excess of one billion US dollars. Perhaps that would present an incentive to remove competition?!"

Fernando replied, "Yes, my good friend. Colonel da Silva of the PF is conducting the investigation. May I connect the two of you so he may interview you and learn what you heard?"

da Silva stood by anxiously, trying to hear the conversation's content.

Fernando handed da Silva the phone, and da Silva and José Vargas agreed to meet soon. The storm continued in strength and delayed da Silva's trip to São Paulo for his contemplated meeting with José Vargas.

da Silva carefully surveyed the apartment to cement the scene in his mind in order that he would remain intent on solving the crime.

Before departing, da Silva instructed his driver to get the car and wait for him at the curb downstairs. da Silva descended to the street, and a surging crowd of celebrants forced him to struggle to cross the sidewalk to the waiting car. The agents he had assigned to guard Fernando's car stepped in front of the stream of people, thus forming a passageway for da Silva. The driver pulled up and stopped and moved to the rear passenger's door and held it open for da Silva. da Silva's raincoat had dried adequately, and the driver took it from him and stored it next to himself on the front passenger's seat.

da Silva thanked the driver and was driven to Galeão International Airport and boarded a commercial flight to Congonhas international airport in São Paulo and then on to the regional PF offices located there.

Upon arrival at the offices, da Silva found a temporary workspace for his coming efforts.

After a delayed two-hour interview in an interrogation room in the São Paulo office, da Silva had obtained the information he required from José Vargas and was able to track down the security guard or bodyguard seen with David Melkor at the consulate party.

Amazingly, the bodyguard was easy to identify and locate. The São Paulo PF staff quickly determined who he must be from José Vargas' description. He was fortunately well-known, and da Silva dispatched a team to collect him and search his home in the Rocinha favela in Rio and collect whatever evidence they might require to tie him to the crime and send it to the lab processing the crime scene evidence. A search warrant was quickly obtained from a sympathetic and friendly judge.

After the evidence collection effort at the crime scene, the evidence was sent to the excellent Rio PF lab for processing. The evidence was being tested and inspected by the expert team at the Polícia Federal Laboratory Galeão Horário, located on Avenida Rodrigues Alves near Galeão International Airport. The effort to find and establish a match with the anticipated evidence to be obtained from the bodyguard's home was commenced.

A crack PF investigating team was dispatched quickly to "invade" and search the bodyguard's home where they took every and anything they could find that could remotely be the source of evidence. Three hours after receipt of the evidence from the crime scene, the lab technicians were combing through the material they received from the investigative team. They believed they had much of what was needed for a positive match tying the bodyguard to the crime. They discovered fingerprints and hair and skin fragments and clothing fibers to later be matched to the evidence collected in the bodyguard's home.

In anticipation of obtaining a successful genetic match and on the strength of his intuition, da Silva ordered the bodyguard's immediate arrest in Rio and transfer to São Paulo to be interrogated by da Silva. He was flown in a PF-operated private jet.

CHAPTER 30

Upon having his suspect delivered to the São Paulo PF offices on the Rua Hugo D'Antola, da Silva began the arduous interrogation effort to determine if the man would confess to having committed the crime.

The bodyguard's name was Rogerio Mendosa; he was a large, muscular, and combatively uncooperative, angry man. He stared defiantly at da Silva across the interrogation room's table while seated opposite da Silva at its center. "Why the fuck am I here?!" Mendosa demanded.

The unflustered da Silva calmly laid his blue-and-white cigarette pack on the table. He motioned toward the two-way mirror, and a subordinate entered the room.

da Silva looked at the young man and said, "Ronaldo, please get some coffees and milk and sugar and an ashtray and matches for me and Mr. Uncooperative here."

da Silva looked Mendosa in the eyes and asked, "Is there anything else you require? Like food or something? We have a busy time ahead of us, and I want you to be comfortable," da Silva said in his customarily charming, personable manner.

Mendosa sneered and replied, "I have no fucking idea why we are talking and have nothing to say to you nor any favors to ask! I am not buying your phony attempt at seducing me with your mock charm! I do not appreciate being taken away from my family and friends on this holiday and am wondering what you could want from me."

"Well, here are some pictures to help satisfy your interest," replied da Silva, showing Mendosa a series of vivid, grizzly, official photographs from the crime scene in Leblon. "This little disaster in Leblon yesterday is why I want your help, Rogerio," da Silva said, staring at Mendosa while looking for some sign of a reaction.

Mendosa didn't blink and responded, "That is very unfortunate. I wouldn't know anything about that specific activity. That's the kind of risk my clients pay me to prevent happening to them."

The sight and presence of his suspect's reticence revolted da Silva. da Silva was an experienced and intuitive interrogator. And he sensed a slight hesitancy on Mendosa's part and continued, "I'm surprised you claim no knowledge of this crime because, by amazing coincidence, we have found your phone has photographs from the same apartment and a crime scene similar to these!" said da Silva, smiling with an "I got ya" look. da Silva continued, "Don't forget, wise guy, our warrant allows us access to your cellphone and all of its contents. Perhaps you'd best cooperate and provide us with the knowledge we require. I'm just wondering how you have identical photographs to ours.?! Could you tell me how that can be?! We have also found fingerprints at the crime scene that match to yours!" da Silva said triumphantly.

"I apologize, Senhor. I don't know anything about this," Mendosa said unconvincingly.

"That is not a credible response, Rogerio. My forensics team has collected every piece of possible evidence from the victims' apartment and your home," said a frustrated da Silva. "Perhaps they have collected evidence that will inconclusively prove you have some guilt in this matter," continued da Silva.

Mendosa's defiance and lack of apparent concern for his being identified as the perpetrator increased measurably. da Silva stared at his captive with contempt and noticed Mendosa could no longer make eye contact. He suspected Mendosa might be about to break. Mendosa fidgeted in his seat and jumped when Ronaldo returned with the coffee and ashtray and matches and milk and sugar. Ronaldo didn't knock and abruptly opened the door.

Sensing weakness on Mendosa's part, da Silva produced a series of photos depicting the deplorable conditions in the federal prisons in Brazil. These included photos of the conditions at Porto Velho Federal Prison in Rondônia that had been taken in the aftermath of the horrific gang violence during Fernando's time at the prison earlier in the year.

Moving the cigarette pack and coffee and milk and sugar and ashtray closer to Mendosa, da Silva said, "We have obtained a search warrant to enter and search your home in Rocinha, and my investigators are there collecting everything they can."

da Silva stood and leaned across the table and looked Mendosa straight in the eyes while moving the photographs into the space on the table in front of Mendosa and said, "You're messing with the wrong guy here, Rogerio. I will find out what I need to know and promise you you'll be in prison for the rest of your life! Look at these photos from federal prison. I'll bet you want to avoid that! We have your family in our custody now. If you saw them last night, that will have been the last time, ever!" The pictures evidently disturbed Mendosa. "Except for a wave at the trial or chat on visiting day at the prison. You will be far away from your loved ones.

If you cooperate, I will do what I can to see you are treated more easily and humanely," implored da Silva.

"Go fuck yourself!" said Mendosa, staring in anger at da Silva.

da Silva laughed. "You're quite the tough guy, Rogerio!" da Silva said, looking Mendosa straight in the eyes. "We will see how tough you are once we see what we can find in the evidence from your home and through questioning your family! Where were you last night at nine o'clock or twenty-one hundred?!" demanded da Silva, based on the coroner's estimated time of the attack.

da Silva's cell phone rang, and he answered and spoke while ignoring Mendosa. He spoke for several minutes and became engaged in a heated discussion with the caller, one of the forensics investigators who were at the PF lab monitoring the lab's progress.

Stepping back in after his call, da Silva continued, "Well, Rogerio, I've got you. We have found your fingerprints on a machete found in your home. Some genetic evidence was obtained from the machete. The effort to establish a match on the genetic evidence and obtain conclusive proof the machete as the murder weapon is underway as we speak. Once we match the genetic evidence to the victims' and to yours, you're in a world of hurt, brother! Now's the time to confess. We also found an additional machete. Your wife tells my men you were out of the house at a social meeting last night until ten thirty. Have you anyone who can confirm your presence at an innocent gathering? If not, well..."

da Silva's acute sense of right and wrong drove him like a relentless machine in his efforts to obtain a confession. Unlike his prey, da Silva purposefully revealed his emotions. He looked at Mendosa like an object that deserved his hatred, and he could see Mendosa was aware of and feared da Silva's success in his drive to collect what was needed to implicate and perhaps convict him.

Mendosa rubbed his bald head and said sneeringly, "Well, João, you're in quite the pickle! Your track record of success is about to be broken! Without a lawyer, I'm not saying shit!"

"Okay, Mr. Badass! We will get you a lawyer. You'd better pray they know what the hell they're doing. If not, you're going on a long vacation at the expense of the United States of Brazil!" threatened da Silva.

Mendosa did not reply but simply began preparing himself a cup of coffee and lit a cigarette in a vain effort to appear cool and relaxed and unconcerned. Studying the Minister in his hand, he looked at da Silva and sarcastically said, "I'd prefer to have Hollywood." He was griping in reference to his cigarette brand preference. Mendosa looked at da Silva and feigned a relaxed smile, the authenticity of which was betrayed by a slight twitch at the upper left corner of the left eye.

da Silva noted the twitch and stared intently at the corner of the eye where it occurred. To da Silva's satisfaction, Mendosa appeared to be greatly unnerved. da Silva ignored him and left the room to allow him to stew.

da Silva received another call on his cell phone, and he stepped out.

He stepped back in and triumphantly told Mendosa, "Well, my friend, you'd best hope your lawyer arrives quickly. We have obtained a clear match of your fingerprints at the crime scene, in addition to on one of the machetes found in your home, and we anticipate an incontrovertible DNA match that proves you were in that apartment last night. We have additionally found blood on the two machetes found in your home and anticipate matching the blood to the victims' along with genetic material we intend to match to yours. We are also processing the machetes, and I am wondering who used the other one. We have identified other different fingerprints on the second machete and cannot wait to find the person they belong to as we are sure they will tell us what we need to know, and that information will be your undoing."

Mendosa shrugged and looked back at da Silva in hatred and was rapidly removed to a holding cell in the PF building. He was to be held for three days until a grand jury returned an indictment for him to be tried for the two murders.

da Silva immediately called his FBI (Federal Bureau of Investigation) contact at the FBI field office located in the US Consulate in São Paulo. The fellow's name was Chris Jones. da Silva told Jones about the crime investigation and link to David Melkor of the venture capital firm of Sandhill Rock.

Jones coincidentally and conveniently knew Melkor was in São Paulo taking receipt of a new Embraer E190 luxury jet and preparing to fly to San Jose, California, to take his new prize home.

da Silva arranged for an immediate flight to São Paulo for Fernando so Fernando could participate in the investigation as reward for his and José Vargas' help in identifying Melkor and Mendosa. Fernando was flown on an Embraer private jet operated by the PF. da Silva brought Fernando in so he could join in the pursuit of Melkor with da Silva and Jones.

CHAPTER 31

Congonhas Airport, São Paulo, Brazil
Afternoon of Friday, June 12, 2020

Upon da Silva and Fernando reconnecting at Congonhas Airport in São Paulo, Jones met them and they drove to Melkor's plane sitting at the Embraer facility at Embraer's privately owned headquarters field, Gavião Peixoto Airport, in São José dos Campos, a city also in the state of São Paulo.

The drive was lengthy, covering some 311 kilometers or 193.2 miles. The drive took well over four hours. Their PF driver ignored the speed limit throughout the drive to accommodate the need to cover the distance and two restroom and coffee breaks. da Silva was concerned they might arrive too late to capture Melkor, and Melkor might depart for the USA before they could stop him. A separate contingent of six PF agents in four cars was dispatched to the airport to watch Melkor's plane. da Silva's PF driver drove over 80 miles per hour or 129 kilometers per hour. da Silva encouraged the speed and reassured the driver he would make sure to have him absolved of any penalty should they be stopped. da Silva's brother, Henrique, was a senior officer in the Polícia Rodoviária Federal or Federal Highway Police. The posted limit was 120 kilometers per hour or 74 miles per hour.

They drove onto the Gavião Peixoto Airport property and quickly spotted and drove to Melkor's plane. Jones had firmly recommended they drive and not fly to Gavião Peixoto Airport. He cautioned their arrival in an airplane or military helicopter with a PF logo might cause Melkor to flee. The already-arrived group of PF agents and their cars greeted them to provide backup and strength in numbers.

Upon their arrival, Melkor was seated in one of his new plane's luxurious lounge chairs and speaking to his executive assistant in Palo Alto, California, on his cell phone. The plane's engines were warming up and abruptly shut down. A group of vehicles emblazoned with the PF logo on their doors had surrounded the plane so as to block its departure. The flight crew powered down and entered the passenger cabin and apologized to Melkor and explained they had received strict orders to stop the plane and open the door to allow the PF to enter the plane and speak with Melkor.

The panicked and angry Melkor shouted an order to the flight crew to depart immediately. The captain explained they were trapped and could not taxi, let alone take off. He and the first officer refused to crash into the police vehicles. The first officer opened the door and deployed the stairs.

A waiting da Silva and Jones and Fernando ascended the stairs and entered the cabin. Melkor was accepting a gin and tonic from the female flight attendant. da Silva had Fernando in tow because he intended to rely upon him to translate the conversation to be held in English between Jones and Melkor for him. Fernando had studied American English at Universidade Católica and excelled in his study of the language.

"Mr. Melkor, we have the authority to take you into custody on behalf of the US and Brazilian governments for your apparent and suspected involvement in a murder in Rio last night," said da Silva through Fernando and Jones.

Jones made an identical statement in perfect time with Fernando's English translation of da Silva's command.

"That is ridiculous," replied Melkor vehemently. "You'd better have your facts straight!" he shouted defiantly. "I intend to depart immediately!" roared the indignant Melkor.

"Mr. Melkor, we have the authority to impound your aircraft immediately," said Jones and da Silva through Fernando. "If you choose to depart, we will surely have one of the Brazilian Air Force's F-15s shoot down your plane. We have informed your flight crew they will be subject to immediate arrest both here and in the US should they fly the plane today, plus they risk death when the plane may be shot down."

Melkor sighed heavily and called to the pilots and told them to relax for the remainder of the day and leave him behind and fly the new plane home to California.

da Silva had Jones and Fernando instruct Melkor to stand up and place his hands behind his back to be handcuffed. His hands were rapidly secured.

"I will sue you all in the courts of Brazil and the United States!" Melkor threatened just as the handcuffs were placed on his wrists.

da Silva spun him around and, with Jones, marched Melkor to the exit stairs and down to the pavement below and into a waiting PF vehicle.

Following Melkor's direction, the pilots settled in to relax and soon took off to head to California with a refueling stop in Miami, Florida.

Melkor was then transported to da Silva's São Paulo PF office where he was informed of his rights and allowed to contact his attorneys in New York. The law firm agreed to arrange to have an attorney from their São Paulo offices come to his aid. He was told a judge had ordered his immediate incarceration, and the attorney was unable to stop the action. Upon her arrival at the PF offices, the attorney admitted she had tried unsuccessfully to obtain a judge's order for Melkor's immediate release. Melkor was then led, shouting threats and insults, to a holding cell.

Rogerio Mendosa had already named Melkor as the individual who had hired him in a lengthy and disturbingly detailed confession that described the events on the night of the murders on June 10. In exchange, Mendosa received an offer of a reduced sentence for his agreement to testify against Melkor at trial. Mendosa additionally provided physical evidence of their agreement and payment of one hundred thousand US dollars in cash in Brazilian Reals he had received for the murders. Mendosa admitted he had used the photos he'd taken at the crime scene to prove his success to Melkor in order to receive his payment. Supporting documentation had already been recovered from Mendosa's home. Mendosa agreed to plead guilty to the murders.

da Silva studied Mendosa with fascination. He detested the man and how he exemplified the decadent, greedy, and violent criminal segment of Brazilian society da Silva had dedicated himself to eradicating. da Silva considered Mendosa less than an insect or rodent vermin he might kill for entering his home uninvited.

A representative from the federal prosecutor's office had been called in to manage the sentencing negotiations. In a conversation with Mendosa's attorney, the negotiations were expediently concluded.

da Silva and Jones and Fernando worked with the prosecutor preparing the case against Mendosa and Melkor.

As a self-serving precaution, Melkor provided a defense attorney to defend Mendosa. Melkor then began a long journey that lasted several months through a trial that ended in his being found guilty and sentenced to thirty years in Brazilian Federal Prison, which, if served in an institution like Porto Velho, equated to a death sentence. Melkor's attorney was valiant in her efforts to have his imprisonment delayed so he could be returned to the US. A panel of judges denied the request, and he was quickly imprisoned with no opportunity for posting bail. He soon found himself in Ariosvaldo de Campos Pires Federal Prison.

In time, Mendosa was also convicted and received a twenty-year sentence with the potential of parole after ten years, a lighter sentence than normally merited under the circumstances. The sentence was given in recognition to his cooperation in the Melkor trial.

An associate of Mendosa who was also involved in the murders was sentenced to thirty years as had Melkor been. Mendosa and his associate were also imprisoned in Ariosvaldo de Campos Pires Federal Prison. The longer sentence than Mendosa was levied in consideration of evidence the man had struck the death blows to the Azevedos.

GastroApp was in disarray, and the board voted in favor of seeking a sale. The process of negotiating a distress sale to Amazon was initiated. Amazon's interest was focused on the potential revenue to be realized through the food offerings purchased by users of the app.

Melkor's career was finished, and he was considered a pariah in Silicon Valley and had no hope of future business activity, as he was in shame and would certainly be away for decades.

On the news of Melkor's arrest, GastroApp's valuation as measured by its market capitalization plummeted to 500 million dollars after several tumultuous days of trading on the Nasdaq. Amazon utilized the drop and potential continuation thereof as leverage along with the Melkor debacle to obtain a purchase price of 250 million dollars in a hostile takeover that left investors with only 25 cents on the dollar compared to the previous valuation of approximately 1 billion dollars. Toward the conclusion of the negotiations, Amazon's management threatened to walk away from the transaction, and GastroApp's board quickly caved to Amazon's demands. The sale was concluded in just over thirty days' time.

CHAPTER 32

FBI field office in the US Consulate, São Paulo, Brazil
Morning of Saturday, August 1, 2020

At the beginning of the month following the Melkor and Mendosa convictions, da Silva and Chris Jones spoke with Fernando from Jones' São Paulo office by phone.

Fernando was visiting his mother and Diamante for a long weekend of relaxation.

They told Fernando the details of the trials and thanked him profusely for his help in solving the demise of the poor Azevedos. They congratulated him for his assistance and asked him to take on a supporting role in pursuit of a case they were looking into. The case involved political corruption and bribery related to Brazil that had international implications.

Fernando agreed to meet with the two in Rio the following morning to explore the request further. He was then flown to Rio and returned to Paulo Coberto's home to pack for travel.

By the following morning, Fernando was awake at around seven o'clock and proceeded to the Grand Hyatt lobby restaurant where he met Director da Silva and Chris Jones for their planned discussion over breakfast.

CHAPTER 33

Grand Hyatt Hotel, Rio de Janeiro, Brazil
Morning of Sunday, August 2, 2020

The two policemen were seated, drinking coffee and eating simple breakfast cakes while waiting for Fernando. Upon departing the Niterói house, The Bishop had donned his customary dark garb, and he garnered several interested stares from the guests seated in the lobby and restaurant. da Silva and Jones rose from the table and greeted him.

da Silva spoke first and said, "Fernando, I am sure you remember this is my good friend and colleague Christopher Jones of the FBI of the USA. He lives and serves in São Paulo, where he works out of the US Consulate. He has now been in Brazil for five years."

Jones was proficient in his understanding of the Brazilian Portuguese dialect and capable of following and participating in the conversation. He relied upon Fernando's command of English to help him work around his relatively few deficiencies' impacts on his understanding of the dialogue.

"Fernando, we are tracking an associate of Lula da Silva and Dilma Rouseff and Michel Temer, the past presidents of Brazil suspected and convicted of corruption in prior years, whom we believe has taken a vast sum of money to Switzerland. The funds were received from the presidents' bribery receipts. The associate's assignment is to hide it all from the authorities," da Silva said, looking into Fernando's eyes. da Silva produced a photograph of a very ordinary-appearing businessman and said, "This is Eduardo Argos, the gentleman under suspicion. We believe he fled the country in a private plane and is now hiding in either Geneva or Bern where he has banking connections. We want you to go to Switzerland, specifically Geneva, and initiate an effort with your criminal contacts to find him for us and help us to arrange his capture and return to Brasília for trial. We also want to get the money back."

"We believe he has well over seven million US dollars," said Jones. Jones continued, "We are convinced a quantity of cash of that magnitude cannot be kept a secret from the underworld, and thus, Argos' activity should be discoverable through your network's connections. We have an INTERPOL contact for you to work with who can arrange for Argos' arrest and capture and deportation to Brazil. He will meet you upon your arrival in Geneva. You needn't worry about the INTERPOL agent's appearance. As you are so distinctive in your ordinary garb, he will undoubtedly be able to identify and find you," said Jones and da Silva in unison.

da Silva added, "The INTERPOL agent will be working in coordination with one of Agent Jones' FBI colleagues in Switzerland."

After a few moments' reflection, Fernando swallowed hard and said, "I love a good challenge. I'm up for it, and it sounds like it could be fun. What is in it for me?"

da Silva smiled engagingly in his personable manner and leaned forward on his elbows with his hands clasped and said, "Well, Fernando, we consider this a perfect opportunity to involve O Bispo. We are prepared to pay you three hundred thousand US dollars if you accomplish your assigned goal. Neither Brazil nor the USA would consider the payment to be taxable."

Fernando smiled enthusiastically and replied, "Well, how do I get to Geneva? I'm all in!"

"We have reserved a seat for you on a flight that will depart quickly for Europe," said da Silva.

Fernando then walked authoritatively through the hotel lobby to the valet and retrieved his SP2 and drove to Coberto's home in Niterói to collect his things on his way to Galeão International Airport.

Fernando had asked da Silva for a written agreement outlining the terms for his effort: a success payment of three hundred thousand dollars for the return of the majority of the seven million dollars in Argos' possession, fixed duration of three weeks for the term of the assignment, guaranteed travel home to Brazil for Fernando upon successful completion or failure to accomplish the task, and payment of the reward to Maria Carvalho in the unfortunate event Fernando wasn't able to collect. Fernando and Jones and da Silva readily agreed, and the three shook hands and ordered more coffee.

da Silva called his executive assistant and ordered the production of a written document commemorating their agreement. In short order, the document was ready for da Silva to pick up at the front desk. He went to pick it up and returned to the table and ceremoniously handed it to Fernando, who read it carefully and signed it and gave it to da Silva who in turn signed it as well.

Fernando then stood and proceeded to the front desk to obtain photocopies of the executed agreement for all present. Fernando returned to the restaurant to give the copies of the agreement to Jones and da Silva and to say his goodbyes to them.

Fernando's bag was sitting next to the table, and he gracefully picked it up and proceeded to a waiting PF car that would take him to the airport and to his flight to Geneva.

Fernando handed the keys to the SP2 to da Silva and spoke while they shook hands: "As you requested during your tour of the car in Leblon, please take care of my baby and enjoy it! Be careful and stay out of trouble," he concluded with a grin and a wink. da Silva smiled like a teenager whose father was trusting him with a favorite sports car. The two hugged each other vigorously.

da Silva had volunteered to keep the SP2 in exchange for the right to use it in Fernando's absence.

da Silva and Jones had arranged for Fernando to fly first class on American Airlines to John F. Kennedy International Airport in New York and then on to Geneva, again in first class. An FBI agent was to meet him along with the INTERPOL contact so they might coordinate the pursuit of Argos.

Fernando spent the flight to Switzerland contemplating his steps upon his arrival in Geneva. He determined to contact an ex-Sombra Preta friend in Portugal who had extensive connections throughout the European criminal community.

CHAPTER 34

Geneva, Switzerland
Evening of Monday, August 3, 2020

After landing, Fernando exited the plane, attracting a great deal of attention in his distinctive costume. Heads turned throughout the airport, and the FBI and INTERPOL agents easily identified him from the description they had received from Jones and da Silva. The two policemen introduced themselves and drove Fernando to his hotel in Geneva.

The three agreed Fernando would have the night to prepare his ideas for the search for Argos, and the two agents would meet Fernando at the local INTERPOL offices at ten o'clock the following morning to complete the plans for the Argos pursuit.

Fernando proceeded to attempt to reach an old friend from the Sombra Preta named Pedro Coelho who now lived in Lisbon, Portugal, and had a powerful network of contacts throughout Europe. Fernando hoped to obtain insight from Coelho regarding Argos' whereabouts.

Coelho answered on the third ring and gleefully asked, "Is that you, Fernandinho?!"

"Yes, it is I," replied Fernando. "How are you, Pedrinho?!" Fernando continued, "I am in Switzerland and am searching for a rat who is here attempting to hide a large sum of money stolen from our dear home country on behalf of those criminal cretins Lula and Dilma and Temer. The man's name is Eduardo Argos, and he is believed to be in Geneva or Bern attempting to obtain a banking connection to quickly and formally hide the money. Can you help me to find him? I am working with INTERPOL and the FBI and the PF on their behalf to find and capture him and recover the money. I could use your help tracking him down. I have a meeting with the FBI and INTERPOL at ten o'clock tomorrow morning and would appreciate your help," Fernando said. "If you're helpful in getting this done, I can give you sixty thousand US dollars, a twenty percent share of my reward I am to receive upon successfully recovering the money."

After carefully listening, Pedro replied, "Okay, you have me interested. It is so good to hear your voice, my friend. We've been apart too long. Where are you? I'd love to come see you."

The two had been close childhood friends in Heliópolis in their early years. They had joined the Sombra Preta together and proved themselves of worth by committing several crimes, some individually and others together. Pedro had demonstrated great skill as a leader and had risen high into the Sombra Preta leadership where he became the boss of the operations in the state and city of São Paulo.

Pedro concluded by saying, "You know I live to help you, Fernandinho! Today is Monday, and your meeting with the cops is Tuesday morning at ten o'clock. Let me have the rest of this afternoon to track down some information. Since it is Monday, I expect people to be consumed with starting the week. I will push hard to get the information you seek. May I call you in two hours to let you know how things are going in my quest?"

"Pedrinho, I will now happily go to a café and drink coffee while I await your next call. I have just checked in to my hotel so I have a place to rest until my meeting with the cops in the morning," replied Fernando.

Fernando went to a café in his hotel's lobby and sat, relaxing and waiting for word from Pedro.

The FBI and INTERPOL had arranged a suite for Fernando at the Grand Hotel Geneva. He checked in and felt a great longing to have Denise Santos at his side in this marvelous setting. The view from his room was incredibly beautiful, and he imagined the conversation they would have while Denise took in the view and sumptuous accommodations. Fernando chuckled with thoughts of thanks to his friend João da Silva and marveled at how his life had come together so well.

He realized he was missing Denise madly and dialed her number on his cell phone; given the time difference, it was then one minute before 2:00 p.m. in Brazil and close to 6:00 p.m. in Geneva. Fernando had dated Denise a couple of times. Twice, they had double-dated with Coberto and Heliana. Fernando had once gone out alone with Denise. Fernando recognized he was very fond of her and was cautious, following the tragic end of his infatuation with Marta Esteves.

Fernando was exhausted and lay down on the wonderful bed in the room. As it was early afternoon, her time, Denise answered, sounding very happy. She was at work preparing for a meeting for her boss. Fernando realized he was developing strong feelings for Denise. He and Denise spoke enthusiastically to each other about the events since they had separated in Rio.

He described his call with Pedro Coelho and pending meeting with the policemen the following morning.

Fernando further described the wonderful circumstances in the hotel, and Denise excitedly agreed they should go there on a future vacation. Her enthusiasm was infectious. Fernando felt an emotional warning sounding in his head. Denise expressed happiness at Fernando's pending potential meeting with Pedro Coelho. She understood his strong ties with his buddies from his youth. Fernando told her he and Pedro had each survived by their wits through some harrowing experiences and would be fine.

Fernando was so warmed and reassured by the sound of Denise's voice he dozed off quickly and awoke to her saying hey and hello in a loud voice. They closed the call by exchanging powerful vows of affection each for the other. Cautious following the experience with Marta, Fernando avoided saying he loved Denise. He carefully referred to his feelings as being a deep fondness. Fernando also said he estimated he would possibly be home within one week, well ahead of the three weeks called for in his agreement with da Silva and Jones.

After hanging up from the call with Denise, Fernando felt profoundly at peace and drifted off to sleep, listening to the noises of the city and street below through a slightly opened window. He slept for an hour and awoke to his ringing phone at seven o'clock in the evening.

He answered in a dreary voice, saying, "Hello, this is Fernando."

"Fernandinho, I have good news, my friend!" exclaimed Pedro. "Your man Argos is in Zermatt now, preparing to meet with a banking contact who will handle the holding and hiding of the embezzled money. He's staying in the Hotel Butterfly, and I have a contact who has eyes on him and will let me know if he moves elsewhere."

"Thanks, Pedrinho. I will share this with the cops at our morning meeting tomorrow, and they and I will plan and decide on our next steps," replied Fernando.

Fernando almost did a capoeira dance-fight move out of excitement and thought it would be best not to as he might damage some of the room's elegant décor.

Fernando proceeded to the hotel's wonderfully elegant restaurant and took advantage of the cops' generous allowance for his daily food needs by ordering a bottle of marvelous Bordeaux from France to accompany his pending food order. He was convinced his journey was about to pay off and felt a smug confidence arising from the strength of his contact network. He studied the menu and ordered a divine beef plate with pan-fried potatoes and grilled vegetables. After consuming the meal and the entire bottle of wine, he checked the time on his phone and decided he'd better proceed up to bed in order to obtain the rest he so needed for a successful meeting in the morning.

He fell into bed at ten o'clock in the evening and awoke without an alarm at six o'clock in the morning to take a run through the streets of the ancient capital. He reveled in taking in the beautiful sights and breathing the glorious early fall air. He returned fully relaxed by the run and proceeded to the hotel's small gymnasium and did an aggressive weight workout. He showered and ordered breakfast through room service.

CHAPTER 35

Geneva, Switzerland
Morning of Tuesday, August 4, 2020

The day had dawned with clear blue skies and a temperature nearing eighty degrees Fahrenheit. At nine fifteen in the morning, Fernando arrived in the hotel lobby dressed in his "uniform" and caught a cab to the INTERPOL offices. He entered the offices at 10:00 a.m. on the dot. Upon his entry, he found the FBI and INTERPOL agents waiting for him with coffee and breakfast biscuits. Fernando gratefully accepted coffee and declined the food, explaining he had already eaten.

The INTERPOL agent quickly began his explanation of the purpose of the meeting. The agent's discussion points covered much of the background Fernando was already familiar with.

Fernando then spoke, "Gentlemen, I have some promising news. I have a contact in Lisbon who has an extensive network throughout Western Europe and tells me Argos is staying at the Hotel Butterfly in Zermatt. I can go there to find him, or you may as well. Which do you prefer? My contact has eyes on Argos to ensure we can track his next movements, if any."

The two agents looked at each other and asked Fernando to excuse them while they stepped out to speak to each other.

Within three minutes, the two stepped back into the conference room in which they were all meeting. The INTERPOL agent spoke first, "Mr. Carvalho, we feel it would be best for you to initially confront Argos with us standing by to assist. Your fluency in Brazilian Portuguese would be highly beneficial in the introductory conversation. We have taken the liberty of arranging transportation for the three of us to Zermatt and have booked rooms at the Hotel Butterfly so we may get close to our target."

Fernando walked with the two agents to the elevators of the office building, and they descended to the garage level and entered a waiting BMW 535xi and drove to the train station and entered a car destined for Zurich where they were to transfer to another train bound for Zermatt.

At the end of the line, they had to transfer to a specialized train for the trip up the steep mountain track to Zermatt. The train operated on a cog track designed to allow a specially configured train to ascend the uncommonly steep rail line into Zermatt. The cogs are laid in a center alignment parallel to and between the tracks. A spoked wheel is set on the drive axle of the locomotive. The teeth of the spokes engage in the cogs and pull the train up a slope much steeper than the normal 2 percent grade achievable by a normal train.

Upon their arrival in Zermatt, the three walked a short distance to the Hotel Butterfly.

The desk clerk on duty was a beautiful young girl of half-Italian-and-half-German heritage. She was so taken by Fernando's handsome looks and intriguing garb she became flustered and seemed confused and incapable of serving the needs of the three men.

Smiling in his powerfully charming Brazilian manner, Fernando asked her if she could locate their guest Eduardo Argos.

She was so overwhelmed by her reaction to Fernando she broke the house rules and, smiling, said, "Mr. Argos is in the lounge now and will eat dinner at around six p.m."

It was then 5:40 p.m., and Fernando proceeded to the lounge and removed his phone from his pocket to look at the photo of Argos he received in Rio. He studied the picture and began his look around at the occupants of the lounge. Fernando spied a man seated by the lounge's fireplace, reading a book and drinking what appeared to be brandy. He looked very much like the unassuming man in the photograph.

CHAPTER 36

Zermatt, Switzerland
Evening of Tuesday, August 4, 2020

The two agents stood watch in the hallway outside the lounge and looked on as Fernando smoothly approached Argos and took the seat next to him and said, "My, what a coincidence, there are two Brazilians in this lounge. Senhor Argos, my name is Fernando Carvalho, and it is a pleasure to meet you. I am assisting the Polícia Federal to locate you and bring you home along with the several million US dollars you have taken from our homeland."

Argos appeared shocked by the strangely dressed man's bold approach and fluency in his mother tongue and knowledge of his intent to hide money. Argos nervously half smiled and looked around as if planning to flee.

Fernando said, "Ahh, ahh, ahh, ahh, Eduardo, there are representatives of the US FBI and INTERPOL waiting in the corridor to grab you if you run. Your best option would be to take us to your room and show us the money and give it to us."

Argos began to sweat and almost shake and replied, "I apologize, Senhor Carvalho, I have associates who would be extremely upset if I were to help you and who might look to hurt you and/or me or your police friends. They are close by now, and I advise against your suggested plan."

"Well, Eduardo, now we have one heck of an impasse here!" said Fernando, tipping his Stetson forward over his brow.

The two policemen, the INTERPOL agent and the FBI agent, approached the table and asked Fernando to translate their English into Portuguese. "Senhor Argos, we are empowered to compel you to take us to the money under threat of arrest and deportation to Brazil to stand trial for your involvement in the embezzlement and dire corruption in your land. Please take us to your room and give us the information we need regarding the location of the money."

Argos relented and stood and invited the men to follow him to his room upstairs. The four walked in the direction of the elevator and then on up to Argos' room.

Argos' ill ease grew to a point where he appeared disabled and prepared to have a nervous breakdown. He fumbled with the key to the door to the room and managed to open it and invited the other three men to enter the room. There was a coincidental loud noise from a neighboring room, and Argos nearly collapsed. Shaking noticeably, he proceeded to the room's closet and removed a large leather case. "Here is what you're looking for," he said, appearing to be concerned some enemy would enter the room with the intent to harm him.

The INTERPOL agent asked Fernando to tell Argos, "Senhor Argos, we have a team of heavily armed agents standing by. If you would feel more comfortable, I will instruct them to come to the room and escort us to a car waiting for us downstairs that will transport us to the INTERPOL offices in Zermatt's police headquarters on the plaza near the train station. My intent is to interrogate you and count the money to ensure it is all here in this bag."

Argos unenthusiastically nodded his consent and appeared to still be under huge stress.

A team of heavily armed and armored officers entered the room and surrounded Fernando and Argos and the two policemen and escorted them down to a waiting Mercedes van.

The scene on the street was very tense, with traffic stopped by the Zermatt police. A group of suspicious-looking men was gathered across the street and stood staring threateningly at Argos and Fernando and the police. One of them moved to pull a weapon from under his raincoat, and one of the armed officers shot him dead on the spot. The fellow fell dead, and an AK-47 fell from inside his raincoat.

Argos and Fernando and the two policemen got into the van and found seats. The van meandered through the streets to the police headquarters.

An ominous-looking black Maybach limousine with blacked-out side windows crept along, following the van, and made no move that exposed its occupants or their motivation. The armed officers followed along in an armored vehicle. Upon arrival at the police headquarters, the armed officers stepped from their armored vehicle and surrounded the van and Maybach to guard the four as they entered the building.

Following the INTERPOL agent, the group found its way to a small conference room. There, a charming female administrative assistant offered coffee and brought in a cash-counting machine and placed it on the table and plugged it in.

The INTERPOL agent asked Fernando to speak to Argos.

"Senhor Argos, this is a routine procedure to ensure the money is here in its entirety. If some is missing, we will be forced to take measures we wish to avoid."

The administrative assistant opened the large case with the money and began the laborious counting effort. This was a lengthy process that continued for over the better part of two hours, as the bills were all one hundred US dollars. At the conclusion of the count, the INTERPOL agent and administrative assistant stepped out for a quick discussion.

The INTERPOL agent returned quickly and took the FBI agent aside. Through Fernando, they addressed Argos, "Senhor Argos, the count totals to six point nine million dollars, or one hundred thousand dollars less than we had hoped to find. There are one thousand one-hundred-dollar bills missing! We have two associates who would like to speak with you and learn more."

A rapid knock came at the door to the conference room, and in stepped João da Silva and Chris Jones.

The sound of gunfire and squealing tires erupted in the street outside while the armed officers engaged and dispatched the men in the Maybach. The men in the Maybach had made an ill-advised, failed attempt to rush to the building and recover Argos and the cash.

da Silva spoke first, "Senhor Argos, I am Colonel João da Silva of the PF, and this gentleman is Christopher Jones of the USA's FBI. My friend here in the cowboy hat and dark clothing is my associate, Fernando Carvalho, whom I believe you have met and spoken with. Our job is to extract the details of your flight from Brazil and recover all of the money and return it and you home to Brazil."

Argos was terribly unnerved by the sounds of the gunfire outside and wasn't able to respond. He stared immobile at da Silva and did not speak a word.

da Silva continued, "Well, Eduardo, we have planned a long flight home to Brasília through New York and Rio. You would be wise to answer our questions and explain the missing money. In New York, Mr. Jones here will have an interrogation team in place to assist our PF experts who have arrived there for your interrogation at the airport in order to help us obtain the information we seek."

Argos looked pale, defeated, and exhausted and didn't react or comment.

As soon as they could, they were escorted by the armed troops back to the train station, and along with the guards, they all loaded into a car on the cog train. And at the next station, the group entered a waiting car on a regular train and were transported in course to the Zurich Airport and onto a flight for New York.

Fortunately, the men looking to harm Eduardo Argos and recover the money appeared to have been dispatched or discouraged, and no others surfaced to threaten neither the group nor their uniformed guards.

Once aloft on their flight to New York City, the exhausted and unnerved Argos chose to speak, "Colonel da Silva, I am not a young man and do not have the will or strength to survive time in prison. I am prepared to tell you everything you need to know. I am prepared to turn over the money I was paid in advance for my assistance in finding safekeeping for the money." Argos proceeded to explain that a second-tier manager at the Brazilian Ministry of Finance named Luis Vieira had given him the bag with the money and his payment. And he, Argos, had not counted the contents upon receipt of the bag. Argos surmised Vieira might still have some of the missing one hundred thousand dollars in his possession.

da Silva immediately made a phone call to Sergio Viana and instructed him to track down Vieira.

Within an hour, Viana called back and reported he had learned through Vieira's office that Vieira was on vacation in Manaus on the Amazon River. Viana reported to Director da Silva that PF agents in Manaus had located and detained

Vieira, and he was in custody and naming names. He admitted to having placed seventy-five thousand dollars of the missing one hundred thousand dollars in a safety deposit box at a bank in Manaus, the largest city in the state. His explanation of the remaining twenty-five thousand dollars of the one hundred thousand dollars was scattered and provided no conclusion other than he had spent it or stored it somewhere. Vieira gave the deposit box key to Viana, and da Silva instructed Viana to obtain a search warrant to gain access to the box.

Viana obtained the warrant and took Vieira to the bank in Manaus and found a large sum of cash. The count was delayed until the cash was securely back in the Manaus PF offices. The count was conducted there and confirmed there were 750 one-hundred US dollar bills.

Vieira quickly told the story of how the money was collected and about all the business and government leaders who had collaborated in a grand conspiracy to protect the money and save it for Lula and Dilma and Temer until their future releases from prison. He confessed to his and the other conspirators' having planned to use the missing money on several personal purchases, including cars and flat-panel televisions and vacations in Europe and the USA.

An enraged da Silva ordered the arrest of all the named conspirators to secure them against potential attempts at flight. The complete lack of inspiration in the proposed use of the stolen money caused him to further disrespect the conspiracy's members.

Upon arrival in Brasília, Argos was imprisoned, pending arraignment and trial. His indictment was virtually instantaneous.

While Argos sat awaiting his arraignment, da Silva and Jones and Fernando set about the arduous task of working with federal prosecutors in assembling the evidence for the trials of Argos and Vieira and the remaining conspirators. Their intent was to submit the evidence to a grand jury for consideration and hopefully obtain indictments for all the conspirators.

After being brought home from Switzerland, Eduardo Argos soon committed suicide in his holding cell at the PF headquarters in Brasília. He took a dinner knife and sharpened it by scraping it against the concrete wall of his cell and cut his wrists and bled to death. He was never tried.

Vieira had made a deal for the return of the missing seventy-five thousand dollars in order to avoid prosecution and, under the terms of a brokered deal between his attorneys and federal prosecutors, was allowed to remain free on bail. While on vacation visiting his parents in São Paulo later that year, a gang member soon shot and killed him in a killing staged to appear as if to be a random act. da Silva suspected the killing was in angry retribution for Vieira's failure to ensure the seven million dollars was secured in Switzerland and for his having held some of the embezzled funds back for his personal use.

da Silva and Fernando did the research necessary to confirm the conspirators named by Vieira were indeed involved and likely guilty. They obtained the evidence they sought. After obtaining proof, the PF released names of the conspirators to newspapers and TV and online news. The result was an explosive barrage of accusations against the two then-apparent-front-runner opponents to Ricardo Voss in the coming 2022 general election. This rendered the coming election to total confusion in the early going.

An ex-governor of the state of Minas Gerais named David Alves was campaigning successfully against Ricardo Voss and Voss' economic reforms. Alves had been a close associate of Lula da Silva and Dilma Rousseff and Michel Temer. Vieira said Alves was instrumental in the effort to transfer the seven million dollars to Switzerland for safekeeping for his friends, the ex-presidents. Director Vargas leaked Alves's involvement to the press. With the news afire with reports of his complicity in the hiding of the money, the disgraced Alves quickly withdrew his candidacy. Days later, a grand jury indicted Alves and the other named conspirators, and the PF quickly went to their homes to arrest them. The Alves arrest was conducted with live television news coverage.

PF Director Marton Vargas arrived on scene by helicopter and made a powerful televised speech about his and Voss' mission to eradicate corruption and violent crime. Soon after his being named PF director, Marton Vargas and his wife Lara had soon moved to a new home on Lake Paranoá in Brasília in the tony neighborhood in which the federal cabinet members all lived. Upon accepting the appointment as director of the PF, Vargas placed the full focus and energy of the PF on eradicating the widespread political and financial corruption and violence that had become rampant under the forenamed ex-presidents. Vargas had been raised up from a senior investigator role, much like João da Silva. Presidente Voss was keenly aware of da Silva's similarity to his boss, Director Vargas. Marton Vargas was a brash and outspoken opponent of criminals and greedy politicians and their activities. He frequently found opportunities to speak eloquently and threateningly against the country's criminals and was violently despised and hated by crime leaders, like Carlos, and their network of collaborators throughout the country and world.

CHAPTER 37

Lake Paranoá, Brasília, Distrito Federal, Brazil
Evening of Friday, August 28, 2020

PF Director Marton Vargas arrived home at his new house and poured himself a day's end cocktail; the pace at work had been tiring and hectic throughout the investigations utilizing Argos' and Alves' information regarding Vieira and the other conspirators thereby discovered.

The weather was clear and the temperature cooler than normal. Vargas wandered his property, admiring the landscaping effort that was well underway and would soon be completed. Vargas' mood was good, and he stopped in the front yard, admiring the house and grounds while marveling at his great fortune to have purchased the property and built the home. In this, he said a prayer of thanks to God for having led him to the PF and into the employ of Ricardo Voss.

Vargas' wife Lara called to him through a living room window and asked him to get prepared to pick up their two daughters from piano lessons in order that they'd be home in time for dinner. He smiled to himself and jogged across the new front lawn and up the front steps to get his wallet and car keys. He went through the kitchen and entered the home's garage and pressed the button to open the garage door. He walked into the garage and took the keys from his pocket and got into and started his black PF Chevrolet sedan.

He failed to notice that another sedan had pulled into the driveway behind him and was facing the garage. Two male passengers and the male driver exited the car, and all three opened fire with automatic weapons. They emptied their magazines quickly and ducked back into their car and prepared to depart.

Vargas' car was riddled with holes, and his fatally wounded body slumped forward, so his forehead rested on the car's steering wheel, causing the horn to sound.

The terrified Lara Vargas opened the door from the house to the garage and fortunately avoided the temptation to close the garage door. Had she done so, her view of the exterior would have been blocked. She saw a dark blue Ford sedan rapidly pulling away from their driveway. She stepped to Marton's car, crying in hysterics, and happily noted their girls were not in the car.

She opened the driver's side door and kissed Marton and checked for a pulse. Finding no pulse, she realized her worst nightmare about her husband's career choice had been realized.

She called the music teacher and arranged to pick the girls up in an hour. She resolved to compose herself and stay steady for the girls.

She dialed João da Silva's cell phone, and he answered, "Hi, Lara. How are you?"

At the sound of João's voice, Lara broke down. "Oh, João, Marton has been killed by gunmen while seated in his car in our garage!"

The stunned da Silva continued, "Oh my God, Lara, when did it happen? Did you see anyone or anything?"

"Yes, João, I saw their car." She described the car as best she could after not having seen any of the car's details.

"Have you called for an ambulance? Have you called the Polícia Federal?"

Lara replied she had done neither.

da Silva placed Lara on hold and continued, "I have called the PF, and they are on their way along with an ambulance. The PF are setting up perimeter roadblocks. Stay right there and wait for and closely follow directions from the officers when they arrive. Are the girls okay?"

"Yes, João. They are at their piano teacher's house, waiting for me to pick them up."

"Give me the address. I will send some officers to get them."

"Oh, João, I do not want them to see anyone before they see me. If a police escort is important, I will wait until the officers arrive."

The PF officers and ambulance arrived minutes later with sirens blaring. The EMTs in the ambulance checked Marton and confirmed his death.

The ranking PF officer on scene addressed Lara, "Senhora Vargas, I am very sorry about this great tragedy. We, the PF and our partners in the PM, have roadblocks and warning notices in place to capture the gunmen. We are putting up a tape perimeter barrier to define where you and your children may not walk while the crime scene investigators conduct their search for evidence. The shell casings in the driveway are not to be disturbed in any fashion. Within the hour, we will sweep them all up to be transferred to our laboratory for inspection. We are placing a drape over your husband's car in order to hide the grizzly truth from your daughters and you. If you wish to say goodbye, do so now prior to the removal of his body by the medical examiners once the investigators having indicated the search for evidence is complete. The medical examiners must determine the precise cause of death in order to align it with the evidence the investigators collect. Colonel da Silva informed me your daughters aren't at home. Please join my associate here, Officer Cesar. She will drive you to get the girls. Officer Cesar and the other officer right over there will escort you, accompanied by the PM, for protection. My partners and I will stay behind to keep you company for the evening here at your home. May we sit in your house until you return with the girls?"

"Of course, Officer," Lara warmly replied.

Lara joined Officer Cesar and the others for the drive to get her children. Lara began to sob and cry uncontrollably.

Cesar tried to console her by distraction and reconfirmed the piano teacher's address. The destination was in one of the city's numerous Eastern-European-style apartment buildings called Super Quadras or Super Blocks. Officer Cesar spoke in an attempt to comfort Lara, "Colonel da Silva says he is on his way from PF headquarters and should arrive soon."

Upon their arrival at the piano teacher's apartment building, they pulled into a parking spot, and Officer Cesar stepped from the car and opened the door for Lara to get out.

The PM escort sat watching protectively from the street. The PM officers got out of their armored vehicle and walked to the lobby and spread out, forming a defensive semicircle.

Cesar escorted Lara to the building's lobby and into the elevator and up to the piano teacher's apartment.

Lara sobbed softly, and tears appeared on her cheeks. "I don't know what I am going to do or say to my daughters." She wiped away the tears and steeled herself to talk to her girls.

Officer Cesar spoke in reply, "Senhora Vargas, I understand you must be terribly frightened and devastated. Please let me talk when we collect your daughters. You should not disturb them at this juncture."

Lara nodded her numb consent.

Cesar knocked on the apartment's door, and one of the daughters opened the door.

"Hi, Mommy. Where is Daddy?"

Cesar replied, "Hi, honey. I am Officer Lia Cesar. I brought your mother to pick you up because your daddy's car isn't working. Would you like to ride in a police car?"

The girls were quite excited about that proposal and followed Lara and Officer Cesar to the car. They returned to the Vargas home and found da Silva speaking to the other officers on scene.

da Silva had brought Sergio Viana and a top-ranked PF crime scene forensics investigation team with him, and they had performed a deep scrub of the garage and Marton's car for evidence. Any sign of bullet damage had been expertly measured and probed and photographed, and those marks in the garage's interior and exterior walls had been covered with Spackle and painted over in order that the Vargas daughters might not see any evidence of their father's awful demise. Both Marton's body and the horrifically damaged car had been removed, respectively to the morgue and the expert PF crime laboratory in Brasília. The forensics investigative team recovered forty shell casings and several bullets that had lodged in the car and garage walls.

To da Silva's and the other officers' and forensic experts' great frustration, they had no suspect or suspects to whom they could try to match any of the forensic evidence.

Within forty-five minutes of the police arrival at the Vargas home, PF and PM officers in tactical uniforms in an SUV surrounded a dark blue sedan matching the vague description provided by Lara Vargas. The target sedan had stopped next to a marsh. The driver of the PF SUV spoke on the vehicle's loudspeaker and directed the occupants to get out and lie on the ground. The three occupants ignored the command and exited their sedan and ran into the marsh and took cover behind some small trees and bushes and grass growing in the wet environment. The seven PF and PM officers in the SUV ran after their prey and quickly caught them. The perpetrators were unarmed, having disposed of their weapons by hiding them in their car and tossing them in a dumpster between the Vargas home and the site of the stop. They surrendered quickly without any resistance and were taken back to the Vargas home to be interrogated.

Lara took the girls by the hands and walked them into the home's kitchen. She had them sit down on the promise she would serve them a snack and a drink. da Silva followed along and stood to the side, awaiting Lara's dialogue with her girls. da Silva and Lara whispered carefully in a sidebar, shortly followed by Lara's talk with the girls.

Lara fought back the urge to sob and cry out loud. With tears streaming down her face, she spoke with a quavering voice, "Dina and Lana, you know I have always warned you about your daddy's dangerous work. I am very, very sorry to have to tell you your daddy was killed this morning, and he won't be coming home today."

The girls looked at their mother then back at each other and began to cry. Lara sagged down, overwhelmed by the weight of her stress and grief.

da Silva stepped to her side and put his arm around her shoulder and looked at the girls. "Girls, I am Colonel da Silva. I worked for your father, and he was a good friend of mine. He always talked about you and your mother and said how much he loved you all. I am convinced he is in heaven and looking down at the three of you and me with a huge smile on his face. Let's help him to laugh! Let's keep him alive in our memories!"

CHAPTER 38

"**M**arton told me a funny story about when your house was under construction and you, Dina, and Lana were playing under the house below the living room and your clothes got caught on exposed screws, and you both began screaming hysterically. He said he called out to you both and explained how to get out. He said he pretended to be very angry to distract you from your circumstance and worry and hopefully to calm your fears."

Lara and da Silva began to laugh. Lana and Dina both burst out laughing at the silly memory.

"You see, the best medicine at a time like this is to remember the happy times and to feel joy over the memory of our lost loved one. I told your mom I will stay for dinner to keep you safe in case some other bad person causes trouble or tries to. I doubt very much anyone could do anything, considering the huge police guard all around the house. I hope that is okay with you." da Silva slid a chair back from the dining table in the kitchen and sat in it, facing the Vargas women with the chair's back to his chest and crossed his arms over the top of the back of the chair. He surveyed the Vargas girls and smiled a silly smile with crossed eyes and his tongue sticking out in a clown-like expression. "Is it okay if I stay?"

he asked in a funny, squeaky voice similar to a cartoon character on a then-popular television show.

Lara and Lana and Dina all started to giggle with relief and tried in vain to clearly reply yes through their giggles.

da Silva continued laughing and said, "Well, I am glad we are all laughing."

They ate a dinner of chicken and white rice and stewed black beans and salad and french-fried potatoes that Lara had prepared quickly using leftovers. They all ate ravenously, and when they finished, da Silva engaged Lana and Dina in a conversation regarding their piano lessons. He encouraged them to demonstrate their skill, and they obliged by playing a selection of Brahms and Beethoven and Mozart. da Silva was greatly impressed by the girls' skill and passion for their playing. He stood and applauded in a standing ovation.

da Silva looked at his phone to check the time and continued, "That was marvelous, Lara. I enjoyed your cooking very much. That was an inspiration, Lana and Dina! Your daddy would be so proud. I am honored you played it all for me. Thank you so much, girls." He grinned at Lara and the girls with a silly face intended to restore their levity.

They all laughed again.

He moved to depart and continued, "I'm going to leave and let you all spend time together, thinking about what you have to do next. We have caught some suspects, and I need to speak to them right away. The suspects are in the driveway, and I will now question them. Lara, Dina, and Lana, it would be best if you stay in the house and leave us to our police duties outside. There are many officers standing guard in the neighborhood so you will be safe. Here is my cell phone number. Please call me whenever you feel threatened or want more company. I live only twenty-five minutes away and will come back should you need me." He hugged Lana and Dina and joked with them again.

Lara accompanied da Silva to the door to the garage from the interior of the house and spoke, "João, it means so much to me and the girls to have had your company. Please give Katia and Andrea my love." She started to cry again and continued, "You were such a good friend and subordinate to Marton. We will all miss him so much! He loved you like a brother. I cannot believe he is gone. Thanks to you, the girls appear settled. They were so pleased by your story about Marton. It really helped! I will include them in the planning for the funeral, and it will take their minds off the loss of our beloved Marton."

da Silva walked through the garage to the driveway and joined the group with the suspects standing in the drive. He motioned to have the suspects placed in a PF van sitting in the street in front of the elegant home.

da Silva got into the van and sat in the front passenger seat and turned to face the suspects seated in the rear of the van. "Well, gentlemen, I am now the acting director of the Polícia Federal. You killed my friend and boss today. I suggest you start telling me about what happened here. If you did do it, you are all definitely screwed. You know there was a time the police would have taken you to a remote ditch and would have you kneel beside it and would shoot each one of you in the head. Those days are over. A trial and imprisonment can be arduous and painful. It is worse now because you are each facing an awful life ahead with years in federal prison. Death might have been a kinder option. Tell me who had you shoot Director Vargas! If you tell me what I want and need to know, I will see to it you are rewarded with leniency."

He stared at the three and watched their stern expressions evaporate in the heat of his stare. They were eighteen and seventeen and sixteen years old and couldn't muster the strength to avoid da Silva's penetrating stare.

After three minutes in the glare of da Silva's eyes, the sixteen-year-old began to cry.

da Silva seized the opportunity. "Gee, son, that must be tough, having to realize you aren't the badass mother you thought you were! Tell me what I need to know and I'll go easy on you! What's your name, young man?!" da Silva demanded of the tearful youngest of the three.

The boy looked terrified and replied, "My name is Teófilo Almeira, Senhor Director."

"Well, Teó, how are you stuck in this awful mess?"

The other boys fidgeted in their seats and scowled at Teófilo.

Teófilo responded, "We are all members of Regimento A, and our families will receive a lot of money for our efforts today."

The boys all chimed in and told da Silva how they had been recruited for the assassination of Marton Vargas. The evidence pointed directly at Carlos. Carlos' new number 2 had been selected from among the group leading Regimento A in Carlos' absence while in prison. His name was William Nelson Vilmar. Vilmar had found the boys in the city of Goiânia in the state of Goiás, the neighboring state to the Federal District near Brasília and bribed or seduced them into attending a recruiting meeting for Regimento A. The boys indicated they had met Carlos face-to-face and had been personally recruited by him. Carlos had made a persuasive appeal to them individually to take the challenge to kill Vargas and thereby enrich themselves and their families.

da Silva was stunned by that admission and called the warden at Porto Velho Federal Prison to see if it could be possible that Carlos were free.

Greatly angered and saddened by the day's events, da Silva motioned to the senior officer on scene and had the boys removed to holding cells at PF headquarters in Brasília. Their car was taken to the lab for a complete search. Weapons and ammunition were located in the trunk. And the effort began to match the bullets and shell casings to the crime scene evidence. The boys directed the PF to the dumpster they had disposed weapons in. da Silva dispatched two officers to retrieve the items and hand them to the forensics team headed for the lab with the other evidence collected in the Vargas' home. The boys' fingerprints were all over the guns and shell casings.

da Silva went to his PF sedan and had the driver open the door so he could sit in the car, making phone calls.

The Porto Velho Federal Prison warden returned da Silva's call to report the commanding officer at Porto Velho Air Force Base had, after some time, learned Carlos was not in his assigned cell nor had routine checks of Carlos' cell been conducted as prescribed. Thus, da Silva's next major investigative challenge began: a worldwide search for Carlos.

The FBI of the USA and PF of Brazil and CIA (Central Intelligence Agency) of the USA and INTERPOL and Brazilian Intelligence Agency or ABIN (Agência Brasileira de Inteligência) were all called upon to provide information and guidance. A subsequent investigation exposed a sizeable bribe having been paid to the guards in the air force base brig who had assisted and purposefully overlooked Carlos' escape days earlier. The officer in charge of the brig was also implicated. All involved were fired and demoted and imprisoned, pending court martials. The bribery funds they'd received were taken from their bank accounts or from hiding places in their homes had they not chosen to store the money in a bank.

*　　*　　*　　*　　*

The ABIN located Carlos hiding on Gregor Stein's private island in the Caribbean. The ABIN's superb senior agent in the Caribbean, a fellow named Diego Guedes, located Carlos. Stein was a Danish billionaire famous for his passionate support of violent and disruptive Communist and Socialist causes throughout the world. It was subsequently learned that Stein was the singular provider of Regimento A's working capital needs. Stein saw Regimento A and its members and leaders to be an ideal means to create difficulty for the Voss administration and perpetuate the destructive corruption that had overshadowed the previous Brazilian administrations. It was subsequently learned that Stein was involved in a complicated conspiracy involving Venezuela and Cuba, whose focus was on undoing Voss' work to clean up Brazil and to additionally remove him from office in the 2022 national election or by force.

da Silva's cell phone rang, and he saw it was Presidente Voss. "Good evening, Senhor Presidente. How may I be of service?"

"Well, Colonel, it is a very sad hour, is it not? Are you at the Vargas home? If you are, I would like to know how the family is doing."

da Silva described the murder scene and his time with Lara and the children. He further described the capture of the boys and their subsequent immediate incarceration. He included the mysterious link to Carlos and Stein.

While speaking to da Silva, Voss listened closely and finished, "Well, Director, that is marvelous. I am so pleased you are there! May I speak to Lara?"

da Silva thanked Voss and walked back into the house. He handed the phone to Lara. He whispered to Lara who the caller was, and the shadow of grief lifted from Lara's face and was replaced with a smile while she took the phone.

"Good evening, Senhor Presidente!"

da Silva heard only Lara's side of the conversation.

"Oh, thank you so much. Yes, we are heartbroken by losing Marton… Thank you very much. We are adequately positioned financially… Thank you so much for your offer. We would love to include you in the funeral celebration. I will await a call from your secretary to make the arrangements… I greatly appreciate your complimentary words regarding Marton and his years of service… Yes, I completely agree with your thoughts about the leadership transition at the PF… I am signaling to Colonel da Silva to stand by and await a call from you."

They hung up.

da Silva hugged Lara goodbye and wished Lana and Dina well and good night.

da Silva's phone rang again, and he answered, noting it was again a call from the president.

CHAPTER 39

Central Brasília, Distrito Federal, Brazil
Evening of Friday, August 28, 2020

"Yes, Senhor Presidente, how may I help? Was your conversation with Lara beneficial?"

"Yes, it was a good conversation, João. I am so grateful you are there to lend support and protect them from, God forbid, more violence."

"Yes, Senhor Presidente, your call and my attention seem to have removed much of the strain on Lara."

Voss waited a moment and continued, "I am so glad to hear that. I plan to go by the property tomorrow to see her in person. João, I don't wish to rush things on the heels of Marton's death. My cabinet and trusted advisors and I all feel it is imperative we secure and announce a replacement for Marton given the extraordinary threats our country faces. The country will need the reassurance a strong leader is at the helm of our greatest law enforcement agency. The murder of Marton Vargas calls out for direction at the top of the PF to coordinate action with the resources we must utilize. I have been giving a lot of thought to filling the vacancy in the PF directorship. I have polled my cabinet and leaders in law enforcement and the military as well as members of Congress. We all unanimously see you as the indisputable choice to lead the Polícia Federal. Your background of dedicated service and success, combined with your marvelous leadership and investigative skills, are much like Marton's and seem to clearly point to you as the only choice for the role."

da Silva was surprised and truly humbled by the president's proposal and replied, "Senhor Presidente, I am honored by your suggestion! I am concerned about how Lara Vargas may react to my taking Marton's place. I am certainly and eagerly prepared to take over the leadership of the PF. I want to check with Sergio Viana and Roberto Cardenas and Fernando Carvalho to determine if they will support me."

Voss chuckled and replied, "João da Silva, your focus on support is of no surprise to me. I have spoken to everyone about your candidacy, and they have given their unanimous enthusiastic support. Lara Vargas was very supportive and said she wants you to complete and honor Marton's and my mission against crime and corruption. She and I additionally want Marton's killer or killers brought to justice and punished. I am convinced the public will be relieved to have the man who caught Eduardo Argos and solved the Azevedo murders and stopped Major Strock leading the PF."

da Silva listened carefully and replied, "Senhor Presidente, I am excited about the opportunity to lead the PF. I am otherwise highly flattered by your confidence in me. I passionately want to continue your and Marton's successful campaign to clean up Brazil. I am excited about the prospect of reporting to you. You have my enthusiastic tentative acceptance of your offer. I want to obtain my wife's and daughter's support and agreement to take on such a demanding and hugely responsible task. We have captured Marton Vargas' killers, and they have emphatically identified Carlos as the force behind the killing. More disturbingly, Carlos did not coordinate the murder from his prison cell. On the contrary, we have learned he has escaped prison. I suspect—as you too must, Senhor Presidente—there may be a number of further heinous acts planned by Carlos and Regimento A to be uncovered and prevented and solved and absorbed. I will dedicate my directorship to containing this potential and to honoring you as the great leader you are and securing your continued success in office."

Voss replied, "Well, thank you, João. I concur wholeheartedly and look forward to hearing what you and your family decide. Thank you for your passionate support of me and our land, my friend."

da Silva had motioned to his driver to depart for his home in central Brasília. He conducted the call with Voss during the drive to his home, and he concluded the call while walking into his house.

Once inside, he proceeded to the kitchen window, looking out on the backyard, and called to his wife and daughter to join him inside. Katia and Andrea soon entered the kitchen on their return from the backyard.

João and Katia had met in school while teenagers. They were deeply in love and had developed a very successful life partnership. Katia had supported João through his demanding weeks in the PF academy. She had counseled him lovingly and supportively through his numerous challenging investigations. In these, he had experienced moments of self-doubt and emotional stress. Katia had been his rock throughout, consistently expressing her love for and confidence in João. João da Silva was fifty-seven years old and Katia, fifty-five. They had been married for twenty years.

Andrea was seventeen years old, having been born in the third year of her parents' marriage. Andrea was, like her mother, a stunning beauty of 5-feet-6-inches or 168-centimeters height with long brown hair set against large vividly hazel eyes, all contrasted and complemented by olive-colored skin that was completely lacking any blemishes or marks. They were each radiant and looked to be a movie star or supermodel.

Katia began the conversation, "Yes, João da Silva, my love, what is it you wish to say?"

"I have terrible news. Marton Vargas has been murdered. Lara and the girls are okay. I am equally stunned to inform you Presidente Voss has asked me to replace Marton as director of the Polícia Federal. I told him my answer is an enthusiastic, tentative yes, and I need the consent of the two of you to formally accept."

"Oh, poor Lara and the girls, this is heartbreaking!" replied Katia.

João described the events that had occurred at the Vargas home that evening. Katia and Andrea teared up and sobbed at their friends the Vargases' tragic turn.

Katia composed herself and spoke, "Well, my dear husband, I know you would enjoy the role and would do a fantastic job. I have strived to be supportive throughout all of the challenging years of your work for the PF. I suspect that our family's and your personal security will be better than ever on the heels of this tragedy."

Andrea offered her opinion next, "Yes, Daddy, I'd bet you'd be the best director ever, and I like the idea, provided you will be safe!"

da Silva chuckled his reply to Andrea, "Well, I do not see how anyone could fill the role better than Marton Vargas. You both know I will try the hardest anyone could be expected to try. I love you both and am ecstatic you are okay with the idea! Let's eat dinner and get a good night's rest before I call Presidente Voss in the morning to tell him the news."

Katia prepared a wonderful dinner of lobster and fried potatoes and salad. They ate heartily while basking in and discussing the new direction for the da Silva family.

At six thirty the following morning, da Silva was up and in the kitchen. Katia and Andrea entered the kitchen later in the morning and found da Silva with a freshly made breakfast of sweet cakes and fruit and sausages and fresh coffee. Katia told da Silva she and Andrea would clean up and disburden him from further effort in the kitchen so he could call the president and do whatever else he needed to do.

da Silva stepped into the backyard, which was landscaped with a concrete patio next to a small lawn and planter beds filled with shrubs native to the Amazon Basin intermingled with poinsettias and pansies and daisies. The flowers were green and yellow and blue and white to reflect the national flag. They were planted in a rectangle with a yellow circular shape in the middle in an attempt to look like the flag.

da Silva sat in a plastic yard chair and dialed Voss' office from his cell phone.

Voss' secretary answered, and Voss was on the line in an instant. "Good morning, João da Silva. How are you and yours this fine morning?!"

"We are well, Senhor Presidente. And you? I am happy to report my wife and daughter are supportive of my taking over the leadership of the Polícia Federal. I believe we have a great deal of work ahead of us, and I want to get to work quickly this morning. I see the priorities to be the capture and return of Carlos to be punished as appropriate. Regimento A and Stein must be completely contained and neutered as well. That effort must be expanded to gain an understanding of who is and was behind Carlos' escape and the murder of Marton Vargas. We then must continue our quest to find and eradicate corruption throughout the land. Additionally, we must fight crime and the way it insidiously seduces so much of the youth in our cities along with people in professional and governmental roles."

Voss smiled while listening, encouraged and reassued by the apparent wisdom of his choice of João da Silva. "Why, thank you, Senhor Director. There is unfinished business to be conducted on your behalf. Please await a call from the *procuradora geral*. I have instructed her to negotiate the terms of your formal employment agreement. I have recommended a handsome salary and benefits package and am hoping it will meet your expectations and inspire you to fill the position and fulfill your duties admirably and courageously."

João da Silva was unaccustomed to such treatment over his decades of service and was careful to not let his self-interest deter him from focus on the job at hand. "Thank you, Senhor Presidente. My expectations are humble. I am dedicated to you and Brazil and the support of my fellow officers in law enforcement."

Voss sat smiling and feeling happy about his decision. They rang off with an exchange of compliments.

Within minutes of the call's end, da Silva's cell phone rang again, and the attorney general (procuradora geral) was on the line. They spoke for forty-five minutes. At the end of their conversation, the attorney general emailed a draft agreement to da Silva for his review and approval. da Silva agreed to the document in a call to thank her. Within minutes, a PDF of the agreement bearing Ricardo Voss' signature arrived in da Silva's email inbox. da Silva printed it and showed it proudly to Katia. Katia was pleased with the terms in the document. She nodded her approval and gave her husband a deep passionate kiss. da Silva signed his copy and scanned the signature page and returned it to the attorney general.

Voss texted a salutation, "Welcome on board my leadership team, Senhor Director da Silva!" Voss called da Silva and continued the conversation verbally, "I am honored to be working with you. Let's honor Marton Vargas' memory by finding and capturing Carlos and stopping Stein forever."

"Yes, Senhor Presidente. I am focused on that very objective. You have my gratitude and allegiance. I am prepared to call Fernando Carvalho and Roberto Cardenas and Sergio Viana to rally our team to the task."

da Silva excitedly dialed Fernando and Viana and Cardenas and told them he had formalized his role as the director of the PF. Next, he called the commander of the PM and told him the news. The commander shared da Silva's passion for eradicating crime and corruption and enthusiastic support for Presidente Voss. All were enthusiastic in their congratulations and pledges to work cooperatively in the effort to capture Carlos and stop Carlos and Stein's disruptive criminal activities.

da Silva conducted the call with Viana and Cardenas as a three-way conference call. In the conversation, Cardenas reported that after hearing Diego Guedes' report that Stein and Carlos were together on Stein's private island in the Dominican Republic he had instructed Diego to not take any action to confront Stein or Carlos but instead to stay in place with his eyes on the two to ensure they could later be located. Guedes had succeeded in being hired as a worker on the island and was frequently in contact with Stein. Guedes reported Stein and Carlos were sequestered in Stein's library in his home on the island.

Cardenas inquired about Fernando's availability, and they all greed Fernando would be best suited to go collect

Carlos. Fernando had developed a well-deserved reputation as a brave participant in action. Cardenas referred to Fernando's familiarity with Carlos and likely desire to bring him to justice. Questions about Fernando's suitability for the work were satisfied by da Silva's animated description of Fernando's action in the Major Strock eradication. They discussed the concern for using Fernando because of his personal investment in the effort to bring Carlos to justice and agreed he showed no penchant for revenge. They debated for some time after which da Silva made a compelling argument in favor of Fernando; Cardenas then decided firmly to give the assignment to Fernando.

In early 2020, a passionate Communist Venezuelan general named Juan Cortez had, at the direction of Nicolás Maduro, launched efforts at infiltrating and disrupting Brazil's political and economic infrastructure. Brazil was the object of envy by the leaders of the failed Venezuelan dictatorial regime of Hugo Chávez and Nicolás Maduro, along with failed despotic leaders throughout Latin America, including the Cuban regime.

Working with General Cortez as his conduit, Stein enthusiastically funded Cortez's efforts in support of Carlos. They saw Carlos and Regimento A as a convenient and easy way to cause difficulty for the Voss administration. Cortez and Stein were passionately focused on delivering votes for Voss' opponents who promised unachievable and ill-conceived and highly expensive programs for which no funding could reasonably be expected to be found. The sum of the costs totaled an amount in excess of Stein's reported net worth of 4.5 billion US dollars. The existing membership of the legislative branch of the Brazilian government could in no way be expected to vote in favor of these programs, were there not a return to the corrupt bribery practices of the past. Stein had committed a fund of 20 million US dollars in support of the bribes and drive to support elections of those who would vote in favor of the programs. The programs were suspiciously designed to enrich a collection of corporations either owned by Stein or affiliated with Stein's network of business contacts.

da Silva and Director Cardenas spoke with Presidente Voss about the development, and they all agreed on a plan of action.

Fernando was flown to Brasília for a quickly called meeting with da Silva and Presidente Voss and Director Cardenas and a representative of the CIA.

CHAPTER 40

Director da Silva's office, PF headquarters, Brasília, Distrito Federal, Brazil
Morning of Wednesday, September 2, 2020

Director da Silva opened the meeting with a somber tone, "Fernando, Director Marton Vargas was killed by members of Regimento A, and we've learned Carlos has escaped prison and is behind the Vargas killing. We have decided to send you to collect Carlos. We feel you are the best choice because you know and understand who and what a threat he is. This is Tom Fielding of the US CIA."

Fielding was a large bald man of mixed race from California who stood 6 feet 5 inches tall and weighed 260 pounds. He was unique in his appearance compared with the typical CIA operative; he wore shorts and a tank top. He had a large athletic frame, and his arms and shoulders exhibited the results of his dedication to weight lifting. For shoes, he wore leather sandals secured by Velcro on leather straps. His arms and shoulders were decorated with tattoos that depicted US patriotic scenes and symbols. These included a bald eagle and a representation of D-Day combat along with a US flag. He was an ex-navy SEAL who'd been a field agent for twenty years and could both defend and advise and train Fernando and provide powerful backup on the mission to capture Carlos.

"Tom is an experienced field agent and extraordinarily tough and smart and should be invaluable as your partner on the quest to bring Carlos back home."

Presidente Voss and Rogerio Cardenas nodded their enthusiastic concurrence.

Voss spoke after Fernando had time to absorb the suggestion and to shake Fielding's massive hand, "Fernando, Senhor O Bispo, our country has been threatened and aggrieved by Carlos' inexcusable acts on behalf of Gregor Stein. The evidence is clear that Gregor Stein has been funding Carlos' criminal activities with Regimento A as well as a developing Venezuelan and Cuban Communist threat to Brazil. It is imperative you and Senhor Fielding succeed and bring Carlos back to justice. As your president, I fully authorize you to use whatever force you deem necessary to bring Stein and Carlos' threat to an end. I believe we would benefit greatly by capturing Carlos so we may learn what we can from him."

da Silva sat next to Fernando and addressed both him and Tom on behalf of the president's assembled team, "Gentlemen, Presidente Voss and Director Cardenas and I have concluded Stein's endeavors must be terminated quickly to stem the advance of his heinous agenda."

Fernando translated the conversation into English in order that Fielding might understand.

da Silva continued, "We are keenly aware of your inexperience, Fernando. We have arranged for you to travel to Stein's island aboard a submarine to go ashore, aided by some MECs who will assure your and Senhor Fielding's safe passage ashore and back to the submarine."

They were to be transported in the submarine *Tikuna*. The Brazilian submarine *Tikuna* was built in the naval yard in Rio de Janeiro by Itaguaí Construções Navais.

In 2020, Itaguaí was currently constructing a nuclear-powered sub for the Brazilian Navy. The nuclear sub was to be named the *Álvaro Alberto*. A treaty between France and Brazil provided for a nuclear technology transfer to Itaguaí Construções, and the Brazilian Navy enabled the project. Álvaro Alberto da Motta e Silva was a Brazilian scientist and admiral. He was a prominent member of the Brazilian Academy of Sciences. He served as the country's representative on the UN's Atomic Energy Commission. His naval and scientific backgrounds made him the logical choice for the nuclear submarine's namesake.

The *Tikuna* was completed on March 9, 2005. It was placed in service on July 21, 2006. Four diesel-electric engines power the *Tikuna*. The GRUMEC are trained to travel to and be placed in their theaters of operations in a submarine.

Cardenas nodded his consent and continued, "Fernando, we have arranged to have two of our top F-15 pilots transport you and Tom to Galeão Air Force Base in Rio. You will be transported by car from the air base to Arsenal de Marinha do Rio de Janeiro. You will then be placed on the submarine *Tikuna* for the passage to Stein's island in the Dominican Republic. Your arrival there is expected to be early on Friday morning.

"Tom, we know you have been away from your family for several months. Once, thanks to God, Fernando's and your assignment is successfully completed, you will both be returned to Rio. We will have you, Tom, flown home to California by one of our F-15s. To speed your trip home and shorten your absence, we have arranged with the US and other governments on the flight path to permit flight speeds in excess of Mach 2.0 so your trip is as quick as possible. Upon your arrival at Stein's island, you will be met by

Diego Guedes of the ABIN who has been there undercover in advance of your arrival."

Fernando spoke next, "I understand the burden you are expecting Tom and me to bear, gentlemen. I am honored and excited about this assignment. I can clearly see Mr. Fielding here will be an excellent partner."

Within twenty-four hours, Tom and Fernando were each flown to Galeão Air Force Base in Rio. They were, as planned, each a passenger in a Brazilian Air Force F-15. The flight was very short. da Silva and Cardenas had arranged to have the pilots fly at Mach 1.0 in consideration of the urgency around the mission.

Within two hours of their arrival, Tom and Fernando were driven in a limousine to the naval base, Arsenal de Marinha do Rio de Janeiro, where they boarded the submarine *Tikuna* that was dedicated to taking GRUMEC troops to their assignments. They were welcomed on board by the MECs (*mergulhadores de combate* or combat divers) and prepared for the several hours' transit to Stein's island.

CHAPTER 41

Waters of the Caribbean Sea off the Dominican Republic
Morning of Thursday, September 3, 2020

The sub arrived at the island at twelve thirty in the morning, under the comfortable cover of darkness.

Upon arrival at Stein's island, Fernando and Tom and their GRUMEC comrades boarded an inflatable rowboat and caught the tide to head to shore. Several additional MECs in diving gear swam along by holding on to ropes on the side of the boat. Fernando donned a wet suit to fit in with the MECs, and after a struggle to locate a properly sized suit for Tom Fielding, they succeeded, and Fielding also donned a wet suit and swam with the MECs.

The island security was sloppy, and they got close enough to shore so they could wade onto the beach. Once on the beach, Fernando and Tom set out in the direction of Stein's private beach where they planned to find their targets relaxing.

A full moon appeared after an opening occurred in clouds. This aided their vision nicely. They had all smeared grease on their faces in order that their skin would not shine in whatever light source they encountered. The night's darkness was enhanced by a thick cloud layer overhead. A loud party was underway some 150 yards beyond their landing point.

The MECs then returned to the submarine to wait for forty minutes prior to returning to the beach to find Fernando and Tom. Three MECs in diving gear remained behind on the island to help Fernando and Tom if necessary. Their names were Doido (Crazy) and Dor (Pain) and Zé (nickname for José).

Stein was Carlos' primary benefactor. The gathering on the island was a celebration of Carlos' escape to freedom.

Diego Guedes found Tom and Fernando by chance and escorted them to a safe clearing on the sand. Tom and Fernando stood with Guedes, eyeing the party. As instructed, Guedes was keeping his eyes on Stein and Carlos, and he noted they were sequestered in Stein's office in the main house.

The island was within the territory of the Dominican Republic. Voss' foreign minister contacted the Dominican government and obtained their permission for Brazilian action to find and secure Carlos on Stein's island.

Guedes was solely an information-gathering spy and therefore was limited from taking armed action unless absolutely necessary. He stepped away to conduct his service duties for the party in order that he might maintain his cover.

While standing in place, Fernando and Tom felt guns placed at the base of their necks and were tapped on the shoulders. They turned and saw they each had an armed fellow behind them pointing toward the main house.

Behind Tom was a giant of a man whom Tom and Fernando recognized from the briefings they had studied on the *Tikuna* that night on their way to the island. His name was Oleg Shostakova. He was a war criminal from the Bosnian and Serbian conflict in the Nineties.

Tom and Fernando proceeded to the main house and into Stein's office as their captors directed. The armed guards recognized Guedes as one of the party workers and motioned him to return to his duties and left him alone.

Stein was seated imperiously behind a grand colonial-style desk. A large gas-fired imitation fireplace was roaring in contradiction to the external tropical environment. The room was intensely hot.

Stein spoke first, "I am sorry to have to meet and greet you in this fashion, Mr. Carvalho, or whatever your name is. I am happy to reunite you with Carlos on this day we celebrate his freedom." Carlos was seated on a couch in the library and grinned like the Cheshire Cat at Fernando and nodded toward him in mock deference, "You and your PF friends are now my and my associate Mr. Carlos' primary targets. You have become major impediments to me and all of us and our plans."

Tom Fielding spoke an angry reply.

Oleg struck Tom a blow with the butt of his gun, rendering Tom dizzy. Fielding shook off the dazed feeling and stood to face Oleg. While attempting to stand up, Fielding collapsed unconscious.

"I apologize, Senhor Carvalho. Your friend's size is too much of a threat, and we believe we'd be safer if we were to tie him unconscious to his chair.

Fernando shrugged in begrudging acceptance.

Stein continued, "I am sorry to say I have no choice except to have you both killed. Nothing would give me greater pleasure than to see you both killed and have your bodies delivered to Ricardo Voss in pieces."

Fernando put his feet up on Stein's desk, which clearly disturbed Stein. Fernando replied, "Gregor Stein, your days in the terror business are over, and your cause is hollow and without point. I will see your corpse well in advance of my death."

Stein sneered in disgust and froze upon hearing auto-matic gunfire from the beach. Within moments, the office door burst open. Fernando had sent a previously drafted text to the dive team commander. Guedes had led the MECs to the office. Doido and Dor rushed in and shot the gunmen behind Fernando and Oleg dead. The stunned Stein fumbled with a desk drawer and produced a revolver and moved to use it in his defense. Fernando pulled his Glock 19 from his waistband and shot Stein between the eyes, killing him instantly. Carlos was unarmed and stood and placed his hands behind his head and knelt in submission.

Zé entered and approached Carlos and handcuffed him and addressed him, "Senhor Carlos, in the name of Presidente Voss, I arrest you on behalf of Brazil. We are to take you to our submarine and return you to Rio where you will be placed in custody to await an indictment and later to be tried."

Carlos sneered at Tom and Fernando and spat on the floor near their feet.

Within fifteen minutes, the island exploded in chaos while the staff and guests reacted to the sound of the gunfire. The MECs engaged Stein's inadequately prepared security force and quickly killed seven of them. The corpses of the deceased were left in place where they fell.

Shortly, a boat operated by the Dominican govern-ment arrived to collect the guests to return them to Santo Domingo to go home to Europe or the US or South or Central America. On board were representatives of the Brazilian and Dominican governments whose task was to document the outcome on the island and to collect the dead.

Back on the submarine, Zé tied Carlos to a seat and shackled his feet and put duct tape with a gag over his mouth to keep him quiet.

The captain announced that Presidente Voss and Director da Silva and Director Cardenas were on the phone, asking to speak to Fernando and Tom. Fernando and Tom joined the call on a speakerphone arrangement.

Voss spoke first, "Well, gentlemen, we are dying to know how your effort went."

Fernando replied, "Gentlemen, I am pleased to report Gregor Stein attempted vainly to engage us in a gun battle and died from a gunshot I delivered to his head. Carlos is in our custody and will be handed over upon our return to Rio. Tom Fielding proved to be a valorous partner, and I have enjoyed working with him. Our 'friend' Carlos is secured here on board and doesn't appear very threatening, except for an attempt at a scary face."

Tom and Fernando spoke together, "It surely isn't working!"

Fernando wrapped it up, "He looks very much like a typical guy from the streets of Rocinha. I'm fighting the urge to cut him so he bleeds and throw him into the ocean for the sharks."

Carlos' eyes widened and darted from side to side, looking for an approaching threat.

Voss spoke again, "Well, I am very pleased by this outcome! Diego Guedes tells Director Cardenas he is on the boat bound for Santo Domingo with all of the island's guests and the remains of ten people, including Stein and his bodyguard Oleg and eight of Stein's mercenary security personnel. Just now we have arranged for Carlos' return to custody."

Cardenas added, "The admiral the GRUMEC report to has agreed to provide a team of MECs to guard Carlos around the clock in a specially constructed building at their headquarters at Arsenal de Marinha do Rio de Janeiro. He will have absolutely no chance of bribing his way out of the facility! Especially now that Stein is out of the picture and won't be available for funding Carlos' needs. We had better hope Vilmar hasn't managed Regimento A's finances carefully and retained further funding to fulfill Carlos and Stein's dreams for future activity. We are further investigating General Cortez's ability to obtain funding from Caracas. Given Maduro's envy driven hatred for Brazil and Presidente Voss, we need to be careful."

Fernando and Tom smiled at each other while noting Carlos' agitated reaction to this announcement.

Cardenas continued, "We are certain all of Stein's staff are on board the boat bound for Santo Domingo as well, and all will be taken to Guantanamo and interrogated by the CIA and ABIN to determine if they are guilty of involvement in Stein and Carlos' criminal activities."

da Silva broke in, "Yes, Fernando and Tom, well done! Fernando, I knew you could be relied upon to make this work! I am sure Carlos is enraged by your having participated in his capture!"

All the men on the other end of the call broke out in loud laughter, as did Tom and Fernando and the MECs and submarine crew. Fernando noted Carlos' face was a brilliant red, and his eyes glared at his captors while his fists were clenched, as was his jaw. The sub set out toward Rio and arrived at the Arsenal de Marinha do Rio de Janeiro at around seven thirty in the evening.

Fernando bid Tom goodbye, and Tom was taken to Galeão Air Force Base for his F-15 flight home to the San Francisco Bay Area. The two embraced like old friends, and Fernando thanked Tom heartily.

Fernando dialed Paulo Coberto and asked him to come pick him up.

Paulo handed the phone to Denise who was effusively excited about Fernando's return.

"Hi, Fernando. Paulo told Heliana and me about your brave work in the Caribbean! The hot tub is all warmed up, and the cocktails are ready so we may all celebrate you as the hero you are. Heliana and I are making dinner, and we all cannot wait to see you, especially me! I am leaving the house now and should be there to get you in about forty-five minutes. Paulo gave me your car's keys, and I'm using it to come pick you up."

Fernando broke into a broad smile; he was very pleased, as he had missed being with Denise.

While he waited, he called Maria and spoke to her about his success. He invited her to come stay with him for a visit to Rio. He offered to take her shopping and out to dinner and to clubs for music and dancing.

The boys who'd killed Marton Vargas were later tried as adults and sentenced to Porto Velho Federal Prison for terms in excess of fifteen years; the sentences were as good as death sentences. All three boys subsequently died at the hands of other prisoners in prison violence in Porto Velho. The boys were simply not big and tough enough to defend themselves.

CHAPTER 42

Paulo Coberto's home, Niterói suburb, Rio de Janeiro, Brazil
Night of Thursday, September 3, 2020

Fernando and Denise were back at Coberto's house within one hour and twenty minutes and joined Paulo and Heliana in the hot tub for caipirinhas. Fernando was grateful to be back safely with his friends and relaxing. He felt the tension from his trip to Stein's island draining away.

Meanwhile, business that would require The Bishop's attention was unfolding in Brasília. The da Silva's daughter Andrea was captured by kidnappers while shopping in a neighborhood store near the da Silva home. The kidnappers were unfortunately very intelligent. They were a four-man team from Regimento A, following detailed orders from William Nelson Vilmar. Vilmar was continuing to act in accordance with Carlos' game plan prepared prior to his escape to Stein's island.

They had studied the da Silva family's security contingent very carefully and determined a means to avoid confrontation. They were masquerading as telephone repairmen in and around the da Silva's neighborhood. They had managed to hack the phone company's work order system and to generate and print fake orders for surrounding residences and a neighboring market. The orders looked deceivingly authentic and weren't questioned by the police guarding the da Silva home and neighborhood. Having been generated in the phone company's system, the orders were easily confirmed as valid. The police called the phone company's dispatchers, and the orders were located in the company's system and confirmed.

A lookout for the Regimento A team observed Andrea da Silva get into a PF car and saw Andrea being driven under guard to the neighboring market. The PF agents guarding Andrea instructed her to call them and they would return to collect her. The criminals then approached the rear door of the market and presented a fake phone repair order. They subdued the store employee they spoke to and tied him up in a corner of the stockroom. They entered the store's front area and found and captured Andrea whom they then placed bound and blindfolded in a mock telephone company van.

Twenty minutes later, her PF driver and guards wondered why they hadn't heard from Andrea. They called her cell phone and, receiving no answer, drove back to the market. They saw no sign of Andrea in or around the market or on the street between the da Silva home and the market. They found the store employee in the stockroom. From his description of the "phone company" men who'd assaulted and bound him, the agents began a desperate search for a phone company van.

Within twenty minutes, the van was indeed located on a side street. To the disappointment of the four agents that found the van, it was completely empty, except for a collection of work orders to be carried out at several homes of prominent citizens. They did find Andrea's cell phone in a corner of the van's internal load bed area. This Andrea had intentionally left to provide proof she had been in the vehicle. The agents concluded the kidnappers must have transferred

Andrea to another vehicle and made a clean escape with their captive. A frantic search of all of Brasília ensued and found no trace of Andrea or a suspicious automobile.

The PF men called João da Silva and explained the circumstance. He ordered the men to expand their area of containment and have all vehicles stopped and searched. Within minutes, he was informed there were five vehicles found to search. None of these had any occupants who had apparently been involved in Andrea's disappearance.

Conscious of the risk of time passing by and allowing the kidnappers to get away or, even worse, very far away, da Silva resolved to get Fernando and his network's assistance.

At the moment of da Silva's resolve to involve Fernando, Fernando and Denise and Paulo and Heliana were all in the hot tub having their before-dinner cocktails and chatting.

Fernando's cell phone rang, and he answered, finding an agitated João da Silva who described the awful circumstance and a demand he had received for a large sum of money to secure his daughter's return and safety. da Silva and Fernando agreed murder might be the motive, and da Silva pressed Fernando for rapid action.

Fernando spoke in an aside to his housemates and explained why he had to step into the house and make some calls. They all were, of course, supportive and agreed to wrap up the cocktail hour and prepare dinner.

Once in his bedroom, Fernando dialed José Vargas' cell phone and explained the problem and requested his help in determining where and with who Andrea might be. José Vargas asked Fernando to stand by while he made some inquiries. Fernando explained he felt some great urgency in resolving his mentor's daughter's problem; Fernando knew Andrea well and was concerned that such a dear child was in a frightening circumstance and obviously in terrible danger.

He was worried she might be severely emotionally scarred by the experience, if not permanently physically harmed.

Fernando returned to the kitchen and roof deck and gave Denise comfort that he was confident in José Vargas' ability to obtain the information needed for Andrea's rescue.

Fernando then called Director da Silva back and told him about the action he had initiated with José Vargas.

"I want you here with me during this disaster, Fernando. Can you come if I arrange to have you flown to Brasília on a private plane?! I would feel so much better if you were here to assist me," said da Silva.

"You know I would love to be there to help you," replied Fernando. "Please allow me time to learn what José Vargas finds out and to talk to my housemates. Once I have a plan, I'll reach back out to you to coordinate."

da Silva thanked Fernando effusively and said he would await word and emphasized how worried he and Katia were about their beloved Andrea's circumstance.

Fernando returned to Denise's side with Paulo and Heliana and explained his conversation with da Silva and need to go to Brasília to help.

Sixty-five minutes after his call to José Vargas, Fernando's cell phone rang. He answered with excited anticipation.

"Fernandinho, I am happy to say the kidnappers are a sloppy bunch that I have been able to identify and locate," said José Vargas. "They are a group of our old Sombra Preta comrades who are helping Regimento A and are camped out on the banks of the Iguaçu River in Florianópolis in the state of Santa Catarina."

Fernando said, "Thank you, my friend. I may require your and Luis Antonio's support in my attempt to rescue the girl. Would you please proceed to Florianópolis and try to infiltrate the camp and stand by for my arrival in a day or so, so I may make the rescue myself?"

Fernando was insistent he'd be the one to execute the rescue since he was convinced of his ability to avoid harm to Andrea and to console her during the rescue. He was certain a familiar face would be calming and comforting to the girl. He further argued he knew he was from the same background as the kidnappers and might know them and, therefore, could understand how to handle them.

Fernando called da Silva and asked and cautioned him to allow The Bishop to handle the matter.

da Silva agreed and told Fernando to expect an air force F-15 to be ready for him the following morning to transport him to Hercílio Luz International Airport in Florianópolis.

Around seven o'clock the following morning, Fernando attended a conference call with Amaraes and the O Banco do Brasil team. Denise was awake with a breakfast and coffee, offering to start their busy days ahead. Before departing the house, he dressed in the outfit of The Bishop and threw a backpack with his Glock 19 and ammunition in the back seat of Paulo's PF sedan. Before driving off, he had calmed Denise's apprehension regarding his taking on a potentially dangerous task. She offered him a packed lunch, and he thanked her and declined, explaining how da Silva always had a van with food and refreshments available at every "adventure."

Paulo drove Fernando to Galeão Air Force Base where he was greeted by an F-15 pilot he was familiar with from a previous adventure.

At around eleven o'clock in the morning, the plane touched down at the airport in Florianópolis. On the flight, he'd received his share of barrel rolls and accelerative excitement.

CHAPTER 43

Florianópolis, state of Santa Catarina, Brazil
Morning of Friday, September 4, 2020

Once the exhausted Fernando was off the plane, João da Silva met him.

da Silva and Fernando then entered da Silva's PF staff car and were driven to the banks of the Iguaçu River near the Sombra Preta kidnappers' encampment.

José Vargas and Luis Antonio and a few of da Silva's PF men greeted them. After a brief conversation and excited hugs and subdued rallying cheers, the assembled men took cover in some brush and small trees and pointed in the direction of a tent they said contained Andrea and her captors.

Fernando went back to the car and got the gun da Silva had given him for his trip to Switzerland, a Glock 19 much like da Silva's own.

da Silva pulled Fernando aside and spoke, "Fernando, these PF officers are some of my best men. I have avoided sending them in out of respect for your belief you are the best choice to rescue my daughter. Please prove me correct."

Fernando smiled confidently at the sight of the campsite and said, "Have no fear. The Bishop is here." He adjusted the Stetson on his head and walked to the tent with his Travolta-like cadence.

Fernando strode in the direction of the tent. As he approached, one of the men in the tent recognized Fernando and called out to him as if he thought Fernando was a fellow kidnapper; Fernando waived back at him and asked if he could see their captive. Confused as to Fernando's purpose, the fellow agreed and showed Fernando into the tent. Seated on the floor was poor Andrea, bound and gagged and looking terrified.

"This is inexcusable!" roared Fernando.

The stunned captors all stared at him in disbelief and surprise and moved to stop him.

With a swift move, Fernando shot the four captors dead with shots to their foreheads and knelt beside the horrified girl and spoke to her, "My dear Andrea, I am your father's best friend. I haven't seen you for years, but I suspect you may remember my name. I am Fernando Carvalho and am called The Bishop because of how I dress."

Andrea began to cry hysterically, and Fernando held her in a comforting embrace, consoling her. The PF men and Fernando's friends and da Silva all arrived in response to the sound of the gunfire.

Fernando walked Andrea out of the tent into the wonderfully warm evening air. She would forever remember the sound of the water in the river at that moment of her liberation and associate it with life and freedom. The river, at that point, is flowing toward the famous Iguaçu Falls on the border with Argentina and has a force so overwhelming its sound conveys the strength and power and grandeur of its final destination at the falls.

Fernando and da Silva and Andrea got into da Silva's car and were returned to the Florianópolis airport. They boarded the private plane da Silva had arrived in and prepared for the return to Brasília.

On the flight, da Silva consoled Andrea and showered Fernando with praise for his success in the rescue. "Well done, my friend! Were it not for you, I have no idea as to what the outcome might have been. I have texted Presidente Voss and Director Cardenas to tell them of your wise and courageous accomplishment. I suspect you should expect further assignments. Director Cardenas is interested in bringing you into the ABIN. He understands your commitment to the bank and Senhor Amaraes. He wants to meet with you soon, following our landing in Brasília."

Andrea sat in silence between her father and Fernando throughout the flight. She appeared as if she were glued to her savior and appeared nervous when Fernando would step away from her and stand up and speak.

CHAPTER 44

Brasília, Distrito Federal, Brazil
Evening of Friday, September 4, 2020

Within a little over two hours, the plane landed in Brasília, and they were driven to the PF headquarters. Presidente Voss and Director Cardenas were awaiting their arrival with a small honor guard with a few musicians.

Voss made a speech celebrating the rescue of Andrea da Silva and emphasized the successful effort by the PF under the leadership of da Silva. He was purposefully silent about Fernando and his involvement because he and Cardenas were hoping to utilize Fernando for future covert work. In the speech, he warned criminals to be careful and beware under his presidency. He further warned those who would be involved in corruption that there was no place for them in Brazilian society. On the heels of the speech, Voss' popularity rating rose dramatically, making him the most popular president in recent Brazilian history. After the speech, Voss and Cardenas and da Silva and Fernando and Andrea adjourned to da Silva's office.

Voss spoke to them, "I am afraid this may not be the end of the challenges from Regimento A and Carlos. Director da Silva's sources report some sobering news. Director da Silva and his PF team and PM partners are concerned with threats from the reinvigorated Regimento A. William Nelson Vilmar has rapidly assumed command upon Carlos' recapture and has been spewing vile threats and vitriol at Fernando and Director da Silva and me. The threats include Regimento A's announcement of their knowledge of Fernando's whereabouts and threat to kill him and Coberto and the Santos women and their parents."

da Silva explained he was working on a plan to draw Vilmar out into a conflict with Fernando, which could provide an opportunity to take him out while in action.

Cardenas reported he had asked the CIA to allow Tom Fielding to return to South America to partner with Fernando as needed. He indicated the potential for the CIA agreeing to the request was very likely and promising.

da Silva emphasized Rogerio Amaraes had agreed to be flexible about Fernando's requisite absences from work in the interest of freeing him up to act on matters of national security. Cardenas offered to employ Fernando in the ABIN with equivalent flexibility for his work at the bank. Fernando smiled at the ideas and offered his acceptance of them.

He was placed in a PF car and whisked to Presidente Juscelino Kubitschek International Airport in the Lago Sul area of Brasília where he boarded the F-15 for his return to Rio. He landed around eight o'clock in the evening at Galeão Air Force Base. A PF car greeted him and drove him to Paulo Coberto's home in Niterói.

On the drive, he called Denise to announce his return and asked her if he were too late for dinner.

CHAPTER 45

Paulo Coberto's home, Niterói, Brazil
Evening of Friday, September 4, 2020

Denise was excited about his return and insisted his timing was fine.

He entered Coberto's home and found the waiting arms of Denise Santos. Paulo and Heliana insisted they all go to the best local restaurant for dinner. Denise pouted and observed she needed time with "her man." Paulo and Heliana laughed and teased Fernando and Denise. They offered to go out for takeout and bring it back to the rooftop deck.

Denise was appearing overtly romantic, and Fernando became concerned.

"Denise, I like you very much but am concerned about developing a deep romance with you. I am living a life full of risks and don't want to burden you with worry about where and how safe I am every time I travel on government business."

Denise stared into Fernando's eyes while making a circle in his right palm with her left hand and replied, "Nando, I understand that being with you could be frustrating, but the trade-off with the wonderful experience when we make love and spend time together is a fair trade. I am in love with you and don't need you to feel the same. I just want to be your girlfriend."

Fernando was relieved and grateful for having told her the truth. He realized he was cautious because of the pain he had experienced in losing Marta.

The PF and PM guard around the Coberto home had been doubled from its previous level, and Paulo and Heliana were delayed and returned with the food within forty minutes of their departure. They all gathered at a picnic table near the hot tub and enjoyed the food. They had purchased a selection of Italian dishes, including ravioli with meat filling and meat sauce and meat lasagna. A Caesar salad and wonderful bottle of Cesari Amarone Chianti were included. They all ate heartily. Denise sat close to Fernando, holding his left hand.

Fernando's cell phone rang, and he saw it was a call from da Silva. He kissed Denise's forehead and stepped away from the table.

She watched him wistfully and realized he was out of reach.

"Good evening, Senhor Director."

"Good evening, Fernando. I am with Director Cardenas. We have some news to share with you."

da Silva placed the call on speaker, and Cardenas spoke, "Well, hello, Fernando. Diego Guedes has been captured in Caracas. We sent him there this afternoon from Rio. The Maduro regime is in collapse and, as you will understand from my explanation, poses a threat against Brazil and Ricardo Voss. General Jaime Cortez has placed Maduro under house arrest and declared himself president of Venezuela. General Cortez and his associates in Cuba and elsewhere have concluded Maduro is an abject failure as a revolutionary. Cortez is in contact with Stein's son, Peter. Peter has pledged a share of the Stein fortune to back the new Cortez regime. We need you and Tom Fielding to go and free Diego. Tom is en route back from California and will meet you at Galeão Air Force Base at four o'clock in the morning. An Embraer jet will take you both to Fortaleza where you are to board the *Tikuna* submarine with MECs who will help you ashore near Caracas on the north shore of Venezuela. You, Tom, and the MECs will need to move overland to Caracas without being discovered. Diego is in a house inhabited by several of Cortez's senior officers who are holding him hostage."

da Silva joined the conversation, "Well, Fernando, you will need to wear a uniform provided by the MECs and avoid your normal costume. This is a very dangerous assignment, and we will keep you and Tom in our prayers. Listen carefully to Tom and Doido because they know exactly how to penetrate the Venezuelan defenses. I remember you studied Castilian Spanish at Universidade Católica and received high scores and are nearly fluent. You will need to be convincing masquerading as a local in your conversations. God bless you, Fernando Carvalho."

"Yes, senhores directores, I am prepared to try to rescue poor Diego. Will Doido and the MEC team have details for Tom and me to study on board the submarine? Director da Silva, please call Rogerio Amaraes and explain my absence is a matter of state security. I will leave him a message now, informing him I have been called away on an urgent assignment from Director da Silva."

Denise sat listening intently with a disappointed look on her face. Fernando stepped to her side and explained he had been called away and would quickly pack to depart for the air force base. Fernando hugged Denise and assured her he'd be back soon and they would spend time together.

Ten minutes later, Fernando was in Paulo's car on the way to the air base.

At the air base, he was able to grab six hours of sleep to make up for having left home so quickly. At four thirty in the morning, he awoke and saw Tom Fielding looking down at him on the cot he was sleeping on. Fielding informed him their plane to Fortaleza was waiting for them. The dawn was hinting at its arrival with a wonderful scent of sea air and touches of pink light on the eastern horizon over the Atlantic Ocean.

Tom and Fernando boarded the plane and were greeted by the pilots. A flight attendant offered them coffee and served breakfast pastries and meats and fruits.

CHAPTER 46

---⋆---

Fortaleza, state of Ceará, Brazil, northeastern coast of the South American continent
Morning of Saturday, September 5, 2020

At 7:00 a.m., they touched down at Fortaleza-Pinto Martins International Airport. Doido and Dor and Zé greeted them with a large SUV and drove to the pier where their submarine sat waiting.

The *Tikuna's* crew welcomed them on board enthusiastically. On the dock, a CIA agent named Tom Bancroft introduced himself. He was a friend and coworker of Fielding who had extensive experience and knowledge in and of Venezuela.

On board the sub, Bancroft proffered a file with photos of the house Diego was captive in. It was a house in central Caracas of colonial style. It was a masonry structure of two stories' height painted white. There was a balcony around the entirety of the second floor. The windows and doors appeared easily accessible from the surrounding ground. Landscaping of large untrimmed bushes surrounded the property and afforded cover for access to the windows and doors.

Fernando and Tom inquired about its occupants. Bancroft explained six members of Cortez's crack revolutionary guard lived in the house and were standing guard over Diego. Diego was reportedly being held in a bedroom on the first floor or in the living room. His captors were reportedly heavily armed. The house was under the protective watch of the Caracas Civilian Police and Venezuelan Army and revolutionary guard. Bancroft observed the guard were trained as much as the GRUMEC troops and were known for being brutal and fanatical followers of Cortez.

Fernando and Fielding spoke together while studying the file and developed their plan of attack. They discussed the plan with Doido and Dor and Zé and a new MEC who'd joined the mission. He was a Palestinian who'd served in the Israeli Army Special Forces. His name was Jamal, and he had a reputation for valiantly and successfully taking on enemies like the revolutionary guard. Fielding had seen him in action in Somalia and urged Fernando to include him on the team to rescue Diego.

The submarine took several hours to get to its destination on the northwestern Venezuelan coast near Port of Spain where they planned to go ashore and make their way inland to Caracas. To cover the well over 350-some-mile distance between the two cities would require a long risky drive in a vehicle of some kind. The risk of being discovered and attacked or captured appeared to be extremely high.

Bancroft and Fielding and Fernando and the MECs all ate a dinner with the sub crew prior to going ashore.

CHAPTER 47

Northern coast of Venezuela near Port of Spain
Late afternoon of Saturday, September 5, 2020

Once in place off the shore of Venezuela, the shore-bound team of Doido and Dor and Zé and Jamal and Fielding and Fernando bid goodbye to Bancroft who planned to remain on board and return to Fortaleza with the team on the sub. The shore-bound team donned wet suits and went on deck and deployed an inflatable raft disguised as a fishing vessel.

The setting sun glinted brightly off the Caribbean Sea as they bobbed in the waves far off the Venezuelan coastline. Oil tankers dotted the horizon. The air was humid, and there was barely any coastal breeze. Looking through binoculars, Fernando peered at the shoreline and saw thousands of mangroves, their stilt-like roots protruding from the water. He could smell the submarine's engine—oil and fuel. The raft had a complement of convincing fishing gear, including fishing rods and reels and nets and a bayonet or hook for securing resistant fish. It was dusk, and they managed to find the shore in the growing darkness. The plan called for them to go ashore and pass through a clean water drainage culvert to get onto the road they would follow into Caracas. It was growing ever darker. They had to make their way carefully in order to avoid being discovered. Every sound caused them to fall to the ground. They had a wet suit for Diego and clothing for them all to appear to be fishermen while returning to the sub. They donned night-vision goggles and went onto the beach in search of the culvert. There was no sign of a Venezuelan guard presence. At one point, a coast guard boat passed by their raft, and three officers on the deck waved to them. The Brazilian team waved back while nervously holding their breath.

"Okay, enough of this socializing nonsense!" growled Doido.

They fell into line and walked along the beach toward and located the culvert. The culvert had a seven-foot diameter concrete pipe that began in a marsh on the side opposite the beach. Dor and Jamal took the front and led the team through the culvert.

At the marsh, they all waded through the water and climbed a slope to the right and stepped onto the road. The sound of an approaching vehicle could be clearly heard in the distance. Jamal and Fielding dropped down on the ground on the shoulder and hid behind some bushes. Jamal took his Colt assault rifle and aimed it toward the road.

A Venezuelan Army truck rounded the curve and approached the hiding place. Fielding motioned for Fernando and Doido and Dor and Zé to fan out in the surrounding underbrush. Jamal could easily see the truck's driver through the night vision on his gun's sight and took careful aim. With one clean shot, he dispatched the driver. The truck rolled to a stop, and six soldiers exited the truck and looked for their attacker or attackers. Fernando and Doido and Dor and Zé engaged the soldiers, while Fielding and Jamal joined in. A fierce gun battle ensued, and the Brazilian team was victorious.

After the Venezuelans were subdued, Jamal and Fielding walked to the truck.

"Take the uniforms from the dead and let's see if we can each find a fit," instructed Fielding.

Shortly, they all had the fortune of finding a uniform that fit. The wet suits and fishing clothing were hidden in a box in the back of the truck. They all got into the truck, and Jamal and Dor took the driver's and passenger's seats and they all started off in the direction of Caracas. Before heading out, they took the deceased troops to the marsh and submerged the corpses in the marsh water, weighed down with rocks.

The drive to Caracas was an edgy experience and took well over eight nerve-wracking hours. They arrived in the early morning hours. They found their way through the city streets, carefully avoiding any sign of military or police checkpoints. On the road to and in Caracas, they encountered no resistance. They passed several civilians who all waved their enthusiastic support for what they believed were troops of their national defense forces.

CHAPTER 48

Caracas, Venezuela
Early evening of Sunday, September 6, 2020

As they entered Caracas, a contingent of soldiers was standing guard in the road. A soldier waived them through, and Fernando shouted a thank-you to the fellow in perfect Spanish with a colloquial accent.

As they entered the neighborhood of the house they sought, Fielding pointed out a single-story brick home. He mentioned it was a national monument and the birthplace of Simón Bolívar in 1783.

They looked at the street signs and soon found the house they sought. Jamal was driving and parked the truck behind some bushes in a vacant lot. They formed a line, and Fielding led the way toward the house. They all crouched while walking.

Fifty yards from the house, there was a sentry post in the street.

"It would be foolish to try to bluster our way past the guards," stated Fielding. "Doido and Zé, please go see what you can see about the house and its occupants."

Fernando and Jamal joined them, and the four took off toward the backside of the house. It was well past eleven o'clock in the morning, and the house was lighted inside. And the sound of music, playing, and laughter could be heard coming from within. Jamal and Fernando crept up to two of the windows and managed to look inside past shades that were drawn loosely. They spotted Diego bound and gagged on a sofa. Additionally, there were six uniformed men who were drinking beer and laughing while a young woman danced erotically in a bikini to entertain them. The men were guarding Diego. One of the men was on his cell phone, and Fernando overheard him ordering a pizza. The team realized they had passed a pizza restaurant on the way into the neighborhood.

Fernando and Jamal motioned to Dor and Zé and Fielding to remain in place and doubled back and watched the door to the restaurant. Within ten or more minutes, a young fellow of Fernando's approximate height and weight exited the store with a boxed pizza. He was wearing a uniform with the restaurant's name and logo emblazoned on the left breast. Fernando and Jamal confronted the deliveryman and pointed their guns at him. He willingly relinquished the pizza and his uniform. Fernando dressed in the deliveryman's uniform.

Fernando and Jamal returned to the house and hid in the bushes. Fernando approached the front door and knocked.

The fellow Fernando had spied ordering the pizza answered the door. He was a large, burly, and gruff-looking character with an unfriendly face. He addressed Fernando, "Well, it's damn well time you got here. Where is Carlos, the regular guy?"

"He has the night off. If you want the fucking pizza, step on out here and get it!" was Fernando's reply.

The big guy chuckled and said, "Well, all righty then, Mr. Tough Guy!" He stepped through the door and was confronted by Jamal's Colt rifle.

Fernando spoke, "Okay, now, Chief, the pizza is on us. If you release the prisoner, I won't shoot you right here."

Fernando held his Glock 19 to the man's back. "Tell someone to release our friend and then, share the pizza. If you don't release Diego, I will shoot you. I'll wait patiently for twenty seconds. That's all the time you get."

Fernando and Jamal were partially inside the front door, holding their guns to the man.

He instructed the others, "Gentlemen, release the Brazilian. I have received other orders."

A surprised fellow guard came forward from inside. "What is going on here?!"

Jamal shot him dead along with the fellow who'd answered the door. Jamal and Fernando stepped around the dead guards and shot four more dead in the living room. The dancer screamed hysterically. With the guards all removed, Fernando stepped to Diego's side and began removing his restraints.

Diego smiled and spoke, "Well, now what took so damned long? It is indeed a pleasure to see you, Senhor O Bispo!"

Fielding and Dor and Doido and Zé all entered the house, and the Brazilians removed the dead Venezuelans to an upstairs room.

"Are you hungry?" Fernando asked everyone.

"I am starved," said Diego.

The others agreed, and they all ate the pizza for breakfast. Fielding expressed concern for their raft being discovered on the beach, and they accelerated their consumption of the pizza.

Fernando consoled the dancing girl and offered to provide an escort away from the house. She accepted.

Fielding spoke, "Fernando, I am pleased you want to be a good Boy Scout, but we need to move quickly here. We have no idea if our handiwork on the road from the beach has been discovered. We cannot swim to the submarine in the event our raft is discovered. The longer we wait, our odds of successful escape become worse."

At that moment, a truck with Venezuelan troops arrived to the rear of the house. The Brazilians slipped out of the front door and into the cover of shrubs in the yard. Fernando quickly walked the girl to a neighboring bus stop and wished her well. They all moved quickly back to the parked stolen truck and got in, and Jamal started the truck.

As they pulled away to head toward the culvert to return to the raft, sirens could be heard sounding in the distance. The newly arrived truck of troops had located the carnage in the house.

Jamal stepped hard on the accelerator and sped toward the culvert. A civilian police car sped past them on its way to the house. Fielding patted Jamal on the shoulder and encouraged him to get to the culvert.

In eight hours, they returned to the Port of Spain area from which they had set out, and to their combined relief, there was nothing blocking the marsh or culvert. Jamal slammed on the brakes, and they came to a stop. The sun was rising, and the heat and humidity were increasing. The thought of reentering the cool ocean water was inviting to the group. The wet suits and fishing disguises were quickly donned. Fernando enjoyed explaining to Diego how they had arrived and intended to escape.

A lone coast guard vessel was seen offshore. They waded through the marsh while carefully avoiding their previous victims. The raft was still in place, and they were soon in the water and pretending to fish. This required actually fishing. Soon, their net was full of sea bass.

They continued in the direction of their arranged rendezvous with the submarine. About 300 yards or 270 meters short of the submarine, the coast guard vessel caught up with them. The vessel had lights and sirens and hailed them to stop. They obliged the order and stopped.

Fernando texted the sub's captain and told him they were being challenged. Fernando engaged the coast guard vessel's commander in a dialogue and protested being stopped while engaged in their day's work. The conversation lasted over five minutes during which time the coast guard boarded the raft and began inspecting the fish and other items on board. Fernando and Fielding and the MECs gripped their hand weapons and braced for a conflict. The coast guard commander was standing on his vessel's deck and ordered them to all strip and prepare to be searched.

Just then the submarine's sixty-millimeter deck gun tore through the coast guard vessel, killing all on board. The vessel began to sink and pulled its deceased occupants down with it. Fernando and Fielding and their team dispatched the coast guard sailors in the raft.

Moments later, the sub pulled alongside the raft and took on the Brazilians.

CHAPTER 49

Aboard the Brazilian submarine Tikuna *en route from northern Venezuela to Fortaleza, Brazil*
Night of Sunday, September 6, 2020

They all went below decks on the sub and were greeted by Bancroft and the captain.

"Well, Diego, my friend, I haven't seen you in years!" enthused Bancroft. "Tom Fielding, it is indeed a pleasure to work with you again, my friend. It's always a pleasure to get in trouble with you!" He continued, "Diego, this gentleman is Fernando Carvalho. He is a new member of the ABIN. He is a close friend of the new director of the PF, João da Silva. He has proven himself to be invaluable by assisting Director da Silva and the PF to solve a high-profile murder case in Rio. He was also instrumental in the rescue of PF Director da Silva's kidnapped daughter Andrea. His cunning was also key to the arrest of Eduardo Argos and the recovery of the embezzled millions Argos was attempting to hide in Europe."

Diego grinned. "Well, yes, I have had the great pleasure of meeting Senhor Carvalho."

Bancroft continued the introductions, "And this giant of a human being is Tom Fielding of the CIA."

Guedes smiled and replied, "Thank you all so much for your assistance in my rescue. I had feared they intended to kill me. I have met Mr. Fielding as well. Along with Doido and Dor and Zé and Jamal. I owe you all my life."

The captain interrupted, "Gentlemen, directors Cardenas and da Silva and Presidente Voss are on the line. You'd best take this call. It is their third since we dropped the team off of the coast at Port of Spain." A speakerphone was set on a desk for the call.

Bancroft answered the call, "Good evening, gentlemen. This is Tom Bancroft of the CIA. I am here with Fernando Carvalho and my CIA associate Tom Fielding and the now-freed Diego Guedes along with four members of your GRUMEC named Doido and Dor and Jamal and Zé."

Voss' interpreter spoke, "Mr. Bancroft, that is highly encouraging. We were very concerned about the safety of those of you on the rescue mission. Senhor Guedes, it is such a relief to know you are free! Were there any casualties on the mission?"

Fielding replied, "None suffered by the Brazilian team, except I seem to have sprained my left ankle. There were unfortunately more than ten deaths on the Venezuelan side. All of those were definitely necessary."

Voss replied, "That is unfortunate but wonderful. Senhores Fielding and Carvalho, you have once again provided Brazil with an excellent service."

da Silva addressed them, "Well, Fernando, you have proven Presidente Voss' and Director Cardenas' and my intuition correct by succeeding here. I look forward to seeing you upon your return to Rio. I will call Senhor Amaraes and report on your success. Perhaps you'd best call him to check in."

Fernando smiled proudly and looked around at all his teammates and replied, "Well, yes, I will do that. I must say that I deserve no recognition for our success. Were it not for the careful and wise planning of Tom Bancroft, we'd have had a very tough go. Tom Fielding and Doido and Dor and Zé and Jamal were all exceptionally brave and focused. In a couple of gun battles, their marksmanship and courage under fire saved us from near disaster."

Bancroft closed out the call, "Thank you, Mr. President and gentlemen. We should be back in Fortaleza by eight o'clock tonight. We are to be flown back to Galeão Air Force Base by private jet and should be there by ten thirty tonight. I plan to fly to Washington DC tomorrow, and Tom Fielding will be joining me. If some of you could join us for breakfast at the Grand Hyatt Rio tomorrow, we could celebrate the victory and Diego's freedom. Tom and I will be staying at the Grand Hyatt tonight. We will be in the lobby at ten o'clock in the morning. I will depart Rio in the afternoon, so a morning celebration would be easier for Tom and me."

Voss spoke in reply, "We would love to meet you there. Fernando, can you attend a breakfast meeting?"

"Yes, Senhor Presidente. I would be pleased to see you and directors Cardenas and da Silva."

"Excellent," replied Voss. "The directors and I will fly in BRS1 and arrive at Galeão Air Force Base in time to meet you in the morning." BRS1 is Brazil's Air Force One, the designation for Brazil's presidential aircraft. It is a modified Airbus A319.

"That is perfect, Senhor Presidente. Thank you," replied Fernando.

Fernando excused himself and was allowed to make a call to Rogerio Amaraes from the captain's berth.

Amaraes' assistant answered the call and found Amaraes immediately.

"Well, hello, Fernando. Presidente Voss and directors Cardenas and da Silva just called me and told me you're becoming a national treasure. They tell me they want you for more patriotic duties. I explained it would be a burden for the bank to not have you full-time. I believe an extended excused absence would harm your learning curve. Presidente Voss and Directors Cardenas and da Silva have offered to assist the bank in paying you a bonus at the commencement of a six-month unpaid, excused absence to serve Brazil. On the next pay date, you will receive a bonus of six months of your base compensation and you will then not receive further payments of your salary. I have emailed an agreement to you reflecting the arrangement. Should you succeed in your governmental assignments, your position with the bank will still be available to you at the end of the six months' absence. Upon your return, you will resume your role and continue your training as if there had been no break. God bless you for your heroic service to our country. Be safe and succeed."

Fernando had been offered compensation for his service to the PF and ABIN. He was surprised and very pleased by and with the bonus compensation offer from Amaraes. "Senhor Amaraes, I am honored and surprised by your generosity. I cannot thank you and Presidente Voss and Senhores Cardenas and da Silva enough! I treasure and enjoy working for and with you and the team and look forward to returning to work. All my best to you and the team."

Fernando was so pleased he returned and rejoined the others on board. They ate a hearty dinner prepared by the sub's chef.

CHAPTER 50

Fortaleza, Brazil
Night of Sunday, September 6, 2020

Within hours, they arrived in Fortaleza. A PF sedan met them and drove them to the airport where they boarded their flight to Rio. Hearty goodbyes and thanks were exchanged.

On the flight, Fernando called Denise and arranged to be picked up at Galeão Air Force Base. He asked her to come get him in the SP2.

CHAPTER 51

Rio de Janeiro, Brazil
Night of Sunday, September 6, 2020

They landed at Galeão Air Force Base at 8:00 p.m. that night.

Upon his arrival, Denise was there, excitedly awaiting Fernando.

Her enthusiasm concerned him because he was afraid of a repeat of his relationship with Marta Esteves. Marta's death had crushed something in him that he intended to leave buried. He had been deeply in love with her and didn't want to risk being hurt again. He was careful to avoid exhibiting enthusiasm. He recognized his interest in Denise was both physical and intellectual. He enjoyed their lovemaking and her extraordinary beauty and athleticism in bed. Her wisdom in business was always on exhibit in their conversations. He considered her a stimulating intellectual equal.

As they hung up on their call, she slipped by saying, "I love you."

Fernando considered taking her to the breakfast at the Grand Hyatt in the morning and decided that would be unfair as it might make her feel he was introducing her as his formal partner. He wanted to spend time with her focused on their friendship to clarify there wasn't a romance.

Fernando bid a warm goodbye to Fielding and Bancroft who were picked up by a PF sedan and driven to Galeão International Airport to catch a flight to New York City, with connection to Washington DC.

Fernando strode to the curb outside the air base and found Denise waiting in his car. He experienced a discomforting recollection of being with Marta.

Denise exited the car and walked to greet Fernando. "Thank God you're back safe and sound, my love."

Fernando controlled his tendency to respond in kind and replied, "Thank you, dear. We had a harrowing, risk-filled morning today, and I could use a drink and some food and your glorious company." He opened the passenger door and held it for Denise to get in. He circled the front of the car and jumped behind the steering wheel and started the engine and kissed Denise deeply. "I am filled with adrenaline and passion following a morning of violence in which my comrades and I were successful. It is so good to see you, my dear Denise! Let's go spend an evening together and unwind. I hope things are well at work for you. I look forward to seeing Paulo and Heliana but intend to focus my attention on you."

"As I will focus mine solely on you, Senhor Carvalho."

As they departed the airport, a PF sedan with Paulo and another officer and PM armored vehicle with PM officers were following to provide cover in the event William Nelson Vilmar and Regimento A might be seeking retribution for the effort in Caracas and killing of Gregor Stein and recapture of Carlos.

They pulled up to Coberto's Niterói house, and Fernando felt a great relief to be home safely. He circled the front of the car and opened Denise's door. They embraced and kissed. Fernando took Denise by the arm and walked her into the entry and into the lower floor.

Paulo caught up, having arrived in the following sedan, providing coverage. The PM armored vehicle that had shadowed the two vehicles could be heard parking in its assigned space to stand watch on the street.

Heliana greeted them at the door, and they all adjourned to change for the hot tub. They met on the rooftop deck at the bar, and the women prepared cocktails. Fernando and Paulo went to the kitchen and began to prepare steaks and salad and pasta for dinner. They took the food to the rooftop and commenced to barbecue the steaks and serve the other items. Quickly, they all clambered into the hot tub with their drinks.

Paulo sat close to Heliana and surveyed the other two. "Well, Fernando, I cannot divulge details for fear of being shot for giving up state secrets. I hear you helped rescue our friend Diego Guedes and are now quite the hero! Your courage and cunning are now becoming legend. It's so good and fortunate to have you back, my friend."

Denise snuggled next to Fernando and looked at him adoringly.

Paulo proposed a toast, "Here's to you, my friend."

"Well, thank you, Paulo. I didn't work alone. I had the fortune of having several wonderful, brave, and smart teammates. Two of them were from the United States and others from the GRUMEC. My success has provided me with a new career path. I have received a substantial bonus from O Banco and will be on a paid leave of absence. In six months, I will return to the bank and continue my training there. I plan to invest my bonus with Rogerio Amaraes' guidance and continue to enjoy being all of your housemate."

Denise smiled broadly and cuddled under Fernando's right arm.

They finished their drinks, and the men served the dinner. They all sat chatting over dinner at a picnic table on the deck. Fernando put on a selection of vintage bossa nova music played from his Spotify account through the stereo on the deck. Fernando thought to himself how fortunate he was to be alive and home and in the company of good friends.

He took Denise by the hand and led her into the house. "My dear Denise, I am so happy to be your boyfriend I cannot tell you. I am sorry I cannot express the romantic affection you seem to feel for me and want from me in return. Please treasure our companionship."

"Oh, that's okay, Fernando. I don't want to pressure you and turn you off. I do treasure our time together. Your sense of humor and intelligence and skill as a lover are more than I could ever hope for. I know you are a complex and intelligent man who is focused on doing great things. I am content to be your friend without overcomplication."

Fernando smiled at her gracious acceptance of his position. "Thanks, Denise, that's all I could hope for."

While they spoke, Fernando had his left arm around Denise's shoulders. He walked her to his bedroom, and they had impassioned sex for the first time in days.

They lay together afterward, and Fernando stared at the ceiling, contemplating his satisfaction with his life. He interrupted the silence, "Well, Denise Santos, you are the best lover I have ever had. Tomorrow I am to learn of a new matter for my focus. You have my word you are my only girl, and I will miss you while I am next gone."

"Thank you, Fernando Carvalho. You are my best and favorite boyfriend in my whole life."

Fernando smiled, and they embraced and made love again.

Fernando interrupted the afterglow, "Denise, I need to sleep in advance of a breakfast appointment at the Hyatt in the morning. I am to meet with Presidente Voss and some senior government officials to learn about my new assignment."

They fell asleep in each other's arms until Fernando's alarm sounded at 7:00 a.m. He arose and dressed in shorts and a tank top shirt and donned socks and running shoes and went for a long run. He returned at 8:20 a.m. and found Denise was still in his room and showering. He showered and dressed in his O Bispo outfit and went to the kitchen and had coffee with his housemates. He told Heliana and Paulo he was likely to receive a new government assignment.

He pulled Paulo aside and spoke to him, "Paulo, I am concerned about your and Heliana's safety along with Denise's, of course. In my absence, please coordinate with and obey the security force around the house. There is concern William Nelson Vilmar and Regimento A are seeking retribution for our rescue of Diego Guedes. I fear that effort may target those close to me. My mother and Carlos Diamante have been placed in protective custody by the PF until such time as the threat abates or is dispatched by the authorities. Please take care of yourself and the women."

Paulo looked in Fernando's eyes with a serious stare. "Yes, Nando, I will. I have arranged for my PF sedan to transport us to the Hyatt to arrive in time for your breakfast meeting. It is waiting outside for us."

CHAPTER 52

Grand Hyatt Hotel, Rio de Janeiro, Brazil
Morning of Monday, September 7, 2020, Brazilian Independence Day

They left and were at the Hyatt valet entrance slower than expected.

It was Brazilian Independence Day, and Voss was making an impromptu speech in the hotel's lobby in advance of the formal celebrations scheduled for that evening in Rio. He emphasized the current state of affairs on all fronts was the best in the nation's 198-year history of independence from Portugal.

A sea of security surrounding Voss' visit had complicated the drive up to the hotel entry. They entered the lobby and found Voss making the speech to an assembly of guests and media reporters. He was focused on the country's history and current economic success. He repeatedly emphasized it was the best time in the nation's 198-year history. He was inspirational while inviting every Brazilian to join him on the exciting ramp-up to the bicentennial in 2022. Voss was a rivetingly persuasive orator, and no one could have missed the excitement generated by his buildup to the crescendo at his conclusion. He mentioned the anticorruption and crime efforts by his administration. He mentioned Regimento A as the prime criminal target. He surprisingly referred to

Venezuela's internal instability with the Cortez drive to unseat Maduro. He warned the country that Venezuelan operatives had unsuccessfully kidnapped a Brazilian official.

Fernando and Paulo saw da Silva and Cardenas seated in the lobby's lounge area and joined them.

Cardenas greeted them, "Good morning, gentlemen. Happy Independence Day. It is indeed a good time to be a Brazilian! Is it not the best part of our work to be led by this great man?!"

"Happy Independence Day!" enthused da Silva. "We have a table reserved in the restaurant and will go there when the president is finished speaking."

They moved to their table in the restaurant.

Voss wrapped up his speech with flair and approached the table and sat between da Silva and Cardenas, "Good morning, gentlemen. It is a pleasure to see you, the fellows who stand guard atop the security wall around our nation. I haven't seen you, Fernando, since your successful rescue of Diego Guedes. Thank you so much for your courage and strength! Thank you for sacrificing your personal life and career objectives to help Brazil! Rogerio Amaraes and I spoke last evening about you and the critical work you are performing for our country. You and your potential at the bank impress him. I regret I cannot mention you by name in public and give you the accolades you so richly deserve. Welcome to your new life as an agent of our ABIN! Director da Silva and Director Cardenas have a new development to share with you. I hope you are capable of assisting to address this new challenge."

Fernando was dressed in his customary garb. He had left his hat at home. In this case, he looked very much like a cleric.

A man and woman in their early forties approached. The man spoke first, "Senhor Presidente, may we interrupt and speak with the father?" The couple had a look of desperate need.

Voss laughed and said, "Well, yes, of course!"

da Silva and Cardenas chuckled to themselves and sat waiting to see how Fernando handled the request.

"Why, how may I help you?" asked Fernando in a soft tone.

The man hugged the woman and spoke, "Father, I am Carlos de Moraes, and this is my sister, Delia. We live in Salvador in Bahia. Delia has stage four ovarian cancer. We are traveling to Albert Einstein Hospital in São Paulo to see what they propose for her treatment. We are not familiar with Rio and are seeking a church and pastor to minister to our emotional and spiritual needs. Can you help us?"

Fernando listened compassionately and smiled and replied, "Senhor de Moraes and Delia, I would be honored to help you. You must know I am a governmental official and here to meet with Presidente Voss and these two gentlemen who are my superiors. While attending university, I garnered the nickname O Bispo for my garb and appearance in it. Some time back, I lost a close girlfriend to a murder. A friend introduced me to Father Silvio at the Church of Nossa Senhora de Copacabana and Santa Rosa de Lima here in Rio. It is close by car. Father Silvio is a wonderful and wise man, and I anticipate he will be of immense comfort and help to you both. I will call him this afternoon and tell him of your need and urge him to help you. The church is a short half hour's drive from here and easily accessed. Mass is given several times each day. Here is my cell phone number. Please feel free to call me if you need further assistance. Please keep me posted on your progress. God bless you both, my friends.

I will keep you in my prayers. Father Silvio is now my priest and spiritual guide and a good friend. Here are his cell phone number along with the church's address and number. Please tell Father Silvio Fernando Carvalho recommended you contact him."

Carlos shook Fernando's hand vigorously. "Senhor Carvalho, you are indeed a man of God. Your generosity and willingness to help match your appearance and nickname."

Voss and da Silva and Cardenas sat marveling at their protégé's performance and ability to offer hope to the couple.

"Good God, man, was I ever correct about what a great person you are!" said da Silva while squeezing Fernando's left shoulder tightly.

With a huge grin, Voss stated, "Indeed, you are an inspiration, Fernando. You continue to be the epitome of what we hope for in our young people growing up in the favelas of our land."

Carlos and Delia excused themselves to go to their room to call Father Silvio.

Voss turned to Cardenas and da Silva and spoke, "Gentlemen, are we planning to inform Fernando about the recent developments?"

"Yes, Senhor Presidente," replied da Silva. He continued, "Fernando, I know you are planning to stay at home and enjoy a break. We have learned some disturbing news. Gregor Stein's son Peter and their company's general counsel arrived last night in São Paulo by private jet. We fear their purpose is to pursue revenge for Gregor's death. The general counsel's name is David Engel. Engel is a Venezuelan by birth who was raised in Havana, Cuba, where he was tutored by and became a favorite of the hard-liners. His father soon returned to Venezuela and was a key lieutenant of Hugo Chávez's during Chávez's rise to power. The elder Engel's first name is Juan. We have evidence he spent a great deal of time with Gregor Stein and General Cortez planning incursions and attacks and crime in Brazil. It is rumored Juan Engel is earmarked for a top role in the Cortez regime. Our concern is David is tasked with doing something in retribution for Stein's death as a means of proving his worth to the Cortez regime. We are told Cortez and his lieutenants are outraged over our success in rescuing Diego.

"Vice Presidente Emanuel Conte and Finance Minister Carlos Aragon are in São Paulo currently, and we are concerned they may be the intended targets. We could easily protect them by pulling them back to Brasília. We will not do that as it would be conceding a victory to our enemies. Our sources tell us William Nelson Vilmar may be there as well to plan future activities with Stein and Engel with the support of the Stein fortune or with the intent of having Regimento A aid in assassination attempts on the vice presidente and minister. Conte and Aragon are speaking at the Independence Day celebration in São Paulo this afternoon.

"People could be deceived to believe you, Fernando, are Emanuel Conte as you are his height and build and look much like him superficially. Conte and Aragon will be speaking in the main hangar at Congonhas Airport. The event is intended to offer São Paulo its own celebration in lieu of the main event planned for Rio this evening. We want you to go to São Paulo and impersonate Vice Presidente Conte in an attempt to draw out the assassins and participate in their arrest or destruction. Vice Presidente Conte asks that you only appear on stage after he completes his speech. You could wave to the crowd once he finishes and appear to be him while he appears to be departing the celebration.

"Once finished speaking, he and Minister Aragon will be taken behind the scenes and moved to an armored vehicle for protection. You will be the decoy intended to draw our enemies out in the open. You are to remain on the stage and provide the impression Vice Presidente Conte is still in the airport. A security detail is to surround you in a mock exit by the vice presidente. We will have eight PM and PF marksmen positioned to address any threat that appears. We believe you will be very safe. The marksmen are to be directed by Paulo Coberto who will join you on this trip.

"The PF jet is standing by at Kubitschek Airport here to take you to Congonhas. The speech is scheduled for one o'clock this afternoon. You should land at Congonhas at noon. A PF car will greet you two at Congonhas and provide ground transportation for you and Paulo."

Cardenas spoke on his and Voss' behalf, "Fernando, you are doing an excellent job as a covert agent. We have asked a great deal of you, perhaps too much. We hope you will take this assignment voluntarily."

Fernando grinned and replied, "Senhores Directores and Senhor Presidente, I enjoy the work and derive great excitement and reward from taking risks. I love this country and knowing and working with and for the three of you. Brazil is the greatest nation in the world, and I serve out of my fervent belief in that. I would fight for the opportunity to perform this and my other duties. God bless us all.

"I am preparing to call Father Silvio for the de Moraes. I am at peace at having found a purpose consistent with the name O Bispo. My choices of nickname and costume have been rewarded."

Voss and the directors all sat smiling with fraternal, if not paternal, pride. Cardenas and da Silva and Voss were all smiling broadly and fully appreciating Fernando's reaction.

da Silva wiped a tear from the corner of his left eye and spoke, "Bravo, laddie. The ceremony is scheduled for one o'clock this afternoon. Paulo is to accompany you and coordinate the PF and PM marksmen and those who will secure the site. You are both to take the PF jet to São Paulo. You should arrive around noon. I have called your mother, Fernando, and she and Senhor Diamante are expecting you and Paulo both for dinner and for the night. Good luck, gentlemen. May God watch over and guide you both."

Voss stood and saluted them both.

They were placed in a PF sedan and soon arrived at Kubitschek Airport and boarded the PF jet. En route, Paulo spoke by phone with the PF team in São Paulo and arranged for him and Fernando to be picked up and taken to the hangar upon arrival.

CHAPTER 53

Congonhas Airport, São Paulo, Brazil
Noon of Monday, September 7, 2020, Brazilian Independence
Day

Paulo and Fernando landed and exited the PF jet and were greeted by a PF agent with a sedan.

The agent greeted them, "Good afternoon, gentlemen. It is a pleasure to meet you. I'm Fred Ontiveiros. I'm taking you to that large structure over there." He pointed toward a massive hangar on the side of the airport. "Pedro Almeida is the PF officer in charge on scene overseeing the marksmen you requested. He has his men stationed on elevated platforms in the corners of the hangar with strong line of sight coverage of the floor and stage. The marksmen are positioned behind tarps with holes at their eye levels for visibility. Pedro will meet you once we enter the building."

They pulled into the hangar and met with Almeida and performed a walk-through. They were introduced to Conte and Aragon and explained the strategy to draw out the criminals and planned approach for their security.

Conte had a detail of the Presidential Guard Battalion. The Battalion is the Brazilian equivalent of the US Secret Service. The Battalion was not specifically assigned to handle Vilmar or Stein.

The senior agent of the detail argued they should grab Vilmar and Engel quickly. Paulo explained Vilmar and Engel were part of an international conspiracy against Brazil. The agent clearly understood the need to kill and not arrest Vilmar and offered to collaborate with the PF and let Vilmar make a move and be instantly terminated. Conte's Battalion detail conferred with Paulo and Fernando, and they agreed on the plan to use Fernando as a decoy. Several of the men in the detail were assigned new posts in the hangar along with PF officers in order to help watch for suspicious activity. Their senior officer presented Fernando with exact copies of the suit and tie and shoes and belt Conte was wearing.

Paulo smiled and patted Fernando on the back and said, "Well, my friend, it's time to get ready for your acting debut. You need to stay here, ready to cover for Conte."

Fernando stepped behind the stage in search of a place to change and wait for his cue to go onstage.

Almeida informed Paulo and the Battalion's senior officer they had a sighting. "My spotters tell me they see Vilmar and a fellow they suspect may be Engel. They are just entering the hangar and are attempting to remain hidden in the assembling crowd."

The men all looked toward the floor in front of the stage. The crowd had grown thick and was surging and pulsing in a way that would make it extremely difficult to identify individuals. Several PF and Battalion agents fanned out in the crowd to find their targets. They had to push their way through the surging throng.

The hangar was 30,000 square feet with a ceiling height of 25 feet. There were 7,000 or more people inside with more entering. The expected attendance was projected to be 10,000. Overflow was accommodated outside the hangar.

The hangar's massive door was fully open to allow those outside to see the activity inside.

After the Battalion spent ten minutes working their way through the crowd on the floor, the national anthem began to play, and gigantic Brazilian flags were unfurled and dropped down at each end of the hangar. A light show started that was timed with the anthem. The display's light and sound caused difficulty in searching through the thickening crowd. One of the men identified Vilmar and pointed him out to the marksmen.

An MC took the stage and drove up the assembling audience's excitement. Fireworks exploded in the ceiling, and the MC spoke, "Happy Independence Day, São Paulo! It is with great honor and excitement I introduce the vice presidente of our great country, the honorable Senhor Emanuel Conte."

Conte strode to the microphone and shook the MC's hand vigorously. Aragon joined them and shook each of their hands, and they waived to the crowd. The law enforcement agents observed Vilmar and his companion checking handguns and replacing them in their waistbands. Immediately, the two moved rapidly toward the stage. Conte and Aragon exchanged greetings, smiling throughout, and commenced their speeches.

Paulo and Almeida noted they had their targets in sight and in safe distance to be stopped. Vilmar looked around him to see if he were in the clear and drew his weapon. Almeida and two of his men rushed forward and grabbed Vilmar. Vilmar swore at them and vainly attempted to shoot toward the stage. He broke loose and ran toward the stage, and one of the officers with Almeida fired, and Vilmar collapsed dead on the floor. The crowd screamed and parted around the bleeding corpse, staring in astonishment.

The Battalion detail surrounded Conte and Aragon and rushed them to their waiting armored limousine to depart in safety.

The MC attempted to calm the audience, "Ladies and gentlemen, the danger has been stopped. Please continue to enjoy yourselves."

The law enforcement officers present fanned out throughout the crowd, looking for suspicious individuals and potential threats.

A popular band struck up a current hit tune, and large display screens began to exhibit a video prepared by the Voss administration exhibiting depictions of current economic successes and Brazilian military troops and equipment. The Brazilian program to construct nuclear-powered submarines was a highlight. It celebrated the Álvaro Alberto., which had been placed in service a month earlier on Friday, August 7, 2020. More nuclear subs were to be deployed by 2029. The video included a promise by Voss to not ever pursue a Brazilian nuclear weapons program. Voss was elected in the national election of October 2018. His next election would be contested in October 2022.

Voss appeared in the video and stated his position against nuclear weapons was consistent with Brazil's embrace of beauty and peace and tranquility. As the video concluded, the audience cheered and chanted Voss' name enthusiastically.

Fernando strode forward to the microphone and did his best impersonation of Conte. He had practiced speaking like the vice presidente on the flight to São Paulo. "Ladies and gentlemen, Minister Aragon and I are unharmed, as are most of you. Thank God. Minister Aragon has safely departed, and I am remaining until a search of the building is completed and it is confirmed there isn't a further threat. Thank you so much for being with us this afternoon. Presidente Voss sends his salutations to you and his wishes you will enjoy and succeed in the current prosperity. God bless you all and our country."

The officers searching through the crowd saw Peter Engel and David Stein creeping toward the stage and "Conte." (Fernando in disguise) They were captured by the PF and transported immediately to Brasília where they were held and interrogated. Following highly publicized trials, they were each sentenced to a long term in the general prisoner population at Porto Velho. Peter Stein's attorneys were subsequently successful in obtaining his release in an appeal to the Brazilian Supreme Court. Engel was unable to obtain his own release. This was ironically the equivalent of a death sentence. Brazil informally and completely ended capital punishment following a controversial execution on April 28, 1876. In his 2018 campaign, Presidente Voss had promised to legislatively eradicate capital punishment permanently.

Fernando and Paulo met with and congratulated the commander of the Battalion detail and the officers working with them.

Fernando and Paulo made sure they weren't required further and departed for Diamante's home to spend the evening with Diamante and Maria. They spent a relaxed evening in the hospitable confines of Diamante's home.

With Vilmar and Engel removed from the landscape, the PF and PM security force around Diamante's building was cut back to a small number of officers, and the building returned to its previously relaxed feel. The remaining security was assigned to observe on a 24/7 watch and to call for backup from the PF and PM as needed.

Paulo and Fernando called da Silva and Cardenas and reported their success. Fernando was instructed to return to Rio and his work with Amaraes at O Banco.

Fernando's phone rang, and it was a number he didn't recognize. "Hello, this is Fernando Carvalho."

"Senhor Carvalho, this is Carlos de Moraes and Delia calling. We want to thank you from the bottom of our hearts. We are with Father Silvio now and are so pleased to be with him. He has provided wonderful advice and guidance, both emotional and physical. Additionally, he has connected us with a marvelous oncologist he knows who works at Albert Einstein Hospital. The doctor is promising to pay special attention to Delia during our visit. The doctor successfully treated one of Father Silvio's colleagues in Porto Alegre who had lung cancer and is now cancer free. You are a great man, Senhor Carvalho. Keep wearing your outfit. It is richly deserved as is your nickname."

"Why, thank you so much for the update, Senhor de Moraes, all my best to you and Delia. I pray she finds relief and hope in the treatment at Albert Einstein," replied a giddily smiling Fernando.

Paulo chuckled and asked, "What was that about?"

Fernando smiled proudly and replied, "Well, my friend, that is what I will regale you and Denise and Heliana with when we are back together!"

The evening held a surprise of sorts. Diamante and Maria announced they were romantically involved with each other. Fernando was very pleased.

Paulo and Fernando were scheduled for an early flight back to Rio on the PF jet. They joined Diamante in his study for after-dinner drinks and talk. Diamante told Fernando how much he was in love with Maria. He continued to tell Fernando how fortunate he was to have such a wonderful mother and role model.

Fernando replied with his thanks and full concurrence. "You are my surrogate father, and I am so fortunate you are in my mother's and my lives!"

Paulo smiled while basking in the warmth of the exchange.

In the morning, they arose at six o'clock and returned to Congonhas Airport and boarded the jet at eight o'clock. Prior to departing the Diamante home, they had breakfast with Diamante and Maria.

At eleven o'clock that morning, they walked into the house in Niterói and settled in to wait for the women to return from work around six fifteen that evening.

Fernando went to his office at the bank to catch up with Amaraes.

CHAPTER 54

Director da Silva home, Brasília, Distrito Federal, Brazil
Evening of Monday, September 7, 2020, Brazilian Independence
Day

The da Silvas were relaxing at home and celebrating the Independence Day holiday with neighbors.

da Silva learned of Fernando and Paulo's successful effort in São Paulo. He started reflecting on his successes with Fernando. For some reason, he felt a nagging concern. He realized they hadn't properly concluded the Azevedo murder investigation. He dialed Sergio Viana and instructed him to go see Rogerio Mendosa in prison and resolve how Mendosa and his partner gained entry to the Azevedos' home.

*   *   *   *   *

At precisely ten o'clock the following morning, PF Chief Investigator Sergio Viana arrived at Ariosvaldo de Campos Pires Federal Prison for an appointment to see Mendosa and his attorney. It was a gray and hot and humid morning. Viana tried to ignore the atmosphere out of concern it might impair his focus and optimism for the outcome of his mission.

Upon his arrival, he marveled at the apparent impenetrability of the facility and wondered how David Melkor and Mendosa and Mendosa's subordinate were doing inside. He was ushered into a boxlike room with a steel table at which Mendosa and his attorney were seated under the watchful eyes of three intimidatingly large guards. High-wattage bulbs in sconces were lighting the room. The light made the white-painted ceiling seem like the sky on a bright cloudy day. The light was reflected in the polished metal of the tabletop. The brilliance of the light elevated Viana's mood.

Viana sat down opposite Mendosa. And the attorney and began, "Gentlemen, thank you for agreeing to speak to me." Mendosa smirked, and his attorney spoke, "Chief Investigator Viana, my client is speaking today on a completely voluntary basis. As we agreed in advance, we fully expect Senhor Mendosa will not be exposed to further prosecution in the event his answers so justify. As I told you in our phone conversation, he will cooperate fully in the hope his sentence and cell arrangements may be softened and improved. How may we be of assistance to you and Director da Silva?"

"Thank you. That is all consistent with the director's and my understanding and expectations," replied Viana.

The continued effort with Mendosa had all but derailed da Silva and Viana's interest in pursuing a wider investigation in search of additional suspects to prosecute. In their phone conversation the evening before, they had agreed to pursue whatever leads the Mendosa conversation might provide without concern for how the potential new information might reflect on the PF's efforts in the Azevedo investigation.

Viana started the conversation, "Senhor Mendosa, the PF and government appreciate your heretofore cooperation and support in our investigation of the Azevedo murders. We have one loose end we wish to resolve in the matter of the murder of the Azevedos. How did you gain entry to their apartment? There was no sign of forced entry by you and your associate."

Mendosa and the attorney began to chuckle and laugh out loud.

"Senhor Viana, would you please allow me a few moments alone with my client to discuss his reply?" asked the attorney.

Viana then replied, "But of course. Please consider my question seriously. The director has asked me to offer a much-improved meal plan and private cell for Senhor Mendosa in the event he is cooperative. Additionally, Senhor Mendosa's sentence is to be potentially shortened. Parole may be considered three years earlier than previously offered." Viana handed the two men a printed menu that outlined a daily meal offering to be specially prepared for Mendosa. Viana excused himself and stepped out to allow the two to contemplate the menu in his momentary absence.

Mendosa and the attorney studied the offering. Through the glass of a two-way mirror, Viana observed the two men discussing his request and the menu in whispered conversation to avoid Viana's eavesdropping.

After a few minutes, the attorney faced the glass and said, "We are ready to speak, Senhor Viana, if you would please step back in."

Viana reentered the room and returned to his seat.

The attorney then spoke, "Senhor Viana, we are very appreciative of your and Director da Silva's generous offer. My client asks that you arrange for conjugal visits for him on a monthly basis so he may reconnect with his wife. He is prepared to talk in exchange for a written agreement documenting your offer and our requests. Senhor Mendosa is concerned about his safety here in the prison and wants access to the art studio to work on his design work and his painting hobby with guards present to keep other prisoners at a safe distance."

Mendosa was smiling broadly in a sarcastic grin and spoke, "Man, were you guys ever sloppy! I have the information you want me to share and will do so happily if we come to an agreement."

The attorney placed his hand on Mendosa's chest to caution against further comments that could be detrimental to a successful resolution of the negotiation.

Viana looked at the two men and responded, "That is an interesting offer and request. Thank you for your time, gentlemen. I have a planned phone call with Director da Silva shortly and will be back in several minutes with our reply and hopefully to collect Senhor Mendosa's testimony."

Viana stepped out and dialed da Silva from his cell phone.

da Silva was pleased with and accepting of the outline of Mendosa's requested changes to the deal and immediately called the field office of the federal prosecutor at the prison to gain their concurrence and have a written agreement drawn up to hand to Mendosa and the attorney.

Thirty-five minutes following his departure from the meeting room, Viana reentered with four printed copies of a document. Viana sat down in his original spot and spoke, "Gentlemen, I am pleased to offer this agreement and hope you will find it acceptable. I will step out now and return when you signal you are prepared to conclude this discussion."

Through the two-way mirror, Viana observed Mendosa and the attorney each smiling and speaking in a whispered exchange.

He stepped back in, and the attorney spoke, "Senhor Viana, I wish to express our sincerest appreciation for this document. Senhor Mendosa has executed these four copies.

One for you and the PF and one for our records and one for the federal prosecutor and court's records. The fourth is for the warden and the prison's records to ensure they follow its directions."

Viana executed the copies as well and indicated he had a court recorder standing by to document Mendosa's pending testimony. The recorder entered with a dictation machine and set up for the coming discussion. Two additional guards flanked the recorder.

Viana began, "Senhor Mendosa, do you agree you are making your statements here today of your own free will and specifically in exchange for the items contained in the agreement we've just concluded and signed here today?"

"Yes, absolutely," replied Mendosa with his attorney's encouragement.

"Senhor Mendosa, our interest here is to learn how you and your associate gained entry to Jorge and Veronica Azevedos' home in Leblon on Sunday, May 10, 2020."

With his attorney's encouragement, Mendosa began to speak, "Our task was simple as we were able to pay the Azevedos' housekeeper a large sum of money to unlock the door for us early on that evening. We arrived around seven o'clock and found the door unlocked for us and surprised the Azevedos who were beginning their dinner. I believe I was clear about all of this in my confession. You and the PF were sloppy in your recording and study of my testimony."

Viana thanked Mendosa and his attorney and stepped out to contact da Silva. Viana explained what he had learned and could hear da Silva searching through his files in his office.

da Silva replied, "Why, yes, I have the housekeeper's name here. Her name is Felicia Ontiveiros, and I have her address right here. I am dispatching a team to find and arrest her for complicity in the Azevedo murders. She lives in the Cidade de Deus favela in Rio."

Viana smiled to himself and returned to the meeting room and said his goodbyes to Mendosa and his attorney.

Mendosa was immediately returned to his cell, anticipating a more pleasing end to his sentence under the terms of the agreement he'd just signed.

Melkor's cell was ironically and coincidentally positioned on the path Mendosa had to follow to the meeting room and back. As Mendosa passed Melkor, he received a hateful stare, and Melkor spat at him and swore a shouted life threat in poorly spoken Portuguese. The guards entered Melkor's cell and incapacitated him with tasers and kicked him while he was on the floor. This was the routine response to Melkor's outbursts toward Mendosa. The guards continued to beat Melkor in the hope he would get their message to shut up and behave. He was then dragged to a solitary confinement cell and left without light or sound of any kind.

CHAPTER 55

*Felicia Ontiveiros' home, Cidade de Deus (City of God) favela,
Rio de Janeiro, Brazil
Morning of Tuesday, September 8, 2020*

The day was warm with clear blue skies. The neighborhood was quiet. Three PF SUVs carrying six officers pulled up to the Ontiveiros home.

The senior officer knocked on the front door. There was no response to the knock. Three additional attempts resulted in no response. The senior officer directed a junior officer to bust the door open with a ram.

They entered the house and discovered no one was home. Following a thorough search, they failed to find any evidence of Senhorita Ontiveiros having recently been in the completely empty home. A thorough search of the living room followed by the kitchen identified a kitchen drawer that appeared to serve as a filing cabinet. A receipt for an airline ticket was found in the drawer. The ticket was for a round-trip flight to Buenos Aires, Argentina. The initial flight to Buenos Aires was on the morning of Monday, May 11, the day following the Azevedo murders. The return flight was open and not scheduled or indicated.

The senior officer immediately called the officer in charge in the PF field office in the Brazilian Embassy in Buenos Aires. An address book and diary were located in the bedroom. The diary indicated Felicia's eldest son was married to an Argentine woman. Their address in Buenos Aires was easily discovered in the address book. The PF field office obtained a warrant for Felicia's arrest and an extradition order to return her to Brazil.

Later that evening, the Buenos Aires Civilian Police found Felicia at her son's home and took her to the Brazilian Embassy and handed her over to the PF officer in charge.

A PF officer rushed Felicia to Ezeiza International Airport where they boarded a flight to Rio de Janeiro. Brazil and Argentina agreed to the extradition between themselves under terms contained in an agreement signed on Wednesday, January 16, 2020.

Paulo Coberto and another officer arrived at Galeão International Airport late that night and met the flight and took Felicia into custody. She was taken to a holding cell to await an arraignment. da Silva and Viana worked closely with federal prosecutors, and within four weeks, Felicia was found guilty and was imprisoned for five years for her part in the Azevedos' deaths. Mendosa was temporarily released from prison to appear as a witness at the trial.

CHAPTER 56

Director da Silva's office, PF headquarters, Brasília, Distrito Federal, Brazil
Morning of Thursday, October 1, 2020

João da Silva was finishing a phone call with ABIN Director Cardenas and Presidente Ricardo Voss. He learned a Venezuelan general named Juan Cortez had seized the presidency of Venezuela.

Cortez had pledged his administration to the purification of Venezuela's political structure to reflect an adoption of a strict Communist regime to be constructed around an outline developed with the guidance of Chinese and Cuban advisors. Cortez believed the Chinese model would provide a path to a much-improved standard of living for the people of Venezuela.

Cortez cited publicly what he deemed to be Nicolas Maduro's abject failure to deliver comfort and well-being to the Venezuelan people. He cited shortages of food and other necessities as the lead examples of the country's decline under Maduro's leadership. In an impassioned speech, Cortez excoriated Maduro and his inner circle for living by a double standard that allowed them to live in luxury without allowing the populace to earn the right to similar or any comforts.

Voss and his advisors and confidants laughed at the ironic turn on Maduro. Their laughter was nervous. The prospect of a neighboring South American regional power becoming stronger and destabilized was unnerving. They were greatly concerned at having learned plans were underway for construction of a Chinese naval base at Port of Spain in northern Venezuela. Diego Guedes had been dispatched to Caracas to see what he could learn. Voss and his cabinet and Cardenas were concerned about the intention of the nascent Cortez regime regarding Brazil. Cortez had issued some vile statements criticizing Voss for his methods to achieve economic success.

Cortez was known to be a fan of military action. He was an ardent student of the military under the Castro regime in Cuba. He had studied under the Castro brothers during his time in secondary school in Havana. His initial statements suggested he wanted to target Brazil.

Despite the Voss administration's efforts to keep Fernando's existence and activities a state secret, it was obvious Carlos had pinpointed Fernando as an enemy and understood what O Bispo was accomplishing. Guedes learned from his Venezuelan contacts that Fernando was indeed a target for revenge. Security around Paulo Coberto's home in Niterói was dramatically increased. Fernando remained at the Niterói home with Denise and Paulo and Heliana.

Denise and Heliana both worked as executive assistants to two senior partners in the largest commercial law firm in Rio. Escorts to and from work were provided by the PF and PM. The escorts were assigned to stand guard during business hours throughout the office building that housed the law firm's offices.

For safety, Fernando returned the SP2 to his Rio caretaker friend. He knew all too well Carlos and his subordinates in Regimento A knew the car was his. Fernando was concerned that driving the SP2 was too high-profile. He feared Carlos' compatriots might target him and Denise in the car.

Carlos remained in the custom high-security building constructed at Galeão Air Force Base in Rio. The building was specifically designed to keep Carlos under wraps and out of touch with his supporters and subordinates. There was no particular evidence that Carlos was in touch with the outside world.

In order to be safe, Directors Cardenas and da Silva were coordinating with the PF and PM as though Carlos was communicating freely. As a result, security activity centered around the potential for an attack on Fernando's life or on the lives of those close to him. There was cause to be concerned Regimento A was looking for Fernando and those close to him to meet out revenge for Gregor Stein's death and Carlos' capture on Stein's island.

Peter Stein remained free in New York City. Peter worked in the Stein corporate headquarters in Manhattan. From his office, he orchestrated a series of investments and charitable and political donations aimed at supporting violently militant Communist and Socialist causes his father had supported. He was known to be in contact with Regimento A and Juan Cortez's team in Caracas. The ABIN discovered Peter was in close contact with the insurgent force near Manaus Air Force Base. One of Peter's close school buddies was a captain in the Cuban Special Forces in the jungle near the air force base.

Fernando purchased a used Chevrolet Camaro with an engine upgrade and a great deal of horsepower. The car was navy blue color with a tan interior. He used it to transport Denise and him on dates and to engagements throughout Rio. He used it twice a week on Sunday mornings to take Denise and him to Father Silvio's mass.

On the evening of Friday, October 2, 2020, Fernando received a call from Director Cardenas. Fernando had elected to drive his Camaro in tandem with Denise and Heliana's armed escorts so he could pick Denise up from work downtown. Fernando surprised Denise with plans for a double date dinner with Paulo and Heliana at the Grand Hyatt.

Fernando's phone rang, and he checked to see who the caller was. It was a call from Cardenas. "Well, good evening, Senhor Director. It's a pleasure to be hearing from you. How may I be of help?"

Cardenas chuckled and replied, "Good evening, Fernando. Fernando, I am with Diego Guedes and Director da Silva. We have a mission to discuss with you."

Fernando took Denise's left hand in his right and listened apprehensively. "Okay, Senhor Director, please let me hear about it."

"Fernando, we need you to return to Caracas."

"Yes, sir, you know I live to serve. What are the details? I am out with my girlfriend now and want to protect my upcoming time to be with her this evening and this weekend."

Denise broke into a smile and reached over and kissed Fernando's right cheek.

"Fernando, our records indicate you knew a Venezuelan woman named Anita Bentley Odebrecht at Pre in São Paulo."

"Well, yes," Fernando replied cautiously. "She was my high school girlfriend. Her father, Guillermo, was a Venezuelan oilman who was in Brazil to coordinate with Petrobras on behalf of the Venezuelan state oil company Petróleos de Venezuela, SA. He was a favorite acquaintance of mine. He was frequently absent on business trips to Petrobras' headquarters in Rio. He chose São Paulo as the city of residence for his family because São Paulo is the center of Brazilian economic activity. He sought out and located contacts with whom he could network. He became well-known for his generous and opulent Sunday afternoon barbecue parties at their estate home."

"Yes, he was the father of the woman we are thinking of," replied Cardenas. "The Odebrechts returned to Caracas in 1998 when Guillermo's work with Petrobras was completed. In 1986, he was sent to the USA to oversee the integration of the fifty percent ownership interest in CITGO acquired by Petróleos de Venezuela. That effort propelled him into the political spotlight in Caracas. Guillermo became close to Hugo Chávez and was in Chávez's inner circle of trusted advisors. I am sorry to report Guillermo was killed by Chávez in 2010. Despite a brilliant series of accomplishments, he fell out of Chávez's favor. Chávez felt Odebrecht was too attached to old capitalistic practices. Chávez drove to the Odebrecht home on a Saturday afternoon, and a heated argument broke out between the two in the street in front of the home. The enraged Chávez personally shot Guillermo dead on the spot. Anita and her mother, Pilar, saw the whole thing.

"Anita had started and was running a successful fashion company in Caracas. The company designed and sold fashionable women's clothing and created and sold fragrances for women and men. In 2014, the Chávez government threatened to nationalize the business and take it away from Anita. She was targeted for her relationship to her father. The fellow from the federal government assigned to work with her on the nationalization acquisition fell in love with her. She so charmed and persuaded the fellow the acquisition didn't go forward. He is a senior lieutenant of Cortez's. He and Anita are now married. Her husband's name is Colonel Pablo Duzon. Duzon is behind much of Cortez's covert terror activities. We want you to go to Caracas and reengage with Anita and obtain her help so you and Diego and Tom Fielding may take Duzon out and eliminate his threat as the strong man for Cortez."

Fernando listened carefully without letting Denise catch on to the discussion. He was tired from his covert efforts and looking forward to a long weekend with Denise and Paulo and Heliana.

Cardenas continued, "For these reasons, we believe Anita is unlikely to hold any affection for her country's government. We hope Anita is disenchanted with the country's dramatic shift to Communism and totalitarianism and will betray her husband out of her distaste for him personally and for his role in the military machine that strong-arms the nation to comply with its Communist direction and that killed her father. There is word Duzon verbally and physically abuses Anita. We hope you can engineer a 'chance' encounter with Anita. You each look much as you did while attending Pre. That should make reconnecting simple. That would hopefully blossom into a rekindled affection and conversation to open the way to achieving the mission's objective."

At the call's conclusion, Fernando agreed to travel to Brasília to reconnect with Guedes and Fielding to receive their orders from Director Cardenas and Tom Bancroft. Fernando was to arrive in Brasília on the evening of Sunday, October 4, and to report to Cardenas' office at ten o'clock on the morning of Monday, October 5. da Silva joined the call late and offered to have Fernando stay at his home on the night of Sunday, October 4. Fernando was to be picked up by the PF jet on Sunday afternoon at three o'clock. Fernando hung up and turned to Denise who was looking very disappointed with the potential of another Fernando absence.

"Well, what about our plans for the weekend?!" Denise demanded with a tear at the corner of her left eye.

Fernando stopped the car in a parking lot to a strip mall at the side of the road and looked her in the eye and spoke, "Denise Santos, I had my heart set on our planned time together. I am very tired from my recent trips and my preparations for work at O Banco. I need time with you to recharge my battery. Let's enjoy our dinner with Paulo and Heliana and make sure every moment we spend is to be treasured in our memories. Make no mistake you are my one and only gal, and I won't jeopardize that." Fernando started driving again.

Soon, they arrived at the Hyatt's porte cochere. The valet attendants opened the car's doors. An attendant took Fernando's keys and gave him a ticket to reclaim the keys and car following their meal.

The attendant asked how long they would be, and Fernando replied, "Just under three hours."

Denise stepped to his side and placed her left arm in his right. She had a huge smile on her face. "Well, lover, that is encouraging. I'd feared you'd be ducking out early this evening. I need your undying attention and physical contact."

They walked through the lobby and into the restaurant.

Paulo and Heliana had a table set in a corner with a bottle of sparkling wine or champagne sitting opened in an ice bucket. Denise put aside her previous melancholy, and they all fell into a typical Friday night conversation among friends who are young professionals, filled with comments about how tired they all were.

Denise told an amusing story about the female partner in charge of the law firm. The partner had had too much wine at lunch. The partner had called an impromptu staff meeting after lunch and climbed on top of the conference room table and began reciting a silly poem she made up extemporaneously. The poem was a salute to everyone's hard work, and she had called out several star performers by name. Denise and Heliana had been among those cited. Denise had her companions in hysterics and laughing out loud. She had an uncanny ability to mimic the woman's voice and mannerisms.

They ordered food and a bottle of wine. By eight o'clock that night, they had concluded their meal and the sparkling wine and bottle of wine and were home on the rooftop in Niterói.

Saturday flew by, and Denise and Fernando became apprehensive of his departure on Sunday.

In bed on Saturday night, Fernando maintained his focus on talking to Denise. "My dear Denise, I know you heard I am to see an old girlfriend in Venezuela on my upcoming trip. She and I were close, and if I am to succeed, I will need to pray on the remnant of our affection for each other. You are the only object of my desire. I will not betray your and my relationship by engaging with anyone else. I am so fortunate to be your lover I will not mess things up."

Denise sat gazing happily into Fernando's eyes. "Oh, Fernando, I don't worry. I can see how devoted you are to me and how happy you are when we are together. I love you deeply. My biggest worry is that you may be injured or killed doing something dangerous. Just remember you carry my heart with you everywhere you go. Should I lose you, I've no idea what I would do."

Fernando was so touched he sighed heavily and nodded his understanding. "Oh, Denise, I cannot go off without telling you how I love you too. I need to be careful because I am at risk of not returning. I don't want to leave you alone and heartbroken should I perish. The way these assignments unfold, it is likely I will be gone for days starting tomorrow. Should I not return, it would be equally cruel to leave you not knowing how much I love you. I think about you a lot when I am working at O Banco and on my covert government activities. You are my biggest joy and closest friend."

He pulled a jeweler's ring case out of a drawer and opened it. He turned it toward Denise. It was a one-and-one-half-carat diamond engagement ring. The diamond was set atop an 18-carat gold band with a floral design. Inside the band was an engraved message: "To Denise Santos with my pledge of love and devotion. Fernando Carvalho, October 3, 2020."

Fernando continued, "Denise, you are the only woman I think about romantically. Please wear this ring as a sign and constant reminder of my devotion to you. I am in no position to propose marriage at this point because of my dangerous living. I will treasure the thought and image of you wearing it and thinking about me."

Denise was clearly thrilled with the ring. Fernando slipped it on her left ring finger, and they kissed passionately.

Denise sat admiring the ring with a glorious smile on her face while rotating it on her finger on her hand. "Oh, Nando, this makes me the happiest gal in Rio or even all of Brazil or the whole world! I love you with all of my heart. Thank you so much for this token of your devotion!"

Denise went to her bedroom for a few moments and returned. She held a necklace she treasured. The necklace had small decorative objects hanging from it. One of the objects was a green piece shaped like Brazil. Another was shaped like the Brazilian flag, perfectly colored and decorated like the nation's flag. Denise took Fernando's hands in hers. "Fernando, I'd love you to wear this necklace as a reminder of me."

Fernando chuckled appreciatively. "I love it, Denise, but I'm not sure that will fit my bulky neck. Perhaps I could wear it as a bracelet?"

Denise took the necklace and wrapped it around Fernando's right wrist and discovered a means to fasten it in place.

Fernando admired it and kissed Denise deeply. "Denise Santos, I will treasure this bracelet and look at it always as a reminder of our love for each other, my love."

At Sunday's breakfast, Fernando and Denise told Heliana and Paulo the news of the ring and the bracelet and Fernando's expression of devotion. Paulo chuckled and Heliana cooed her enthusiastically happy envy.

Paulo pushed Fernando in jest and spoke, "Well, Mr. Hard to Get, it's damn well about time you embrace your affection for Denise! Heliana and I had worried about what we would have to advise Denise to do in the event a promising suitor approached her. Now you will be safe! We will make sure she is left alone and remains available for your return."

Denise blushed and kissed Fernando. "You needn't worry, Senhor O Bispo. There cannot be another I'd love or pay attention to like I do you! You can bet big money I will be here with my ring patiently awaiting your return."

The weekend progressed nicely. The couples spent Sunday at Flamengo Beach, relaxing. The weather was perfect with crystal blue skies and temperatures in the low eighty degrees Fahrenheit; the humidity was low, adding to the day's comfort.

In the afternoon at three o'clock following a fun pizza dinner at Pizzaria de Icaraí in Niterói, Paulo and Denise and Heliana dropped Fernando at Galeão Air Force Base. There he boarded the PF jet he usually flew on. It was an Embraer E190 modified as a personal business craft.

At five o'clock that evening, the plane arrived at Kubitschek International Airport in Brasília. Upon landing, the plane sat awaiting dispatch orders on its next destination. Fernando called da Silva and told him he'd arrived. They chatted briefly, and da Silva confirmed he was arriving at the airport. While Fernando waited on board, darkness arrived. The sun set around six thirty, and it quickly grew dark.

Fernando called Denise to tell her he had arrived safely. As a security precaution, the outdoor lighting at the airport had been dimmed to safely obscure Fernando from visibility from the perimeter. Concern over the potential of an attack by Regimento A remained high. The PF realized the likelihood of Regimento A locating Fernando was very low. They resolved otherwise to take him from the plane secretively. A stairway was rolled to the plane. A PF agent with a flashlight came to the plane stairs and guided Fernando to a gate where João da Silva greeted him with a PF sedan.

They drove to the da Silva home where they spent the night. They stayed up late talking until da Silva remarked about the hour and their morning commitment with Director Cardenas. Andrea and Katia were overjoyed to see Fernando. The da Silvas were all enthusiastic about Fernando's news of the ring for Denise.

They admired the bracelet, and da Silva smilingly spoke, "Well, young man, this is fantastic news! We are all so pleased and happy for you and Denise."

Katia and Andrea giggled their approval.

da Silva and Fernando arose early the following morning and prepared to go to Director Cardenas' office for Fernando's assignment meeting. da Silva and Fernando arrived at the ABIN offices at exactly 10:00 a.m. Cardenas and Guedes and Fielding and Tom Bancroft were all seated at the conference table in Cardenas' conference room off his office.

Cardenas stood and closed a folder marked Top Secret. "Thank you for coming, Fernando and João. Please take these open seats and open the folders in front of them." The folders were copies of the top-secret folder Cardenas had in front of him. Cardenas continued, "Tom Fielding has agreed to accompany you and Diego on this mission, Fernando. Tom Bancroft has provided his excellent insight and helped us with the planning."

Hearty greetings were exchanged all around.

Fernando and da Silva and the others sat and opened their folders. Inside were photographs of Anita and Pablo Duzon and their home in Caracas with brief bios of the two. They learned Duzon was a career army officer who was fifty-five years old. Anita had just turned thirty. Pablo had trained with the Red Army in Moscow and Cuban Army in Havana. He was an ardent Communist and avowed enemy of Capitalism. He and Anita had a son named Pablo Jr. who was twenty-one years old. Junior, as he was known, was also an army staffer. Junior was Pablo's son by a previous marriage. Junior was a master sergeant and served with his father's crack special forces team.

There were additional photographs. These were aerial pictures of Cuban and Venezuelan special forces troops in the jungle near Brazil's Manaus Air Force Base in the Amazon. The CIA and ABIN and US and Brazilian military commands had monitored the troop movement and validated their origin by taking photos of the men in their uniforms on the ground in the jungle. The photos captured details of the men's uniforms. These confirmed their origins as Venezuelan and Cuban. Russian and Chinese military advisors were spotted working with them. The CIA and ABIN and Brazilian and US military commands were convinced the troops' intent was to disrupt the air force base with an armed campaign against its planes and personnel and infrastructure.

Cardenas spoke, "Gentlemen, we aren't sure about the timing of any planned attack. What we do know is all of the Venezuelan and Cuban men in the jungle near Manaus AFB have sworn an oath to defend and support Pablo Duzon and Juan Cortez and Venezuelan Communism. We believe Pablo Duzon's capture by us or death at our hands would crush the heart and spirit of their mission. Once Duzon is removed, our intent is to have our air force attack the insurgents and weaken them from the air. We will then have the GRUMEC and Brazilian Army and US Navy SEALs and US and Brazilian marines and US Green Berets close in and eliminate them to the man. Presidente Voss and US President Monica Mallory have been advised to expect a protest from the OAS and UN. They say they couldn't care about either organization since neither seems concerned about the resurgent militarism in Venezuela. Fernando and Tom B. and Tom F. and Diego, you are to leave for Rio soon to regroup with your GRUMEC comrades on the *Tikuna* submarine bound for Port of Spain. Tom Bancroft has a plan to help your ground travel in Venezuela. Tom, would you please explain?"

Bancroft addressed the men, "Thank you, Senhor Director. Gentlemen, please turn your attention to the next items in your files. One of our CIA agents is working in Port of Spain. He has been able to hire this fellow in the photograph with the pickup truck. Tomorrow afternoon, the truck's owner will leave the truck near the culvert you passed through on your last visit to Venezuela. He will leave it with a full tank of gas. He will leave it unlocked with the keys in the glove box. You are to return it to the exact same spot with a full tank of gas when finished with it. The house in the next photograph is the Duzon home in Caracas. It is in the same neighborhood as the home Diego was held in. The address is on the next page."

The picture was of a modest stucco-covered structure of one story in height. The men felt comfortable with approaching it after their successful rescue of Diego in the neighborhood on their previous Venezuelan foray. As with the home Diego was imprisoned in, the Duzon home was surrounded by thick unkempt foliage that offered cover.

Fernando listened carefully to Cardenas and Bancroft and nodded his understanding of the outline of the effort. "Senhor Cardenas and Mr. Bancroft, this is precisely the type of opportunity I relish. The chance to work with Tom and Tom and Diego and the GRUMEC again is enticing. I'd also like to be able to help Anita. Seeing her again would be a rewarding experience. You can count me in."

Cardenas smiled and replied to Fernando, "Well, that is wonderful! You are all to depart for Rio tonight to board the *Tikuna* at Arsenal de Marinho do Rio de Janeiro. Good luck to you all!"

da Silva stood and hugged Fernando and whispered in his ear, "Well, laddie, be careful. You need to keep your word to Denise and return safely to her side in Niterói. Remember we all love you too. Make your country proud and safe."

Fernando and Fielding and Bancroft and Guedes were driven to Kubitschek Airport where they boarded the E190 and were flown to Rio. They landed at Galeão Air Force Base and were transferred secretively in an armored PM vehicle to the *Tikuna* at the naval base.

While they boarded the *Tikuna*, the captain and the crew and Doido and Dor and Jamal and Zé greeted them. They ate a hearty meal of feijoada with the crew and were shown to bunks where they might rest on the long trip to the Venezuelan coast.

At ten o'clock that night, they were underway. The throb of the diesel-electric engines was hypnotic. The team all lay down to nap. With full stomachs and with the engines' rhythmic sounds and vibrations, they fell fast asleep. Fernando felt comforted by the smell of diesel fuel and the engines' throbbing.

At six o'clock on the morning of Tuesday, October 6, the sub's engines became quiet. The captain came through, announcing they were near Port of Spain and breakfast and coffee were ready. Bancroft arose quickly and called to the team to join him for breakfast and preparations to go ashore. The captain had offered the team the use of his conference room for breakfast and their preparations. The team all dressed in frog gear they'd received upon boarding and checked their weapons carefully. Bancroft laid out a plan to again go ashore using inflatable boats disguised as fishing boats. Again, they had fishing poles and nets and other equipment to complete the deception. He cautioned the men that following the Guedes rescue, the Venezuelan Coast Guard was more vigilant than they had been previously. The men placed clothing to look like fishermen in waterproof packs they were to carry ashore. A crescent moon was disappearing on the horizon. The smell of the engines' exhaust reminded the men they were breaking away from the secure environment of the *Tikuna*.

Bancroft and Fielding searched the horizon on the ocean and shore with night-vision binoculars, looking for any sign of threat, and saw none. They saw mangrove trees mingled with palms all swaying in a light breeze. They signaled to their companions to get underway. The men had also packed clothing for their activities in Caracas. They hoped to pass for locals. They used packs intended to protect their weapons as well.

At seven thirty in the morning, the team went on deck and placed their "fishing boat" in the water. They luckily found themselves in the midst of a teeming school of sea bass. Their net was soon filled to capacity. The sea was calm, but there was a drenching rainstorm that began suddenly. They proceeded to dress in their fishing disguises and turned toward their culvert destination. Soon, they were all convincingly drenched as any fishermen should be in a similar circumstance. They hid their frog gear carefully in a burlap bag that appeared to be for fish storage. The floor of the boat was quickly filled with over thirty writhing fish. They approached their landing target, and suddenly, a coast guard vessel approached.

Bancroft called the sub's captain and made sure the crew was watching with their deck gun ready to provide cover and safety.

The coast guard came alongside and swept the "fishing boat" with a searchlight. The guardsmen appeared relieved by the sight of the fish and sodden fishermen.

"Looks like you've got our dinner. Thank you for your hard work!" shouted the ranking guardsman on the cutter with a laugh.

Fernando and Diego laughed too. They were capable of passing for locals. And Fernando replied, "Yes, there's enough for us all. How many are you there? Please tell us how many you all plan to feed at dinner tonight! We are obliged to share with you who protect our great land from enemies."

The coast guard crew laughed and replied with their head count.

Dor and Zé stepped aboard the cutter. Jamal and Doido handed across fifteen large fish to the crew. Quickly, Dor and Zé reboarded the fishing boat. The senior guardsman became serious and demanded their fishing license. Diego pulled his wallet from his pants and produced some expertly forged documents he'd received from Bancroft, a fishing license and

a national identification card. The entire team also had identification cards. For safety's sake, Diego also had a driver's
license. The coast guard thanked them for the fishing license
and identification cards and motioned they were fine and
dismissed.

There appeared to be an opportunity to pull away. The
MECs placed the oars in the water and began to row vigorously toward shore and the culvert. The coast guard crew
waved their thanks enthusiastically.

Fernando called out as they departed, "Please enjoy the
fish with our compliments and salutations, gentlemen!"

There was a small village on the shore near the culvert.
The MECs pulled ashore as if to be headed for it. The cutter
sounded its siren in thanks as it pulled away.

CHAPTER 57

North coast of Venezuela near Port of Spain
Morning of Tuesday, October 6, 2020

The siren caused the Brazilian team some anxiety. They all pulled their weapons from their swim bags and held them close.

They beached their boat and called Bancroft to report they were on land. At nine o'clock in the morning, they pulled the boat through some bushes into a clearing and covered it with palm fronds from nearby trees and left it covered. They pulled a burlap catch bag out and filled it with the fish and carried them along in search of locals to give them to. They changed into dry clothes and donned boots designed for hiking and running. They marched across the beach, attempting and succeeding to look like simple fishermen.

They found the culvert and proceeded through to the marsh. While they waded through the marsh, Doido joked about wondering if their victims from the army truck they'd ambushed on their last visit might still be submerged there. Dor replied their remains must have been picked clean by whatever creatures may have found them.

Once across the marsh, they found the pickup truck precisely where Bancroft promised it would be. Jamal called Bancroft to report they had the truck. The truck was a nicely preserved 1985 Ford F-150 with only eighty-five thousand miles on the odometer.

Diego inspected the truck carefully. He noted it had a current registration and a government inspection tag that was current until January of 2021. Diego insisted he should drive because of his intimate knowledge of the area. Diego opened the glove box and found the keys. The engine started easily. The engine sounded to be in perfect repair. Rain continued to fall heavily. The windshield wiper blades worked perfectly and appeared to be brand-new. Diego looked at the gas gauge. He pointed at it, smiling. It read full.

Fernando and Fielding sat in the cab with Diego. The MECs loaded into the load bed with the fish for cover.

At nine thirty, the rain increased in intensity. The relentless downpour drenched the men in the load bed. Diego turned south toward Caracas. The cold wet of the rain was made more uncomfortable while the temperature rose to eighty-three degrees Fahrenheit. The humidity exacerbated the MECs' discomfort by rising to 84 percent.

The storm was a hindrance to their progress on the trip. Certain parts of the road were washed out or submerged. The trip should have taken eight hours but instead took ten. The pickup performed nicely, and they stopped for gas in a small town on the way. The town was named Bolívar after the country's most famous son, Simón Bolívar. The passengers in the cab were protected from the rain.

The police or military did not stop them even once. They appeared convincingly to be fishermen driving home. The cab's air-conditioning effectively defeated the external heat and humidity. They entered the outskirts of Caracas at eight o'clock at night.

They found the Duzon home easily. Fernando and Fielding and the MECs got out at a small hotel near the house and checked in. Diego went to park the truck and agreed to return to the hotel to join the others. To avoid suspicion, they told the front desk clerk they had been fishing and needed a place to rest up and shower. They each had the national identification cards Bancroft had had forged for them. Their home addresses indicated they lived in the fishing village near the culvert where they came ashore. The cards were required to be shown upon checking in. The clerk seemed unsuspicious and fully accepted the men as Venezuelan fishermen.

They offered the remaining sea bass to the clerk so he might share them with whomever he wished. They got to the room and showered quickly and dressed in the casual street clothes they had brought. Fernando and Fielding stretched out on the beds for a quick nap.

Dor and Zé and Doido and Jamal went back out onto the street to watch the Duzon home. They hoped to see Pablo or Anita. They located a small café near the house and took a table by the window and ordered coffees. Within twenty minutes, Pablo Duzon exited the house and got into a car with a driver and was driven away. Soon, Anita walked out and into a small grocery on the street.

Zé and Jamal jogged back to the hotel and told Fernando where Anita was. Fielding and Fernando got up. They followed Jamal and Zé back to the café. The MECs pointed out the grocery.

Fernando walked into the grocery. Passing the front window, he saw Anita standing at the vegetable counter. He entered the store and walked up next to her and began studying the tomatoes. In his perfect Spanish, he spoke, "Well, what a surprise to see you, Senhorita Odebrecht."

The stunned Anita stared dumbstruck at Fernando and smiled. "Senhor Carvalho, what a surprise and pleasure! What are you doing here?!"

Fernando smiled broadly and turned to face Anita. "Well, I have been fishing. I am with friends, and we are all at the café nearby. Would you care to join us?"

"Oh, Nando, why are you here?! I haven't seen you in so long!"

Fernando noticed the store clerk was watching intently. He stood close to Anita and leaned toward her left ear and whispered, "Anita, I know you are married. I am here on official Brazilian state business to try to stop your husband's current insurgency effort in Brazil."

Anita smiled and replied, "Okay, Nando, I would love to join you and your friends over coffee."

Fernando took Anita by the right arm and walked her across the street and into the café. He introduced her to the team.

Anita bowed and addressed the others, "Gentlemen, I am not a fan of my husband's political and military focuses. How may I be of help?" Anita spoke in a low voice and watched the street outside nervously.

Fernando smiled and folded his hands in front of him on the table. He studied Anita closely. Her eyes opened wide as she noticed Pablo's car delivering him home. He entered the house. "It would be best if you went home now, Anita," said Fernando.

Diego caught up, and Fernando pointed at him and continued, "This fellow is a close associate of mine. He and I will go to the grocery and buy an assortment of the vegetables you were looking at. He will bring the vegetables to deliver them to your house. He will knock on the door. Please stand clear when he enters your house. We intend to kidnap your husband. Please understand he means harm to Brazil and its people. We need your cooperation and, if possible, will not harm you or Pablo. Once Pablo is removed, I will have time to spend with you and catch up."

Anita nodded her agreement and walked to the grocery with Fernando and Diego. They went to the vegetable counter and selected tomatoes and potatoes and onions and avocados. Anita paid for them while chatting with the clerk. She handed the bag to Diego and looked at Fernando and winked. She exited the store and walked to her house. The MECs watched her from the café.

Soon, Fernando rejoined the café occupants. Shortly, Diego walked from the grocery to the Duzon's house with the grocery bag and knocked on the front door. Anita and Pablo answered. Diego was greeted graciously and shown to the kitchen where he placed the bag on the counter.

Within several minutes, Jamal and Fernando and Fielding knocked on the door, and Anita let them in. Duzon was at the sink in the kitchen, filling a teakettle.

As Jamal and Fernando and Fielding entered the kitchen, Diego stepped behind Duzon and placed his gun in Duzon's ribs. "Senhor Colonel, I don't wish to harm you but please do as we say."

The stunned Duzon made a move for an alarm under the kitchen counter.

Fernando placed his right hand on Duzon's forearm and stopped him. The teakettle went tumbling to the floor where it came to a stop in a pool of the water it had spilled. A tea bag and bottle of honey Duzon was planning to use to make his evening tea remained on the counter.

Fernando spoke in Spanish, "Now, Pablo, you don't want to upset your neighbors by causing a ruckus. We are determined Brazilians bent on stopping you and your vile efforts. Please follow my friends here."

Diego and the MECs guided Duzon to the front door, and Diego guided them to the pickup truck.

As he exited the house, Duzon erupted in rage, "Did that whore of a wife of mine help you with this?!"

In the street, Duzon shouted for help. Fielding hit Pablo on the head with the butt of his revolver, and Duzon went silent and sagged and went limp.

Fernando and Jamal put Duzon's arms around their shoulders, and they walked him like a friend who'd drunk too much. As they approached the pickup truck, they placed the unconscious Pablo in the load bed and placed his head on the piled-up fishing net. They secured his hands at the wrists and legs at the ankles and placed a gag in his mouth.

As preagreed among the Brazilian team, Fernando stayed in the kitchen with Anita.

Anita started to cry with relief and hugged Fernando. "Oh, Nando, I've been so miserable with that man!"

"I can only imagine," replied Fernando. "Are you ready to go back to Brazil?"

Anita nodded her consent. Fernando asked her to collect some clothes and personal items in a small bag.

Anita ran to her bedroom and collected some things. In a moment, she returned to the kitchen. "After my father's death, Venezuela has held no attraction for me. I'd love to leave with you."

Fernando smiled at her and replied, "Anita, I am seeing someone and cannot be your boyfriend. I'd love to help you escape this Communist madness. Where and how is your mother?"

"She is well, Nando. She still lives in my parents' old home some blocks away from here."

"I see," said Fernando reflectively. "Will she be okay if you depart Venezuela?"

Anita teared up slightly and replied, "Unfortunately, I'd guess Juan Cortez would try to punish her for my departure and Pablo's disappearance."

Fernando realized a complexity had arisen in the Brazilians' plans. It would be impossible to get Anita and Pablo and Anita's mother Pilar out of the country altogether safely on that one night.

They walked to the intersection where the pickup was parked and found the Brazilian team waiting for them. It was now past ten o'clock in the evening. The rain persisted. Fernando opened the cab's passenger side door and put Anita in the seat and joined the MECs and Fielding and Duzon in the load bed.

Fielding sat cradling Duzon's head in his lap. Pablo stirred, and his eyes opened, looking wild with rage.

Fielding stroked Pablo's forehead sarcastically and whispered, "Hush," softly in Pablo's ears.

Fielding tightened Pablo's gag, and Fernando spoke to Pablo, "Well, Senhor Colonel, it appears we have the upper hand. Please be patient. We intend to place you and Anita in our submarine and take you both to Brazil. Your little foray in the Amazon near our Manaus Air Force Base is all but over."

Duzon struggled violently in his restraints. Fielding placed a rag soaked with chloroform under Pablo's nose, and Pablo fell into a deep anesthetic sleep for the duration of the drive.

CHAPTER 58

The rain continued and provided cover for the Brazilian team in the pickup truck.

Diego stopped again in Bolívar and purchased gas. He had made a mental note of a gas station near their landing on the shore and there refilled the tank again as Bancroft had instructed.

At eight o'clock in the morning, they pulled into the parking spot in which they had found the pickup. They returned the keys to the glove box and left the truck unlocked so its owner might get it back. Pablo was still out cold, and Fielding lifted him out of the truck and threw him over his right shoulder.

At eight forty-five in the morning, they all walked to their hidden "fishing boat." They were relieved to find it still safely under the palm fronds. They loaded in Anita and Pablo and pushed the boat into the surf and started to row for the submarine. Anita looked at Pablo and cried tears over her wasted years with the violent man she had married. They found the *Tikuna* easily resting in the spot they had left it.

At nine thirty, Bancroft and the captain greeted them from the deck. Three sailors stepped toward the boat and helped lift Anita and the anesthetized Pablo on deck and down the hatch and into the sub. Pablo was laid in and secured to a bunk. Fielding remained standing and watching the captive. The captain offered Anita his berth. Fernando and Diego debriefed the captain and Bancroft on the mission.

At ten o'clock in the morning, they were underway for Rio. They all found bunks and were shortly well asleep to the sound and vibrations of the diesel-electric engines.

At five o'clock in the afternoon, Pablo awoke from his haze and started shouting.

Fernando stepped next to Pablo's bunk and addressed him while pointing at Fielding. "Pablo, if you aren't quiet, I will have my friend Mr. Fielding here put you back to sleep. Don't forget you're on a Brazilian Navy submarine. There are six officers and over fifty crewmen on board. I will resist telling them they may do what they wish with you, an ardent Communist and anti-Brazilian. I doubt they've had the pleasure of launching a living enemy from the torpedo tubes."

Duzon struggled against his restraints, and his eyes exhibited terror and frustration. Tears formed at the corners of Pablo's eyes.

Fernando chuckled and continued, "Well, Pablo, I am sure our plan for you will be much worse than killing you. When we arrive at the naval base in Rio, you will be handed over to interrogators from the Brazilian ABIN who want to learn what you and Juan Cortez and your allies from Russia and China and Cuba are up to on Brazilian soil."

At seven o'clock that night, the Brazilians had dinner with the sub's crew.

Fielding took a plate to Pablo and helped him eat. Pablo's constraints made feeding himself extremely difficult. Fielding fed him slowly and offered him a glass of orange juice.

"Well, what have you capitalist pigs got planned?!" inquired Pablo.

Fielding smiled and replied, "Senhor Colonel, I am going to anesthetize you again so you may sleep for the duration of our voyage."

Duzon looked angry again and spoke, "You will all be sorry by the time my comrades take action in Manaus! Tell that traitorous whore of a wife of mine I will find a way to obtain justice for me and for Venezuela!"

Fielding rolled his eyes and filled a handkerchief with chloroform and held it to Duzon's nose. Pablo was quickly back unconscious.

CHAPTER 59

Caracas, Venezuela
Night of Tuesday, October 6, 2020

Juan Cortez tried twice unsuccessfully to call Pablo Duzon. A critical planning meeting with the insurgent troops in Brazil was scheduled for three o'clock on Wednesday morning. It was unusual for Pablo to not answer a call from Cortez, and Cortez became concerned and sent a car to the Duzon home to find out where Pablo was.

In the car were three members of military intelligence with policing experience. At midnight, the three officers knocked on the front door, and no one answered. They broke a pane of glass in a rear door to the kitchen and entered the house. A panicked thorough search of the home yielded no evidence of anything except a struggle in the kitchen. The senior officer called Cortez and reported there appeared to have been a kidnapping.

Cortez gasped and almost dropped the phone. He radioed the troops in the Amazon and reported Duzon could not be found. A Cuban general named Ochoa was in command and offered to stand in Duzon's place in the upcoming planning meeting.

Cortez was overwhelmed with the idea someone had penetrated his capital city and kidnapped one of his top men and the man's wife. He thanked the Cuban for his offer.

"General Ochoa, I need your help and apologize for having you stand in for a colonel. I will call you when the planning meeting begins."

Ochoa replied, "Thank you, Senhor Presidente. I am not offended to be taking the place of an inspirational Socialist warrior like Pablo Duzon!"

The planning session concluded hours later, and the Venezuelans present were fired up by the news of Duzon's abduction. A plan of action was agreed upon. The troops were to attack Manaus Air Force Base and inflict as many casualties and as much damage as possible.

Pablo Duzon Jr. was enraged and saddened by the news of his parents' capture. He rallied his comrades to a fury of inspired anger.

CHAPTER 60

Amazon jungle near Manaus Air Force Base
Night of Wednesday, October 7, 2020

General Ochoa and Cortez had decided the plans were to be best executed under the cover of darkness. At ten o'clock in the evening, Ochoa ordered three Russian Iskander short-range ballistic missiles to be launched toward Manaus Air Force Base.

The USA and Israel had installed and were manning a ground-based Patriot antiballistic missile defense system. The US and Israeli forces identified the inbound missiles and destroyed them expertly in the air. US Navy SEALs and Brazilian GRUMEC troops and US and Brazilian marines were prepared to engage the insurgent forces. US Army Rangers also participated as did the Argentine Army, Compañia de Comandos 602. The Compañia de Comandos is the Argentine Army's special forces unit. It was formed during the Falklands War in 1982.

The pro-Brazilian troops approached the insurgent force and trained laser targets on the missile battery and insurgent troops and their other equipment. Three Brazilian F-15s from Galeão and Manaus air force bases swooped in and fired air-to-surface laser-guided missiles and inflicted serious harm on the insurgents. The pro-Brazilian troops closed in and engaged the surviving Communists. A fierce ground battle ensued and lasted forty-five minutes.

General Ochoa and the senior Russian and Chinese officers fought in the battle and died bravely defending their positions. Pablo Duzon Jr. was also killed, as were ten of his Venezuelan comrades. The base's defenders executed a brilliant flanking move and surrounded the insurgents. In so doing, the Brazilian and US and other troops surrounded twenty-five surviving insurgents, and they surrendered and were all captured and taken prisoner.

Juan Cortez listened to a live radio communication from the battle scene. Cortez's dream of a glorious victory for Communism over the greedy capitalist nation of Brazil was crushed. He was demoralized and called the Cuban president in Havana, and Cuba and its allies agreed to withdraw any remaining forces from near Manaus.

Presidente Voss monitored the events in Manaus closely and called Bancroft and the Brazilian army commander, and the three discussed the situation and were ecstatic.

CHAPTER 61

Arsenal de Marinha do Rio de Janeiro, Rio de Janeiro, Brazil
Morning of Thursday, October 8, 2020

At eight o'clock in the morning, the *Tikuna* arrived home and docked.

Fielding and Fernando had revived Pablo Duzon and were preparing to take him to the dock to hand him to the ABIN. Tom Bancroft and Tom Fielding bid Fernando goodbye and were taken to Galeão Air Force Base to catch a flight home to Washington DC. Anita had awakened and freshened up. She joined Fielding and Diego and Fernando and Pablo and Bancroft, and they all ate breakfast together with the Tikuna's captain and his senior officers. Pablo was included in the meal and throughout stared wild-eyed at Anita, muttering to himself and looking somewhat rabid.

At eight thirty, Diego and Fernando took the Duzons onto the dock. Three ABIN agents, two male and one female, met them.

Anita was assigned to the female's custody. The female agent held a master's degree in psychology and was experienced in handling psychological trauma and physical abuse victims.

Pablo erupted violently, swearing at Anita and the Brazilians. He went into a political rant and railed against Voss and capitalism and his captors and poor Anita. Despite his restraints at the wrists and ankles, Pablo attempted to fight his captors. Diego rolled his eyes and smiled at Pablo and placed another chloroform-soaked rag under Pablo's nose. Pablo was soon out cold and ceased struggling.

The ABIN men carried the unconscious Pablo to their waiting car, and they drove him to Galeão Air Force Base and placed him on a private flight to Brasília.

CHAPTER 62

The flight carrying Pablo Duzon and his ABIN guards arrived in Brasília at two thirty in the afternoon. ABIN Director Cardenas and a security detail greeted them. Pablo was rushed from the airport in an armored vehicle and delivered to the ABIN headquarters in Brasília.

At the headquarters, Pablo was placed on a cot in an interrogation room and offered coffee and a light lunch.

After allowing Pablo forty-five minutes to rest and revive, the ABIN's top interrogator entered the room accompanied by a male nurse and interpreter. The nurse checked Pablo's vitals and general cognitive condition. The nurse confirmed Pablo was adequately revived from the chloroform and could be expected to handle the questioning safely. Pablo was found to be in adequate shape to be interrogated. His blood pressure and oxygen level and reflexes were good, and he appeared aware of his surroundings and circumstances. He answered simple questions correctly. The questions were the current date and his name and age and date and place of birth and home address. He answered all clearly and correctly. At the interrogator's request, the nurse administered a small dose of sodium pentothal.

Director Cardenas observed the process through a two-way mirror. The room was gray with gray furniture consisting of a metal desk and file cabinet and gray metal-framed chairs. The chairs were covered with gray-colored plastic coverings on the cushions. The cushion coverings were made to appear like leather. The lighting was intentionally very low.

The interrogator sat next to Duzon with the interpreter leaning in close. "Colonel Duzon, I am Henrique Duterte. I am the senior interrogator for the ABIN. You are in the Brazilian capital of Brasília." Duterte could see Pablo was becoming groggy from the sodium pentothal and began his questioning. "Colonel Duzon, I will now count backwards from one hundred. When I am finished, I want you to agree to cooperate with my questioning."

Somewhere inside his mind, Duzon tried to fight back. He managed to curse at Duterte, "Go fuck yourself, you lapdog of the Voss capitalist regime!"

Duterte smiled patiently and replied, "Now, Colonel, that will not get us to where we need and want to be!"

Duterte nodded toward the nurse, and another injection of sodium pentothal was administered. Duterte checked his watch and waited five minutes for the drug to take hold. Pablo began slurring his speech, and his head lowered so his chin was on the top of his chest.

Duterte placed his face close to Pablo's and spoke, "Senhor Colonel, what is the purpose of the Venezuelan and other troops assembled near Manaus Air Force Base in Brazil?"

Duzon managed to find the strength to respond. "They are the first wave of a glorious effort to destroy the insidious capitalist government of Ricardo Voss!" replied the defiant Duzon.

"What interest do China and Russia have in this effort?!" continued Duterte, with the interpreter speaking forcefully into Duzon's right ear.

"I cannot tell you my allies' secrets!" managed Duzon, admirably fighting off the sodium pentothal's impact.

Duzon attempted to curl up in his chair and go to sleep. Duterte carefully poured a pitcher of ice water over Duzon's head. Duzon made a whimpering response and tried to avoid Duterte.

Duterte and the interpreter closed back in on Duzon's face and right ear and continued, "Listen to me, Colonel. I hold all of the cards here. We have your wife and know your son is on our land. You won't be going home to Juan Cortez and your sad little life of Communist confusion ever!"

Duzon began to mumble an incoherent angry reply.

Duterte tried to not become angry in return and continued, "Okay, Colonel, you must tell me the details of the Russian and Chinese presence in the Amazon! I am about to step out for a half an hour. If you decide you don't like things, you can stop them by simply sitting up and calling for me to step back in."

Duterte and the nurse guided Duzon to the cot in the room and laid him down. Before placing Duzon on the cot, Duterte poured more ice water over Duzon's head. In so doing, Duterte was careful to not get the cot wet. He handed Duzon a towel to dry his hair. Duterte and the nurse stepped back out and turned the lights down quite low using a rheostat.

Duterte went to the adjacent room and watched Duzon through a two-way mirror. Duzon was evidently desperate to fall asleep and curled up on the cot with his left arm across his eyes. Duterte opened a laptop computer connected to speakers in the ceiling of the interrogation room. He surveyed a menu of sounds to pipe into the room. He selected a fog-horn combined with the sound of a screwdriver blade being dragged across a metal surface producing a screeching sound. After fifteen minutes, Duzon attempted to escape the room by pulling on the locked door handle. He soon returned to the cot and attempted to find sleep while covering his ears. Five minutes later after not succeeding in finding rest and silence, Duzon stood and motioned for Duterte's attention.

Duterte spoke into a microphone piped into the room, "Yes, Colonel, what do you need?"

Duzon replied, "Okay, I know how this game is played. I desperately need my sleep. I am ready to talk."

Duterte stopped the sounds and got the nurse and interpreter, and they reentered the interrogation room.

"Okay, Colonel, you said you know how the game is played. I'll let you sleep for one-and-one-half hours. If after that time you tell me what I demand to know, I'll let you sleep all night without that little symphony of noises. If you let me down and don't tell me what I want to know, I'll recommence the sounds and will relentlessly prohibit your sleep."

The nurse rechecked Duzon's vital signs and confirmed he was okay. Another injection of sodium pentothal was administered, and Duterte and the nurse lowered the lights to a dim glow. The Brazilians exited the room. Duterte took his position observing through the two-way mirror and set a timer for ninety minutes.

Director Cardenas had departed. He called Duterte and received an update on the interrogation. The call lasted thirty minutes. Duterte checked his watch at the call's conclusion and stepped out to get a coffee.

At the coffee station, he encountered Director da Silva smoking a cigarette and fixing himself a coffee. The two sat chatting idly while drinking their coffees. They spoke until the timer sounded. Director da Silva departed.

Duterte stepped back into the observation room and observed Duzon was soundly asleep. Duterte and the nurse and interpreter stepped back into the interrogation room and turned the lights back to full brightness. Duzon sat up looking disoriented and extremely tired. He rubbed his eyes. He looked terribly forlorn and worried and frightened. The nurse again checked Duzon's vital signs and nodded his approval.

Duterte addressed Duzon, "Okay, rise and shine, my friend. I am a man of my word. If you are ready to talk and satisfy my need for information, you may go back to sleep when we are done. Is that clear, Colonel?"

Duzon appeared defeated both physically and psychologically and nodded his concurrence and replied, "Yes, Senhor Duterte, I am ready to talk, but please let me sleep longer!"

Duterte responded, "No bullshit here, Colonel. I will happily turn the sounds back on! Don't disappoint me!"

Duzon sighed heavily. "All right, I am prepared to betray my country's and its allies' secrets!"

Duterte placed a small recorder on the table between them. Duzon proceeded to speak for over an hour and gave great detail. He filled his talk with agitated extreme Leftist rhetoric.

After the more than one hour of talk, Duterte learned Venezuela and Russia and Cuba and China had designs on the strategic advantage they could gain by placing a massive jointly operated air base and naval yard near Port of Spain. The construction was planned to begin in January of 2021. Aerial photography by the Brazilian and US air forces had confirmed large shipments of earth working and construction equipment having arrived in Port of Spain from China and

Russia. Additionally there were unassembled prefabricated buildings and paving and concrete materials. The objective was to utilize the base for military action intended to convert much of Latin America to Communism influenced by Cuba and Venezuela and China and Russia. Their intent appeared to not be so much politically evangelical in nature. Instead, their intent was to frustrate and threaten the USA and its Latin American allies. Duterte learned Brazil and Argentina and Chile and Columbia and Mexico and the Dominican Republic and Jamaica and Haiti were all targets along with much of Central America. Russia had no particular Socialist or Communist agenda but simply favored the potential for disturbing and threatening the USA and its allies.

Duterte was quickly on a call with Cardenas and Voss and US President Monica Mallory. President Mallory and her director of national security and secretary of defense expressed their concerns.

President Mallory spoke first, "Presidente Voss and Senhores Cardenas and Duterte, thank you very much for this detailed and powerful and disturbing insight. We will present these findings to the UN and push for severe economic sanctions against Russia and Cuba and China and Venezuela."

The US secretary of defense concluded the US comments, "We are prepared to wait to see the outcome of the proposed sanctions. Should they prove unsuccessful, we have prepared a military response. Our definition of success is the complete withdrawal by China and Russia and Cuba and to obtain their joint public announcement they are abandoning their plans to attempt an incursion into the Western Hemisphere."

On November 1, the United States and Brazilian ambassadors to the UN made a presentation to the general assembly of the UN. The presentation contained the details derived from the Duzon interrogation. The aerial photography depicting the construction activity was presented too. The missile attack on Manaus Air Force Base was included in the presentation.

The reception was lukewarm. Key allies like Great Britain and France and Italy and Japan and Germany and Australia and New Zealand and Canada all readily agreed to participate in the imposition of sanctions. The sanctions presented a potentially crushing economic blow to the targets. In the ensuing weeks, Russia and China informed Cuba and Venezuela they could not provide adequate financial aid to offset the sanctions' overwhelmingly adverse impact on the Cuban and Venezuelan economies. On November 10, 2020, Venezuela and its allies announced the plans for Port of Spain were being ended. Juan Cortez's government was faltering as a result of a widespread failure to address the continuing economic shortcomings Cortez had cited regarding the Maduro regime.

A populist movement arose in support of Mateo Hernandez. Hernandez was a Caracas attorney and law professor and longtime outspoken critic of the country's shift to totalitarianism.

The beleaguered nation fell into disarray while Cortez resisted the pro-Hernandez direction and wishes of the people.

Venezuela's oil production ground to a halt, and Venezuela teetered closer to the brink of economic collapse. Hernandez found a supportive audience in the Venezuelan Army. Cortez rallied support in the military and swore he wouldn't accede to the populist groundswell. A civil war broke out and propelled Venezuela into a dark era of violence.

CHAPTER 63

Anita Duzon, née Odebrecht, was living with the female ABIN psychologist caring for her. Fernando called her to check in.

Anita answered excitedly, "Hi, Nando. It's so good to be hearing from you!"

Fernando smiled and replied, "Hi, Anita. I have spoken to your psychologist and am very pleased to hear you are progressing well. Have you been following the developments in Venezuela?"

"Yes, Nando, I have. I am praying Mateo Hernandez will be able to attain the presidency. I have been unable to reach my mother to check on her."

Their conversation continued, and Fernando agreed to speak to Director Cardenas about freeing Anita's mother.

On Friday, November 20, Diego and Fernando and Tom Fielding and their MEC companions were back in Caracas. They found their way to the Odebrecht home. Pilar was under close guard.

With Tom Bancroft's guidance, they had developed a plan to approach the home through the clean water sewer in the neighborhood. Fielding's size and strength were invaluable in opening and manipulating manhole covers. He was able to climb the ladders integrated in the sewer walls and push the covers up and out of the way. Tom had practiced the effort repeatedly in his career. He was able to move the covers in a fashion that made their movement hard to discern from any distance over several yards. He also did so without making any loud or disturbing noise. The guards in and around Pilar's home had no warning of Tom's and the Brazilians' approach.

The team entered the home through a door that opened on a short alleyway behind the house that served as its driveway. Guards in the house and on the front porch were terminated with silenced handguns.

Pilar was found in the kitchen preparing a cake she was going to bake. Tom Fielding and Diego Guedes and Fernando approached Pilar. Pilar looked terrified by the surprise entry of gunmen in her home. Pilar was overjoyed when she recognized Fernando. Fernando told Pilar about Anita's circumstances. He comforted Pilar she would soon be reunited with her daughter.

On the morning of Wednesday, November 25, the *Tikuna* returned to Arsenal de Marinha do Rio de Janeiro and docked. Anita and her psychologist caretaker were present to receive Pilar. Fernando spent twenty minutes with Anita and Pilar and satisfied himself by learning the psychologist believed they were in good condition both psychologically and physically.

Paulo picked up Fernando at the navy base, and they returned to Niterói. Soon, Fernando was home with Paulo and Denise and Heliana for dinner.

Fernando monitored Anita's progress thereafter and was pleased with the outcome. Anita was ultimately successful in moving her design firm to Rio and began dating Luis Antonio. Luis Antonio moved to Rio and took a director level position in Anita's firm. He was assigned the director of security role.

Luis Antonio and Anita moved close to Niterói and were frequent visitors at Paulo Coberto's home. Fernando and Anita became comfortable with behaving like surrogate brother and sister. Denise fully understood Fernando's dedication to Anita, and she and Anita became close friends. Anita hired Denise as her executive assistant.

Fernando and Diego and Fielding and their MEC companions were given several additional assignments in Venezuela that centered on the civil war and Hernandez's political aspirations. The Communist-centered political branch of the Venezuelan military soon expired from lack of the support it had had from Cortez. The unique and luxurious lifestyle benefits showered on the military soon became impossible to deliver, and the benefits' termination undermined Cortez's influence. The military splintered into two equally strong factions. One supported Cortez, and another supported Mateo Hernandez and the anti-Cortez opposition. Brutal battles broke out between the supporters of Cortez and Hernandez. Cortez fled to Havana and was no longer visible.

At the peak of the civil unrest in Caracas, the inhabitants of the Brazilian Embassy were evacuated home to Brasília. Two female employees of the embassy staff had married members of the Venezuelan Army. The Cortez government refused to allow the women to participate in the evacuation. One of the women was Director Cardenas' niece. She was the daughter of his youngest sister. The two women were known to be hiding in one of their homes. Tom Bancroft arranged to have them escorted to a safe house on the coast near Port of Spain where they were to await the arrival of a Brazilian team assigned to extract them. For the effort, Bancroft engaged the pickup owner who assisted with the extraction of Anita.

*   *   *   *   *

At eight o'clock on the morning of Monday, November 16, the pickup pulled up to the Brazilian women's hideout. The driver had a fabricated false business name emblazoned on the truck's door. It identified him as an on-call handyman. He exited the truck dressed in coveralls and extracted a tool case from the load bed and walked to the front door and knocked.

One of the Brazilian women let him in. He instructed the two women to go out and get into the truck's cab and wait. He immediately followed them to the truck and got in and started the engine. He turned the truck toward the road to Port of Spain. Their trip was slow but uninterrupted. They stopped once in Bolívar and purchased gas. They arrived in the fishing village near the GRUMEC's landing point near the culvert at five o'clock in the afternoon.

The safe house was a small bungalow on the main street of the village. The truck owner's wife had arrived earlier and had cleaned the house and made the beds and placed fresh towels. Upon their arrival, the driver's wife was in the modest kitchen, hard at work on dinner. The extraction team arrived at six o'clock in the evening.

Diego Guedes introduced himself and his MEC comrades to their Venezuelan hosts. The Brazilian women were ecstatic at the sight of their fellow countrymen. A rousingly cheerful dinner ensued. There were nine people in attendance: Diego, Doido, Dor, Zé, Jamal, and the two Brazilian women from the embassy plus the truck driver and his wife.

At eight o'clock in the evening, the truck driver and his wife departed for their home in Caracas. Diego paid them ten thousand US dollars in cash, which was the prearranged price for their help and subsequent silence.

At six o'clock the following morning, the MECs and Diego awoke the two Brazilian women, and they all walked three hundred yards to the culvert and waded through the marsh and boarded their "fishing boat" and were on board the *Tikuna* at ten o'clock in the morning.

On the morning of Wednesday, November 18, the *Tikuna* docked at Arsenal de Marinha do Rio de Janeiro. The two women from the embassy in Caracas were flown quickly to Brasília where they were taken to the foreign ministry. A reception was held at the foreign ministry. The women were reunited with the ambassador to Venezuela and the rest of the evacuated personnel.

At the time of the reunion, Fernando was at work at O Banco do Brasil in Rio. Ronaldo Amaraes had assigned Fernando to a research project. The intent of the project was to trace the origin of suspicious amounts accumulating in certain of the bank's accounts. The transactions were believed to be related to the funds movement that wound up with Eduardo Argos. The research was a mind-numbing challenge. Over fourteen individual and corporate accounts had accumulated the suspicious money in them. Fernando had to create a road map of the flow of the money.

On this particular morning, he was completing his analysis. He was perplexed by the obvious conclusion: someone was gaming the interest calculated on depository accounts. Carlos Aragon and Emanuel Conte were benefitting from the activity Fernando discovered.

Finance Minister Carlos Aragon and a collaborator on the bank's staff had clearly created accounts to capture the truncated results of rounded interest calculations. A majority of the bank's accounts were interest bearing. The practice of providing interest on accounts arose as a means to protect the principal balances in depository accounts during the eighties era of hyperinflation. The interest calculations could produce results of several decimal places in length. The program that made the calculations would shorten the calculations by dropping the ends and rounding them down to the nearest decimal place. The shortened results were simpler to track and understand in account statements compared to the longer untruncated results. The amounts so removed were then placed in accounts belonging to Argos and Conte. An interest calculation of .035779 would be changed to .035. The .000779, thus removed, would land in an illicit account. The interest calculations were continuous and thus made thousands of times each month. The accounts with the funds receiving the interest calculations held the equivalent of millions of US dollars. Argos and his collaborators on the bank's staff created fictitious entities that were named as the accounts' holders.

No one at the bank had questioned the validity of the accounts. Fast-growing business accounts were highly desired by the bank and thus went unchallenged. In addition to the accounts with the largest balances were accounts that belonged to a wide array of bank customers with interest-bearing depository accounts. The truncated amounts were not large enough to have been noticed as missing by any of the account holders. Those accounts received none of the truncated amounts. They did receive the interest that remained after the truncation. As a result, no material test of the interest earnings on the accounts would identify an issue.

At the peak of the fraud, there were in excess of one hundred million USdollars providing the basis for the interest calculations. By the seeming magic of mathematics, the infinitesimal amounts truncated in the interest calculations would accumulate to substantial amounts. Over the course of several years, the effort netted over five hundred thousand US dollars in accounts secretly belonging to and controlled by Finance Minister Carlos Aragon and Vice Presidente Emanuel Conte.

Fernando was shaken by the implications of his discovery. He had a standing weekly one-on-one meeting with Ronaldo Amaraes scheduled for that afternoon. Fernando made the finishing touches to a PowerPoint presentation he was to give to Amaraes in their afternoon meeting. He went through the presentation and carefully rehearsed the comments he would deliver to Amaraes. He was concerned about the impact on the Voss presidency by exposing the complicity of the vice president and finance minister. He put that aside after reminding himself his duty was entirely to Brazil and not one individual. He went to lunch at a neighboring restaurant and returned refreshed to the office. At three o'clock in the afternoon, he went to Amaraes's office.

Amaraes began the session, "Well, Fernando, how are you progressing with your project?"

Fernando cautiously replied, "Well, Senhor Amaraes, I have made a disturbing finding that should be of great interest to you and Director da Silva and Presidente Voss." Fernando set his laptop computer up to project his PowerPoint presentation on a big-screen television in Amaraes's office. He took Amaraes through the presentation.

The bank's senior compliance officer had been involved in the fraud and had purposefully steered the compliance team away from questioning the accounts receiving the truncated amounts. At the completion of the presentation, Amaraes appeared shaken by the news that two of Voss' senior team members and a trusted bank staffer were involved in the corruption.

Amaraes stood and moved to the door to the office and spoke again, "Well, Fernando, this is staggering news. I need to call Director da Silva and discuss our next steps. You have done a marvelous job, young man. Director da Silva and I knew you had great promise when we met you at Roberto Cavalcanti's party."

Amaraes sent da Silva an urgent text to find out where he was and arranged a call.

Director da Silva was wrapping up his day in his office at the PF headquarters in Brasília. da Silva called Amaraes almost immediately and began the conversation when Amaraes answered, "Good evening, Ronaldo my friend. What is the nature of your urgent communication?"

"Hello, João. I apologize for interrupting your evening. Our young friend and protégé Fernando has been working on a special research project for me. In the effort, he has uncovered some disturbing news. His findings indicate that Emanuel Conte and Carlos Aragon have received over one-half million US dollars they obtained through a bank fraud they executed with the help of one of my senior team members. We believe you and Sergio Viana should receive Fernando's presentation with his findings so you may determine what to do. Are you available for a video conference soon?"

da Silva checked his calendar on his phone and thought for a moment. "Well, Ronaldo, my morning is packed tomorrow, and I'm busy with Katia and Andrea this evening. How about tomorrow morning at eleven o'clock?"

Amaraes had a sidebar discussion with Fernando and returned to his discussion with da Silva. "Yes, João, Fernando and I will meet with you then."

"My executive assistant will send you a Zoom conference invitation prior to the meeting." da Silva was disturbed by the potential impact on the Voss administration and slept poorly.

During the night, he wrestled with how they would break the news to the president. Like Fernando, he concluded he would hold to the country's best interest and proceed.

*   *   *   *   *

At four o'clock in the morning, da Silva realized he was angry at Conte and Aragon for their betrayal of their offices' responsibilities. He arose at six thirty and showered and dressed for the day. He had breakfast with Andrea and Katia and drank several cups of coffee. His PF car and driver arrived at nine o'clock.

da Silva was in his office and drinking his fifth cup of coffee for the morning at 10:50 a.m. His assistant reminded him the Zoom conference with Fernando and Amaraes was set to start in a few minutes. Sergio Viana arrived at 10:59 a.m. to listen in to the presentation.

At 11:00 a.m., da Silva and Viana sat in front of da Silva's computer and joined Fernando and Amaraes in a videoconference.

Amaraes started the discussion, "Good morning, gentlemen. Thank you for agreeing to hear Fernando's presentation. What you will learn is that despite our collective efforts under the direction of and with the inspiration of Ricardo Voss, financial corruption and fraud haven't been extinguished in Brazil. The findings imply the fraud persists high in our government and the senior staff of O Banco do Brasil. I have this very morning received and accepted the resignation of Juliana Pereira, the bank's director of compliance whom as you are about to learn was not acting properly in her official capacity."

Fernando and Amaraes screen shared Fernando's presentation. Fernando made the presentation. da Silva and Viana listened with rapt attention.

At the conclusion of the Zoom meeting, Amaraes and da Silva called Presidente Voss with the news. They included Fernando on the call, and he walked Voss through the findings in his presentation. Voss was stunned by the news and angrily agreed to pursue Conte and Aragon for prosecution. da Silva cautioned Voss to not contact either suspect directly.

At the conclusion of the call with Voss, Viana departed and reached out to a judge to obtain search warrants to go to Aragon's and Pereira's and Conte's offices and homes to search for evidence.

At two o'clock that afternoon, Viana arrived at the executive office building in Brasília and proceeded to Conte's office in the annex building to Palácio do Planalto, the official presidential residence.

Conte stood and faced Viana while Viana entered. Viana handed Conte the warrant. And Conte slumped into his chair while studying it and spoke, "Senhor Viana, I will in no way attempt to complicate your effort here today. I have disgraced our country and our president." Conte opened his computer and showed Viana where his email trail regarding his and Aragon's efforts with Pereira was located. Conte began to cry.

Three PF investigators had accompanied Viana. The investigators spread out throughout the office, searching hard-copy files in Conte's desk and a filing cabinet. They focused heavily on Conte's smartphone and computer. Conte moved to a sofa in the office and sat studying the investigators as they progressed in their effort. After two hours, the investigators and Viana had what they needed. After one-and-one-half hours, Conte offered a full confession. In it, he implicated Aragon and Pereira. A PF team was dispatched quickly to the Pereira home.

Juliana had just arrived home and was in hiding, following her termination by Amaraes. The PF took her into custody and soon placed her in a cell, pending an arraignment. The televised media had gotten word of the activity and captured Juliana's arrest in video.

Viana and his investigators proceeded to Aragon's office. Pereira had called Aragon and warned him there was legal action being taken. When the PF arrived, Aragon's assistant called him to announce the PF's presence. There was a loud noise from the office. The assistant let Viana and his men in. Aragon's body was slumped forward on in his desk chair and his head laid on the desktop. A huge pool of blood had formed out of a massive self-inflicted gunshot wound to his right temple.

Viana had his investigators search Aragon's phone and computer and office files. The medical examiner arrived and took Aragon's body away to conduct a formal investigation into the cause of death.

Conte was also placed in a cell. In his cell, Conte wrote his letter of resignation:

> Over the recent two years, I have had the pleasure and honor to work with and for Presidente Ricardo Voss. I must now confess I succumbed to greed and worked with Finance Minister Carlos Aragon and Juliana Pereira of O Banco do Brasil on a fraud to obtain money from accounts at O Banco. We acted out of greed and arrogance and never thought our crime might be discovered. Carlos and I hold Ricardo Voss in the highest esteem and intended to in no way disgrace him or his administration. He is a man of great personal character,

and our nation is fortunate to have him
as its president.

The confession was released to the media.

Fernando and Paulo and Denise and Heliana watched the report on the evening news while relaxing before dinner. Fernando mesmerized his companions with his detailed explanation of how he discovered the fraud. Denise stared at Fernando with reverence while he spoke.

Presidente Voss later made a nationwide announcement regarding his selections of candidates for a new vice president and finance minister. For the vice presidency, Voss proposed the female governor of the state of Bahia. For finance minister, he nominated Ronaldo Amaraes. Voss emphatically explained that Amaraes had no involvement or blame in the fraud at O Banco. Voss explained his personal sense of loss over Conte's and Aragon's involvement in the fraud. He eloquently reemphasized his administration's dedication to cleaning up corruption. He came across as very sincere and honest.

Voss' approval rating in the polls rose dramatically following the speech. A calm settled over the country, and everyone went about his or her business with a sense of comfort and optimism for the future.

CHAPTER 64

At six o'clock in the evening, Carlos received his dinner in his private cell inside his custom prison structure on the navy base. A note was taped to the bottom of the tray. The note was William Nelson Vilmar's replacement's response to a request from Carlos.

The Regimento A team had found and seduced a kitchen staffer to channel Carlos' communications with Regimento A. Regimento A had discovered the identities of all the kitchen staff.

The fellow passing the communications was a dishwasher and food preparer who'd been tailed to a bar in Rio on a Friday night. The Regimento A team approached their target and offered to pay him one full year's worth of his salary to be the conduit for Regimento A's written communications with Carlos.

Carlos remained angered over his capture in the Dominican Republic and the deaths of William Nelson Vilmar and Gregor Stein. Carlos had asked the Regimento A team to target and kill Fernando and Denise and Heliana Santos and Paulo Coberto.

A Regimento A scout reported the targets were routine users of the Rio subway system or Metro. To their hunters' great frustration, the targets rode the train accompanied by heavily armed members of the PF and PM. Fernando and Paulo and Denise and Heliana were known to ride the trains on Friday evenings in order that they might get from the central business district to restaurants and entertainment venues south of the city's center. Riding the train removed the need for driving while intoxicated. Public transit also removed Fernando's having to drive the SP2 or Camaro, each of which risked his being easily identified. The PF and PM escorts were easily accommodated in the trains' seats and sat awaiting a call to action.

On the night of November 28, a Regimento A assassin named Roberto Pena was assigned to take out the targets; he became overly anxious about fulfilling Carlos' assignment. On the evening of November 29, he received confirmation his targets were on a southbound train. He went to the southern terminus of the line in the borough of Ipanema. There, he blended in with the crowd and stood awaiting sight of his targets.

A crowd was assembled on the train platform. The train came to a stop, and the guard contingent stepped from the train. The guards visually identified Pena. Fernando and his companions had followed the guards off the train. Pena foolishly exposed himself in a vain search for his victims in the crowd.

The lead guard, a captain in the PM, spoke to his comrades through his communication setup, "Easy, gentlemen, we must protect our assignments. Let me handle the contact."

He approached Pena cautiously. "Roberto, I am Captain Ricardo Galera of the Polícia Militar. Please place your weapon on the ground in front of you and place your hands on top of your head. We know what you are doing! We do not want you to be successful, and we don't want to harm you! Please do your family and friends a favor and surrender to us immediately!"

Pena paused awkwardly for a moment and reached for his gun in his waistband. One of Galera's men who'd moved three feet behind Pena shot him two times in the back of the head. Pena's lifeless body sagged to the floor of the train platform. A woman standing nearby let out a piercing scream. The passengers on the platform surged rapidly toward the exits.

Fernando and Denise and Paulo and Heliana moved quickly to the nearest exit and walked onto the crowded neighboring street and hailed a cab. Within minutes, they were home on the rooftop in Niterói and relaxing in the hot tub.

CHAPTER 65

Morning of Saturday, November 28, 2020
Caribbean Sea near Port of Spain, Venezuela

Captain Juan Ochoa of the Cuban Navy, the brother of General Pablo Ochoa who perished in the battle at Manaus Air Force Base, was patrolling in search of any sign of Brazilian or unauthorized naval activity near Port of Spain. Captain Ochoa's ship was an aging surplus Russian-built destroyer assigned to find and sink any Brazilian or unwanted foreign vessels, submarine or otherwise, it might encounter. The ship was named *The July 26, 1953*, in tribute to the start date of the over five-year revolution. That swept Fidel Castro into power on January 1, 1959. Cuba's and Venezuela's militaries were concerned regarding foreign intervention in support of Mateo Hernandez's effort to obtain the Venezuelan presidency.

Diego Guedes was on the *Tikuna* with his usual MEC companions. Caracas was reported to be in the throes of civil unrest, if not war. The pro-Cortez Venezuelan military was fearful of being overwhelmed by Hernandez and his supporters. Guedes and his team were headed for Caracas in support of a CIA mission to extract and rescue Mateo Hernandez and evacuate him to Brasília.

Captain Arturo Franc of the *Tikuna* was apprehensive about the mission. He knew Venezuela and Cuba were angered by the previous Brazilian efforts in Venezuela. He'd successfully navigated into the Port of Spain vicinity with Diego and his GRUMEC passengers on several occasions.

The sailor manning the sonar station called to Captain Franc. "Captain, we've been spotted by the Cuban ship, and they have locked on us."

The *Tikuna* had been retrofitted with advanced electronic equipment provided by the USA. The *Tikuna* was in open water at a depth of 150 feet.

Captain Franc frowned and felt a surge of inspirational adrenaline. "Never mind, gentlemen, we will succeed against our opponent. Brazil doesn't need to be the lapdog of any other power like our Cuban opponents. Their ship is outdated Russian surplus. They have struggled to build their own ships. The result is fishing trawlers converted into pathetic excuses for warships. Our opponent is Captain Juan Ochoa, a seasoned naval veteran with extensive destroyer experience on *The July 26* with its previous Russian commanders. Thanks to the independent ingenuity of Brazil, we built this, our own submarine. We have the extraordinary benefit of advanced electronics, courtesy of our friends in the USA. Senhor Pereira, please execute a zigzag pattern to confuse our opponent. We must then rise to seventy-five feet of depth and prepare to launch three torpedoes toward our Cuban opponents."

Franc pulled a stopwatch from his right pants' pocket and started it and watched, intending to measure out five minutes' time. He anticipated it would take Ochoa five minutes to get in position and launch his anticipated depth charge attack on the *Tikuna*.

On board *The July 26*, Captain Ochoa was laboriously moving his ship carefully into position to drop depth charges aimed at the *Tikuna*. In so doing, he and his crew mistakenly exposed the ship's starboard side to attack. In a moment of anxious self-doubt, Captain Ochoa and his crew lost track of the *Tikuna*.

Captain Franc repeatedly received distance and activity updates regarding *The July 26*. His crew watched him nervously while he studied the stopwatch and thought. When the stopwatch got to four minutes, Franc calmly ordered the conclusion of the zigzag pattern. This he followed with several cunning depth and course adjustments. When the stopwatch reached six minutes, Franc recognized *The July 26* had mistakenly exposed its starboard side. The seaman manning the *Tikuna*'s sonar excitedly reported three depth charges had been launched. Captain Franc reset his stopwatch and started to count the time since the depth charges' launch. The crew waited breathlessly while Franc patiently counted out twenty seconds. Franc calmly directed the helm to reposition the sub. When Franc's stopwatch showed thirty seconds, the three depth charges exploded some three hundred yards from the *Tikuna*. The sub handled the shockwaves from the explosions well. Captain Franc ordered three of the *Tikuna*'s eight torpedoes fired in the direction of the Cuban vessel.

Captain Ochoa remained distractedly engrossed in positioning *The July 26* to drop further depth charges. *The July 26*'s deck watch called out the approach of the torpedoes.

When seven minutes had passed since Franc's first start of his stopwatch, all three of the *Tikuna*'s torpedoes struck *The July 26* at the waterline on the starboard side. The torpedoes breeched the ship's hull and detonated the weapons in storage in its hold. A massive fireball roared up from the explosion and engulfed the bridge in flames.

Ochoa fell through a three-foot-long opening that had been torn in the floor of the bridge and perished instantly in the inferno below decks. *The July 26* began to take on water rapidly and sank at the stern. The weight of the water pulled *The July 26* under, engulfed in flames and explosions of its ammunition. The ship disappeared below the surface and sank to a depth of 1,800 feet where it broke in two and plummeted to the ocean's floor at a depth of 24,250 feet. Its demise was rapid and took two minutes and forty-five seconds from the torpedoes' impact. The sinking to the ocean floor took well over ten minutes. All the souls on board were lost and entombed in *The July 26*'s twisted wreckage. A huge oil slick formed on the surface above *The July 26*'s descent. A total of 150 died—149 crew members and a political officer tasked with overseeing the crew's compliance with Cuban Communist Party political philosophy.

Captain Franc had ordered the *Tikuna* to rise to a depth of 25 feet and soberly observed the sinking and damage through the *Tikuna*'s periscope. When the ship disappeared, Franc noted eight minutes had elapsed since he had first started the stopwatch for the initial count. He ordered the *Tikuna* back to a depth of 150 feet and set a course toward shore.

In reply to *The July 26*'s numerous calls for help and backup, several Cuban and Venezuelan warplanes and warships soon filled the sea and sky in search of the *Tikuna*. No survivors of *The July 26* were identified or rescued by their Cuban or Venezuelan comrades or the *Tikuna*.

Captain Franc expertly avoided discovery. He prepared to defend his ship and its crew and its mission. He had been ordered to avoid any escalation of combat. It was feared escalated fighting might delay or postpone the rescue of Mateo Hernandez.

Franc took the microphone and addressed his crew, "Well, gentlemen, I am once again reminded of how fortunate and honored I am to be serving with all of you. We needn't celebrate at the expense of our opponents' lives. Please join me in the Lord's Prayer in tribute to Captain Ochoa and his crew." Franc crossed himself and prayed.

The entire crew of the *Tikuna* and its passengers from the GRUMEC and ABIN prayed with Franc. At the prayer's completion, the crew and passengers applauded Franc and sang the Brazilian national anthem. Franc asked the men to be quiet for fear another vessel or a submarine chaser aircraft might discover them. The men were sobered by Franc's cautioning tone.

Thirty-five minutes after *The July 26* sank, the *Tikuna* surfaced cautiously near the Venezuelan shore, and Guedes and his MEC team boarded a raft and rowed toward shore. A heavy cloud layer provided a cover of darkness. They made their way undetected and went ashore near the culvert and marsh they'd previously passed through. The pickup truck was in the spot where they'd previously left it. The owner had returned it as he'd promised. They piled into it after confirming the gas tank was full. Guedes drove them toward Caracas.

While they approached Bolívar on the highway, they encountered no opposing troops or police and later came across Tom Fielding and a team of Hernandez's supporters. Mateo Hernandez was with them and was pulled into the truck's cab. The road was filled with military vehicles carrying troops loyal to Hernandez, providing protective cover and escort. The troops shouted their support for Hernandez.

Guedes and his companions bid goodbye to Fielding and Hernandez's supporters. They managed to find an open gas station and refueled. Guedes followed a side road Tom Fielding had recommended and returned to the pickup's parking place. They encountered no adversarial troops. They soon were wading through the marsh and walking through the culvert to the beach. They uncovered and boarded the concealed raft and rowed toward the *Tikuna*.

Captain Franc and his crew welcomed Hernandez aboard, "Senhor Presidente, welcome aboard! Presidente Voss asks that we call him once you're safely aboard."

Hernandez smiled and replied, "Thank you, Captain. I am very pleased to be with you and to be the guest of the people of Brazil. I think I am now ready to speak with Presidente Voss."

Captain Franc escorted Hernandez to the captain's conference room.

Presidente Voss and Director Cardenas were called on a speakerphone.

Voss spoke first, "Well, Senhor Presidente, congratulations on your successful escape from Caracas. I will meet you tomorrow evening in Rio and bring you to Brasília in my airplane. We are completing a structure in Brasília that can serve as your formal offices in absentia. My people and I are ecstatic about your assumption of the Venezuelan presidency! We have additionally found a home in Brasília suitable for a man of your stature. The CIA and our troops and Ticuna Indians are currently evacuating your wife and cabinet members through the Amazon. They're due in Manaus within eight hours. They should be in Brasília in time to join you and me tomorrow evening. Your supporters, both civilian and military, are rumored to be routing the pro-Cortez factions from Caracas. The fighting is said to have been brutal. Fortunately, reports from the CIA and ABIN indicate conclusively the violence is tapering off. It is reported that Juan Cortez and his family have fled Caracas to Havana in search of refuge. Hopefully, Juan Cortez will have no opportunity to return from Havana to Caracas and reclaim his failed leadership. My and US President Mallory's expectation is you will be able to return to Caracas and assume your presidency in its rightful place. In advance of that wonderful day, the Brazilian offer of a location from which you may govern in absentia stands."

Hernandez listened while smiling a relaxed smile. "Thank you, Presidente Voss. I look forward to working with you and our mutual allies on rebuilding Venezuela! God bless you and the people of Brazil for your interest in our cause!"

CHAPTER 66

Amazon forest, four miles from Manaus, Brazil
Morning of Sunday, November 29, 2020

Tom Fielding and Dave Cooper of the CIA were with several MECs and Brazilian marines. They were escorting Hernandez's wife, Senhora Dona Hernandez, and several members of Mateo Hernandez's newly formed administration through the forest to be evacuated through Manaus.

Members of the Ticuna tribe were guiding the group. The Ticuna were expert at finding their way secretively through the forest. Members of the Venezuelan and Cuban marines and Special Forces were in pursuit. The Ticuna managed to frustrate the pursuers and avoid discovery. They dispatched many of the enemy with traps consisting of sharp stakes at the bottom of holes covered with tarps covered and disguised with pieces of native plants. The unwitting victims ran across and fell through the tarps to their deaths. Several others were killed with bows and arrows and by darts with poisonous tips delivered by exhaling through tubes pointed at the targets. The pursuers exploded into a confused panic and vainly tried to run. While running, they fell into the hidden traps and ran into the Ticuna and Brazilians' weapons' ranges. Within forty-five minutes, the pursuers were eradicated. The Ticuna are the most numerous indigenous people in the Amazon.

Senhora Dona Hernandez and the administration's staffers were all safely delivered to Manaus Air Force Base at one o'clock in the afternoon. They boarded an Embraer C390 transport and cargo airplane and were in Brasília by four o'clock, just in time for a celebratory dinner at the presidential palace in Brasília.

Presidente Voss and Presidente Hernandez had arrived earlier on BRS1. The Venezuelans had a joyous reunion. The Brazilian government and US had planned to establish a shadow government for Venezuela and to install Hernandez as the county's leader in absentia. Presidents Voss and Mallory and their military commanders were developing plans to return Hernandez to Palacio de Miraflores in Caracas, the official workplace of the Venezuelan president.

The official presidential residence at Palacio La Casona was similarly to be protected for Hernandez. There was a reasonable concern about loss of lives because the pro-Cortez military faction had surrounded the buildings and stood protecting them for Cortez's potential return from Havana. It was learned that Cortez had been secreted away from Havana and was in hiding in luxurious surroundings in Beijing, China.

On Monday, November 23, 2020, the US secretary of state traveled to Beijing and negotiated Cortez's relinquishing any claim on the Venezuelan presidency. Under the terms of the deal, Cortez was offered a luxurious residence in Caracas. He additionally received a chauffeured limousine and government-paid health coverage. Learning of the agreement, Cortez's supporters thankfully agreed to allow Hernandez access to the governmental buildings. In exchange, Cortez was allowed to retain substantial bank accounts he had accumulated offshore in the USA and Caribbean and Europe. Cortez was further allowed to run for office in the Venezuelan National Assembly. Cortez agreed to not actively interfere in the Hernandez administration. In this, he was told he could definitely work legislatively to counter Hernandez.

On Monday, December 2, 2020, Mateo and Dona Hernandez and their cabinet members were returned to Caracas and to their residences and the official offices for their positions. The cabinet, although never having governed, was made up of a collection of Cortez's opponents from the pre-Maduro and Chávez and Cortez business and academic communities.

An estimated two million Venezuelans turned out on the route from the airport to central Caracas and cheered their new leaders' arrival. The populace and military that had been beleaguered and betrayed by the Cortez and its predecessor regimes celebrated enthusiastically.

The Brazilian ambassador and embassy staff were returned to the embassy. The two women embassy staffers who'd been evacuated were returned and reunited with their husbands.

Presidents Voss and Hernandez later formed a wonderfully powerful alliance between Venezuela and Argentina and Chile and Paraguay and Peru and Bolivia and Uruguay and Mexico. The alliance focused on restoration of human rights and political freedom throughout Latin America. An era of great prosperity and public contentment spread throughout the region.

CHAPTER 67

Office of Presidente Ricardo Voss, Brasília, Distrito Federal, Brazil
Morning of Friday, January 1, 2021

PF Director João da Silva and Presidente Ricardo Voss telephoned Fernando Carvalho on his cell phone.

Fernando had just dropped Denise off at Anita's office building.

da Silva started the conversation, "Good morning and happy New Year, young man. I am feeling an enthusiastically positive motivation to challenge you to help with youth development here in Brazil," enthused the cheerful da Silva. "Presidente Voss and I have scheduled a conference in Rio in March."

Voss cut in, "Yes, happy New Year, Senhor Carvalho! We plan to have over two hundred thousand people attend the conference at Maracanã stadium on Monday, March 1, 2021. The attendees will be young people from all walks of life throughout the eastern regions of our country. The attendees will be seated in the stadium, and accommodations for the potential overflow shall be provided in the streets. The streets will have large-screen displays with a public address system for sound presenting the activity in the stadium. We hope to have strong representation from the favelas and impoverished rural areas. We are further encouraging wealthy and middle-class attendees.

"Director da Silva and I want you to speak about your successful rise up from your impoverished beginnings in Heliópolis. We want to capitalize on the current era of positive economic momentum and inspire the nation's youth to work hard and succeed. We firmly believe that the effort could broadly benefit the entire economy of our land. Additionally, the current strong economy may very likely offer opportunities for young people to be employed and succeed. We also believe young people will relate to and see you as a role model. Since Carnival ends in late February this year, we are confident there will be the momentum of a carryover of positive sentiment shared widely. May we rely on you to prepare a speech and share it with us in advance and deliver it at the event?"

Fernando thought carefully about his time commitments and replied, "Gentlemen, that would be a huge honor and pleasure for me. Since your timeline gives me two months to prepare, I am convinced I may accommodate your deadline. I will have an initial draft of my speech to you within two weeks. I will focus on my nickname and choice of my costume and dedication to good work and to living up to the nickname O Bispo. I will describe my criminal activity as an unfortunately normal bad choice for a young person struggling to become a participant in our materialistic world. Happy New Year, gentlemen. I will reward your generosity and faith in me.

"Have you heard the great news? Paulo Coberto has proposed to Heliana Santos, and she has accepted! I am to be his best man, and Denise will be Heliana's maid of honor. Father Silvio will conduct the wedding ceremony and the wedding mass. Denise and I are very excited for them and cannot wait to see you both at the ceremony and reception."

da Silva responded enthusiastically, "Yes, Fernando, I heard about the proposal. Katia and Andrea and I are very much looking forward to both the wedding ceremony and mass and reception. I had intended to discuss the wedding with Presidente Voss today and to find out if he and Senhora Voss might attend."

Voss chuckled and replied, "Well, since you are both such favorites of mine, of course, I will be there. My wife and I will want very much to see Fernando and Denise in their roles in the wedding."

*   *   *   *   *

Carlos observed the arrival of the New Year in his cell at the navy base. A message from William Nelson Vilmar's replacement as head of Regimento A arrived taped to the bottom of his breakfast tray: "Carlos, I am sorry to report Roberto Pena was killed while attempting to fulfill our order to remove Carvalho and Coberto and the Santos women."

Carlos wadded the note up and threw it angrily into the corner of his cell. He pulled out a small notepad and wrote his reply furiously, "We must eradicate Carvalho and his housemates! Instruct Pena's brother, Marcos, to carry out the killings!"

Upon receipt of his boss' directive, Vilmar's replacement contacted Marcos Pena and assigned him to the task.

Word had spread of Paulo and Heliana's wedding. The directive encouraged Marcos to hit his targets at the gathering. They soon learned Presidente Voss and Director da Silva would be in attendance. The likelihood of having to confront the Batalhão da Guarda Presidencial and a certain large presence of the PF and PM led them to alter the plan.

Regimento A and Carlos' research had discovered Coberto's mother's home address in the Donna Marta favela in Rio. Paulo and Heliana were known to visit her for dinner every Sunday afternoon. The Regimento A leadership concluded their best chance for success would be to ambush Paulo and Heliana during one of their Sunday visits.

The research further indicated Fernando and Denise would spend their Sunday evenings alone together on the rooftop of the Niterói home. They would lounge in the hot tub and barbecue their dinner.

The Regimento A leadership and Marcos concluded their best hope of accomplishing Carlos' assignment would be to kill Paulo and Heliana on their way to and into Paulo's mother's home. They envisioned gaining access to a roof near the Niterói home on a Sunday evening and killing Fernando and Denise from there. Then they'd be in the good graces of Carlos who still exerted a great deal of influence over Regimento A. The membership of the gang would be hard to direct without accomplishing a big objective like the removal of Carvalho and Coberto and the Santos girls.

Vilmar's replacement recognized he desperately needed to reassure Carlos and the Regimento A membership he was the rightful choice to lead the gang. He handpicked three top Regimento A gang members to assist Marcos. They were experienced in fighting with the Sombra Preta. They had been imprisoned with Carlos and Fernando during the violence at Porto Velho. They were known for their ruthlessness and cunning and determination. Marcos was welcoming of the help because he knew how heavily guarded his targets were and would be going forward.

CHAPTER 68

irector da Silva's executive assistant finished connecting Director da Silva and Presidente Voss and Fernando together on a conference call. da Silva and Voss had received Fernando's draft of his presentation for the gathering scheduled for March 1 at Maracaná stadium.

Maracaná has a capacity of just fewer than eighty thousand and is similar to London's Wembley Stadium, which has a capacity of ninety thousand.

Voss began the conversation, "Well, Senhor Carvalho, you are indeed The Bishop again! Your presentation is exactly what Director da Silva and I had hoped for."

Fernando listened and blushed while smiling.

da Silva chimed in, "Yes, laddie, you've made us so proud of and confident about our trust in you. Your presentation is fantastic!"

Fernando replied, "Thank you, Senhor Director and Senhor Presidente. I am so pleased you both like it! It is entirely from my heart and soul. I look forward to presenting it on March 1!"

Paulo and Heliana's wedding was scheduled for Sunday, March 6. On Sunday, February 27, Paulo and Heliana were on their way to Paulo's mother's house to finalize the plans for the wedding.

Heliana and Denise's parents were in Rio for the planning. The reception was to be held at the Grand Hyatt. The elder Santos were staying at the hotel.

A front desk clerk who was sympathetic to Regimento A and Carlos notified William Nelson Vilmar's replacement of the Santos' presence. Vilmar's replacement directed Marcos Pena and his assistants to stake out the lobby and await the potential arrival of Paulo and Heliana.

Paulo and Heliana arrived around noon and were greeted by Fred and Senhora Santos. The four went to the lobby restaurant and were seated for lunch. An entourage of PM and PF guards was accompanying them.

Marcos became anxious and agitated and left his assistants in the lobby and entered the restaurant and asked for a seat. He was seated a few tables away from the elder Santos and Heliana and Paulo's table. Marcos was an insecure fellow with dreams of achieving prominence in Regimento A. His anxiety overcame his logical thought processes. He sat nervously, trying to identify a means to effectively attack the elder Santos and Paulo and Heliana. The waiter asked him if he wanted a beverage to start. He was so preoccupied he couldn't answer. He fumbled around and ordered an ice water. The waiter delivered the water, and Marcos was unable to decide what to order to eat.

Captain Ricardo Galera of the PM was leading the protective guard detail that was present. The guards had taken tables near the Santos and Heliana and Paulo. Captain Galera watched every one of the fifty other guests in the restaurant carefully. His intuition told him the visibly fidgety man seated at a nearby table was a source of potential trouble. Galera leaned next to his second-in-command and instructed him to watch Marcos as well.

Marcos stood to relieve his anxiety. He mistakenly exposed a gun secured in the waistband of his pants. Galera motioned to his men to remain calm and allow him to address Marcos. Galera stood up and walked toward Marcos. All the guards on Galera's team stood as well and surrounded Marcos with their weapons drawn.

Galera looked at Marcos and pointed toward the floor and spoke, "Senhor, I am Captain Ricardo Galera of the PM. Please don't place the good people in this restaurant and yourself at risk. Remove your gun from your waistband and lie facedown on the floor with the gun at your side."

Marcos thought if he were to shoot, he'd avoid betraying the Regimento A and Carlos and Vilmar replacement's faith in his performance. He was wholly conflicted and confused as to what to do. He thought about his brother's recent death at the hands of the PM. He reluctantly withdrew his gun and lay nose down on the floor with the gun at his side.

Galera stepped over Marcos and kicked the gun away to one of his men. Captain Galera stood Marcos up and handcuffed his hands behind his back at the waist. Galera's second-in-command marched Marcos out and through the lobby to the porte cochere where Marcos was placed in a PM car and driven away. Marcos' assistants observed the action and moved to rescue their leader. The PF and PM backup for the PM team quickly moved into the lobby and had all the criminals surrender and placed them under arrest. Galera called for police vans, and the prisoners were removed to the PM's pretrial lockup in Rio where they joined Marcos to await indictments.

Fortunately, no shots were fired, and no one was hurt. Paulo and Heliana and the elder Santos caught a cab and departed for Paulo's mother's home. They took a catering department representative with them to finalize the reception planning. Galera and three of his men followed in an official car to provide cover.

*   *   *   *   *

Later in the evening following a successful planning session, Fernando and his housemates were at home and relaxing.

Fernando was walking Denise through his presentation for the March 1 event. He had developed a new idea. He enthusiastically observed, "Denise Santos, my dear, one of the major problems in our land is the divide and misunderstanding between the economic classes! When I was at Pre, there was an exchange student from California who had come through an organization called the American Field Service or AFS. There were other exchange students from the USA elsewhere in Brazil who'd been placed by AFS. Brazilian students went to the USA as well. The students would stay with families that volunteered to host them. The hosts would provide the students with food and housing and access to school. The students would attend a local school in their hosts' community. They were compelled to learn the hosts' language and be immersed in the host country's culture. The result was appreciation for each other's country and culture by both the guest students and their hosts.

"AFS began as the American Ambulance Field Service in 1915. It was a US volunteer ambulance corps in Étrelles, Brittany, France, during World War I. At the end of World War II, they got together and asked themselves how another war could be prevented. They believed everyone in the world would benefit by having future generations learn that people everywhere are the same. Thus, ignorant bigotry and hatred could be expunged. They concluded that enabling exchanges of secondary-school-aged children between countries could help teach people to appreciate each other and to understand differences aren't dramatic or indicators of evil. They believed idealistically the ignorance and hatred that drove world wars and genocide could thus be removed.

"I think we need exchanges of kids within Brazil! Kids from favelas could learn that middle-and-upper-class people have the same passions and desires and values as they and their families. Some time in a home with a supportive focus on studies and material security could well teach them values and incent them to focus and work hard much as I did from my time at the Diamante home. In the alternative, kids from the middle and upper classes could learn lessons about how the poor of Brazil are focused on family and religion and succeeding. I believe I can gain Director da Silva and Presidente Voss' support to include the concept in my March 1 presentation."

Fernando could usually be notably stoic. His enthusiasm and passion in describing the exchange idea impressed Denise.

She smiled and patted Fernando on the shoulder and kissed his forehead. "Keep on dreaming and thinking, my love. Your energy and drive will likely make a huge difference in our beloved Brazil!"

The next morning, Fernando telephoned Voss and da Silva on a conference call and described his idea and vision. The two were equally inspired by the concept, as was Fernando. With Voss and da Silva's approvals, Fernando revised his presentation for March 1. Within twenty-four hours, he circulated his revision to Voss and da Silva and received their approval to deliver it on March 1.

The March 1 event received the full and enthusiastic support of the Catholic Church. The archbishop of Rio de Janeiro appeared onstage with Fernando and Presidente Voss. At the event's conclusion, the archbishop awarded Fernando the honorary title of priest in recognition of his wonderful work. Father Silvio was also present on stage and hugged and kissed Fernando. Fernando later joked sarcastically with Denise that she so aroused and inspired him he would gladly break his vow of celibacy.

Fernando assisted Father Silvio at Paulo and Heliana's wedding on March 6, 2021.

The exchange program concept was later implemented and proved a big success. Fernando became successful on the Amaraes team at O Banco do Brasil and continued his covert activities. He was able to balance his time between his covert activities and work with Amaraes and charitable focus on youth development.

Fernando and Denise and Paulo and Heliana spent the month of March 2021 relaxing in the home in Niterói. Life settled into a relaxing and comfortable pace for them all.

Anita's business was very successful, thanks to a Voss-engineered economic boom.

On March 20, Anita delivered her wedding gift to Paulo and Heliana. The gift was two round-trip first-class tickets on American Airlines to New York City along with three nights in a suite at the Manhattan Sheraton Hotel plus tickets for two to two hit theatrical musicals. Paulo and Heliana departed on the morning of Wednesday, March 21, and returned on Sunday, March 25.

CHAPTER 69

Paulo Coberto's home, Niterói, suburb, Rio de Janeiro, Brazil
Morning of Saturday, May 1, 2021

Fernando answered a call from Director da Silva, "This is Fernando. How are you this morning, Senhor Director?"

da Silva replied, "I am sorry to say I am not happy, Fernando. But it is good to hear your voice. I am calling regarding another challenging crime I need your help to solve."

Fernando was intrigued and replied, "My dear Senhor Director, what is the crime, and how may I be of assistance?"

da Silva paused for what was an uncustomary length of time for him while collecting his thoughts and responded, "This is a tough one, Nando. There is a serial killer or killers in Rio. The murderer or murderers routinely target attractive young women. The killer or killers rape their victims and then disfigure the bodies by using a knife to remove the facial features. The crimes are committed in the victims' homes. There were two murders last night. Sergio Viana is in Rio working with the civilian police to collect and evaluate the evidence from the crime scene from last night. I thought you'd be interested to know both murders occurred in the building Marta Esteves lived in in Niterói."

Fernando thought back to Marta's death and cringed. "That is awful! I am available to meet with Sergio and discuss how I may help."

da Silva responded, "That is wonderful and more than I could have hoped for, Fernando! Sergio is on the third floor of the building in the unit next door to the one that was Marta's."

Fernando nodded and prepared himself to tell Denise he was going to disturb their planned quiet day at home. He opted to use the Camaro since the SP2 was still at the home of its caretaker. He drove to the apartment house and parked in the adjacent surface parking lot. He approached the front door with trepidation and entered the modest lobby and took the elevator to the third floor.

There, several officers he recognized greeted him. Sergio Viana was in a conversation with the neighbor woman who had previously identified Marta Esteves' killer's car. Fernando listened in and learned the woman had no valuable information to share. Fernando made his way around a perimeter tape the police had placed around the apartment concealing the two victims.

A woman arrived and identified herself as the mother of one of the victims. Viana obtained the permission of a neighbor to interview the woman in the neighbor's apartment. His request was granted. He took Fernando and the woman into the apartment and learned her name was Silvia Alves and her daughter's was Victoria Alves. Sylvia was very nervous and distraught, nearing hysterical and Sergio began, "Senhora Alves, I am so sorry I have to ask you questions. Please understand we need to learn a great deal to find out who or what is to blame for killing your daughter and her roommate. Why did you come here this afternoon?"

Sylvia was holding an advertisement and shaking visibly. She began to sob and managed to speak, "I came here because Victoria and her roommate, Kara, had replied to this advertisement. They called me this morning very excited because the company had advised they were sending a talent scout to interview them. I arrived at ten o'clock as we had agreed. But when I arrived, the front door was ajar. Then when I entered, I found them on the living room floor!" She broke down, crying uncontrollably, and the advertisement fell from her right hand to the floor.

Viana picked up the advertisement and read it: "Wanted beautiful women who can dance and sing to appear in an upcoming movie to be filmed here in Rio." It closed with the name of the alleged director; a fellow named Francisco dos Santos of Filmes Suldense and an email address and phone number. Viana dialed the number, and the call went to voice mail. The recorded answer was "Hi, this is Francisco dos Santos of Filmes Suldense. Please leave a detailed message with your name and phone number and address, and I will get back to you as soon as possible. Thanks for calling."

Viana told Fernando what he had heard. They spoke for ten minutes. At the conclusion of their discussion, Fernando volunteered to have Denise help set a trap for Francisco or whatever his real name was. He took down the phone number and called and asked Denise to call Francisco's number.

Denise called. At the completion of the voice mail introduction, she said, "Hi, my name is Denise Santos. I am very interested in your offered role in a film." She gave the address of Coberto's Niterói home.

She received a call back from the number she had called. "Hi, this is a Francisco dos Santos of Filmes Suldense. I am very pleased by your interest in our opportunity. May I come by in twenty or so minutes and meet with and evaluate you?"

Denise answered an enthusiastic yes.

Fernando spoke to da Silva and made an arrangement. The security around the Niterói home was increased. Fernando drove there and within twenty-five minutes, a female PF officer in civilian clothing arrived; she was strikingly attractive and bore an uncanny resemblance to Denise and Heliana. Fernando and a male PF officer took up positions in a closet near the living room and stood guard. The female officer turned on the television and sat in a chair. The front door was left ajar.

Within an hour of Denise's call with Francisco, there was a knock on the front door.

The female officer went to the door and opened it fully. "Hi, I am Denise Santos. Are you Francisco?"

'Francisco' smiled and entered. "Well, yes, I am, Senhorita Santos. I am very pleased to meet you. Are you wearing underwear? I would like very much to see you without your clothing so I may evaluate your appearance."

The officer blushingly replied, "Well, yes, I am wearing underwear. I am slightly uncomfortable with your request. It seems slightly hurried."

'Francisco' smiled patiently and responded, "You are correct, Senhorita Santos. I'd like to see you dance first so we may progress at a reasonable pace. Might you have a speaker or sound system I may use to play a song for you to dance to?"

A Bluetooth speaker was sitting next to the TV. 'Francisco' connected his phone to the speaker and started a current dance hit by Ivete Sangalo, and the female officer danced to it.

'Francisco' smiled appreciatively. "Well, Denise, that is marvelous. Let's have you sing along to a favorite song of yours."

The officer asked to sing "Antonico" by Gal Costa. 'Francisco' started it, and the officer delivered a perfect karaoke rendition.

'Francisco' smiled again and continued, "Well, Senhorita Santos, your dancing and singing are much better than I had hoped! If you are more comfortable now, please undress so I may evaluate you physically."

The officer was genuinely nervous and complied by unbuttoning the top buttons of her blouse. 'Francisco' leered lecherously and stepped too close behind the woman and placed his hands on her shoulders. He pulled a knife from his waistband and positioned it in preparation for later use. He pulled a rag from a plastic bag he removed from a pocket and placed it under the female officer's nose; she became unconscious and fell to the floor. 'Francisco' knelt and continued the unbuttoning of the blouse.

Fernando and the male officer stepped from the closet and into the room. Fernando spoke first, "That's it right there, Senhor dos Santos!"

'Francisco' was shocked by the appearance of the two armed men.

Fernando continued, "Please take your hands off of the woman and step over here beside my partner and me."

'Francisco' appeared to lose all energy and glumly stepped beside Fernando and the male officer.

The male officer spoke, "Senhor dos Santos, you are suspected of murders committed in Niterói this morning. We are placing you under arrest as the suspected murderer. Please place your hands behind your back at the waist."

'Francisco' complied and was handcuffed. Another male officer entered, and the officers escorted 'Francisco' to a PF car, and he was removed to a pretrial cell.

Denise had been hiding on the rooftop and returned once 'Francisco' was removed; she helped to revive and calm the female officer, and the day returned to approximately normal.

Fernando called da Silva and Viana and spoke to them on speakerphone. They were very pleased with the outcome and applauded Denise's help.

da Silva spoke to Fernando and Denise, "Wow, you two you are quite the crime-fighting duo!"

Fernando chuckled in response, "Careful now, Senhor Director. Denise makes much more than I and must remain employed by Anita! We are each very pleased to have helped to remove that cretin 'Francisco' from circulation. Please give Senhora Alves our condolences for her loss."

On Tuesday, June 1, 2021, an anti-Communist uprising broke out in Cuba. Several hundred Brazilians were in the country as tourists or conducting business and became trapped when their requests and attempts to leave Cuba were denied. Fernando and Tom Fielding and Diego Guedes and the MECs were back in action. The USA provided Brazil with access to its airstrip at Guantanamo, and an air evacuation was possible.

On the morning of Wednesday, June 2, da Silva was preparing to leave his home for work. And he received a call from Sergio Viana who had spoken with the warden at Ariosvaldo de Campos Pires Federal Prison.

Following his threats toward Rogerio Mendosa, David Melkor had apparently attempted to attack Mendosa during an exercise yard break and hurt him to the extent Mendosa had to be hospitalized after being cut badly by a makeshift weapon Melkor had managed to create and/or obtain. Melkor had snapped and was sweaty and agitated and stammering and looked deranged. Subsequently, friends of Mendosa surrounded Melkor and beat him mercilessly. Melkor later died from massive internal and cerebral injuries. The guards looked away and feigned concern in a feeble attempt to appear to try to rescue Melkor.

Viana closed by noting Amazon had tired of their acquisition of GastroApp and were selling it for a tidy 350 million US dollars to another retailer. This marked the final chapter in Melkor's pathetic and futile life.

da Silva thought back to the Azevedos' murder investigation and shook his head in amazement at the misery one man had wrought so widely.

He picked out a bottle of wine when he arrived home and sat with Katia and Andrea, relaxing in their backyard. He felt wholly relaxed and decided to call Fernando and invite him and Denise to be the da Silvas' dinner guests the following Saturday. He looked at his wife and daughter and wondered at his good fortune in life.

Fernando continued to be successful at O Banco do Brasil. Directores da Silva and Cardenas continued to work cooperatively with Fernando's bank obligations while using him on a continuing variety of covert adventures.

Fernando and Denise's relationship remained strong and passionate for years.

Ricardo Voss' presidency was a huge success as measured by his achieving continuing high scores in popularity polls. Under his leadership the Brazilian Economy grew strong and was envied widely by other governments.

Mateo Hernandez governed wisely and oversaw a return of Venezuela's economic strength. The economy was strong enough to provide benefit to every Venezuelan; the days of Chavez and Maduro were soon dim unfortunate memories.

ABOUT THE AUTHOR

Mr. Brownlee experienced a severe stroke in early 2014. He lost the use of his left arm and leg and has overcome cognitive difficulty completely. Thanks to surgery received in late 2020, he anticipates some modest recovery of his idled limbs by late 2022.

He wanted to write fiction throughout his thirty-plus years as a business professional. He lived in Brazil for one year as an exchange student.

He thought up his protagonist as a character a favorite Brazilian actor could portray.

He is a retired businessman who served as a CFO and CEO and COO in several businesses in the Western and Midwestern USA.

Following his graduation from College with a degree in accounting he worked for Price Waterhouse; he received a California CPA license in the early 1980's. Thereafter he worked as a controller and ultimately as a CFO.

CPSIA information can be obtained
at www.ICGtesting.com
Printed in the USA
LVHW091506150222
711201LV00015B/734/J